Awaken

Awaken

G.R. Thomas

To Rochelle Maya Callen,
But for you, I would not have put pen to paper.
Thank you.

THE WORLD OF A'VEAN GLOSSARY

Terms and names that appear across *The A'vean Chronicles Series*

A'veans: (Watchers and Eudaimonians) Originate from the creation planet, A'vean

Amais: (a-may-us) Eloi council member. One of the first Watchers deployed to Earth.

Am'iel: (am-ee-elle) Watcher.

Av'ael: (a-vay-elle) Hybrid. Eudaimonian child with a special connection to Sophia.

Brennan: (Bren-un) Watcher. Also known as Bren'ael (Bren-ay-elle), which he hates immensely. He prefers the name Brennan.

Cael: (kay-elle) Watcher. Watched over Sophia as she grew up along with Enl'iel and Brennan.

Dash'iel: (Dash-eel) Watcher. Prefers to be called Dash.

Enl'iel: (En-lee-elle) Hybrid (Eudaimonian). She is relatively young - born in the 1700's.

Gal'iel: (gelle-ee-elle) Watcher.

Gedz'iel: (Ged-zee-elle) Watcher. Leader of the Eloi council and benevolent Watcher who chose to stay on Earth to guide his brethren, even though he had not over-stepped I'el's rules.

I'el: (I-elle) Supreme and prime creator of entire living universe. First energy to obtain consciousness and from himself, life was propagated over the entire universe. Referred to as a He, but has no gender. I'el is everything and nothing all at once.

Kea: (kee-ya) Watcher. Also known as Ke'arel (Kay-a-relle). Watcher who has secretly protected all those around Sophia from the time she was rescued and hidden as a baby.

Koi: (koy) Watcher. Trainer of warriors, directly reports to Ged'ziel.

Matias: (ma-tie-us) Eloi council member. One of the first Watchers deployed to Earth.

Neren'iel: (Nah-ren-ielle) Hybrid. Wife of Nik'ael, killed by high angels of A'vean. Sent to cleanse the Earth of the Eudaimonians; hybrids of Humans and Watchers.

Pathos: (path-oss) Eloi council – the first five A'vean Watchers sent to help pull ancient humans from the swamps and breathe souls into to them.

Rik'ael: (rik-ale) Brother to Sophia.

Serail: (sir-rail) Eloi Council member. One of the first Watchers sent to Earth.

Soph'ael: (sof-a-elle) Sophia. The long-awaited Earth-born angel and saviour for the A'veans trapped on Earth.

Theus: (thoos) Eloi Council member. One of the first Watchers sent to Earth.

Ty'rael: (ti-rail) Watcher.

Uriel: (you-re-elle) Powerful Archangel. Monitors the progrees of the Fallen angels and keeper of the prophecy of Enoch.

Archimedes: ancient Greek mathematician born 287-212 BC. Lived in Syracuse, Italy.

Enoch: (e-nok) Biblical character professed to be the only human to ever leave Earth to visit A'vean body and soul with I'el. Chosen to encapsulate secret knowledge, since he was a human who lived an exemplary and peaceful life; the life that I'el had wanted for all humanity.

Ilir: (eye-lear) Human, cook, nurse maid, and overseer of the running of the Katoika sanctuary Around 300 years old. Kept young for over two hundred of those years by the power of the Watchers.

Jasmine: (Jaz) Sophia's best friend.

Kristen: One of the most experienced Human warriors. Descendant of the humans who sheltered with the Watchers during the Great Flood.

Thomas: Brother to Kristen. Helps train human warriors.

Xavier: Human warrior

The Six Satans: (The Unseen) Watchers who rebelled after I'el banished them to the Earth. Also known as 'The Unseen' because they work their evil from the shadows, through dreams and human possession.

Asbel: (as-belle) Weakest link of the six Satans.

Anjou'elle: (on-ju-elle) Sister and ally to Neph'reus.

Belial: (be-lie-al) right hand man to Nik'ael.

Ged'erel: (ged-relle) Most trusted ally of Yeqon.

Kasadya: (Kas-ahd-ja) Oldest of the Daimon.

Lilith: Formerly human, not a hybrid, but a monstrous being evolved over thousands of years into the mother of vampires through drinking the A'vean blood.

Neph'reus: (nef-ray-us) Sister to Anjou'elle.

Nik'ael: (nik-ale) The last of the Satans to be recruited during the Great Flood.

Pineme: (pin-em-ay) One of the six satans.

Yeqon: (ya-kon) Leader of the Six Satans.

Other Terms And Places

Alchemae: (el-kem-ay) Healers of the Watchers and Eudaimonians.

Afflicted: Watchers and Eudaimonians who have become addicted to the drug Thanratos. They become a slave to whomever feeds it to them. It makes them violent, unpredictable and emaciated.

Asmodai: (as-mo-die) Creatures from the Daimon realm that are a conglomerate of many souls. They seek memories from others to grow in strength to regain a physical form.

A'vean: (a-vay-ahn) Immensely huge planet that keeps all the souls ever created by I'el.

A'vean: (a-vay-en) Descendant of I'el.

Archangels: Third rank below I'el. Keepers of peace and order. Messengers of I'el.

Cavern of Souls: Upon the death of their mortal body, a Watcher or Eudaimonians soul returns here deep within the earth. Their energy is too great without a body to safely walk amongst Humanity. They await here for the portal to A'vean to be reopened so they may return home.

Daimon: (Day-mon) Watcher or Eudaimonian that has turned evil.

Derinkuyu: (dery-ink-u-you) Factual tunnel system near Kaymakli in Turkey.

E'lan: (ee-lahn) The universal elemental current that connects all energies, both conscious and static. This current is utilised by those of A'vean decent as a means of communication, flight, transference (travel across distances within seconds) and a source of weaponry.

Eloi Council: (ee-loy) The first five Watchers who were deployed to Earth and Ged'ziel. They oversee that Watchers and Eudaimonians adhere to strict rules regarding their behaviour on Earth and keep vigil on the activities of the Daimon.

Empyrean Realm: (em-pie-re-ahn) Parallel dimension created by the Daimon. It is where they hide and travel to and from the mortal realm. It is a place of desolation, death and suffering. Only leeks, onions and apples grow in its tainted soil. It is inhabited by many creatures that hitched a ride to Earth from other worlds with the first Watchers to arrive on Earth. This is the realm of Hell, a reflection of the planet Tartarus, where all souls, whether they be human or other, go as punishment before they are allowed redemption to return to A'vean.

Eudaimonian: (you-dye-moan-e-an) Hybrid of Watcher and Humans.

High Angels: Soph'ael (Sophia) is a High Angel. One rank below I'el in power. She is the daughter of A'vean.

Kaladai: (Kal-a-die) The ancient key that opens the portal between Earth and the rest of the universe. Destroyed by I'el tens of thousands of years ago, because the Watchers interfered with the development of the human species too much.

Katoika: (ka-toy-ka) Ancient training and living sanctuary of the Watchers and Eudaimonians located deep below ground in country England.

Kaymakli: (Ky-mar-klee) Factual ancient underground tunnel system in Turkey near the town of Nevsehir.

K'ufili: (ku-filly) Similar to a kiss. When those of A'vean heritage touch their mark of A'vean against another's in greeting.

Mark of A'vean: All descendants of A'vean have a swirling marking across their right eye, forehead and cheek. It is unnoticeable when hybrids are born and only becomes prominent when they Awaken at age twenty-one. Pure A'veans; Watchers and Angels have this mark as a signature of who they are from the moment they take a physical form. It is a biological identification and communication anomaly unique to the A'vean spirits that take human form. It glows when they are threatened and also when they greet each other.

Middle Realm: Parallel earth created for the souls of good-hearted humans to dwell until the portal to A'vean is restored and they can then return to A'vean, where all conscious energies and souls dwell.

Nevsehir: (nev-sha-hish) Small town built along the hillside below ancient Ottoman ruins in Turkey.

Psynostris: (sin-os-tris) The term given to a state of sleep Watchers go into once every week. They do not sleep every night, only one coma-like sleep every seven to ten days.

Pterugia: (ter-roo-jia) The A'vean name for the wings of light energy that Watchers and many hybrids possess.

Rogue: Zombie -like creations created by the Daimon. They feed on blood.

Tartarus: (tar-tah-russ) The planet of punishment for souls that have committed evil acts. Hot and dry, barren and dank. Many levels exist on it depending on the gravity of what a soul has done during its physical lifetime.

Thanratos: (than-ra-toss) Ground up bones of ascended Watchers, Eudaimonians and Afflicted. Powerfully addictive when ingested, it gives the recipient an immense sense of power and is hallucinogenic.

Thyros: (thy-ros) Entry and exit gate to the underground chambers of the Empyrean realm. Comprised of enchanted standing stones above ground and a receiving chamber below ground.

Watchers: Warriors and protectors. Sent to various worlds, where they take the form of the inhabitants to enforce law and order and watch over the natural evolution of species.

Zythros Stone: (zyth-ros) E'lan laden gemstone rock at each and every sanctuary both Watcher and Daimon that facilitates entry into and out of sanctuaries as well as a communication portal across the world.

Prologue

12,000 years ago

As charcoal clouds mustered on the horizon, the sun still shone bright and warm from behind the billowing mass. With sleek, muscled arms, Nik'ael gripped at an overhanging branch leaning out from the shade, plucked a hard, green olive, and inspected it. Perfect! Beads of sweat glistened at his temples; the heat of summer was at its peak. A white linen chiton kept him cool as it flapped in the breeze against his thighs. He let go of the branch and unclasped his water pouch from the woven belt strung loosely around his hips. He drew a long, refreshing gulp. The rolling clouds mirrored across his sparkling blue eyes as he caught sight of his reflection in the silver clasp, reminding him all too well of what he was. Nik'ael smiled as his alabaster hair blew around his square jaw as an emerging breeze rustled the leaves above his head.

A storm was brewing; he would have to cut short his walk today. These long walks were pleased him, where he surveyed his crops. It rested his mind amongst the peaceful quiet of the orchard. Nik'ael's broadening smile deepened the dimples on his golden cheeks. The harvest was plentiful. They would all eat heartily this year. A rumble of thunder in the distance set him on his way down the grassy hill towards home. The unripened olive rolled between his finger and thumb as he went.

Nik'ael surveyed expansive plains as he descended from the rise of the hilltop. *This is a paradise on Earth,* he thought. He contemplated the small village that was his home—a collective of family and friends who lived and worked in harmony. An eclectic mix of people who laughed and loved, regardless of who or what they were. Illness was rare, lives were long, and the land upon which he stood sustained them well. Nik'ael looked skyward and wondered why, even now, he and his kindred still could not visit their true homeland, despite all their good works for the human population.

Many years had come to pass since life was breathed into the first soul on this world. Distant thunder rumbled deeply as he took in the parched surrounds, and he thought about his ancestors. They were sent to watch over this new mortal species called humans. It had been a blessing and a curse. For, once on Earth, these Watchers of the Kingdom of A'vean succumbed to the impulses of the human condition, breaking the law of the Kingdom. They discovered urges of the flesh that they had hitherto never known. They fell in love and lusted after these weak but beautiful beings, creating offspring such as he, Nik'ael, son of Toth'iel.

These offending Watchers were sent to Earth to oversee and protect humans, nothing more. Breeding with them was considered heinous by the Throne, a great betrayal of the innocence of humankind. The Watchers were banished without recourse to live amongst humankind, forever unable to return home. New afflictions beset the Watchers, no doubt punishment for their weakness. Bitterness and anger brewed within many of them. A new scourge which they suffered in the human form, and which divided them into factions. Nik'ael was one of the Eudaimonia—the Flourishing Ones—hybrids who had merged through necessity into a peaceful life on Earth among the humans. They continued to teach and care for man and woman whilst learning from their ancestors' painful experience to no longer mix their progenitors' bloodline with mortals.

Realising the damage they had caused, many of the offending Watchers had largely removed themselves from contact with humans, preferring to retreat within the shadows into a hidden life. A select few stayed to guide their Eudaimonian offspring in the ways of the ancestors in the Secret Places hidden throughout the world. They protected the descendants from themselves and their enemies.

As strong as Nik'ael was, even he feared the others, those in exile who became The Daimon—vengeful Watchers who had vowed to rise against A'vean. Reviled by their predicament, they disappeared, not heard from for centuries, but remained ever-present, ominous and unseen.

As Nik'ael travelled home, leaving behind him the olive trees he loved so much, something touched him lightly upon his shoulder. He turned, and his eyes widened in surprise for a moment. In his three hundred years, he had never seen such a being. Uriel, an Archangel from the High Council of A'vean towered over him.

Nik'ael bowed deeply, eyes cast down.

"Stand, young Nik'ael, I wish you no harm. I wish only to speak with you."

"Kindred, you have my ear and my heart, but I cannot stand in your presence," he quietly responded as he laid his arm upon his bent knee.

"Many years have passed since we could consider ourselves kindred, Nik'ael, yet I bring you a warning at the peril of my divine soul. You are descended of my brother Toth'iel who sinned along with the others. I have watched with regret his fate and that of his lineage. Entrenched in the mortal realm eternally is truly horrendous." Uriel shook his head in despair. "You, Nik'ael, have lived with dignity amongst humankind and have not followed in your father's way."

Nik'ael cringed inwardly at the insult. His father had been a great warrior who had made one simple mistake. He was too scared to share these feelings. He did not know the temperament of an Archangel first-hand to dare to contradict one.

Uriel continued. "I have heard your confessions of remorse for the sins of your forebears. Your undertakings to be of service to the

Throne in protecting man and woman from further degradation have not gone unnoticed."

Nik'ael attempted to speak, but Uriel struck him silent with the wave of his hand.

"For this reason, I grant you a small mercy. I am here on the orders of the Throne, directly from the great I'el, to warn our humble servant Noah of a great flood. It shall deluge the Earth catastrophically, so as to purge all of the evil from this once beautiful creation. Take refuge Nik'ael. Warn your worthy kindred, for I pity your poor souls."

Nik'ael was silent for a moment, his mouth hung slightly open in shock. He looked upwards, barely daring to meet the eyes of Uriel. Surely this could not be? His Creators were not vengeful. Were they not benevolent, especially to those who shared the spirit and power of A'vean running through their veins? His mind raced for answers.

Uriel rose into the sky as glaring white light and heat emanated from behind him. His eyes swirled like supernovas, a mishmash of coloured, sparkling light. In a booming voice, he called out, "You have been warned. Dismiss me at your peril."

He was gone in a blinding flash that left Nik'ael reeling from the aftershock, thrust back onto the ground with the breath knocked from his lungs. As he recovered from the encounter, he drew himself up and fled.

Despite a superhuman speed, he worried his mortal legs would not get him home fast enough to warn his village. Against all his instincts, he forced himself to stop, close his eyes, and relax his mind. Connecting with the elements, he drew in the energy surging on the breeze, and rose into the sky just as Uriel had. Nik'ael felt the ripples of energy surging from within, an instinct he had suppressed more often than not. Doubt plagued him as his back burned and his muscles flexed. He could never match the power of an Archangel, yet he knew he possessed an immense strength, which was unusual for a hybrid. He comforted his confidence with this thought as he let himself relax. Nik'ael flew upon the cooling breeze, through the ever-darkening sky. The ground flew by below, but not nearly fast enough in this moment of desperation. He quietly cursed himself for not practicing his higher abilities more often. He never really needed to. By the time he reached the valley where he lived, an ominous and heavy rain was drenching the landscape.

Nik'ael called out frantically to his family as a feeling of doom suddenly overwhelmed him. Neither human, Eudaimonian, nor Watcher responded. The bang of a door against a nearby house set him on edge as the breeze screeched wildly through the village, like the howls of monsters in the pits of Hell. Distressed chickens clucked and squawked as they dashed for cover. A cow had pulled itself free from its tether and seemed disorientated, nosing through barrels of grain, the whites of its eyes bulging.

Searching every home and field, he found nothing but signs of hasty retreat. The rain pelted his body. The streets already ran with torrents. In the distance, through the hideous sounds of the angry storm, he thought he heard a scream. He felt fear and pain, but not his own. Drawing as much energy as he could, he crested the rocky hill that protected his village from the ocean winds, only to be confronted by a scene of utter horror.

There, upon the beach and bathed in a blinding light, were his family and friends being slaughtered by High Angels. Humans were being thrown like sacks, smashing their brittle bodies into barely recognisable remnants. The odour of blood made his stomach lurch with nausea. The unnatural redness running into the sea foam was hard to watch, yet he could not look away. Watchers and Eudaimonians had their spines ripped out, rendering them unable to commune with the elements. Fresh muscle and bone littered the sand, leaving them vulnerable and paralysed, unable to save themselves through flight or transference. The dark blood of the Watchers and the crimson of the humans, congealed into pools of horror before it was lapped up by the incoming tide. Nik'ael hid behind a large rock, watching the bloody murder with disbelieving eyes. He was frozen in place. He could not have moved from his hiding spot, even if he'd wanted to.

As though time stood still, this scene seemed to last forever, as though it was occurring in the slow motion of a nightmare. The paralysis of shock numbed him, and his body was immovable from the ground.

When all of the humans were dead and the Earth-bound Watchers rendered completely defenceless and unconscious, the avenging Angels ascended up to the clouds and disappeared, their mission complete.

Torrential rain fell with a deafening roar. Nik'ael's hair plastered to his face. His tears and the hammering droplets of rain were indistinguishable now. Shock had heightened his senses. Every hair on his body stood frozen, every cell intimately aware of the suffering below. Pain shot through him as though he himself was under attack. His stomach heaved at the metallic odour of the inconceivable torrents of thick, glistening blood as it drained from the sand into the ever-encroaching tide. What was once pristine white was now stained a dark, sickening red.

Nik'ael slowly rose out of his hiding place, shamed by his cowardice. *Uriel warned me too late*, he thought to himself. They had no chance at all. Was that his intention? Was he being fooled by design? Was he to be punished by bearing witness to such carnage?

Still in shock, he made his way unsteadily by foot down to the beach. Stepping through the masses of bloodied bodies, he kneeled by a human companion, a young man so broken from within that he was now a mere sack of skin. Lifeless eyes looked up at him. Poor Evane, such a kind soul. He scanned the beach, short of breath from the sorrow as he found himself surrounded by hundreds of lifeless and dying corpses, most of whom he knew. The wind blew hard into him, whipping at him from all directions. The sea spray burned his eyes and the sand bit hard at his skin as he searched on. He was unable to heal the mortal wounds of his kindred by himself. There were too many, and the poor humans had no hope at all.

Furthest away from the menacing tide, high up on the beach, he came upon a figure whose familiarity brought him to his knees instantly.

Lying atop a small rise of craggy shoreline rock, a female lay prone. Her back was flayed wide open, her beautiful earthly body completely ruined. Nik'ael crawled to her on hand and knee, such was the effect that the sight had upon him. He reached out to her still warm but ghastly pale flesh and rolled her over into his lap. He knew who she was even before he saw her beautiful face. He could tell by the curve of her body, the impossibly long plaited white locks, now bloodstained and cascading down her lithe physique. Across his lap, mortally wounded and limp as a rag, was his wife, Neren'iel. Her soul was no longer with him. As a half-breed, she could not withstand the immense power of an avenging Angel, and these wounds could not be healed. He gently picked up her hands and kissed her fingers, already tinged blue by the touch of death. He wanted to die right then and there with her. Pulling her up higher into his lap, he cried out, his head thrown back in anguish. Hot tears cascaded down his face, mirroring the rain pounding upon his back. The physical droplets of his grief diluted the blood that encrusted her angelic face. He could not feel her energy any longer. He could not feel anything at all.

After a time, Nik'ael was forced to carefully lay her back upon the ground. A soft and lingering kiss was placed upon her cold lips, a whisper of eternal love promised into her unhearing ears. He ran his hand one last time down the length of her hair, caressing her soft, pale skin under his trembling hand, embedding her visage and feel into his memory. He rose into the sky, weakened by what he had seen on the ground. The ocean was rising and raging at an incredible speed. Tsunami-like waves crashed further, eating deeper into the peninsula, engulfing everything in sight. Were any of his kind able to survive this? He turned his back, no longer able to look. In the distance, he saw her. She was fleeing over the farmland. Had she sat there like him and done nothing, too? He closed his eyes. He was utterly alone, deserted, betrayed.

Nik'ael flew for what felt like an eternity, his own tears adding to the steadily filling oceans. The sky overhead was smudged crystalline by the icy comet that had exploded above the earth, now raining its remnants down. He found small ports of rest on the peaks of the highest hills and mountains not yet engulfed by A'vean's wrath. Nothing made sense. I'el was peace, A'vean the ultimate place of oneness, or so he had been taught as a child. His confusion slowly turned to the beginnings of anger.

Finally, he spotted out at sea a vessel of such magnitude that he thought for a moment he was hallucinating. His body was weak and ravaged. Following the ship's path for a time through the roiling waters, he finally flew down and rapped on its doors.

An oaken porthole opened on the side and an aged fellow thrust his head out, looking about for the disturbance. The wind and sea spray blew savagely into his greying hair and beard.

He glared in surprise at Nik'ael, who cried out to him, "Noah, beloved of The Most High of A'vean, please, will you offer me sanctuary? I was warned too late by the Archangel Uriel, of this horrific tragedy. I've witnessed my family slaughtered. I am lost." The human weakness deep within him surfaced as he begged for help.

Noah looked at him momentarily, then wordlessly shut the window.

Shock, abandonment, utter misery, and loneliness assaulted Nik'ael's senses.

He clenched his eyes and fists, his mouth thin with building rage. All the muscles of his body rippled beneath his golden skin. Tossed around in the sky by the cyclonic winds, he threw back his head and let out a scream so primal, so loud and reverberating, that it penetrated every corner of the Earth. His veins strained against his skin through this outpouring of passion. The swirling mark upon his face lit up like a beacon, blazing across the waters below. Something snapped within him. When his energy was finally depleted, he quieted. Nik'ael opened his eyes wide and clear. He looked back up to the furthest reaches of the sky and spoke with an unnerving calm.

"I will have my revenge against you. A worthy servant was I to you and of all those seated by your table. You reward me, a victim of circumstance, with such betrayal? I curse all that follow the Throne of A'vean, and I vow to cause chaos and harm for the rest of my days."

Nik'ael drifted silently through the air, his head low in defeat. Through bloodshot eyes, he glared at his reflection in the glassy water below. Angry tears worked their way slowly over his flaring nostrils, then languidly dripped from the edge of his locked jawline. His shadow and reflection suddenly disappeared as the dull sunlight was blotted out behind him. He spun around, still dominated by fear, and his hands flung back in defence. There before him hovered five malevolent figures. Instinctively, he knew them.

Yeqon, Ged'erel, Asbel, Pineme, and Kasadya. The Five Satans, forever present but always unseen.

Yeqon moved forward and spoke. "Brother, we heard your grief from every realm. We are one and the same. Take my hand. Join us. Together, our power combined, we shall avenge all that have wronged us."

Without hesitation, and in a moment of pure weakness, Nik'ael reached out and grabbed Yeqon's hand.

A powerful, dark energy shot through Nik'ael, piercing every cell in a nanosecond of pure agony. His eyes turned from blue opals to black, and his heart went from feeling, to stone cold.

Nik'ael was now the sixth Satan.

I always knew I was different. Not weird or quirky, just different... well maybe a little weird, but weird is completely okay. I look just like everyone else my age, mostly. On a deeper level though, I knew that what made me human was more ethereal than I was comfortable admitting, even to myself. Snippets of my abilities had been shining through my entire life. What I thought I was, and the truth of its meaning, were about to bring me crashing down into a level of chaos I could have never imagined.

One

Cockatoos screeched like washerwomen shouting orders for the day as I emerged from the fog of sleep. A blaring alarm, getting louder by each ignored minute, nearly imploded the iPhone by the bedside. Finally, I slipped my hand from under the duvet, touched the dismiss button, then flung the whole device across the room.

Refusing to open my eyes, I slithered from bed. In a well-practiced routine, I made my way to the bathroom by feel alone. Flipping the light switch on, glare reflected in the mirror, forcing wakefulness upon me.

"Ugh!" Who invented mornings? Were they thinking straight?

Turning worn brass faucets on, I waited for the shower to heat. The gentle spray of water on the curtain and rising steam beckoned. I stepped in, leaned against the wall and relaxed.

Shift work. The early starts and night shifts were the pits, but it's what I did, because I loved my job. Nursing rewarded that selfish part of me that liked the indulgence of making a difference, of saving a life, and knowing that it was my actions that did it. I would have preferred it though if people could choose their moments of sickness to occur in more socially acceptable hours.

Healing came naturally to me from my earliest memories. Anyone I saw in pain, be it a person or a poor creature found on the side of the road, I had to care for them. A legacy bestowed by my family.

Generations of healers, seers, mystics, you name it. Everyone, according to Nan, experienced something different as their gift. We could probably open up a sideshow at a carnival, except that our powers were more than a money-gouging stunt. They were organic and real, but hidden. On the hospital wards, I could gently and discreetly unfurl small amounts of my secret gift as it developed. A nursing career allowed me the freedom to be me, Sophia Woodville, without standing out too much.

After a few minutes, feeling slightly more human, I stepped out. Lavender moisturiser melted into my still-warm skin. I swiped the steam from the mirror and slid in my contacts. Warm brown eyes reflected back. I slathered on some foundation, a sweep of mascara, and aloe lip balm. A touch of makeup was necessary whenever I left the house, just enough to cover the large swirling tendrils of the birthmark that covered my right eye and cheek. I'd never been ashamed of it, but the veil of light beige saved strangers from staring or voicing the odd, awkward question. It wasn't a particularly bad birthmark. In fact, Nan instilled in me that it was beautiful; another part of my heritage.

My ordinary, covered up reflection stared back. I saved a little rebellion for my hair; I wasn't a complete bore. Rainbow tinted tresses slid through my brush as I wound hues of pale blue, pink, and green into a messy bun. I smiled. It reminded me of my rotation in paediatrics. A nurse who looked like a fairy broke down all the scary barriers that kids hid behind. It was an icebreaker and a crowd pleaser, especially if you were five years old. I thought Nan's proper old-world ways would object, but she was surprisingly modern by suggesting that it looked enchanting.

Back in my sunlit room, I threw on aqua scrubs and a worn pair of running shoes. Dropping to the floor, I fished under the bed for my ID lanyard when it occurred to me I hadn't received my regular, silence-shattering 5:45am wake-up call from my bestie, Jasmine. Then I remembered why when I caught sight of the smashed phone in the corner, resting on the ever-growing pile of crumbled clothes.

Crap, another one. Annoyed, I grabbed it off a red top, finding my ID underneath. That's the third time I'd assaulted an innocent phone to death this year. I offset this aggression with the fact I didn't do it to living things. It was becoming a costly character fault though.

I rummaged around on my bedside table, looking for the landline under a pile of books, when my door creaked open. Within seconds, a mass of black and white fur flung me to the ground.

"Shadow, you smelly old thing, no morning breath kisses!" Plastered to the floor, I snuggled my Alaskan malamute and constant shadow, hence the name. I wriggled out from under his sloppy, love-struck licking and pointed to the bed.

"Go on now, back to bed." All seventy kilograms of dog heaved up onto the bed. He snapped the quilt in his mouth and pulled it up over himself, resting his head ceremoniously upon the pillow. I giggled, thinking I should've You Tube'd that.

Dusting off his fluff from my scrubs, I dialled Jasmine's number.

"Hey you, what's up with voicemail?" she demanded. "Don't tell me you're not coming in today. It's our first day in the ER, and I'm sweating bullets here. I need you as my wingman, or person… or whatever!"

Ride of the Valkyries blared in the background of her phone. Jaz presented herself to the world as a hard-core emo, gothic chick. She closely guarded her true self, even from me. I'd learned never to question her secret stash of classical music.

"Morning Jaz. Calm down, I just murdered another phone!" I confessed. "I'm going to have to pad my walls to protect the next one that succumbs to my morning wrath."

"You're going to be working just to fund new phones," she said. "We've got to work on your morning mood," Jaz laughed, vastly improving my attitude in an instant.

"If you're lucky, I'll pick you up in twenty." I then mumbled through my parting goodbye, "Isn't it about time you got a licence?"

Avoiding the third last step with the betraying creak, I snuck downstairs and peeked in on Nan. All was quiet. The purr of the cat was whirring away on the end of her bed. As with every morning, I set out a teapot of English breakfast leaves and a blue willow teacup and saucer. I filled the kettle so that when Nan woke up, she just had to press a button, wait 60 seconds, pour, and enjoy. I slipped a ladybug design tea pot cosy, knitted by Nan, over the pot, grabbed my keys and handbag, knitted by Nan, a slice of sourdough bread, and headed out the door.

The air was cool. The crunch of my steps along the gravel path disturbed a delicate dawn silence. My Mini Cooper started with a welcoming rumble, setting some birds to flight from nearby eucalypts. Pressing the radio on, I reversed out of my forested home in the Dandenong Ranges.

A flurry of early cars passed by. As I waited to merge, I unwound the window, took a deep breath of the crisp morning air. There was an unearthly magic in the surrounding mountain ash forests. Creatures of all kinds dwelled in the shadows. Even the sound of the breeze caressing its way through the trees cast a spell over me. When I was young, I was so very positive that I could hear fairies whispering in the treetops.

Turning out, the familiar flashes burst through the pulled drapes of Brennan's house. A photographer, a pretty nice guy who worked all hours on his art. He'd given me a few beautiful nature shots as gifts for running errands for him. He'd had an accident in the past, was now paraplegic and seemed content living in solitude. It seemed such a shame. He was young and gorgeous, but never graced the wider world with his presence. I was determined to get him out of the house at some point.

A few kilometres along, I tooted the horn a couple of times outside Jaz's place. I drove right up to the front door. Bellbird song kept my mind from nodding off as I waited. She never came out on time.

I recalled the day Jaz and I met. We first found each other when we were twelve. We'd both started a new school the same day. I'd been home-schooled until then, so hadn't a clue about how to navigate the formidable social terrain of junior high school. Jaz, on the other hand, had been to seven different schools, had three expulsions under her belt, and knew how to establish herself as the top dog in three minutes flat. She was a nightmare, unkempt and foul-mouthed. We had an almost-fistfight on our first meeting at lunchtime. She did the chasing whilst I sent her dizzy circling a tree. That's how we became best friends.

The front door finally opened. Expecting Jaz to come bounding out, I tooted the horn to annoy her, but it was her brother Ben, ducking under the doorframe. He looked over at me as he headed to the garage. He paused a second, wiped his hands down his work pants and walked over.

"Hey."

"Hey," I replied, fiddling with my lanyard.

"Big day today?" He leaned on my door and smiled. It immediately felt a little warmer.

"Yeah, bit nervous. What about you?"

"Just more of the same. Picked up a nice old Fat Boy to do up."

"A fat what?"

"A Harley, Soph! Picked it up for a song. Unfortunately, it needs a heap of new parts. We'll have to scale back on the partying."

"Yeah, hard core ravers, aren't we? We'll have to tone down those crazy popcorn-filled movie nights," I said, secretly wishing that would not happen.

Ben leaned in a little closer. He smelled of grease and spice.

"Maybe I just need to cut back crawling after Jaz. Costs me a fortune ferrying her around." He jutted his chin at the house, eye on her bedroom window.

"She'll exhaust herself out eventually. At least you've got me. A hot tea, Netflix binge and I'm sweet. I'm a cheap date." The lanyard snapped. I could have died right there; the earth should have swallowed me whole.

Ben smiled, his chin dimpled. He pushed back from the car. His eyes hooked me just long enough to make me squirm.

"I love those nights, Soph," he said as he stepped away. The space left between us was an unwelcome void.

"Me too,"

Ben tucked his black, shoulder length hair behind his ears and left.

"Catch you later, Soph," he waved, disappearing into the garage to work on this latest motorbike. My cheeks burned, whilst he seemed so unaffected walking away, calm and measured.

You are an utter embarrassment, Soph.

Eventually, Tinkerbelle's emo cousin emerged from the house, thankfully interrupting my self-deprecation. Jaz sprayed deodorant on the run. She grumbled her way into the car, cursing to herself about pigs, brothers, and missing clothes.

"Just shows you that genes count for something. He's such a bloody slob. My scrubs were under his filthy socks!" Jaz pretended to gag. "I'm convinced I descend from a more sophisticated heritage. His parents clearly came from Slumland." She rolled her eyes and grunted.

"He's not so bad Jaz, just a regular guy. None of them care about clean socks!" I laughed and took the peppermint she offered me every day for 'un-kissable breath.' Jaz remained in a state of half-dress, pulling impatiently at her shoelaces and finger-combing her hair.

"Floor it, Soph." She kicked something at her feet. "Oh my God, you too? Is that last week's noodle box? You're a slob, just like him!"

"Again, licence, car, get one. My car, my space!" This was standard character bashing for us, but it was our routine, our love language.

It was a smooth drive down the tree-lined, winding roads, listening to random breakfast radio. Making good time, we detoured for a coffee. Miss Marples was a favourite haunt; the cutest little teahouse on the mountain, with amazing coffee, and scones the size of your head. I'd worked there from age fifteen as a server. Alfie and Harriet Fraser were my bosses back then. Alfie currently ran the place on his own since poor Harriet fractured her hip. Being a back of the house handyman, he never looked too comfortable as a barista, but surprisingly, made a mean short black. Alfie was a wiry man with a strong Scottish brogue, despite being a forty-year expat. Every kid around here grew up knowing that he was Santa, ringing the bell through the streets of the shire every December. He was brash and loveable; one of a kind.

As we parked, Jaz grumbled about how Ben had spoiled another 'opportunity' the previous night, following her around a nightclub. She didn't understand that he was just watching out for her. Bad boys were her poison. She didn't want to hear me defend Ben, and went inside the café ahead of me whilst I grabbed my bag and locked the car.

The back of my neck tingled as I crossed the carpark. A chill slid under my skin. I pulled my handbag closer to my body and quickened my pace. An intrusive, sharp pain fired through my head. The unnerving sensations had me instinctively look over my shoulder, examine every shadow. The café backed into dense forest; its frontage packed with bountiful gardens... plenty of places to hide. I felt for my phone in my bag, triple zero on my mind, before remembering I'd smashed it an hour ago.

A branch cracked. I spun. A mass of wisteria trailing down the roof of the café shifted, despite the air being perfectly still. Dawn blushed the horizon orange and purple, but night still claimed its place. Everything was too still. Not a bird cried. I ran to catch up to Jaz, kept the strange incident to myself, hid my trembling hands in folded arms.

We pushed through the glass-panelled doors. The perks of being a former favourite employee meant I could pop in before opening time to grab a coffee whilst the fresh morning scones were baking.

"Morning, Sisters of Mercy. Come to cure my ailments?" called a booming voice. Alfie used the same line every single time.

"Morning, Alfie. And no, no one could cure your ails. There are too many. Can we please have the usual?" I asked sweetly.

Jaz whispered sideways, close to my ear, through her teeth.

"If his ails didn't live in a bottle of Glenfiddich, he'd be just fine!"

I elbowed her in the ribs. "Shut up and be nice. He's harmless."

For a girl most would cross the road to avoid, Jaz had some pretty ironic social standards. Alcohol and Jaz didn't mix. She had little tolerance for its use.

The old man with sparse grey hair fumbled around at the counter. As ever, Alfie proudly wore a piece of clothing bearing the Fraser family colours.

"No kilt today, Alfie?" I asked.

"Ahh, too nippy for the nether regions these days," he answered in a most matter-of-fact way.

"That's more detail than I needed, but thanks." I made on OMG face at Jaz. She rolled her eyes, disgust clear and present.

Alfie wore a tattered green and red vest, proudly ironed, with polished silver buttons.

"How's Harriet today?" I asked.

"Oh, she's never better, never better. Especially since your dear old Nan come see 'er. Bless her. She's an angel, that woman."

"That she is," I responded as he topped up the coffee grinder.

We waited on a window bench seat out front whilst the intoxicating smell of arabica filled the room. Miss Marple looked down upon us from every direction. A hundred framed photos covered richly papered walls, an homage to the great British mystery sleuth.

"So," Jaz began, "We need a night out in the city. There's a great band playing at a new club on Flinders Lane. I've got to make up for last night. Bloody Ben!"

"Just the two of us?" I asked. "In the city? I don't know, Jaz." Embarrassment clawed up my neck. "I'll stay in, you know Nan. She's so overprotective."

Yes, yes, I was a young woman in the prime of life, and used to enjoy the odd clubbing experience. I'd just lost interest in the nightlife scene since my last experience. My idea of fun was being outdoors, surrounded by nature. I know sounds like a tick off the bucket list of a retiree, but I didn't care. It killed Jaz. I was sure I was her social faux pas.

"C'mon Soph. Ben will be there, unfortunately for me, but fortunately for you. I'm sure mister sticky-bloody-nose will be all over the place. Even though we know he's a pussycat, no one else does.

You've seen six-foot-six trouble back away from him at a glance. You'll be in expert hands. Hopefully, I'll be in hot ones!"

I smacked her leg. "Be nice!"

"Never!" Jaz winked.

I smiled and shook my head. As long as she was safe, what business was it of mine?

"Anyway, you could tell Nan that you're spending the night at my place, a girls' night in." Jaz grabbed my hands. "C'mon Soph, you've got to let your hair down, and I mean literally. Have I ever pointed out to you that you never actually wear it down? If you let that rainbow mane down with me by your side, we'll look like Helena Bonham Carter and Barbie on a date! That's action done and dusted!" She laughed wildly at her own joke.

"Jaz, I know you think I'm a geriatric in a twenty-year-old body but…"

"Yes, and your point is?"

"Hmm…" I frowned jokingly. "Downtown isn't my thing anymore. All those sweaty bodies squeezed into dark spaces. I can't breathe." I pulled the collar of my shirt to waft in some air. "I'm claustrophobic just thinking about it." I smacked her arm. "And I'm not going to lie to Nan." I eyed her disapprovingly. God… I was a geriatric.

She rubbed her temples in exasperation. "Sophia, I love Nan, I know she means well, hell, she was right about that last dipstick I dated. But you have to actually live a little, get outside your comfort zone and her shadow. What do you want to do? Go to work, come home, make tea with Nan, and knit your own line of handbags for the rest of your life?" Jaz shrugged her shoulders.

I hugged my handbag to my side in mock shock.

"You can't go to the same two pubs up here for eternity! That's a very small gene pool to dip into. You're young, gorgeous, and never had a boyfriend, girlfriend, or whatever your thing is. Seriously, you don't realise what you're missing out on!" She grabbed my hands as I felt my cheeks burn from the unintended insult.

"You owe yourself a bit of room to take a risk and enjoy yourself. Not everyone's out to get you! There are some nice people out there. I know what happened last June gave you a fright, but that's not representative of every experience." Her eyes were sympathetic, though her words were trying to galvanize me into action.

"You're still trying to hook me up! I'm not interested, not just yet," I sighed dramatically. "Unless you can deliver Theo James to my front door, forget it!" I clutched my heart; she rolled her eyes. Jaz needed a partner constantly. She hated quiet, never liked her own company. I was happy to wait for the right one, not just anyone. I never felt the need for constant companionship the way she did. Well, I'd certainly reconsider that stance for Theo, though.

The conversation reminded me of my last experience in central Melbourne. We'd caught a train downtown to the new Docklands development. A boutique club had opened up, and Jaz had procured a few opening night tickets from some poor sap who was after her. Unfortunately for me, Ben was under strict instructions to stay out of her face that night. If he hadn't, my night may have turned out differently.

It had been a nice place, actually. A modern medieval-chic feel. Jaz's taste, down to the finest detail. The crowd looked loaded, and not just with money. Glassy-eyed, distant stares surrounded us as bodies moved hypnotically to the reverberating beat under minimalist lighting. It wasn't quite the crowd we were expecting. That kind of partying was totally not our scene. We'd stuck by the bar for a while until the Sap turned up and summoned the guts to ask Jaz to dance. She loved the seductive power she held over people.

"You all right for a while?" she'd asked.

"I'm fine. I'll just be here, admiring the stoners. Try to show some class tonight, Jaz. Just one girl or boy at a time tonight?" I asked in my best motherly voice.

"Always." She blew a provocative kiss, batted her eyelash extensions and disappeared onto the dance floor.

After a while, a guy in a black hoodie sat next to me and started the usual small talk. Oddly, he stared straight ahead at the mirror behind the bar, not looking in my direction at all. Face shielded by the hood, he seemed underdressed for the place. He picked at a coaster through black gloves.

"You here with anyone?" His voice was strained. He coughed to clear his throat.

The hairs on my neck rose like internal alarm bells. I edged away.

"Yes, actually. My boyfriend is just in the bathroom." My voice wavered with the quick lie.

"Thought you walked in with that chick over there?" He jutted his head in Jaz's general direction.

"My boyfriend is her brother. He brought us in, okay? Look, he'll be back in a minute. I'm not interested. Can you please leave me alone?" I'd searched for Jaz, but she was nowhere to be seen.

He stopped talking at that, got up, and walked away with a limp.

Nervous sweat had sprung down my back. This creep has been watching me. The value of having a boyfriend right then seemed to suddenly skyrocket.

My head ached, and I felt a little nauseous. I needed some fresh air.

I made my way down a dimly lit hall to find the ladies' room, catching my heel on a ripple on the rug. As I bent down to reposition my shoe, a large gloved hand clapped over my mouth. Someone dragged me out through a door into an internal corridor.

"Don't even think of making so much as a squeak!" The words rumbled cold and wet into my ear.

Immediately, I was sure it was the guy from the bar. His voice was the same. I struggled, twisted and kicked, but I couldn't see him or wrench myself from the iron grip. There was no chance to scream. His hand pressed hard into my mouth, blood coated my tongue. I fought with all I had, thinking that this was it. I'm going to be tomorrow night's six o'clock news. He dragged me into shadows, pushed me face down onto a concrete floor. He felt me up, all over my back, down my arms and legs. My skin crawled with revulsion, nausea burned my throat, my mind swam. He flipped me over.

"Move and your throat will open like an oyster shell!" Images of all the worst possible things that could happen to a girl in this situation flashed through my mind. My pulse pounded in my ears.

What actually happened, though, was as terrifying as it was bizarre. He leaned forwards; his face still hidden by the hoodie. He took ragged, laboured breaths, the odour sour. He moved with urgency; his head swung around frequently to check that we were alone. He sniffed at the air, like a dog trying to pick up a scent. My limbs froze when he reached for my eyes. I could barely draw a breath; his weight was too heavy on my chest. I squeezed my eyes closed; my lips trembled wildly. The cold of his gloves pried my left eyelid wide open. His head tilted, face still unseen, inspecting my eyes. For what, I didn't know. He grumbled, seemingly annoyed. His breath was hot and more rancid by the second, each breath gurgled and bubbled. Next came a flash of silver. I struggled for my life then, regardless of his threat. He growled like an animal when I freed an arm, reached up and grasped at the silver weapon with every ounce of my strength. I punched his face, shoving it back into a glimmer of light, immediately wishing that I hadn't. His hood slipped back. A bald, sallow-skinned face with dark, unforgiving eyes glared back. His lips were pale and bloodless, as lifeless as a corpse. I frantically lashed out and registered the coldness of his skin.

He overpowered me again. The weapon slashed at my arm, making sharp, deep contact. A screamed erupted from me. His weight shifted off me. He scrambled up and gazed at his small, scalpel-shaped blade. I shuffled away, taking quick advantage of the freedom. I frantically looked around for an escape route, glanced back at his position, just in time to see him lick my blood off the knife. The bile that had been swirling in my throat ended up on the floor. Limbs a tangled, jellied mess, I tripped over myself, fell against a wall, but exploded into a run, expecting another grab to finish me. Something bright flashed from behind me. It reflected off of the metal door I was yanking open. I looked back momentarily to see my attacker spreadeagled on the floor, a large gash across his head. Dark fluid seeped slowly from the wound. Repulsed, I ran. As the door slammed behind me, I heard a malicious laugh, his voice in my head.

"Now, now, I know who you are. I'll be seeing you real soon, sweet angel. Mmmmm. Yum, yum."

The night was a blur after that. I'd dragged Jaz out and screamed practically the entire way home. It took me two days to tell her what actually happened.

"Soph! Soph? Oh, don't go thinking about that, please? He was just a pervert, high on some kind of dust trying to scare you. He's probably dead or someone's girlfriend in prison by now." Jaz's voice pulled me back from the vile memory.

"Will you at least go somewhere, off the mountain at a minimum, just to get away from here?" She held her arms wide in an exaggerated gesture, indicating the general vicinity around us.

"How about a compromise?" I offered as I pushed the memory far away. "We'll go down to The Mill in The Gully after work tonight to celebrate our first day in the ER. I'm sure the crowd aren't the Neanderthals you think they are."

Her expression brightened slightly at my concession.

"But you have to come for a hike in Sherbrook Forest with me on our next day off together."

"Oh, come on! That's not a fair deal. Nature and bugs and ugh," she grumbled. Outdoorsy was not her thing, just like clubs weren't mine. It was a miracle we were even friends.

Thankfully, Alfie interrupted with steaming cups.

"You girls goin' out on the town tonight?" he asked, ever the eaves dropper.

"Yes, Alfie. And yes, I'll mind my manners." I gave him a gentle squeeze on the arm.

"It's those boys who need to mind their manners nowadays. You be sure 'n take that Ben with you; he'll keep their grubby hands off of yer. Yer hear me?" Alfie's eyes sparkled with a little moisture.

"Don't worry yourself, old man. She's a big girl now. We can look after each other. C'mon, Soph. We're going to be late."

Jaz shuffled me out of the front door, the bell tinkering as it opened and closed.

"If you go listening to old McDougall there and his nonsense, you'll end up a spinster, living in a house full of cats!"

"Rude! I like cats!"

I peered back to wave at Alfie, catching him taking a swig from a silver flask hidden under the till.

Chapter Two

The horizon of warm weather loomed in early December. Soon the dry heat of an Australian summer would arrive. I loved the heat of the sun on my skin. It was comforting and familiar, and I didn't rock winter clothes.

At 6:50am Jaz and I arrived in the staff room of the ER at St. Xavier's Public Hospital. Judy McPhail, the mentor for graduate nurses, was waiting by the door with the allocations for our first shift. We were both nervous. Anything could roll through those doors, and that kind of unpredictability was daunting. I may have had a natural healing gift, but that didn't mean the horrors of what could happen to the human body freaked me out less than anyone else.

"Okay, Jasmine Armitage. Good morning." Judy's face exuded warmth, and with a broad smile, she handed Jaz a welcome pack. "You are going to work alongside me today in the Short Stay wing. We should get a few sprains and fractures, and there's usually a lot of suturing to do down at that end. Have you helped with stitches before?"

"No, but that sounds sensational!" Jaz was determined to work in the high stress and pace of the ER. An adrenaline junkie, Jaz had only had one speed, and that was full throttle.

"Sophia Woodville…" Judy flipped her notepad over, scanning the staff roster. "You will be partnered with Cindy Beal. She's in the resuscitation bays today, so that's going to be a real eye-opener for you.

Take in as much as you can. There's always a handful of heart attacks, so keep your eyes and ears open. You should learn a lot today."

I was sure my life force left me then and there. Dealing with people on the edge of life and death was terrifying. I glanced at Jaz; my eyes wide with unadulterated fear.

"Whoa, you're like a super nurse already. Just don't zap yourself with the defibrillator!"

"Thanks, friend!" I said and headed out the door to what would become the day that started it all.

What I thought was going to be the most terrifying experience of my life actually turned out the opposite. Cindy was a patient and kind educator. Twenty years of experience and not at all jaded.

By lunch I'd done numerous electrocardiograms, taken enough blood to satiate a vampire, and roused more than a few overindulged ravers. I'd actually confused a few of them, as they happily thought they'd arrived in Fairyland when they woke up with me in their faces. Thank you rainbow locks.

The mayhem of the place was overwhelming though. People of all persuasions came and went, nonstop. Groaning, crying, screaming and arguing; countless eruptions of unpleasantness spilling on the floor seemed par for the course. Lunch with Jaz was a welcome break for me and an expletive-filled venting session for her.

"That was so not what I was expecting! I've been showering stinking old winos all morning. I was yelled and spat at by a woman complaining that aliens stole her methadone, and she needed more before they came back to abduct her!" She blew her fringe from her eyes with a look of disgust. She pinched her nose, attempting to rid her memory of all the offensive odours.

"That wasn't the worst of it. I was sent into the kids' wing to relieve the staff for morning tea. All the little rug bunnies cried and hid from me. Couldn't even get a temperature taken! What the actual…?" she complained as she popped the top of her Gatorade.

"Have you looked in the mirror lately?" I giggled. "Smudged black eye liner, blood-red lips, emo hair? Not exactly a fairy party for the kids, Jaz! You'd do better where I've been today. You'd frighten the OD's into not risking death anymore if they woke up to your pretty face!" I scoffed playfully. She pursed her lips, one eyebrow kinked up in annoyance.

"You literally stop my heart with hilarity. I am choosing to ignore your insults. So, what about you? Any hot docs to drool over while stabbing in adrenaline?"

"Oh, for God's sake, turn off your hormones. I'm trying to eat!"

"That crud is not food. Nothing remotely delicious there. Here, have my apple." She rolled it across to me.

Whilst she bit into a pastrami and cheese toasty, I tucked into my quinoa and vegetable salad. "Do I ever look like I'm lacking energy?"

"No, but you'd be easier to order for on pizza night!"

"There is such a thing as a vegetarian pizza you know!"

"Why bother?" Jaz stuck her fingers in her mouth, pretending to vomit. "Anyway," she drawled, "Remember that cute new intern we worked with on Southward? You know the one, all muscle, no brain? Well, there must be some brain since he's an intern, but I tell you, one look from me and he's just a hormone with legs!" She had her sultry, come-hither face on.

"Leave the poor docs alone. They don't understand that you are the lioness and they're the gazelle."

Jaz smiled deviously.

"I've got a date with him tonight. Do you hate me? Do you mind if he comes with? He's offered to pick me up. I hope his car is cleaner than yours."

"Whatever makes you happy, Jaz. I'll stay in. I wouldn't want to crowd you." I was kind of relieved. I'd been feeling more exhausted than usual. I stirred slowly at my coffee, taking a bitter sip, forgetting I hadn't actually sugared it yet. Jaz groaned as I ripped open a small stick of sugar.

"God, you're such an old bag! Sister, you're not getting out of it.

You better be there tonight, too!" She stood up, pointed her water bottle at me. "Be there, woman!"

"Okay, okay," I said. "But just for a little while. Satisfied?"

"Excellent!" Jaz's eyes widened. "Oh crap, I need to wax!" She winked provocatively.

"Ugh, how much is he going to see on the first date? Actually, don't answer that!" I flashed her my palm.

Soon the clock ticked on the half hour, cutting short her reverie about which lippy and black dress she should wear. I pushed out from the table, gulping my coffee down.

"See you Jaz. Hope you find some hot wino to wash this arvo to rev you up for tonight," I giggled and ran from the swipe of her hand, just vaguely hearing a string of insults as I whipped out the door.

Back in Resus, it was quiet for all of thirty seconds. Cael, the RN in charge, called out to me with an Irish-tinted voice to prep a patient bay for a 'screamer.' It seemed like Jaz might have hand balled one of her 'fun' patients to me. As I was double-checking the bedside equipment, a growing howl of what sounded like a cornered wild animal echoed up the corridor.

Heading up the ambulance gurney as it wheeled through the door was Cael, his eyes wide with amused alarm.

"Sophia, ready for some fun?" A devious grin dressed his face. He was going to enjoy my inexperience.

"Um, what do you…" I didn't need to finish my sentence when I caught a glimpse of our patient. My heart raced with uncertainty. Pulling up was a thrashing mess of arms, legs, and blood spatter attached to a body that had seemingly ripped out its own hair. Fistfuls of long auburn locks entangled the fingers of what I now realised were female hands.

She was screaming; howling a name.

"Annie! Annie! Annie!" Heavy panting followed a rumbling growl. Bloodshot eyes looked desperately left and right for an escape route.

Lashing out at anyone daring to approach, even scratching herself with blood-caked acrylic nails, she was a fearsome sight. Anything she could grab hold of was fair game. The attending registrar reached in to give her a shot of Valium to calm her down. Bad move. Lightning quick, she grabbed his wrist, twisting it with a sickening crack. The syringe flew across the room. The doctor fell to the floor, screaming and grasping his flaccid hand. I pressed the emergency call button. The black harness securing the patient to the ambulance trolley kept her body down, but she fought so fiercely that the entire gurney shimmied across the floor.

"Get me out, get me out! Get me a corpse!" she screamed. The paramedics looked more than pleased to be depositing her with us.

"Do you think we need a psych consult, Cael?" I asked rhetorically amid the incessant howling. He had meanwhile called a code grey, indicating the presence of an aggressive patient. This received an immediate response as more medical personnel entered the room, backed up by some burly security guards.

"Considering she was found trying to scratch some poor sod to death at Ferntree Gully Station, that'd be a yes," Cael answered over the noise, preparing more Valium as he spoke. "That ain't just her blood under her nails. I paged for the consult when we got the heads up from the ambos while they were in transit. Hope he'll be here sooner rather than later. Having fun?" He winked at me as he leaned in to hold the patient's arms down, hopefully preventing more fractured staff. His smile was calm while my heart pounded with both thrill and fear.

Whilst Cael tried to calm her down, there was a wet *pfft* sound. She spat in his face.

"Oh, come on, woman, that's just not nice!" he growled. I grabbed a cloth and antibacterial lotion, wiped his cheek, glad that I wasn't the one in the line of fire. The woman writhed more ferociously, panting like a dog. Saliva and blood trickled down her chin, drizzled onto her clothing. A few more spit bombs were dodged by all but the contorted face of the poor registrar, who was still in agony on the floor.

"I didn't sign up for this shit," he said through clenched teeth as another nurse put ice and a splint on his arm.

The woman mumbled and growled to herself, straining vigorously at the chest restraints. Her neck arched back unnaturally. Her pulse pounded so hard it bulged rapidly on her neck. She struggled desperately, the air thick with sweat, urine and the musty tang of blood. Cael eased off her for just a moment, watching her closely.

She had no ID, but as I looked through the fearsome façade, there was evidence of a previously well-kept woman. Remnants of neatly applied makeup still stuck to her face. A single gold earring dangled from an ear. Her clothes looked expensive. Apart from all the bloodied rips, she probably worked somewhere corporate.

Her attention hooked on me for a moment, grinding her teeth and chewing at her lips.

"Don't be scared. We're all here to help you. Try to calm down," my voice was shaky, lacked the conviction of a seasoned nurse, and I was met with the gnashing of her perfectly white teeth.

"You, remember me? Hmmm?" Her bloodshot eyes widened. She smiled broadly; her expression maniacal. "Mmmm, you tasted so delicious." Her voice was melodic; the creepiest sing-song tone. She wore a crooked and impossibly scary smile. I involuntarily took a step back from the bed, felt a chill prickle the back of my neck.

What the hell? It can't be. I rubbed the silvery scar from the attack beneath my sleeve. Without warning, and her with eyes fixated on me, she yanked her arm back towards her face. She began biting deep chunks out of her own flesh.

"You are not worth this torture, though. Argh! Get me out of this thiiiing!" she screeched through a mouthful of muscle and skin, her eyes still glued to me. Arterial blood splattered the roof and walls. I copped a spray across my chest.

"Oh my God, stop! Stop!" I yelled, grabbing at her wrist to stop the self-mutilation. She spat blood and tissue at me.

"You burn, you bitch! Get your filthy hands off me. Argh!" Annie wrenched her wrist from my grip, large blisters pillowed from where I'd touched her.

"Holy hell!" said Cael.

He moved with lightning speed, grabbed both her arms, held them firmly across her chest.

Throughout this horrific episode, she screamed non-stop. Attacking herself and begging for mercy all at once. For a split second, her eyes cleared of their glazed, fanatical stare. She glared pleadingly at Cael.

"Help me! Please?" A milder voice begged, choking on the bloody mess in her mouth. It was as though there were two people battling each other within one body.

"Settle down, Ma'am, settle down. You're safe. Relax, listen only to me and I'll help you." Cael soothed in his liquid voice, "I see you; I know the pain you are suffering. Let me help you."

In the next moment, her eyes reverted to a berserk, bulging stare. The menacing voice returned, along with continued attempts to chew any part of herself that she could reach.

I grabbed some fresh bandages nearby to cover her wounds, if at all possible, never letting my eyes leave the scene in front of me.

She glared long and hard at Cael, whose expression was now deadly serious. "No one can help me, I am dead!" she screamed. "You're burning me, bastard, bastard, let go of me!" Her thrashing escalated. Between us all, we each held a limb down with immense effort. She was tiny, her strength disproportionate to her size.

As if perfectly timed, a psychiatrist arrived, eyes glued to an iPad. He addressed us briefly with a curt nod, barely making eye contact with anyone, least of all the patient. Cael, still leaning heavily on the now physically subdued woman, gave him the limited information he knew.

"Send her to H ward. We will assess her in the morning when she has calmed down and her wounds have been attended to." The psychiatrist's voice was monotone, his expression cold.

Ward H was not where you wanted to be allocated. It was locally known as Hell Ward, because that's what it was like to work there. It was the locked down section of the hospital, where prisoners and violent patients were securely treated.

"Keep her restrained. We'll sedate her for assessment up there. She's in no condition at the moment to be interviewed by those police." The psychiatrist jerked his head towards the hallway.

He looked my way for the briefest moment whilst I was trying to put a pressure bandage over the pulsing wounds of the Annie's arm. The edge of his mouth quirked up. Not in a smile, but in a crooked way that set a new chill slithering through my skin. He returned his focus to the patient. Exhaustion seemed to have settled upon the her. She panted a little slower through clenched teeth now, her crimson lips peeled back with the strain.

"Can you tell me who you are? What is your name?" he calmly inquired of her.

She considered him for a moment, grinned, and then spoke in a foreign language. It sounded like Greek, but throatier. She spoke in a careful and calculated tone.

"Anyone speak Greek?" I asked.

Cael's expression read deadly serious. "I speak a little," he answered, his eyes glued to the woman.

"That isn't any Greek I've heard, and I'm Mykonos born," interjected a pot-bellied security guard.

"It's a dialect. Perhaps you missed it growing up?" Cael answered quietly.

"I'm telling you it's not…"

"Quiet. If you can't help, just be quiet while I concentrate." Cael snapped at the guard.

"No need for translation," said the psychiatrist, clearly impatient. "She is highly distressed and needs to be calmed down before we try to make sense of her. Call the orderlies for an immediate transfer. I've called ahead. She's booked into bed 13."

He moved to leave the room, but stopped at the door, looking back as the woman began muttered randomly again.

"Annie, Annie, Annie!" she panted, pointing at the psychiatrist with a restrained finger. She spoke briefly at him in the strange language, her tone terrifying. She then reverted to English.

"Her blood is on all of our hands. Get it, get it now! You will answer to him if you do not do his bidding!"

My hair would have stood on end had it not been in a bun.

Something seemed to wash across the psychiatrist's face. Was it understanding, or perhaps fear?

He left without another word. The orderlies arrived and were given their instructions by Cael. They gingerly manoeuvred themselves around the patient to avoid the renewed onslaught of spitting and wheeled her out. Her screaming echoed down the corridor until it was cut off by the closing of the elevator doors.

I took a deep breath, the back of my gloved hand pressed firmly against my forehead. I leaned against the wall, exhausted.

Cael raked his hands through his pale hair, his face to the corner.

The pot-bellied guard was ghostly pale.

I asked the guard if he was okay.

His lips initially moved silently, making his double chin wobble. "She was, as Cael suggested, speaking some dialect of Greek that I've not heard before, but I could pick up enough." His voice was shaky; haunted. He hitched up his pants, "She said, '*You know me,*' then something else I couldn't understand. Then she said, '*I am Deumos, loyal servant. Get me out, trapped, pull me, wretched thing.*' And also, '*Peel this flesh from me.*' It sounds crazy. The last thing she said was, '*I bring you the Earth-born.*' There were some other words I couldn't make out. Then, '*Bring the blood, or pay with yours.*' She repeated these same phrases over and over. Freaky shit, oh sorry miss, um… freaky stuff, you know?" He made a quick exit after that, leaving just Cael and I in the room.

"Peel this flesh from me! What the hell? Do you think it's some new drug?" I asked, rubbing the goosebumps from my arms.

Cael responded in a kind of bland way, "Not sure, Sophia, but I wouldn't want to be the one trying to draw blood for a tox screen. Seems like she's the one doing the bloodletting!" he laughed, but not with his eyes. Worry shadowed their blueness.

I picked up the Valium syringe from the bloodied floor and noticed the thin red wheel lines tracking out the door. Cael called my name, pulling my attention from the foul sight.

"Hey, look at that!" He pointed to the wall clock, a little more animated.

"It's only fifteen minutes to knock off. What do you say we grab the other grads and meet at The Mill for drinks tonight? I could use a debrief after today in the shape of a shot glass!"

"Actually, I was going to meet up with friends there tonight, anyway."

"How about I pick you up, so you don't have to drive alone? Is 5:45 ok? Text me your address."

"Oh, um… that'd be great!" I'd rather arrive with someone than walk into a packed club alone, so this was unexpected, but welcome. "Here," I passed Cael a paper hand towel with my address written on it. "My phone needs repairing," I said with a smile.

I arrived home after dropping off Jaz and took a quick shower. My scrubs and shoes went straight in the garbage. I wasn't going to bother washing those. Annie's face was etched in my mind, and I needed to eliminate all traces of that experience.

My wardrobe was a disaster. I surveyed the crammed mass of fabric and accessories. Having little care for fashion, I settled quickly on a pair of black skinny jeans with a simple white shirt. Patent black flats with a bit of bling on the toe were my only 'good' shoes, so on they went. To make my bestie happy, I straightened my hair and left it down. The multi-coloured layers nicely pepped up the muted tones of my outfit. The indigo on the top was due for a touch up, the pale natural blonde was showing through, but the colours still popped enough.

Nan was out on one of her charity days, and as she didn't 'do' mobile phones, I left her a note on the kettle. It's the first place she goes when she arrives home.

Tea is the essence of the Gods, Sophia. Her motto and life philosophy.

Right at 5:45pm there was a rev in the front garden. Footsteps crunched towards the house, and finally a knock at the door.

I opened the door just as Cael removed a motorcycle helmet. Afternoon sun glinted off shoulder-length, pale blonde hair. Distressed denims, a white t-shirt with a black stallion on it, and a retro aviator jacket had him looking like a Calvin Klein commercial on my front porch. From hospital scrubs to this. Wow! Words died in my throat for a moment.

"Are you going to let me in, Sophia, or do I need an invitation like a vampire to step over your threshold?" he asked with a bemused smile.

"Oh, God. Sorry, I'm just flustered. I was, um, rushing to get ready."

He stepped in, practically ducking through the doorway. Clearly no jockeys in his family tree, I guessed.

"Nice house."

"Thanks, I'll just grab my bag."

I dashed upstairs, rummaged through the clutter on my bed, and found it. I returned to find Shadow, tail wagging, flat out on his back, Cael scratching his belly.

"Wow! He generally goes all attack dog with anyone other than Nan or I, he's even sus on Ben and Jaz." I was impressed. Shadow was my nice-o-meter.

"Animals know who the good guys are," Cael said.

He stood, headed towards the door.

"Come on then, let's go and unwind a bit."

I looked dubiously at a red motorbike parked near the front door.

"2012 Ducati. This is *my* pet. Here, put this on and jump on the back."

I wrestled a silver helmet onto my head and mounted the pillion behind him. My arms sheepishly slipped around his waist.

"If you don't want to go flying off around the bends, I suggest you hold on a little tighter. I don't bite."

I gripped tighter around his abs, wishing it was someone else.

We roared off at an alarming speed, so much so that I deduced the speed limits and Cael were foreign to one another. After realising he did have control of the bike, I actually enjoyed the thrill of the speed, the feeling of the wind against my skin. I hugged tighter into him, let myself relax.

About half way down the mountain, my head became fuzzy, swam with dizziness. The tighter I held Cael, the more pronounced it became. It wasn't female hormones causing me to girl crush on him; it was different. If I pulled slightly back, the feeling dissipated. When I leaned into him around the bends, my head began to thump. *Weird.*

We pulled up to The Mill in Grand Prix record time. Whilst Cael looked stunningly wind-swept, I tried to smooth down helmet hair. The carpark was full, the music already pulsed into a foggy, dusk air. It was a cute place. A two-storey bluestone building with a pub downstairs and a concert venue upstairs. A blue neon entrance light blinked eerily through the blanket of dusk. A poster by the door advertised the night's band, a Pink tribute called Moore Pink.

Pushing through the double doors, immediately there were a few familiar faces from St. Xavier's. We veered to a table near the entrance to the beer garden and joined them. I greeted Gus, Jane and Olivia, all from the ER, whom I'd only met briefly that morning. Cael rescued me from an awkward silence after the hellos, ordering a round of drinks and some tapas.

After some general chit chat, Gus asked us about the woman who had come in.

"I hear it took two hours to get her sedated enough to get her under control," he said with raised brows.

Jane nodded. "The cops have already sent in forensics to scrape her nails and intend to charge her with the attack at the train station. Apparently, her victim was a seventeen-year-old girl. My mate Pierre has been nursing her. Apparently, the poor kid copped a hundred stitches down her back and another fifty around her eyes. What kind of animal does that?" She shook her head in disgust.

The squeal of my name interrupted the conversation. Jaz entered with a googly-eyed young boy. I say boy because this intern looked like he'd just stepped out of high school.

"Soph, you came! I so thought you'd wimp out!" I received an over-exaggerated hug. She had her cutie-pie façade in full effect. The one she dazzles all of her fresh catches with before she goes in for the kill. I noted that she'd toned down her look tonight. She'd gone for a less vampy lipstick, and covered her tattoo with a long-sleeved dress, black of course. A little less intimidating for the poor guy, probably. He was cute, but way out of his depth with Jaz, and I think he knew it.

"I didn't see your car out there," she said. "That's why I'm so surprised to see you."

"I got a lift with Cael, actually."

"You minx, I knew there was a tiger in there somewhere. Word is, he's very, very single." Jaz punched me playfully in the shoulder.

"It was just a lift," I sighed and steered her to our table.

After a delicious meal, we heard the band doing a sound check upstairs.

Jaz was the first to get up. "Who's going to join us?" She pulled her pet to his feet, and they sauntered over to the staircase. Jaz grabbed at his backside.

"I'm on an early shift," said Cael, "But I'll stay for a little while. Do you need an early night, Soph?"

Despite feeling exhausted, I was having a nice time.

"I'm good for a while, let's go."

We set off up a packed staircase. Cael grabbed my hand, guided me through. My skin was instantly on fire. My head swam again, and I had to grab the banister to remain upright.

"You okay?" He reached to steady me but I shook my head.

"I'm fine, let's go," I pushed him on ahead of me.

The first set had just begun. The lead singer was probably not the best Pink lookalike, but her voice was spot on. Jaz was dancing, amongst other things, with Mr Googly Eyes. The rest of us danced as a group. Cael stayed close, reaching for me every now and then, making sure I was okay.

After a while, we drifted into the flow of the crowd and started dancing separately. The thump of the music vibrating through me helped me relax and forget the day's worries. Despite a persistent headache and the fact that Cael was strangely keeping very close to me, I was having a great time.

In the middle of the song, *'So What'*, I caught a fleeting glimpse of someone in the crowd staring at me. I looked behind me to see if there was another person he was looking at, but everyone had their backs to him. The intrusive stare became heavier as I turned back to see he was a step closer. Dark eyes. Pale skin. He was jostled back by the crowd, becoming a silhouette behind a support post. He disappeared behind a group of girls. I arched my neck to see who it was. I kept spinning around slowly until I caught sight of him again.

My heart raced; fear instinctively crept up my spine, sweat pooled in the small of my back. Visions of the other club came to mind. Anxiety plucked at my skin. I continued dancing, trying to appear normal, despite feeling completely creeped out. I tried to get a better view with every move I made. He darted away each time. Shivers slithered along my skin, despite the heat beating off the crowd. My head craned left and right, standing on my toes to see where he went. The flashing of the disco lights flickered the room like a black and white movie.

I saw him weaving in and out of the crowd, peering back and forth at me. He was close, then far, then close again. I was just about to tell Cael when there was a loud crack. An overhead light exploded, raining down over the crowd, who screamed and scattered to get away. The lights went out. People surged in panic as the band called out to hold on until the power fired back up. I was jostled around, felt someone rush past me, cold and way too close. A hand grabbed me as an emergency spotlight turned on, revealing the panicked crowd looking for the way out. I searched for Cael but couldn't see anyone I knew as I was bumped around some more. Another grab at my arm. I was freaked out now, and searched desperately through the mass of bodies for whoever it was. The lights blared back on. I spun around, trying to find my bearings, looking wide eyed for this freak who was watching me. I turned and ran almost face first into Ben. I'd ended up by the doorway to the stairwell. Ben glared at me; arms crossed. He often looked broody, but his expression was especially dark. The shadows of his face underpinned anger or hurt. I couldn't work out which.

"Ben, I'm so glad to see you. I was just…"

"Soph, I think it's time to go," Ben said.

"Where's…" I was going to ask if he'd seen Jaz when I felt a gentle tap on my shoulder. I turned, smacking straight into Cael's expansive chest.

"Hang on, Cael, I'll just be a sec." I spun immediately back to see what was wrong with Ben, but he was gone. In the space of a fraction of a second, he'd disappeared into the thickening crowd. Something was up with him. Ben frequently came out with us, but he always hung with the group. I'd never known him to skulk alone in the background. His perfect smile always made a bad night feel good. No smile this time, and it left me with a nagging worry. Could it be that I was with Cael?

"Are you stalking me?" I asked Cael, forcing normalcy to hide my still-shaking voice.

"Just checking no one is hassling you," he replied, grabbing my hands and pulling me back to the group. An electric shot seared up my arm, causing my breath to catch in my throat. *What the hell?*

"No one's hassling me. I just thought I saw a friend," I lied. The irony of Cael's concern wasn't lost on me. I could have told him about the weirdo in the crowd, but I chose to keep it to myself for now. Cael didn't seem to notice my shakiness, so I left it at that.

Jaz emerged as the crowd thinned on the edge. Unsurprisingly, I couldn't see her face as it was so deeply glued to Googly Eyes' mouth. Perhaps that's why Ben had a thundercloud expression. He was way too protective of her.

Still slightly dizzy from the strange feeling I'd had, I tapped Cael on the arm.

"I'm gonna go home, Cael. I'll grab an Uber," I said, checking my pockets for my phone, forgetting I'd killed it that morning.

"No way. I'll drop you off, I insist. I've got a couple of things I need to catch up on before I call it a night, anyway," he said.

We said our goodbyes quickly. I didn't bother with Jaz; she was now mauling Googly Eyes in a booth at the rear of the dance floor.

The ride home seemed to clear my head, push the strange feelings away. The air was sweet and fresh, and the evening had cooled considerably and it plucked at my skin. The steep mountain road at night was pitch black. Only the small light of the motorbike hinted at the forest that surrounded either side of us.

Pulling up to my house, Cael, ever the gentleman, walked me to the door.

"Thanks for coming, Sophia. It was a good to see you smile." He leaned in towards me.

Oh God! My heart thudded in my ears. He edged closer. I smelled his cologne, fresh and light, like the ocean. I shivered as his warm breath fanned my ear.

"Don't move," he whispered. My heart hammered.
I tensed automatically. He reached behind my head, then swiped left and kicked something out into the bushes.

"What was that?" I asked, extremely alarmed.

"I thought if you turned around and saw a massive huntsman spider on the doorknob, it would spoil your night. I hate those things," he said with an exaggerated shiver.

"Well, thanks. You've saved a damsel in potential distress," I laughed, thoroughly relieved I hadn't put my hand on a spider.

"See you in the morning. Don't be late." Cael waved goodbye.

Through the revving of his bike, Cael called out.

"Lock your doors, Soph," he flicked me a thumbs up, then disappeared at alarming speed, leaving nothing but moonlit dust in the air.

I watched him ride off. There was something about him. Something I couldn't quite put my finger on. I didn't want him to leave.

Cael suddenly felt very familiar, and I didn't know why.

Chapter Three

The soft beeping of a heart monitor broke the midnight silence. The room was dark, other than a small stream of light striping the wall from an overhead nightlight. Nurses chatted quietly in the distance as they busied themselves with the night shift routine.

A large silhouetted figure slipped quietly and unseen into the intensive care room. It made its way to the deeply sedated patient. Her thickly bandaged arms were shackled to the bedside. Blood leeched through the white crepe. Her legs were secured to the foot of the bed. A blood transfusion dripped slowly through a large IV in her neck, replacing the volume of blood she'd left on the floor of the ER that morning. Oxygen tubing lay slightly askew under her nose.

The figure reached down, straightened the tubing so that the gas was flowing correctly into her nostrils. The monitor began to alarm, its rhythmic patterns became chaotic. A palm waved across the screen. With a brief flash of white light, the monitor silenced.

Beep, beep, beep.

The individual placed a hot hand across the woman's chest. Her body jerked up, as if shocked by electricity. Her eyes flew open. Inky orbs glared back. They were venomous, but her body was so heavily drugged, only her eyes could react with the hatred that dwelled inside.

Wordlessly, the figure placed his hand across her entire face, gripping gently with the edges of glowing fingertips. The woman's head arched backwards, not of her own will, but from the energy being infused forcefully into her brain. Her mouth gaped open with silent screams. Her eyes bulged, begging for mercy. The blackness within them slowly receded, revealing a hint of jade. An inky substance oozed from her nose, mouth, and ears. It amassed upon the pillow; haloed her head.

The smoky entity rose up, attempting to take form. Before it had a chance, the silhouette by the bedside thrust two hands within its depths and released a maelstrom of electrical energy. The room lit up briefly with the intensity of the force. A miniature thunderstorm raged silently above the woman's head. The thick blackness swirled and writhed in defiance. Only the individual inflicting the attack could hear its screams as it collapsed within itself, on its way to oblivion.

Once more, hands were gently placed upon the woman. One over her heart, the other upon her head.

Glowing bright and warm upon her skin, those hands infused a healing force. In the distance of her consciousness, the woman heard a message.

You are free.

The room was now quiet and empty, apart from Annie. She lay still in the bed, serene, peaceful, and healed.

Chapter Four

Another early morning wake-up went as well as yesterday, except that this time, I had to mind my manners. Nan was my alarm clock today, so I couldn't very well throw anything at her. My regular call from Jaz was a bit more surprising, though.

"I don't need a lift today, Soph. I, ah, already have one."

"Did you go home last night?' I asked, unable to suppress a smile.

Silence.

"Good luck explaining that when you see Ben. By the way, he was there last night, looking pretty peeved. You have to stop sneaking out on him."

"Sorry, I didn't see much, other than Adrian's face, among other things. Ben will live. He's a big boy. He needs to get himself a girlfriend. He needs to stop panting over what he can't have." Her tone was unsympathetic. The last part irked me.

"You're so mean; I'll see you at work." I hung up. Jaz was pretty awful to Ben sometimes, yet he never complained. I got the feeling this part of their dynamic dated back to her childhood. Most of it was a mystery to me, even now. All I knew was that they were foster kids and had looked after themselves since their foster parents died. They'd done it pretty tough, but always had each other's backs. Well, except when Jaz was prowling for a hookup.

It was a matter of life and death that I needed a large mug of coffee when I arrived at work. The staff room was empty, save for the cleaning lady who politely waved hello. I was ridiculously tired lately and seemed to get more exhausted every day. Yet it still took me ages to get to sleep at night. My mind constantly raced with empty thoughts; my heart pounded in my ears. I'd only had two drinks last night, but I had a killer headache now. There'd been no time for Miss Marple's this morning, so I suffered the crappy, generic instant hospital-issue coffee. With enough sugar, though, the hot liquid was bearable and caffeinated me appropriately.

I'd barely made it out of the door when I was knocked to the ground by a gurney as it sped through the ambulance doors. My head smacked on the doorjamb as I went down. Blackness and stars peppered my sight as I was quickly hoisted up.

"You ok? Sorry, sweetie." Gentle blue eyes glistened with worry.

I rubbed at the back of my head and leaned against the wall. "I think so. I… what happened? You normally drag-race patients through the doors?"

"Ha, humour, you must be fine. In that case, follow me. We need all hands on deck, we've got family here. I'm Kea, by the way. Come on." She guided me down the corridor.

We arrived at the resuscitation bay. What did she mean 'we've got family here'? When then slipped behind a curtain into mayhem, not the usual methodical calm. A huge medical team circled a bed. The air was rich with the sickly metallic odour of blood; lots of blood. It pooled on the floor, seeped into the soles of shoes. More blood than Annie yesterday; exponentially more disturbing. My stomach lurched. Not the best weakness to have as a nurse. I caught snippets of conversation.

"Where was he found?"

"The police said he was hanging over the top of a two-metre-high statue inside Rickett's Sanctuary. The caretaker found him when he opened up this morning. Had to call in the fire brigade to haul him down."

Monitors beeped and alarmed constantly.

"Apparently, the place was a mess. Trees ripped up, one of the statues smashed to rubble. Like a tornado had been through the place, so they say. Found his bike smashed up further down the tourist road, just back from the shopping strip, so weird."

"That's got to be a couple of kilometres away. How did he get to where he was found?"

"I've never seen an injury like this. This is no motorbike accident."

My attention spiked. Motorbike accident? I knew two people with motorbikes, Ben and Cael. I pushed forward, heart pounding in my head, trying to see who it was.

"What the hell?" someone exclaimed.

"Looks like it's just been ripped out!" said another shocked voice.

"Crank up the oxygen, blood's too dark. He's hypoxic. Draw a sample and send it to the lab."

A doctor in navy scrubs pointed to me. "We need an extra set of hands. Get some gloves on, and stand here. Put pressure over these wounds."

I froze for a moment.

"Well, come on girl, get over here!" he grumbled.

Shaking myself out of a fugue, I fumbled with the gloves, my hands sweaty, my fingers just wouldn't slip in; the gloves snapped. I grabbed another pair, hands trembling. My head ached more painfully the closer I moved to the bedside. That bang to my head… that had to be the cause.

My skin prickled, head pounding like a drum when I saw the patient. My vision blurred at the edges, and that wave of nausea rolled through me. I had to grasp the bedside for a moment to regain control of my balance. *Blip, blip, blip.* The cardiac monitor sang harmoniously next to me, but it seemed a thousand decibels too loud.

A naked male, face down, was exsanguinating quickly. A gash on either side of his spine gaped wide. My head throbbed harder. I squeezed my eyes shut for a second. Rough hands grabbed mine and pressed them down firmly over one of the spinal wounds.

"Press here, and don't move until I say so. Got it?"

I nodded to the doctor, trying to mask my efforts to slow down my panicked breathing. Exposed vertebrae shone pearlescent white up the left side of the body. I was both mesmerised and horrified all at once. Blood pulsed rhythmically with the beat of the cardiac monitor. As the blood oozed up through my fingers, I was sure, but quite possibly concussed, that it actually sparkled.

His skin was torn and ragged, as though hacked by a saw. Muscle flailed with every breath the patient took. The bloody mess made a sucking sound. The insides were too far on the outside.

The doctor was cleaning out the other side of the wound whilst inspecting it. The distraught sobs of staff unsettled me further as they frantically busied themselves with various jobs around the patient.

"I'd swear to Jesus Christ himself that this guy has had his spinal bone ripped out! Look! There's exposed spinal nerves that look exactly like cord tissue, yet the central column is intact! I want a Neuro consult!" This was the senior ER registrar, Dr Davis. He seemed nice enough, but his face was in such a contortion of confusion right now that I was sure he was feeling like he'd landed in Oz with no yellow brick road to follow.

He packed the wound heavily with gauze to stem the bleeding, calling out, "Nancy, call the OR. He needs exploration and patching up. Book a CT on the way. I need to see what's going on in there. Draw more blood for trauma panel and get some O-neg blood down here ASAP!"

Nancy nodded wordlessly and moved with a well-practised precision.

Davis looked at me. "You're new. What's your take on this?"

"I, ah, well… ah, it's horrific, it's… oh um, it's bloody, very bloody." Why was I so dumbstruck? My skin bloomed with humiliation. I was an honours grad, for crying out loud! Where were my neurons hiding?

"Don't bust a brain cell! Take your hands off there. I'm ready to clean that side out now." He moved around to my side of the bed.

Kea quietly appeared and placed her hand on my shoulder. She whispered sympathetically in my ear, "Hon, don't mind him. He tends to lash out when he's frustrated. Why you don't stand up at the top end and note the poor boy's vitals every five minutes? That'd be a great help, and I'll take over here."

I removed my bloodied gloves, quickly washed my hands, and grabbed a pen and chart.

The victim's vitals were all normal, other than an elevated temperature, which was perplexing, given the exposure he'd had in the elements and considering the amount of blood he was still rapidly losing.

Davis snapped again, "Neuro status? His pupils, have you checked them? Has anyone checked this guy's pupils?" he yelled.

"I checked them on the way in," said Kea. "They were fine then. Sophia, could you check them again?"

I pulled out my penlight and knelt down so I could get to his face.

"Oh no… no, no, no! It's Cael. Oh, my God!" I welled up.

"We all know who it is!" Davis barked, "So get on with making sure our teammate has the best chance of recovery."

Cael's face was battered but serene, his breathing steady. He was utterly ripped to shreds. From last night to this, how could it be? Just hours ago, we were laughing and dancing.

I nervously reached toward him, removing a twig stuck in his muddy, matted hair.

"What happened to you?" I whispered to no one but myself. I reached for his eyelid, very gently opened it, fingers shaking and tingling. I shone the torch's beam in, and then felt a blow as though a bomb went off at point blank range. Blinding light shrouded me. Pain seared through my back and my face. Indecipherable images flashed through my mind. Crashing waves, black eyes, women and children, intense white light. Arms reached out to me, dripping with blood, grabbing at me. Terror punched into my soul. I couldn't move or speak.

Then all went quiet.

Chapter Five

A loud knock on the door drew Diane's attention, only because it was frantic and clearly, they'd forgotten to press the intercom buzzer to request entry.

Being morning tea time, she was alone in the pathology lab, and as gross as it sounded, she'd happily snack by herself amid the sight of the various specimen containers. Annoyed, she pushed out from her desk and opened the door. A clearly inexperienced intern was standing there with a pathology bag full of tubes.

"Is this where I drop off urgent blood samples?"

He was quite a looker, but clearly not at the top of his class, because right in front of his face, a bold sign read, 'Deposit samples through chute. Please press intercom for urgent samples. Thanks, Pathology.'

"Yes, thanks. How quick do you need it?" she asked.

"Straight away. It's for Cael from the ER. He's been badly wounded in an accident, and Dr Davis needs results immediately," he blurted breathlessly. He'd obviously taken the stairs down, not the elevator.

"Oh no! Poor Cael. I'll get onto this immediately. Let them know I'll bring up the results myself."

Diane had known Cael for a number of years. He was one of those really decent guys, the kind who looked after his staff as well as his patients. For someone so young, he was of a class of gentleman long forgotten.

"Thanks," the intern puffed as Dianne shut the door in his face, threw her sandwich in the bin, and headed straight to the work benches.

Despite feeling distressed about Cael, Diane immediately prepped the slides and tubes with careful precision. The first analysis indicated that his blood-oxygen level was at 100%, which was very strange. The blood appeared to be severely oxygen deprived. It was dark blue in colour, when it should be a bright shade of red. She was slightly excited by the possibility of a mystery on her hands, but felt immediately guilty because of whom the sample belonged to. The routine in the lab could get a bit dull, so something challenging was pathologist porn. Sad, but true.

All of the other elements of this blood sample were at the highest end of normal as well, so she just needed to work out why the blood was so dark... something wasn't right.

Popping her hair back in a headband and a new set of gloves on, Dianne got comfy in her chair. More slides at the ready, she carefully slid them into her microscope. After a few adjustments to the scope, she leaned in to get a good look at this mysterious blood.

As her eyes adjusted, she sat back up and furrowed her brow. Was something swirling and sparkling on the slide? Diane made another adjustment to deepen the image and sharpen the focus. She leaned back in to look, and screamed. A bloodcurdling, horrific cry.

The chair rolled away from under her as she fell to the ground.

"Help! Help me! Help, please, oh, God, help!"

Dianne pressed her hands hard into her eyes. Blood dripped down the side of her face as she knelt, bent over. She panicked, knowing all too well the aroma of that metallic tang.

Colleagues came running from the tea room.

"What's going on?"

"Is that you Dee?"

"Oh, Dee!" Jamie, her supervisor, placed a gentle hand on her back. The emergency fluid spill kit by his side. She barely acknowledged him. He leaned in closer.

"Diane, it's me, I'm here. What happened?"

"My eyes! Oh, my eyes!" she whimpered.

"Did you get a blood spatter?" he asked.

"No! No, nothing. I just looked at it and, oh God, it hurts. I just looked!" she gasped.

With that, Diane collapsed to the floor, unconscious.

"Call a Code Blue, Amy. We need some help here!" Jamie ordered. He checked her pulse and breathing, which were all fine, then repositioned her carefully onto her left side. He removed her hands from her eyes; sucked in a shocked breath. Blood trickled from them, pooling in her ears.

"What the hell?" he gasped.

"Oh my God! What's happened?" exclaimed his intern, Sarah.

Sarah placed two squares of moistened gauze over each eye. Jamie put an oxygen mask onto Diane's face and checked her pulse again.

The code team entered with an experienced calm. Senior ER nurse, Kea, lead the team.

"What's the story?" she asked.

"We don't know. Seems Diane was examining some blood slides during her tea break, and suddenly she was screaming on the floor with blood pouring from her eyes," Jamie answered, shock hitched his voice.

Kea leaned in while other colleagues hooked Diane up to a cardiac monitor. She removed the gauze and pried open one of Dianne's eyes. She recoiled at what she saw. She opened the other eye and saw the same thing.

Kea sat back; concern creased her brow. "Jamie, what chemicals have you got down here? Could anything you use do this?"

Jamie raked his hands through his hair, eyes red-rimmed. Diane was more than just a co-worker. This was his wife on the floor. He panicked.

"Oh my God! Shit, shit, shit! What the hell is going on? Nothing, there's nothing. Help her, please!" Jamie choked out the words.

He turned to Sarah and spat out, "Go see what samples she was looking at and cover that microscope. Don't let anyone use it."

"There are some tubes here with Cael's name on them," Sarah said.

Kea looked up sharply at that, then back to Diane. "Don't let anyone else use that scope, or examine those samples. Shut down all the machines that have come into contact with them. Quarantine everything until we know what's going on."

Jamie stared at his wife, colour drained from his face. Her eyes were pure white. No iris, no pupil; colourless.

Chapter
Six

Flashes of light and dark flickered. A groan and a sickening thump sounded to one side of me. Trees rustled in a breeze I could not feel. Thump, thump, thump — crack.

"Argh!" An agonising scream roared. Groaning; mumbled curses I couldn't make out. Two silhouettes clashed, floating in the air. They threw themselves at one another mercilessly. Blinding flashes of light exploded each time they made contact. Both figures panted, exhausted, as though this had been going on for some time. Each time there was a burst of light, I tried and failed to recognise who it was.

The brighter figure flung its arm forward, an explosion of lightning exploded from its palm, slamming the dark creature to the ground so hard it seemed to be half buried. But that did not end the fight. The dark one, the more terrifying of the two, clawed back out of the ground, rose up into the air. Huge trees silhouetted in the moonlight. The dark figure raised its arm. Fire, hot and stinking of sulphur, burst from it, hitting the lighter being in the chest. The contact spun it around, rendering it prone on the ground. Advantage gained, the dark figure quickly descended and knelt by its victim. It grabbed the head of the overwhelmed being, wrenching it backwards. A pale, glowing trident stabbed down around its neck, pinning it helplessly to the ground. A third figure emerged from the darkness, leaned over the defeated one, and spoke in a cruel tone.

"She is mine."

The creature atop the defeated one ran its hand slowly down the wretched one's body. It plunged its hand into the other's back and ripped upwards. The tearing of sinew and crunching of bone, tinged with the smell of blood, filled the air.

I screamed.

"Stop! Please stop, whoever you are, stop!"

The helpless creature groaned as its light faded. It turned its face and stared straight into my eyes. It extended a hand toward me, palm up. An image of concentric circles glowed white. It was him; it was Cael!

The creature that I now knew to be pure evil stepped back from Cael's limp body and faded into the night. The other dark being focused its attention onto me as it stepped over Cael's body. I wanted to run, but my limbs wouldn't budge. This new evil presence advanced upon me quickly. It grabbed hold of my arms with merciless strength. Barely restraining itself from breaking my bones, it leaned forward, pulled me close to its muscular body. Black eyes pierced into mine, its form frighteningly familiar. It caressed my hair in a strangely loving gesture. It breathed slowly, controlled, as though in contemplation, and then said,

"You are mine, Sophia."

I willed myself back to consciousness, heard the distant call of my name.

Help me, I screamed in my mind.

"I think she's coming round," said a familiar voice.

"Sophia, Sophia, it's me, open your eyes."

"Call a doctor," another voice instructed.

My eyes wouldn't open, and I thought I was still in the grip of the evil thing; a dark silhouette, masculine in shape, indistinct other than those black eyes.

"Sophia!" a shout close in my ear jolted me awake. Thrashing my arms and legs, I tried desperately to be free of this dark terror.

"Soph, it's me, Jaz. Nan's here, and Ben too. It's okay now, you're all right." The odour of disinfectant assaulted my senses.

"Sophia, I'm here now, dear. You are safe," spoke a smooth, familiar British voice.

Nan's with me, I thought. Ok, I'm ok.

Slowly, my eyes cracked open to the glare of bright lights and many faces peering down at me.

I tried to sit up; my vision blurred as it adjusted to the brightness.

"My contacts? Where are they? I can't see," I mumbled, my tongue felt thick.

"They're still in, dear," soothed Nan. "You've been unconscious for an hour or so. Relax, let your eyes adjust. You're safe now."

Nan rested a warm hand across my head, instantly soothed the remnants of fear. Her energy willed calm into me. A spark passed between us, though I wasn't sure if it was going from her to me, or the reverse.

Fully alert now, I peeled the blood pressure cuff from my arm just as it began to automatically inflate. Thank God. I was just dreaming about that thing pumping up on my arm. Just a stupid nightmare. Nothing had hold of me after all. I barely convinced myself of it, remembering the image of Cael's face as he lay on the ground, ripped to pieces.

"Well, thank Christ for that. I thought I was going to have to buy a new black dress. Geez Soph, are you trying to give me a frigging heart attack? You that hard up for attention?" Jaz's version of sympathy was unique.

"Just diverting you from the poor interns," I said.

"Ugh. So funny!" she grumped.

Her smudged eye makeup betrayed dried tears. Never one to let her prickly exterior show weakness, I must have given Jaz a decent fright. She gave my hand a reassuring squeeze. Another shock zapped between our hands. She yanked hers away. My face and right arm left burning hot.

"Ow, Soph, did you feel that?" she asked. "No, what?" I lied, panicking, rubbing the strange feeling in my hand.

"You okay Soph? Ben asked from the end of the bed. He looked pained.

"I think so." I wasn't sure it was true, but all limbs seemed intact and working, so I figured I must have been alright. He moved closer, as though to say something else, but the moment was interrupted when a nurse with a severe crew cut entered the room. She checked me over, put the blood pressure cuff back on, and noted my vitals down on the bedside computer.

"Hi there, Sleepyhead. You're awake!" She stuck a thermometer in my ear. "Your temperature is quite elevated; 39 degrees. How are you feeling?" Her bedside manner was far softer than her appearance.

"Fine, I think, a little dazed, perhaps. My head and back ache, but otherwise, I think I'm okay." My voice sounded sleep drunk.

"In light of this high fever, I'll be back shortly to take some blood so we can see what's going on. It might explain your fainting episode. I'll alert your doctor and be back shortly. You just lay back and rest, Honey." She gently patted my hand and gathered my charts. I snuggled back into the pillow. I'd never had blood taken before; I'd never had an ill day in my life.

After the nurse left, Nan spoke.

"Well, that won't be necessary at all. We like to keep our fluids in our own vessels in this family. Come on, Sophia, we are going home. I'll have dear old Esme tend you."

"Uh, Nan?" Jaz piped in. "Something really weird happened to her. You don't just fling three feet across a room into a wall, lay unconscious for an hour, and then go home for afternoon tea!" She shrugged, mouth agape in confusion.

She had guts back talking to Nan like that.

Jaz continued. "What if she got an electric shock or something?" Jaz looked at me, still rubbing her hand. "Shouldn't you let the experts check her out properly first? Is that 'fluid in the vessel' thing some religious guilt you peeps have never told me about? I didn't think you were the religious type!" Jaz rolled her eyes.

"Experts? Lord preserves me, Jasmine!" Nan smoothed her platinum hair, her effort at composure. "Have I taught you nothing, young lady? Although Sophia and yourself choose to work in these mechanised, disease-ridden institutions of drug intoxication, I have no time for them. You know perfectly well that we are more than capable of providing our own health care!" Exasperation with a plum tone was Nan's specialty.

"Yeah, yeah, natural healing mumbo jumbo," Jaz ducked. Nan's glare was about as tangible as a clip around the ears.

"Leave it Jaz, I'm fine," I said, giving her an encouraging smile.

Not wanting to cause a fuss though, I did as Nan said. I'd never gone wrong with her healthcare to date, so there was no valid reason in my mind why I should stop taking her advice now.

As I was easing out of bed with Nan and Ben on either side of me, a different nurse entered the room with an equipment-laden trolley. The fluorescent lights suddenly intensified my headache. The room spun for a moment as she parked the trolley next to me.

"You shouldn't be up out of bed yet. I need you lying down whilst I draw the blood in case you become lightheaded," the nurse snapped. She didn't have the comforting bedside manner of the previous one. Her arms and her neck were inflamed with some form of lumpy rash. She scratched them raw before donning gloves. She looked like she needed the bloodletting, not me.

"Where's the nice nurse?" asked Jaz, crossing her arms, sneering in the way only Jaz could.

"She had to attend to another patient," the nurse replied, avoiding eye contact as she opened a syringe.

Her smooth intake of a calming breath prefaced Nan's next sharp, yet polite interjection. "With the greatest of respect, we will not be requiring anything further from yourself or this… " she looked around, waving a limp hand through the air, "…ponderous place. I will be discharging Sophia in a moment's notice, thank you."

Taken aback, the nurse sought out a response, scratched some more, mumbled weirdly to herself, and finally said, "But I must take her blood." She had a strangely determined expression on her heavily wrinkled face.

"I understand. But we have the right to decline treatment, and are exercising it today, thank you." Ever so polite, my dear Nan was. Watching this exchange was as amusing as it was unnerving.

"I'm going to get the doctor to discuss this with you. I need your blood." She left quickly, wringing her hands as though she were nervous. So hasty was her exit that she banged into her trolley, sending blood collection tubes rolling across the floor.

"'I need your blood!'" mimicked Jaz in a Dracula accent. "Freakin' ghoulish!" she exclaimed.

"What's the big deal, Nan? It's fine. I take blood from people all the time. I can survive losing a few drops," I said, hoping to ease Nan of the worry.

Now Nan was patting down her lilac morning suit. *Oh dear.* Whilst Nan, with her soft appearance, elegantly tall 'stature, and knitting proficiency, might lead others to believe her to be mild and meek, I knew otherwise.

"Sophia, you are indeed an adult, but believe me, there are lessons you have yet to learn, and perhaps at this very moment you are now realising that?" She stared at me intently before turning away and gathering her handbag.

Was she referring to the energy that passed between us? The unsettling zap I gave Jaz? How could she possibly know?

Nan continued speaking as she picked through her bag for something. "You should heed my advice on this matter. Now, unless you wish me to have a conniption in front of your friends, get up and dressed immediately."

"Fine." I reached out for Ben. "I feel a little lightheaded."

He moved to my side. "I've got you," he said. His muscles trembled with the effort of holding me ever so carefully as my toes hit the cold floor. He smelled so nice, so familiar so — I don't know. I wobbled.

"See!" exclaimed Jaz, her hands raised in vindication. "She's dizzy. She needs to be monitored a bit longer. It's not like I'm a nurse or anything."

"Jaz, cut it out," snapped Ben.

"Since when are you the qualified nurse, Benny boy?"

"Don't be a smart mouth. I'm not qualified in much, but I think she looks okay. She's just a little weak, that's all. Nan's right, she'd be better looked after at home."

Ben gripped my hand a little tighter as I planted my feet firmly on the floor. My stomach lurched, my head spun again, and I lean back against the edge of the bed. Ben sat with me, and after a brief moment, he stood, let my hand go. The dizziness dissipated.

"Jaz? Maybe you are better at this nurse stuff?" Ben moved away, leaving a lonely space between us. Jaz smirked and huffed at him in vindication. Ben backed away to the far wall. He rubbed his hand over and over. He stared at me with an odd expression. No electric jolt this time, but he certainly felt something pass between us. What was it? This day was getting stranger and more surreal by the minute.

The door banged open, revealing a familiar face.

"I understand you are refusing essential medical care, Ms Woodville?" It was the psychiatrist who took Annie away yesterday. He fiddled with his ID badge. The picture was nothing like him. Unease shifted through me; my pulse thudded a little harder.

"And you are?" Nan questioned him authoritatively.

"Dr Hyde, head of psychiatry, and I'm here to assess Ms Woodville's state of mind to see if she is fit to make her own medical decisions. She has suffered a concussion, has a high fever, and therefore most likely not in a fit state to refuse important diagnostic care."

"Doctor Hyde, oh my God!" Jaz giggled in my ear. "It'll be Doctor Jekyll next!"

A smile tugged my mouth.

"Excuse me, doctor, but I am her grandmother, and I have made the decision to discharge her from your care."

The dark-haired doctor closed his eyes, rolled his head side to side as though trying to release a tense muscle. He glared at Nan, not a hint of emotion in his expression or voice.

"As she is an adult, you have no legal say in the matter, I'm afraid. If you are going to be difficult about this, I'll have security escort you out."

He focused on me, his dark eyes cold and beady. "You must understand it is in your best interest that we ascertain that you are fit and well. Don't you, Sophia?"

The way he spoke my name tugged at a memory that had my flight response fully armed. Ben's head snapped up; eyes sharp. He stood to his full height, moving quickly in front of Jaz and I. Nan placed her handbag back down and faced the doctor, putting herself between us as well. Her hands were clenched behind her back, fingers lacing in and out of each other. She was reading him. I'd seen her do these many times before. It was her sixth sense to know a good energy from a bad one.

Nan leaned around, mouthed something, but I didn't catch her words. I was more focused on the sheen of sweat that coated her temples, the nervous waver in her voice. Nan was the most composed person I knew. My heart thudded faster.

"Soph, what's going on?" whispered Jaz, seemingly oblivious to the building tension. I ignored her, as I was unable to take my eyes off the doctor.

Ben moved closer behind Nan.

"You need to leave; you're not needed here now. We're taking her home," he said.

The doctor frowned; looked confused.

"It's all right Ben, I have this under control. Go fetch the car, Dear." Nan handed him the keys.

Ben nodded, shoved past the stonily silent doctor, firmly shouldering him as he went. As he made contact, the doctor's image stuttered like static on the TV. His face became nondescript, his features seemed to swirl within the oval of his face.

"What the…" my words faded. Ben moved quickly, pushed Nan out of the way, and jumped protectively in front of me. I felt like I'd gone back into a dream-like state.

The doctor's guise evaporated, revealing a bare-chested man with eyes so dark, so cruel, they could burn through your soul. His olive toned skin shone ethereally. He wore pants and little else. He seemed blurred around the edges, no definitive lines to his shape. He seemed there, but not there.

My limbs froze.

I had to be delirious. I was clearly seeing things; the bump to my head was worse than I thought. Two dark horns erupted from his black hair, curled backwards to a sharp point. This was a mythical creature, something out of a scary fairy-tale from my childhood. This was my insanity.

What followed next happened in seconds.

"I knew it was you." Nan spoke calmly. "I've sensed you for days." "No time for reunions," he responded.

At that moment, he lurched at Ben's throat, lifting him high into the air. He slammed Ben to the ground, limp. "I'll deal with you later; you weren't meant to be here, boy!" The doctor or whatever he was, growled at Ben's body.

Jaz and I screamed in unison. She ran at the creature, black polished nails bared at it. I remained frozen. No use to anyone.

The creature eyeballed Jaz and spoke one simple word: "Unsee."

Jaz screamed, fell to her knees, rammed clenched fists into her eyes. Blood oozed down her cheeks. In that instant, I knew what Nan had whispered to me earlier. I threw myself over Jaz's body, both of us falling heavily to the ground. I don't know whether I was blinded by the headache or something else, but either way, I couldn't see anything for a few moments.

With Jaz struggling in pain and frustration underneath me, I heard a scuffle behind me. Voices argued in that strange language Annie spoke yesterday, and there was a sudden rise in the room's temperature. The lights flickered, a snap, and then a loud crack.

A male groaned.

"Leave him be!" yelled Nan.

"You betray me over and over," the creature said.

"You betray yourself," Nan replied.

"What the hell is going on?" screamed Jaz.

"Quiet, shh," I whispered to her.

An emergency evacuation alarm sounded. The pounding of hundreds of feet vibrated the floor as the hospital converged to respond.

The pain in my head suddenly dulled. I somehow knew this meant that the vile creature had gone, but where, and for how long? I looked behind me to make sure it seemed clear. I pulled Jaz up from the floor, my arm around her shoulder for support.

"What the hell just happened? Are we in the prison ward by mistake? He threw something at me!" Jaz sobbed, wiping her bloodstained eyes on the sleeve of her shirt.

"We must leave immediately. It is not safe." Nan still spoke with an unnatural calm, as though nothing supremely paranormal had just happened. She beckoned us out the door.

We followed Nan without question. I wanted to be as far away as possible. I supported Jaz; she could barely see through swollen eyes. She stumbled beside me. Emergency alarms blared an ear-piercing whoop, whoop sound. This was not a fire drill, it was real. Smoke sucked into my panicked breaths. Fearful voices rang out as people rushed past, pushing patients in beds and wheelchairs towards emergency evacuation points. I stopped running and gasped.

"We've forgotten Ben!" I screamed.

"We can't stop, Sophia. You don't understand the danger we are in. I'm sorry, but you must leave him!" yelled Nan over the noise as she ran on.

"What? Ben, we've lost Ben?" Jaz pulled away, stumbled, into oncoming evacuees as she ran back towards the room that we had just fled.

I ran after her despite Nan screaming for me not to. I yelled for Jaz to stop. After twisting and turning through a few corridors, pushing through the fleeing masses, I found her back where we started. Jaz stood still as a statue, unflinching. An evolving emotion of utter confusion and horror marred her pale face. I followed her gaze. Where the creature had assaulted Ben, there was a human-shaped scorch mark burnt into the linoleum.

Someone touched my arm. I spun; it was Nan.

"This is the reason you must follow my every word, Sophia," she said.

Chapter Seven

Running at full speed, through the labyrinth of corridors, I was in a state of shock every bit as real as the pallor that had stripped the life from Jaz's face. Running panicked scenarios through my mind about Ben, I ran behind Nan while dragging Jaz, who resisted every inch. My mind raced for answers, achieving no port of call. Something stirred in my gut, like a cord about to snap. Talons of fear clawed my insides. The corridors had thickened with smoke. Fear invaded every screaming cell of my body. It was a struggle to keep my eyes focused and clear enough to follow Nan. I tripped over something, pulling Jaz down alongside me.

"You trying to bloody kill us? Let me go!" Jaz screamed.

"We've got to get out together! Come on!" I pulled Jaz up, coughing on the black cloud that burned with every breath. Nan was just ahead, looking back for us through the haze of smoke and people. Panic paled her face. Perhaps the first time in my memory. Instead of heading out an emergency exit, Nan pushed through the heavy door of an internal stairwell.

"Come, Sophia! You must hurry. We are running out of time; we need to get out of this place!" she yelled back as she raced down with an alarming speed.

Jaz fought me the whole way. "Let me go! I'm… going to… find…my brother!"

Jaz swung a fist. I dodged and pulled at her harder. "I don't know what the hell is going, but we've got to get out of here. Stop fighting me, God damn it!" I yelled.

Her screams were manic. I pulled at her with a renewed strength, half-tumbling down the stairs. I grabbed the balustrade, lurching us both forwards.

The lights flickered on and off, the buzzing of the incandescent tubing menacing.

What were we running from? Fire, that thing?

It was madness, careening down a staircase, hospital gown flapping behind me, running from something unknown... something I wasn't altogether sure was really there. At the final landing on the ground floor, everything went dark. I ran into the back of someone and screamed.

"It's me, Sophia. Hush, be still and be quiet," Nan whispered. Her voice echoed inside my mind.

The lights burst on, and there stood that same creepy doctor. Still blurred, ghostlike, he blocked our exit. He spoke in that strange language. A language foreign to me yesterday, but now I understood it as though it were English.

"Enl'iel, put your ancient soul at ease. Finally, we have found the one sought for so long. Stand down and give her to me and all will be well. We shall have peace between us and be once more among the exalted and our kindred." His voice dripped like honey laced with poison.

Nan replied in the same language. My mouth fell open.

"I know your true intent with this child. Your course is misguided. You are clouded by an eternity of hate. You know not the correct path to our salvation. I choose the path of light. I am a seeker of repentance, and I am the keeper of the Earth-born child. Stand aside, rest your vengeful and wearied soul. Let us pass!" Nan spoke with authority.

"Leave this place, and get out of our way!" Nan demanded.

"Nan?" My voice hitched. "What's' going on?"

"Fucking let me go!" Jaz struggled against me. "I'll kill it if it hurt Ben."

I slapped a hand over her mouth, instinctively felt the graveness of the situation.

"Quiet, please, Jaz… shut up!" I hissed into her ear and stepped us a little further back.

The doctor shimmered. His features morphed in and out of focus. A great heat and light emanated from behind him. Blinding whiteness pulsed outwards, shaping into a familiar form, like wings but made of light.

These wings of light rippled and pulsated. He elevated into the air. At this point, Jaz fainted, either from exertion, shock or both. I really wasn't sure. I felt like I could repeat the gesture as I eased her down behind me. I crouched, checked her pulse with trembling fingers; she seemed fine for now.

The creature hovered closer; intense heat radiated from it. I covered Jaz with my body.

"Get away from us!" I yelled. "Nan run! Run!"

A gusty wind blew up inside the stairwell. Howling like a storm, the high-pitched screech deafening. Lights flickered faster, some exploding, causing micro shards of glass to spray upon us. I knelt over Jaz's body to protect her.

The figure faced off with Nan and it spoke again.

"You possess the key to our salvation. I will have it now, or the wrath you will face from my brothers will make the curse we have endured seem a mere jest. You know not the danger you are in. We are unseen, yet ever-present around you." How could something so beautiful be so very ugly?

As my fear for Nan heightened, my entire body began to shake, feverishly heating up from head to toe. I'd never felt such fear, confusion, or dread. As the scene played out, my mouth became desert dry. I couldn't swallow, and was too afraid to release screams of terror building within me.

Nan stood her ground, reached out her right hand. "You will leave this place!" she bellowed.

Her hand glowed white, and without so much as a flinch, a shot of crackling lightning exploded from her palm, straight at him. Like a bolt from the sky, it hit the creature; the smell of burning flesh hit me. He reeled, recoiled and looked down at the scorch mark upon his heaving chest. His black eyes glowed crimson, and he, too, reached out a glowing hand, threatening the same gesture to Nan.

"Don't test me, Enl'iel! Your kind can never defeat me!" His voice was thick with rage. With a quick flick of his hand, Nan was flung across the small landing; her skull cracked on the wall. She slumped over, silent.

Before I could react, think, or move, he came for me. My body felt like it was on fire, my limbs were jelly. How am I going to fight this thing? Gasping for air in the burning stink, my body seemed to react as he edged closer. My backbone screamed, felt like it might peel itself from within my body.

He lunged for me. I dodged, circled back around, and pulled Jaz out of the way, dragging her closer to the bottom stair.

"Come, child, don't fear your destiny. It will be in your best interest to come willingly." He reached out again, curling his fingers, trying to entice me. I could barely breathe. Pain tightened my chest. I grabbed my heart, the pain shot through, front to back.

I fell to my knees.

"Please… don't. Please?" Breaths were too hard. "Leave me… alone." My voice was thready; barely there.

He laughed heartily.

"Oh child, there is no chance of that. It is what is written, and so it must be done," he laughed again and lurched forward with one flap of the immense light wings.

An explosive, lava-like heat seared up my spine, and I was suddenly pulled into the air. I thought the figure had me for a moment, but his face was a picture of shock. My body felt strange… lighter. I looked down at my dangling legs in disbelief. My arms flailed as they sought support that I quickly realised I didn't need. White light glimmered on both sides of my body, the light of it softening the shadows, pushing away the caustic air. Impossible heat coursed along my right arm, up into my face and back down again. Without conscious thought, my arm shot out as Nan's had. A burning, crackling energy exploded from my palm towards the shocked creature. The right side of my face throbbed, my pulse thundered in my ears. Another nuclear bright crack of light shot from within me a moment later. My own free will was not present, as all of this happened to me. All I could do was watch on as the creature faced off with my rebelling body. This man, or thing, growled like a cornered animal. He backed away, face livid, then advanced once more, and my body intuitively reacted in exactly the same way.

He roared and advanced again. This time, he made it close enough to grab at my neck, cutting off my air supply. I gasped; pressure built up in my head. Panic overrode my ability to think. My vision blackened around the edges as his grasp became hotter and tighter by the second. He spun me around, elevated me a little higher as though to slam me onto the floor. A quick glimpse of my unconscious Nan drew a renewed strength and anger from deep within me. My body burned agonisingly again; it shot lightning bolts in every direction. I felt like I might actually combust. The monster dropped me as his hand singed to blackness, recoiling from the heat onslaught, and for a moment, he receded into the shadows.

I collapsed to the ground, exhausted. I felt as though I'd been kicked in the gut by a horse. In fact, it was more like I'd been under a whole stampede of them. Agony wracked my body. My hair, glued to my face with sweat, veiled my vision as I crawled to Nan. She lay still and unconscious. I placed my shaking hands on her smooth face. She was warm, her life force strong. I glanced back at Jaz, who was stirring behind me. With horror, I saw him standing above Jaz. Hundreds of swirling black puffs of smoke danced around his body.

A beautiful, deadly smile spread across his face.

"I, Belial, servant of The Six, am in awe of your power. I underestimated your emerging strength, Earth-born. Enl'iel has protected you well. I will not risk myself against your untrained power on this occasion, but I shall give you an incentive to offer yourself to us willingly."

"Pick it up," he spoke to the black swirls, which immediately congealed into an opaque, featureless, human form; a person made of smoke. They descended upon Jaz, enveloping her. They swirled and pulsated until no part of her was visible at all.

Was I screaming out loud, or in my head?

The chaos I was witnessing was so surreal that the line between reality and delusion was too blurred to know what I was doing. I half ran, half crawled to Jaz, not thinking of the danger. In a few paces, I was within reaching distance and grasped through this swirling, miasmic mass. My fingers ran through it like water; there was nothing to grasp within the putrid-smelling thing engulfing her. The blackness began to rise, and there, within it, arms flung aside as if in crucifixion, was Jaz. My skin chilled.

Jaz was still, her eyes closed, she looked serene. The wind streaming down the stairwell increased intensity, a whistle in its song. It forced me back, the thing with Jaz untouched inside it. Debris picked up, swirled ever faster. Stinging glass shards bit into my flesh. I struggled hopelessly against the onslaught, unable to help my friend. Then, with one last blinding flash, the smoke monstrosity was gone, all that was left on the painted red floor at the bottom of the stairs was a burn mark, Nan, and me.

I collapsed, sat in utter stillness for some time. Comprehension and shock merged into an emotion that was indecipherable. I crawled numbly back to Nan and laid my hands upon her heart and forehead. Through stinging tears, I weakly drew from within and around me the elemental power of the Earth's magnetic fields. I willed all that was positive into her. My hands warmed; they glowed as though a light was shone behind them. It was nothing like what had just happened to me. That… well, I didn't know what that was. Nan roused, a thick trickle of blood ran down her neck. It rapidly dried up and shimmered into nothingness. She wordlessly took my hand, pressed it against her cheek. She spoke with her eyes. She knew what this was.

Nan gathered herself up in silence whilst I stared at the blackened patch of ground where Jaz had been. I ran my fingers slowly, disbelievingly, over the charcoal stain. The roughness pricked sharply. I placed my hands flat on the floor, shaking uncontrollably. I could feel what was left of Jaz's energy in the cold, hard concrete. I pressed harder until my knuckles whitened and my hands ached, willing her back. I cried silently.

"Nan, what's going on?"

As the words left my quivering lips, footsteps echoed down the stairwell. I got up, backed away fearfully and protectively towards Nan.

"Let's get out of here," I whispered. She grabbed my hand.

As we turned for door, it opened with a loud bang. The exit sign fell to the ground. Kea, the ER nurse, stepped over it, dangling keys in her hand. "Hurry, follow me!"

The footsteps on the stairs stopped. I felt another presence behind me. I glanced back fearfully; it was Ben. He was dishevelled and pale-faced, dark circles under his eyes, but alive.

I threw myself at him, exhausted. He returned the gesture with a fierceness that shocked me.

"Are you okay?" Ben held me back, looked me over carefully, his warm hands cupped my face.

"I don't know," I sobbed as he drew me back into his familiar embrace.

"Where's my sister?" he asked softly.

I looked over his shoulder to the scorch mark on the floor, then back at him, lacking any form of explanation. Tears pooled in my lashes.

His grip tightened as he scanned the room.

Before he could speak further, Kea interjected.

"Enl'iel, I'm your only safe ticket out of this hellhole today. Come with me."

"I don't know you," said Nan. Curiosity, not fear, laced her voice. "Who are you?"

Kea shook ever so slightly. She shimmered. As she came back into focus, she straightened into a tall and regal posture. Her dark hair faded into purest white; swirling opalescent eyes sparkled above a gentle smile.

I reeled. Ben stiffened, and Nan breathed a sigh of relief.

Chapter Eight

It must have been close to midnight. I don't remember how I got into the car. Everything was a blur of pain and confusion. Ben held me close, an intimacy we'd never before shared. His familiarity was the only common sense. I looked up at his face. The moon was high in the sky, its light touched the silvery scar along his chin.

Ben's hand didn't leave mine, even for a moment. A sheen of sweat beaded across his face. I hadn't the energy to ask him if he was in pain. I didn't need to, anyway. I could feel it tremble in his body. All I could do was hug tighter into him. As I nestled my head into his shoulder, that strange lurch in my stomach returned. As though he felt it too, he slid away, set me on the seat on my own.

"Nearly home," he whispered gently, but he seemed suddenly remote, like a stranger, as he physically distanced himself. It was so confusing, along with all of the other frightening events I had just endured. I was overwhelmed, to the point of complete physical and mental exhaustion. Although I fought it, my battered body betrayed my will to remain alert. I fell asleep against the car window listening to the quiet murmurs of Nan and Kea in the front, and the sound of Ben breathing softly, ever so controlled, next to me.

I roused as the car eased to a stop. Doors opened and closed. Footsteps followed. More murmuring outside, then heard a new voice in a mix of the familiar ones.

"I'll carry her up." Ben's deep timbre pulled me further into wakefulness.

The cool night air was eclipsed by the strong arms that slid around me. Warm breath whispered into my ear.

"It's just me, Soph. I've got you, relax."

And I did. I found that I did not have the strength to do to anything but relax. I felt like I had the flu. My skin burned, my head spun and ached; and I felt sick to my stomach. I let myself melt into Ben's warmth. He was safe and familiar. He carried me carefully, with gentle, measured steps into our house and up to my room.

The kettle boiled and cups tinkered downstairs as Ben pushed the door open with a shove of his hip. Laying me on my bed, he hesitated ever so briefly, watching me with a pained expression as he pulled a blanket over me. He opened his mouth as though about to speak, then checked himself and turned to leave.

"Ben, stay. Please?" My voice a whisper.

He looked back, his eyes anywhere but on mine.

I reached out for his hand. He sat on the very edge of my quilt and took it. His hand trembled, didn't hold on like he did earlier. That long silver scar on his jaw seemed more prominent as his cheeks burned with an emotion I was unable to decipher.

"Jaz… I… she… I don't know what happened to her. I saw something, but I can't… I don't know what I saw. I tried to save her, I was reaching for her, but I just couldn't grab her. There was black smoke everywhere. I couldn't see where she was, and then she was just gone!" I was babbling as I sobbed my heart out to him. His fingers curled a little tighter over mine. He leaned forward, and to my utter surprise, he kissed me ever so softly on my forehead. The gentle touch sent shockwaves through my whole body. He jerked back quickly enough that told me he'd felt something too. His red-rimmed eyes glistened; he swiftly wiped them with his sleeve.

"You need to rest, Soph," his emerald eyes found mine again. "Esme is here. She'll be checking on you soon."

"What happened out there? Did you see what I saw? I can't be losing it, I can't. You were there, and then you weren't. Jaz was there, and then she was gone. I was… God, I can't even say what I was doing. It's just plain madness."

"You're exhausted. I didn't see anything until I found you at the bottom of the stairs. I'll find Jaz. She probably ran off in fright from the alarms. She nearly died in a house fire as a kid. She was probably just freaked out. She's disappeared before — you know that. Jaz puts on this bravado, but she's just a lost kid on the inside. Whatever you both saw has probably triggered memories she'd rather forget. I'm not doubting what you saw, Soph, but you whacked your head pretty hard. It was dark and chaotic during the evacuation. The black smoke… well, there was a small fire at the hospital. You're not mad, Soph. You've just had a really crappy day. Don't worry about Jaz. She'll turn up tomorrow, I'm sure of it."

"But, that doctor, he wasn't normal. And Kea, she did that thing with her hair and eyes!" I slumped deeper into the pillow, too exhausted to argue with him, and also slightly offended that he'd politely accused me of imagining what I'd seen. Then again, if I were him, I probably wouldn't believe me either. "Ugh, you're probably right." I threw up my hands, resigned to my sudden madness. I gave in to what was sensible as I rubbed my eyes. "Thanks for looking after me. Let me know when you hear from Jaz, okay? I'm so worried."

"No problem. You know I always look out for you guys. You're my only family." He squeezed my hand, pulled it away, leaving my skin cold and wanting the heat of his again.

"Rest up. I'll come check on you tomorrow." His weight lifted from the bed, and he left, leaving the lingering scent of sweet ashes and spice, like the smouldering embers of incense.

I gathered up my quilt, pulled it tightly, and rolled to my side to have a self-indulgent sob.

I'm lying in my bed. Cicadas murmur and click outside the window. Slits of moonlight slice through the shutters, cool light stripes my bed. I feel as though I'm going to get up, but when I try, not a muscle will move. Only my eyes can open and close. The cicadas are suddenly silent. Everything is silent. I see a shadow glide past my window, breaking the pattern of moonbeams on the bed. Heat rises inside me. My heart thunders behind my ribcage, my arms and legs still leaden.

The door that leads to my balcony creaks slowly open, even though it is always locked. I watch it helplessly from my paralysed state. A shadow enters, moving unnaturally. Not walking, not gliding, but jittering back and forth, as though stuck between this world and another. I am now in a place of horror. I don't want to look, but can't take my eyes from the sight. It stutters its way silently towards me, a recognisable figure emerging from the darkness. A female vision in an ethereal, flowing black gown. Head cast down; it hovers at the end of my bed. Silent. Menacing. There is a sense of sadness emanating from it. I feel its lonely energy, fear, and regret. She is somehow communicating with me through emotion. Then she raises her head. I scream, but not out loud. I am still frozen.

Jasmine stares at me. Her blackened eyes look at me with sorrow. I hardly recognise her. She is weeping. Oily tears slip down her face, spilling over ruby lips, pooling onto the floor. Drip, drip, drip. She leans her head from side to side while she looks down at me, as though she is contemplating something. I will her to hear my thoughts, to understand that I will find her. I would do anything to find her.

In a voice that is not hers, a faint, scratchy whisper; she speaks.

"I am lost."

I squeeze my eyes shut for a second, and when I open them, her face is inches from mine. Her eyes bore into mine, black as night. A growl emanates deep within her. She screams a single word.

"Awaken!"

Chapter Nine

The toxic heat of volcanic energy emanated from the depths below the plain. Mountains in the distance shimmered like a mirage.

Great expanses of red and black crumbled with desolation. An ochre, cloudless sky blazed overhead, undisturbed but for the ashen gases spewing from the mountainous peaks engulfing the horizon. Pungent, sulphuric odours permeated every corner, every rock and grain of sand. Long dead tree carcasses, silent sentries, lined the length of an avenue leading to a platform of pumice. Upon this altar, an incongruity to what was natural to any known world, stood The Six.

Six tall figures, powerfully built, proud and brooding. Bare chested males, each gripping a weapon in his left hand. One, a blackened sword, as long as he was tall. The second, a trident spear that glowed like molten metal. The third, an orb of pulsating light, balanced upon his palm. The fourth a cross bow knocked with six bolts of lightning arrows. The fifth, an axe head of the clearest crystal… and the sixth, nothing at all. His weapon was hidden and decidedly more destructive — the power of manipulation. With an unnatural stillness around them, silence reigned as they contemplated the situation that had driven their every move, every thought, and decision for millennia. An endless battle, created by their own actions, plagued their sanity.

"It is increasingly evident that finally, we have found the Earthborn," said the sharp tongue of the first.

"We must strike now, while she is in our sight," added another.

"She is well protected. Her power is unbalanced, and lacking control. She nearly killed Belial without knowing what she was doing. I say we wait until she awakens. We should draw her out, see her power for ourselves, then find a weakness. We already have the leverage we need. There is no need to rush in like fools," added a third.

"Why the concern, my brother? Belial is but a servant, a pawn in our war. He barely deserved the title of Watcher even in the beginning. His loss for her gain would have been well worth it. You have a weakness in you, brother. Worry not for others when it concerns our mission," the first retorted.

"This is the best time to strike. She cannot overcome us; she has no control of her power. I say we take her and force her awakening. Then she will become ours, available to use at our leisure. If we bring her here, no one else can stop us." Frustration dripped from this new voice.

"I am tiring of this. My time has been long away from home. We have wasted too much energy foolishly chasing false leads. Are we sure she is the one? Do we really understand how to harness her power?" The words rumbled from the deepest and most aged of voices. A mumbling of acknowledgment to these questions resounded with the nodding of horned heads.

The third voice spoke again. "She shows all the signs and has been protected since birth by the most powerful of Watchers and Eudaimonia. There are unprecedented energy signatures spiking around the world. My spy informs me that there are increased gatherings in the sacred places, all discussing her. We have never seen such activity. But I know we are missing something. We have one part of the solution, which is her in the flesh, but I am certain there is something else that we are missing. In all of these years, we have always been a step behind, blinded by our own rage. This is the time to think clearly and shield our wisdom from our vengeance so as to bring this war to an end. There is more to this prophecy than we first thought.

We must wait and watch. We have misinterpreted something, I'm certain of it now. We should not draw her out before the entirety of the advantage is on our side." Before he continued, he glanced to his left at the figure suspended in a sphere of swirling black mist. A girl, young and serene, who, in this world or that, was now a player in a game far beyond her comprehension.

"Brothers, you are wrong about Belial. He was wise to protect himself. He is an immensely powerful ally. He is entrenched with the closest of ties to her protectors. This keeps us within an arm's reach. He is invaluable to us." He bowed reverently to the others as he said this.

The first contemplated this for a time. He turned to survey the realm he called home with an unabashed disgust. It made even Tartarus look luxurious. He inhaled deeply, his expansive chest widening. Taut, powerful musculature strained under smooth, golden skin. He turned back, ashen hair billowed down his back. His face was chiselled with angelic exquisiteness.

Beauty had never been so skin deep as with he.

"As you have gained so much insight with your many years of reconnaissance, and an equal amount of opinion, it is to you that I charge the task of unravelling that which we do not know. Immerse yourself to the fullest in that wretched place and find the answers that elude us. Take the Rogues, send them far and wide. Use whatever resources you can find. I will have no more mistakes. My patience has been wrung through. I am sick to the core of my dealings with this forsaken human world. It once amused me to meddle in their evolution, but now they just cause me to wretch. The mere thought of another day spent looking down at them wearies me. What a waste they were. A'vean has done so much better on the other worlds and none of those has brought such reckoning upon us. Why these humans hold such standing will for eternity be a mystery to me. The Throne is entrenched with fools!" He struck his trident hard into the soil, causing a rumble deep within the earth. Screams reverberated from somewhere far off.

With that, the first, his voice echoing off the mountainous ranges, raised his arms to the sky and called, "Belial, come forth!"

Rumbling thunder, like a storm on the horizon, filled the air. The sky darkened dramatically over the heads of The Six. Wind raged around them; they stood, unmoving. A distortion in the air about them developed into a spinning vortex. Red and white swirls of electrically charged energy clashed. Static buzzed in the air. An opening in the sky emerged, revealing the blackness of space on the other side.

"My Masters, I am your humble servant." Belial appeared, stepping casually but reverently through the fresh opening between time and space. Ferocity dripped from him like beads of sweat.

"Get rid of that!" The first pointed a finger at the girl. "You know what to do with it."

Belial glanced at the foul-mouthed girl, who he had only just transferred there, a tactical move he hoped would be pleasing to his masters.

"Yes, Master, as you wish." As he moved to leave, Belial thrust his glowing white trident into the dusty earth beneath him. A crack appeared just wide enough for him to squeeze his hand into. He reached down and fished around, immersed up to his elbow. Screams emerged, growing louder as he slowly withdrew his arm. In his grasp was a writhing mass of black smoke, flashes of light popping out from within it. Tortured faces appeared and disappeared. They snapped in and out; trapped in the smoky haze. Gruesome mouths gaped wide, a look of horror in black eyes. Agonised cries resonated from within the billowing blackness.

"You will all do nicely," Belial responded to their pleas of mercy. He pulled a piece of smoke out of the mass and threw it towards the girl. "You know what to do, if you know what's good for you." He laughed to himself.

He turned to the Six, bowed deeply, only grimacing with malice towards them when he was low enough in submission that they could not see his face. He stood up proudly before them, reaching a hand toward the levitating girl and beckoned, "Come."

The swirling smoke surrounding the girl sparked with life. It moved, dragging her with it, and followed Belial back through the portal.

Chapter Ten

As I awoke, I realised the gut-wrenching screams were coming from me. The horrendous images of my nightmare dissipated all too slowly. I shimmied to the head of my bed, pulling my knees up tight, hugging them in self-comfort.

My bedroom door opened with such suddenness, I imagined that they had been camping outside my door. Nan and Esme entered wearing equally concerned expressions. Esme sat on the bed close to me, while Nan wrung a fresh washcloth into a basin, before patting it across my head.

"Child, Esme's here. You're safe now. What troubles your sleep, my sweet?"

Esme was the most beautiful soul, and someone I'd known my entire life. Descended from the Wurundjeri people, she'd called me her spirit child for as long as I could remember.

Her beautifully soft, ebony hand caressed my face. "Baby girl, you tell Esme what you've seen. I see fear in those eyes." Her voice was velvety sweet, but edged with concern. "You're burning up, Sweet Pea. Nan, boil the kettle. She needs some 'o my special tea. And my bag, would you please bring it up? Got some magic in my bag o' tricks. I musta known strange things were gonna be going on here tonight." Esme smiled, but her gentle eyes were fraught with something else.

"Of course. I'll be back shortly, Sophia." Nan kissed me lightly on my head. Her necklace fell forward, the large white gem she always wore grazed my cheek. It vibrated softly on my skin. For the briefest moment, my headache eased, but just until she stood back up. What was that about? Nan let me play with this gem as a child when I was frightened or unwell, to distract myself from my worries. I'd always cherished it, but never known it to do that. My mind raced with thoughts both rational and not.

Esme leaned over me. "Esme will have you feeling better real soon, Honey Pot. You tell me what's got those eyes like saucers when you're good and ready. But first, let's get you up and out of that God-awful hospital rag and into something nice. What you think about that, eh?"

"Ok," I mumbled.

"A shower is a fine start, I think. I'll get one running for you. When you're done, you'll have some nice Kakadu plum tea. Then I'll tuck you up, snug as a bug."

"Esme, I think I'd like to sleep downstairs for the rest of the night."

"No, girl, you'll stay right here with me. I'll sit by you all night. I'll keep those restless spirits away." Esme soothed as she smoothed my hair back.

"How do you know that's what's upset me?" I asked.

"Sophia, I told you many a time that I've a deep connection with my land. These ranges are where the spirits roam. I feel 'em, and I especially feel that one's been here tonight, but it's a strange one. Somethin's not right about it. Not one bit." Her head was slowly shaking. Whilst she mulled over this thought, deep concern wrinkled her face.

"Yes, something is so very not right about today. Tonight. Everything!" I added, exasperated.

Nan arrived back from the kitchen with a brewing teapot on a tray and a weathered brown bag slung across her shoulder. "Do as Esme says, Sophia. Take her remedies, get some rest, and we will have a long overdue discussion in the morning."

Nan sat by me for a moment and rested her hands across mine, infusing her energy beneath my skin. It was warm and tingling, so familiar. It gave me just enough fuel to heave my aching mass out of bed. Nan swiftly left the room again before I could say anything more.

As I stood, I caught sight of a photo of Jaz and I when we were sixteen. Me, all girly in pink, and Jaz, already in the goth phase, with her newly tattooed right arm pulled tight around my neck. She was planting a kiss on my cheek. You couldn't see her face in the picture, though, it was obstructed by her mane of dyed blue and black hair. I picked up the homemade mosaic frame and rubbed my fingers across it. A tear slipped down my face and dropped onto the glass, blurring the picture.

"What happened to you?" I whispered to myself.

By the time I pulled myself together enough to walk to the en suite, Esme was busy humming an enchanting indigenous lullaby to herself while she tested the water temperature for me.

"I miss hearing that song. It brings back nice memories." My words caught each time I tried to speak. "It's still comforting."

"Course it is, that's old Esme's purpose, Sweet Pea, to soothe all of my children. There now, you hop on in. I'll wait outside the door, just right here if you need me."

Esme closed the door behind her, and I stepped into the shower. The sting of the water woke me right up. I coveted sleep, to be away from this unsettling reality, but feared returning to that nightmare. The heat and moisture eventually soothed my aching bones. I used an abundance of soap, trying desperately to wash away the horror of it all. The suds stung my back. My spine was on fire. I concluded that I'd bruised it during the myriad of falls in that one twenty-four-hour period. Or, let's be honest, whatever the hell happened in that stairwell. The floating thing, the lightning shooting out of me… that couldn't be good on the body. Just thinking about those events made me feel on the verge of losing it.

Perhaps I was still dreaming? Could I be that lucky?

I towel-dried my hair, and wiped the steam from the mirror. I barely recognised myself. The reflection was alarming. My hair had faded. The rainbow of colours now a pastel palette, the boldness just a memory. Redness glowed angrily along the inside of my right arm. I hesitantly touched it. The skin was painfully raw. Most shocking though, was the birthmark on my face. The mocha swirls were now maroon welts, raised and ugly. They too were terribly painful to touch. It was like my life had become a horror movie, with me as the gruesome star.

My lips trembled; tears welled. Before I could indulge in a fresh cry, my entire back began to itch. *What now?* It felt like ants were crawling under my skin. I grabbed my back scrubber, hooked it around, and gave my back a good hard scratch. Wrong move. It hurt like hell. Pouring vinegar on an open wound would have been more pleasurable. The room spun; acid coated the back of my throat. I had to lie down. It was all too much. I removed my contacts, and with blurred vision, felt my way back into my room, wrapped only in my towel.

"Don't look at me, Esme, I'm a freak show!"

"Oh, Sweet Pea, there's nothing about my dear Sophia that would ever worry 'ol Esme."

She was waiting for me with a clean set of pyjamas and didn't flinch at the sight of me. It was as though I'd always looked this way. She smiled warmly as I shimmied into the bottoms. I turned my back on her to discreetly put the top on. It was then that I heard a sharp intake of breath.

"What is it?" I asked, immediately fearful.

"You feelin' a little itch on your back there, Honey?"

"Yes! It started in the shower. I tried to scratch it, but it hurt too much. I'm red and sore all over. Can you see a rash there, or some bruising? Anything?"

"Don't you go scratchin' that itch any more. I'll get you something for it, just a touch o' this and that."

"What is it, Esme? What can you see? You're freaking me out!"

"Don't you worry now Sweet Pea, just relax while I grab a couple extra things downstairs. I need some fresh boiled water, Petal. I've got a little sage and lavender burning for you by the door an' window. It'll keep the spirits away. Your big 'ol fluff ball is sleepin' outside your door, too. He's stinkin' up to high heaven. That smell would keep the devil himself away!" Esme laughed heartily. "You best give him a bath tomorrow. Pee-ew!" She waved her hand in front of her nose. "I'll be right back to see to that back and then we'll settle you in for the night, all nice and cosy, eh?"

Although I was terrified of being left alone, I also didn't want to seem childish, so I nodded and she bustled quickly out of my room.

For the first time in my life, I felt like I was seriously ill. I actually needed healing myself for a change. I was about to snuggle back into bed when I heard Nan and Esme in what sounded like not so much a disagreement, but certainly a fervent discussion of differing opinions.

I couldn't help myself. If they knew something I didn't, which I was fairly positive was the affirmative, I was going to find out.

I tiptoed to my door, stepping lightly so that the floorboards didn't give my movements away.

I kneeled, placed my ear gently on the wood, and listened.

"I really insist we wait until morning. I need time to prepare, and I would like Brennan's support." Nan's tone was firm and unyielding.

"Enl'iel, she's entering the Change, and I see it's a Quickening. I saw it on 'er back just now. She's gonna need to know before too long. I can soothe things somewhat, but that girl's gonna get a fright if she awakens suddenly and doesn't know what's goin' on! Poor child."

That word again. Awaken. What the hell did that mean? I was wide awake!

"It's all too early. She hasn't reached her comin' of age, and her body isn't ready yet! It hasn't had the right kind 'o preparation," Esme added, sounding distraught.

"Yes, you are correct, of course, Esme. It is too early, but I have my suspicions as to why. I too believe she is experiencing a Quickening, and I believe Cael has sparked this. She is the one we have been waiting for, Esme. We have known this for twenty years. Unfortunately, she has grown up very human, and it will take care and training in the right way by the correct individuals to prepare her properly."

"Yes, yes, I see your point. My heart cries for what that poor girl might go through. She's like my own flesh 'n blood baby, Enl'iel. I'm frightened for her."

"I never would have been able to protect her so well without you, my dear friend. I know you love her every bit as much as her own mother, myself included. You and I are on the same side, but there are encroaching forces that are working ever more fervently in opposition. Please, tend to her wounds and let me make the appropriate arrangements? I need to work out what to do with Ben and Jasmine as well. They were never meant to be a part of this. Stay near Sophia, Esme. We must dull this Quickening as best we can until she is in a safe place to awaken. Here is most definitely not safe."

"All right then, I must trust your judgement. I just don't want lie to my baby."

Esme's heavy footsteps plodded back up the stairs.

I nearly fell over myself trying to run back to bed, tripping over my floor rug as I went. I'd barely made it into bed with the covers up when there was a knock at my door.

"Sweet Pea, it's just Esme. You ready for me to come on in and tend to that troublesome back?" She asked sweetly.

"Yes, come in," I answered, trying to mask my breathless voice. I lay in such a way as to give the impression that I'd already dozed.

Fear, anger, and betrayal hit me all at once. Is there a name for that emotion? What did they mean I'd grown up 'human?' Who was Enl'iel? What was that talk about Ben and Jaz? Being frustratingly non-confrontational in nature, I just bit my lip before I blurted out something I'd regret. I needed Esme to be in and out as quickly as possible so I could attempt to process their conversation. I needed to make some sense out of this strange, evolving madness.

Softly closing the door behind her, Esme entered, carrying a tray covered with fresh eucalypt leaves, some white cloths, and a steaming pot of water.

"Here now, my sweet baby, a nice cup o' plum tea for your aches."
Esme poured a large cup. "Drink up." I took it from her as she
dropped her bag onto my bed. The tea was hot, sweet, and fruity. It
burned satisfyingly down my throat as I watched her ready whatever
preparation was coming my way. She hummed to herself, and I
detected an undertone of nervousness in the melody.

"Esme?"

"Yes, dear?"

"What are you making?"

"Oh, just a bit 'o this an' that. A nice eucalypt compress to calm that
fever, and a soothing tea tree lotion for your back, dear," she answered
as she pounded a mortar bowl, not meeting my eyes.

"What's wrong with my back? Is it bad?" I watched her every move.

"Oh no, Honey, no! Just a bit of a rash. I expect it's all from stress.
You're always lookin' after everyone but yourself."

I needed to know what she'd seen on my back, but I needed to do
so without raising her suspicion.

"I've just got to go to the bathroom while you're finishing that,
okay?"

"Yes, dear," she replied, seemingly lost in her own thoughts.

I did one of those walk-run things that you do when you're trying
not to appear to be in a rush. The bathroom door clicked shut I and
nearly hit the roof as I was met with a pair of glowing green eyes.

I flipped on the light, and for a change, it was something normal,
rather than another heart-stopping apparition. Our cat, Pumpkin, sat
perched on the vanity. Undoubtedly, he'd been licking drips from the
tap. His wet orange fur a giveaway.

"Hey puss, I've had enough scares today." I picked him up, giving
him a brief snuggle before putting him down on the floor to purr away
with satisfaction.

I ruffled at the toilet paper roll to convince Esme that I was doing
what she expected, then grabbed a hand mirror from the second
drawer. I slid off my top, and my skin instantly pricked with a chill,
despite my feverish state. I manoeuvred around so that my back faced

the large vanity mirror and I could dangle the handheld one in a way that helped me get a reflection of my back.

After a bit of adjusting, I saw it. I drew in a none too silent breath of surprise and dropped the mirror. It cracked.

"You okay in there, Sophia?" called Esme.

"Ah, yeah, I'm fine. I just knocked something over. All good," I lied.

I picked up the mirror with a quivering hand. Things definitely weren't good at all.

I took a slow, deep breath in and repositioned myself again.

In the now warped reflection of my hand mirror, I gazed hypnotically at the vision within it.

Either side of my spine was streaked deep red. A raised, fernlike pattern fanned out from my backbone. It curled around the edge of my shoulder blades. It was symmetrical, as though etched by an artist. The inflamed skin was punctuated with small regular bumps. It was like looking at something or someone else, not me.

I must have stood there too long, mesmerised by the sight, because the door suddenly opened, and there was Esme.

"Oh, Sweet Pea!" Her voice dripped with sadness.

She guided me out with a swift gentleness.

"Nan, you better come on up here!" Esme called out calmly.

I was awake, but felt like I was moving in a dreamlike state. How much can a body take in one day? How much can my sanity endure? I had questions, so many questions. I wasn't sure I knew how to compose the right words to ask for answers to things I didn't comprehend at all.

Next thing I knew, I was in bed, face down, and feeling a distinct wetness on my back. I tried to get up, but a gentle hand pushed me down with a comforting, "Shh."

"Just lay while I finish the compress to your back. It's burning up and needs settling down," Esme soothed. "Be still. I know there's a lot going on in that pretty head o' yours right now, but it's near on five o'clock in the morning and you need to rest."

In a drunken kind of voice I slurred. "W-where's Naaan?"

"I'm here, Sophia," replied a hollow voice to my left. My head lolled her way. An expression of sorrow was on her face, the likes of which you only see when there's been a death. Was it Jaz? Was it my own?

"I don't want to know, Nan. I… don't want… to know," I drawled.

"I know, sweet girl, I know. We will talk after you have rested. The time has arrived to tell you the truth. It has, however, come sooner than I anticipated. You have a future that you could not possibly imagine, Sophia."

I didn't want a new future. I just wanted to go back to yesterday, back to when everything made sense. Back when I had a wild best friend trying to pimp me out to potential boyfriends, and a career that brought me happiness. Back to hanging with Ben, helping him put his bikes back together. I wanted to un-see the things I had seen and un-feel the rebellion going on inside my body. I wanted sleep now, to forget it all. I gazed past Nan, out into the darkness of my window. I stared into the nothingness of it and willed it all away as I drifted off to the sensation of Esme rubbing my back. In the furthest reaches of consciousness, where you know you can't turn back from sleep, I heard Pumpkin hiss and Shadow growl.

Eleven

The shadowed figure hung in the predawn air, looking down upon the three women in the room below. He'd been there every night for twenty years, observing his charge. The two older ones he could just wrench to pieces right now. The other one though, he would bide his time as he had done for so long. Her death was coming; it was imminent, unstoppable. Necessary. She was merely a player in a larger game, yet she was the queen, the most powerful piece on the board, and she did not even know it. What happened today or tomorrow mattered not.

The two older figures hovered annoyingly in his line of sight. They fussed over her endlessly. She was never alone long enough for him to get as close as he wanted to. Out here, he was less detectable. That Enl'iel was painfully strong for a half-breed, and cloaking himself from her had become a true art form, though it drained his energy greatly. And that witch-woman burning her God-awful smells made him retch. He might dispatch with her sooner rather than later.

"Why were you at the hospital, Belial? Did Yeqon send you?"

"Yes, he grows impatient," answered Belial from behind an overhanging jasmine bush. "The Rogues are sloppy when left to themselves, making mistakes the humans will pick up on. One of them infected a live human. They will have us exposed before too long. Brainless filth. He sent me in to right the mess. It was a coincidence she was there at the same time. Almost poetic, don't you think, brother?"

"The time is not right. I told them that."

"Indeed. She is too human, yet her power great. She is dangerous."

"Perhaps we should bring her in, Belial? We could observe her until her awakening. She couldn't hurt anyone in the Pits. I question whether she would be any use at present though."

"That is what Master Yeqon wants. He was displeased I did not return with her. I have been given orders."

"I understand. Carry them through as you must. I have a plan of my own."

"As you wish, Nik'ael."

"Did you return the human girl?"

"Yes."

"Good."

"You enjoyed roughing up that boy in the hospital today. Miss the old days of war and torture?"

Belial laughed in response.

"Get out of here!"

Belial obliged by vanishing instantly.

Nik'ael dared to venture a little closer to the upstairs window. As she rested serenely upon the bed, half naked and face down, he watched. A muscle flinched across the bare expanse of his chest. He would follow his own plan. He sighed in frustration as the old hag covered her back with lotions and healing leaves. The young woman's beautiful form, slowly hidden from his sight. He was mesmerised by her. She had grown into such a beauty inside and out. He'd become impossibly enchanted by her. Nik'ael fiddled with the wooden bracelet around his wrist as he wrestled with these unwelcome thoughts. Strong fingers pinched forcefully at the little brown beads. It was tempting to let her live a little longer, to savour her presence. But that was not his call. He was just one — the whole made all of the decisions together; well, most of them.

She must be entering the Change. He could see the redness glowing under her skin; her energy tracts were emerging along her spine. From what Belial had reported, her powers were beginning to pulse, so her body must be in complete agony. He remembered that feeling all too well. A hint of sympathy tugged at his heart for the briefest of moments.

Nik'ael watched and listened to them console her. She had no idea what she was. They thought she was being protected by keeping her in the dark, but it actually made her exquisitely more vulnerable. It would take her too long to harness her power, as her humanness had left her body and mind weakened. She did not and would not know her own strength before he took her. This made his mission seem all the easier to complete, and time now seemed less of the essence.

She turned her head to face the window. He instinctively drew back to guard himself from being seen. Her eyes gazed out as though she were looking directly at him, into him. Without realising it, he had moved forward again to look deeper into those eyes. She would not see well without her human-made enhancements, not yet. But soon — soon she would see into the furthest depths of the universe with those beautiful eyes. He imagined that they were actually looking into his own. The Mark of A'vean burned deeply on his face. His hands clenched white-knuckled by his sides. The desire to reach out and touch her crept up on him again, to run his hand along the smooth curve of her body. Her soft skin, warm under his touch. His fists trembled. He held his breath as his dark heart quickened, rebelling against him. He shook his head to clear his thoughts and glided backward again, accidentally brushing against a tree branch, rustling its dewy leaves.

A growl from below and a hiss from the sudden appearance of a cat's face in the windowpane surprised him. He was getting sloppy. Thousands of years of no results and chasing false hope across the world could do that. It could make you just a shell of what you once were and leave you a mere ghost of your old self. Desperation was something he never used to feel, but it was an affliction that the passing eons had brought out in him exponentially.

Nik'ael was tired.

He moved off to leave, taking one last look over his shoulder at her. He touched his right hand to his head and vanished in a flash of light.

94

Chapter Twelve

I opened my eyes and, for a beautiful moment, forgot what had happened yesterday. Then, all too quickly, it crashed back down like a tidal wave pounding at the shores of my memory. Poor Cael and Jasmine. What the hell was going on? My heart thundered in an immediate panic. I rolled onto my back and reacquainted myself with that searing pain in my spine. I sat up, let my legs dangle over the bed, my head in my hands. It pulsed mercilessly, too. Thoughts of escape washed through me as I felt something wet on my feet.

Shadow was dutifully kissing my toes. "Hey boy." I gave him an unenthusiastic scratch behind the ear, which was still met with a thumping hind leg and a groan of pleasure. Dried eucalyptus leaves and towels lay neatly folded on my side table, a tangible reminder of last night's events.

I seemed to be alone. Gingerly, I made my way back to the bathroom and threw some cool water over my face. I slipped my contacts in. Moving like an old lady, thanks to the nerve war in my spine, I picked up a glass shard from my hand mirror. I didn't recognise the face staring back at me. I sighed, not really wanting to, but took a quick glance at my back in the vanity mirror. Still there in its garish, inflamed glory. Not a dream, God damn it. My heart thundered. Those strange red capillaries seemed brighter and thicker, like hives from an allergic reaction. At least the itching had subsided.

I leaned heavily on the wash basin and considered running away, right there and then. I looked deeply into the eyes staring back at me. They were fearful and brimming with tears. Despite myself, my lips trembled, and I let my head hang loosely. Finally, I released a sob. It rattled deep in my chest. Blurry tears slipped slowly down the basin, towards the drain. They glistened like liquid diamonds as they trailed away.

For a moment I gave into the fear and ran in a panic back into my room. The morning sun lacked its normal comfort as it streamed across the room. The air itself felt heavy, suffocating. My breaths came too quickly. I leaned against the end of my bed.

Could I trust Nan? I didn't know at this moment of irrationality. I just had to get out. I stumbled to the window. No one was outside, the yard a clear path of exit. I flicked the window latch, ready to jump out that way, knowing the groan of the balcony door would give me away.

I squeezed under the bed to grab any old bag I could find. Shadow thought it was playtime and yanked the backpack in my hand. "No Shadow, not now! Let go!" He backed off but stayed annoyingly in between my feet when I threw open the wardrobe and crammed an assortment of clothes in. On the way back to the window, the picture of Jaz and I, still smeared with last night's tears, caught my attention. Shadow pulled at my bag again. "Stop it!" But he pulled it clean out of my hands with a loud rip. The contents flew everywhere. "Look what you've done! Bad dog!" I growled at him and knelt to pick it all up. I stopped just as quick, slumped on the floorboards, stared at the small peels of paint curling off the wall.

What was the point? Where was I going to go? The picture of Jaz hooked my eye. It was so simple then, two friends just messing about, having fun. It suddenly dawned on me that I was helpless and vulnerable. Just like Jaz, just like Ben. I wasn't so sure about the rest of them. If I ran, who knew what was out there waiting for me? Where was I going to go, anyway? Did I run in ignorance and leave everyone behind? No! That wasn't me. I wasn't so much a fighter as I was loyal.

I couldn't just disappear like a coward and leave those that I loved, no matter what hand they may have had in all of this. "Ugh! Damn it!"

My fists balled; I kicked the wall in frustration and shoved the remnants of the bag under the bed.

"You win Shadow." I gave him another scratch behind the ears. His tail thumped. I breathed deeply, in and out, to compose myself.

"All right, Soph. If it doesn't kill you, it makes you stronger." The potential killing part worried me. I wiped my eyes clear on the back of my hand. The clock ticked over to 11:45am. Death. The thought had me recounting what I'd witnessed at work. Had the place burnt down? Had anyone else been injured? Was that creature going to come back? I decided in that moment that running was definitely not the right choice. I had to know what was going on, to protect myself at the minimum. I needed to find out if Cael was okay, and even though I didn't know where to begin, I was determined to find Jaz. Besides Ben and I, there wasn't a soul on Earth that would notice her absence. She needed us. I hadn't even told Nan what happened to her. She knew Jaz was missing, but she was out cold when that thing abducted my best friend. How I was going to ask about a smoke monster-abductor was something I'd have to think long and hard about. I wasn't even sure I could discuss it with Ben after what he said last night. I felt vastly alone.

I rummaged through my cupboard again and found a light, floral sundress to throw on. Without bothering about my hair, I took another calming breath and left the room, not in any way ready for whatever was about to come. At the bottom of the stairs, I forgot about step number three, and it creaked predictably. The noise had Nan out of the kitchen in a flash.

"Good morning," she spoke softly. "Would you like breakfast?" She smiled sweetly; her hands wrung nervously through her apron.

"Just tea." I was short with her and she noticed it. My belly growled, but I didn't feel like hanging around her for too long. I'd eat later. There was too much clouding my mind for idle chatter over porridge.

The silence was awkward as Nan brewed the tea. Normally, we would be gossiping like parrots, but today the silence flowed like molasses, slow and painful.

"Where is everyone?" I asked. "From last night, I mean."

She paused a moment, then said, "Esme went home. Ben left as well, with Kea keeping him company. He wants to be there when Jaz finds her way home."

"I'm not so sure she will." My voice trailed off. The smoke monster haunted my mind; the smell of the hospital, the burn of my back, all pushed me to confront Nan.

"I didn't know you knew any of the staff at the hospital. How do you know Kea? You seemed to recognise her when she did that changing… thing?" I fluttered my hands in the air to demonstrate. "Actually no, don't answer that. I can't handle any more surprises right now." I'd asked questions that I didn't quite know I wanted answers to.

Nan maintained an uncomfortable silence before putting a steaming teacup in front of me. She felt my forehead simultaneously.

"You're still burning up. How does your back feel?" she asked, almost sheepishly. Her tone annoyed me.

"How do I feel?" I snapped. "I feel as though my life has just taken a tumble into Weirdville. My body is trying to both combust and rip itself apart simultaneously. That's how I feel! And to top it off, my best friend has seemingly disappeared into oblivion, abducted by some possessed cloud-thing and a goat man!" I yelled at her, smacked the table, spilling the tea. Nan opened her mouth, but I held up my hand to stop her. I stood; the chair tipped to the floor.

"Whatever it is, I don't want to hear it, not now. I can feel it's something that I will never be able to un-hear, so please just give me today, just one day to pretend I have a normal life." Tears pricked my eyes, but I blinked them back, overwhelmed by this unfamiliar anger surging. I needed to get away.

"One day, Nan. Just one day, and then I'll listen to you," I ached to scream again, but I pulled my anger back to a cool simmer.

I left the kitchen without looking back, fairly sure she was in open-mouthed shock. I never spoke to Nan that way. The veranda door slammed behind me as I grabbed a dried corncob from the half-barrel by the back steps. I also slipped a peppermint from a sweet jar into my pocket. Barefoot, I made my way towards the back of our property, trailing the lavender-hedged path. My fingers grazed across the purple buds, upsetting the bees dining on them. They buzzed with annoyance. Crisp leaf litter atop velvety grass was soothing underfoot. My feet were the only pain-free body parts I seemed to have. I stomped harder than necessary down the stone steps towards the back paddock. Anger buzzed under my skin, but it felt damn good to let it out.

Ten acres of bushland provided me with a childhood alien to many twenty-first century kids. I lived and breathed the outdoors. Too much time inside was suffocating. With the sun streaming though the treetops, eucalypts on the breeze, the serenity of my surrounds had my nerves calming slightly.

My pace hastened past the shed; a run-down wooden cube precariously erected upon the edge of a large pond brimming with goldfish. Another year of neglect and it may well join them on the silty bottom. The building leaned like an aging monolith. The windows were whited out with grime, and a peeling green door rotted at the base left it a sorry sight. It was a creepy kingdom for the only creatures that I struggled to love — spiders. I tried, but no, I could not shake that goose bump inducing, get-the hell-outta-there feeling when one of those hairy puppies crawled by. That shed was huntsman central, so I never ever went inside it. Not ever. A wide berth was always necessary, just in case one was out sunning itself.

About fifty meters further down, I saw *him*, and the remnants of my anger instantly melted away.

"Hey Grey!" A magnificent grey head with a show-stopping mane swung up from knee high grass. Grey trotted over with a hopeful nicker, knowing that a treat was surely coming. "Good morning, my sweet boy," I whispered. He dipped his velvety muzzle into my treat-laden hand. I leaned against his warm body, inhaled in his horsey scent.

"Beautiful boy." I kissed his neck. It was warm and soft, and just plain good.

Seventeen hands of gentle storm-coloured equine enthusiastically crunched on a corncob whilst I stroked his neck. When he'd finished his treat, I asked him, "May I?"

He snorted, bobbed his head and shuffled his hooves, indicating he was ready for a run. With a handful of his mane, I swiftly hoisted myself onto his bare back with a long-practised ease. I leaned forward, rubbed his neck and whispered, "Off you go, handsome." He launched forwards.

Riding Grey was like an extension of myself. I did nothing, just moved with him. If he walked or galloped, it was up to him. Today he took off through the wooded acres as though he felt a need to run off the nervous energy that was coursing through me. I leaned into him as warm air skimmed my skin, tugged my hair. His warmth and power thrummed underneath me as he sped towards the rear of our property.

Sun filtered through the canopy of towering Mountain Ash channelling pops of summer heat. Grey's hooves pounded with the beat of my heart. The air rushing past created a calming white noise, and for a moment, time stood still. The chirping of the birds slowed, the sounds all around me dulled as I let go of it all. My head relaxed back. I lifted my face to the sky and slipped briefly out of reality. His pace was slow motion; I held on for dear life as my old life crumbled away. Somewhere deep inside of me, I always knew that my life was never going to be ordinary, no matter how much I wished for it. Bucking most of the trends of conventional living was always going to set me apart. Always wondering the fate of my parents and living with Nan who gave little away, left many unanswered questions. My life was set apart in so many ways from others, and what happened yesterday was a sucker punch, jolting awake the part of myself that had been happily hibernating.

Grey slowed to a trot, then a gentle walk at the rear perimeter of our property. It jolted me from the calm. We skirted a small stream that crossed the back corner. I slid down, kissed his neck, slipped a peppermint into his mouth. He lumbered off to slurp in the clear water.

Where sunshine struck a soft patch of grass, I laid down, closed my eyes and listened. A trickle of water was chorused by a family of lorikeets screeching in the distance. The sun soothed my pains. I snuggled deeper into the ground and curled onto my side, wishing it would swallow me up, at least for a time. From my earthen bed, I listened to the rustling of a miniature world that lived in the leaf litter. The musty smells of another realm, of life invisible to the naked eye, but comforting to me.

The warmth pushed me into a lazy and comfortable nap.

The sounds of nature entwine with the ancient language of the forest in my dream. I'm running, arms open wide. My fingers graze lavender bushes, scattering butterflies as they try to land for lunch. I am young now, maybe six. My pale hair streams wildly as I giggle that joyful, carefree laugh that the innocence of childhood keeps only to itself. The fairies swirl around me, tickling my ears. They want to play hide and seek. I run from them and hide behind the retaining wall by the pond. I struggle not to laugh, press my hand to my mouth, trying to keep impossibly quiet. They always find me — that was the fun of it. I poke my head around, peek up the steps, and a bright, floating white light pops out at me. It whizzes through my hair, creating more of a mess than before. I run, laughing and squealing, as a whole cluster of my fairy friends chase and tickle me until I reach the back steps of the house. My dress is now crusted in mud and leaves. I turn to wave at them before I go inside. They cluster into the shape of a heart before darting off with immense speed, disappearing into the forest. I hear the whinny of a horse and put my hand over my eyes to shield them from the bright sunlight. Then I look off into the distance. Someone is in the shadows of the forest, but I can't make out who it is. I call, but no sound escapes my mouth.

Another loud whinny brought me out of the dream, the glare of the sun that was now burning hot. I woke with my mouth halfway open, as though I was still calling to the mysterious person in the shadows. I hadn't seen my fairies in a long while. I missed them. I was always sure they'd been real; despite the mocking I'd received from Jaz and Ben when I shared my secret with them.

Grey whinnied again and I sat up, shielding my eyes from the glare. I screamed in surprise as someone loomed over me.

"Hey you, it's just me."

"Ben?"

"Sorry, yeah, I didn't mean to scare you."

He knelt next to me, his dark hair covering his eyes as he studied the ground. I bombarded him with questions.

"What are you doing here? Nan said you went home. Are you okay? Have you found Jaz?"

"Slow down, Soph. One question at a time." He half-smiled, raked a hand through his hair. For some reason, it made my heart flutter just a little quicker.

He studied me intently for a moment, then reached towards me and gently tucked some stray hair behind my ears. Aware of what he was seeing, I shoved his hand away and pulled my hair back down, pressing it firmly to the side of my face. It suddenly mattered to me how I looked in front of him. I turned away to watch Grey grazing on his favourite ferns. Not sure what he'd seen, not sure what to say, not sure why I cared. Self-deprecating humour spilled out.

"I've just got out of bed. I might scare you half to death!"

"Soph. You're beautiful, no matter what," he responded, a gentleness in his voice.

He tipped my chin up, pushed my hair back.

"I only see a tired girl in need of cheering up." He reached for my hand.

He may well have been lying to save my dignity, or really hadn't noticed the glaringly obvious scarring over my eye. Either way, there was a comfort between us and my hand slipped into his. He pulled me to my feet, a stomach flipping hum hit me as our skin touched.

It felt like the strange feeling with Cael, but different. With Cael it was a calm familiarity, but with Ben, I wanted to run towards and away from him all at once, and it scared the hell out of me.

"Come on Soph, let me cheer you up." Ben's liquid voice yanked me out of my thoughts. His fingers wrapped around mine as though he was scared I might disappear if he let go.

"How could you possibly cheer me up?" I asked, shielding my annoyingly sensitive eyes from the sun's glare.

"Just follow me."

We wandered slowly back to the house; it was really the only speed my body would allow at present. Silence was heavy between us. The gentle padding of hooves kept us company as Grey followed behind like a puppy. I snuck glances at Ben. His face was taught, brows drawn in thought.

Since he wasn't divulging anything about yesterday, I couldn't contain my silence anymore, or stand the strain between us.

"What happened yesterday? You just disappeared!"

He sighed, raked his hair again. It felt like he was buying time.

"I don't know. I remember the drive home, putting you to bed. Other than that, a vague recollection of waking in a hospital hallway with a killer headache."

"That's it? You can't remember anything else?"

"Bits and pieces, but nothing that makes sense. There were screams. At first, I thought it was all the people running to get out, but then I heard Jaz's foul mouth through an open doorway, so I followed that down the stairwell. That's where I found you." Ben squeezed my hand softly. "Glad you're okay."

"That depends on your definition of okay."

"What do you mean?" He stopped and looked me over. "Are you hurt?"

I panicked and changed the focus. I couldn't let him be dragged into this any more than he already was.

"No, no, I'm just exhausted. You're okay though? Let me see where you hit your head."

"I'm fine. Nan checked it last night. Speaking of her, she's made you some weird, vegan dessert thing." He smiled. I liked his smile.

He pulled me into a run. My body screamed in defiance, every sense on high alert. Movement teased each nerve ending like pinpricks. The smell of lavender, crepe myrtle, and eucalyptus rushed through my senses as the landscape seemed to come alive in a way I'd never noticed. Something was unfurling within me.

When we arrived in the kitchen, Ben didn't let go. "I know how to make you feel better." He guided me into the lounge. I squealed and dashed towards a mass of black hair and dragon-tattooed arm that dangled over the sofa.

"Jaz!"

She was tucked under a knitted blanket, coffee in hand, with Nan fussing about her. A plate of untouched avocado chocolate mousse lay crusted over on the tea table. How Nan thought she'd eat that, I'd never know.

I hugged her so tight she squealed. "Easy, sister. I've got a concussion. I don't need a fracture as well!" Her attitude seemed intact. That was a good sign. Her hair had the lingering smell of smoke. Was it from the hospital fire, or those black entities I knew I saw engulf her?

I hugged her again; she pulled away quickly. "You look like crap, Soph!"

"Where have you been? What happened to you? Did you, um… do you remember?" I asked, visually checking her over for cuts, abrasions, anything serious. Despite the rain of glass that had poured over us, her skin appeared perfectly intact. The only evidence of anything untoward was her eyes. They were bloodshot and puffy, a hint of dried blood caked into her mascara-smeared lashes.

"More than I care to discuss right now. Let's just say, what I've seen makes Twilight seem like Sesame Street." She looked straight at me in a way that said, *please don't make me remember it.*

"Please, Jaz. I know it's hard, but I need you to tell me the last thing you remember?" I was desperate for her not to have seen what I had… at the same time, I needed to know I was not out of my mind.

"Again, not feeling like an Oprah spill-my-guts sesh, but if you must know, my most vivid recollection is Alfie's face a mile too close to mine! And it wasn't coffee breath I was smelling!"

"What's she talking about?" I looked at Ben and Nan.

"Alfie found her unconscious at the back of the café this morning when he was getting supplies from his storeroom. Apparently, she was sleeping at the back door. He nearly tripped over her. He wasn't too impressed. *Too much partying, not enough working,*" Ben mimicked Alfie's accent perfectly.

"Huh, he's one to talk! Mister, one shot coffee, two shots whiskey!" snapped Jaz.

"Jasmine, there's no need for that. Alfred is an old man; he could have hurt himself." Nan frowned at her. "Apart from you, dear Ben, whose amnesic episode, thank the heavens, has protected you, we have all witnessed some rather frightening events over the past twenty-four hours. It has been shocking and confusing, I understand. I myself have been overwhelmed, as I know Sophia and Jasmine in particular must be. The reality is, though, you are all in danger because of it. I need you girls, and you too, Ben, to trust in me that I will explain what I know where and when I can. Trust in me that I will protect you."

There was a moment of tense quiet.

"What's going on?" asked Ben. He edged closer to Jaz, one hand brushing gently through her hair. "I don't understand what you're talking about. Aside from wanting to smack my irresponsible sis for running off — again!"

I grabbed Jaz's hand that was flying up to smack him.

"What exactly is going on, Nan?" Ben's eyes were wide, his mouth a thin seam of frustration. He leaned heavily on the edge of the couch.

"Ben, your ignorance keeps you safe at this stage. Be grateful for that. The girls were unharmed. We are all very lucky. I am expecting a couple of acquaintances any moment now to help me sort out this mess. I just need you to do as I ask for now. Please?" Nan politely fobbed off his questions.

Ben sighed, banged a fist against the couch. "You know something. How can I protect you guys when I'm kept in the dark? What's going on with Soph? Please tell me?" His neck flushed; he slapped the couched again.

"The less you know, the better. Trust me on this. I will keep you all safe, Ben. Faith is difficult when you feel in the dark, and can't find anything tangible to hold onto. But you *must* have faith in me." Nan tried to console him, but he turned away, pressed his fingers to his temples, trying to cool his temper.

"Well, this is starting to sound like a B-grade movie plot." Jaz rolled her eyes and moved to get up from the couch. "I'm outta here. I'm sure there's a party somewhere. Tell Alfie he can go fu…"

Ben pushed her back down. "Sit down, sis! For once, shut up and stop being God-damned pain in the arse!"

Jaz glared at him, smacked his hands way. "Sorry the middle of my sentence interrupted the beginning of yours, Ben! *I* was speaking. Get your God-damned hands off of me, *brother*! I'll go wherever the hell I want. Who appointed you my parent? I'm 20 years old, not a fucking toddler!"

I rested my hand on Jaz's shoulder, pushed a wisp of healing towards her. It hurt. Pain sang down my arm as the energy flowed, catching my breath.

"What are you doing, Soph? Will everyone please stop touching me? Leave me the hell alone!" Jaz grimaced and sniffed at me. "You stink, too. What kind of perfume have you got on, eau de puke?" Her words were unusually venomous. Something was not at all right with her.

My hand slipped away. "I'm sorry, I was just trying to help." I forced calm into my voice where panic reigned. "We've been through something horrible. We should stick together, like always?" I said softly. "We've got to make some sense out of this." I glared at Nan. Clearly, my last day of oblivion was not meant to be. I needed to know what was going on in this little world of ours, and now.

"Yeah, well, keep your hippie healing crap to yourself!" Jaz's expression was vicious. I sat back, trying not to feel hurt. Ben's attention slid from Jaz to me and back again, his jaw feathered over and over. The air in the room was thick with frustration.

A knock at the door interrupted the mood momentarily. Nan discreetly placed her hand on the door to feel the energy on the other side. We didn't need a peephole. I realised she was still in her nightwear; it was very out of character. She was also not herself.

"About time," Nan sighed and unlocked the door. In walked Esme, followed by Kea, who was pushing a wheelchair with Brennan in it.

What in the world was the neighbour doing here? And, a random nurse from work?

They entered quietly, almost reverently, like it was a Sunday service. I was right back on a razor's edge. Nan guided them over, scooted me closer to Jaz's end of the couch and sat by my side. Jaz edged away from touching me, pulled her blanket up to her neck.

"Ben, dear, would you mind heading to the market to grabbing a few things for Jasmine? Here's a list." She pulled it from her pocket, pre-pared as though she had the morning set out. He grabbed it, scanning it from top to bottom, brow arched. His eyes darkened towards Brennan.

"Hurry now, Jaz needs a good hot meal, and the kitchen is a tad bare." Nan pointed Ben to the door.

"I'm not eating your…"

Nan cut her short, "Hush, dear. You've been through an ordeal. Relax and let me care for you, as your mother would."

"Mother? Don't talk to me about mothering. I've always taken care of myself just fine!"

"Jaz! She's just trying to help! Calm down," I exclaimed.

Jaz averted her eyes to the floor.

Nan waved her hand. "It's okay, Sophia. It takes more than a snappy mouth to upset me." Nan turned back to Ben. "You and I shall have a chat when you get back, Ben. Kea will keep you company, just in case you still feel a little under the weather from yesterday. Now be a dear and grab those things for me, won't you?"

"Sure, no worries, and I feel just fine for the record," he said, grabbing his keys, his face pinched with annoyance.

Kea picked up her keys, too. "Nuh-uh, you're co-pilot today, buddy."

"I'm not your buddy," he snapped, eyes hooking on me briefly as he followed her out the door.

Jaz piped up again to say something as the door slammed shut, but Nan, clearly frazzled now, laid her hand across Jaz's forehead and commanded, "Sleep," and out she went.

Chapter
Thirteen

With Kea and Ben gone, it was just Brennan, Esme, Nan, a snoring Jasmine, and I left in our tiny living room. Brennan was strangely unaffected by the strange goings on.

"How long have you put her out for, Nan?" I asked. She used to do this to me when I'd had nightmares as a child. If I couldn't get back to sleep on my own, she would help. Nan bordered on the cusp of a magician, rather than healer.

"Long enough, dear," she said. I tucked the blanket back around Jaz's neck. She looked peaceful.

Brennan broke the ensuing and uncomfortable tension in the room. "Hey, Soph. Jaz will be fine, don't worry," he said, all too casually. I frowned, still wondering what the hell he was doing here.

"I'm guessing you're not here to ask me to run out and grab you some milk?" I said dryly.

"No, Soph, I don't need milk today." Brennan wheeled his chair a little closer. Esme followed quietly behind, lacing her fingers nervously.

"I suppose you're wondering what your recluse neighbour is doing here?" he asked.

"I don't know why any of you are here, to be honest."

"Well, your Nan needs a hand. There's something about your past you don't know, and it's time for you to know. I happen to be able to help with that," Brennan responded.

My skin prickled; my fingers numbed. "You know what this is all about?"

He nodded, eyes sliding to Nan then back to me. "It's something she's been dreading and looking forward to since the day you were born. I know that must sound utterly ridiculous."

"Okay," I drawled in that way you do when you think either yourself or the person who's talking to you is not quite settled in reality.

"You're not losing the plot. Don't worry about that. I'd be the first to tell you, if you were! We are all perfectly sane, I assure you. Well, I can't vouch for Kea, but…"

"Brennan, please!" Nan snapped. She wrung her hands more urgently. "Sorry." He inclined his head, put his hand up in apology.

"Sophia, you are perfectly safe and normal. Well, kind of."

"Brennan!" Nan exclaimed again. Esme sucked her lips in, trying not to laugh.

"Okay, it's been a while, En… uh… Nan." Brennan apologetically raised hands again. He closed his eyes, took a breath. "Soph, there's something we need to tell you."

There it was. I stood, cold clung to my skin. I couldn't sit to receive bad news; I was pacing before I realised, moving between the bookcase and sofa, wringing my hands just like Nan. Esme slipped onto the couch to comfort an indifferent snoring Jaz.

My attention landed on Nan, but hers remained fixed on Brennan, her complexion a little ashen.

"Soph, you have a heritage that you have never known about. We've allowed you to grow up in the human world, oblivious to it, in order to give you the best start to your life," he said.

Breath punched from my lungs. My knees gave way, and I slid to the floor. "We… human?" I muttered. Nothing made sense. I pinched the back of my hand… I wasn't dreaming.

"You, little princess, have a future and abilities that you could never even imagine. Concealing it has been for your protection, not to simply keep you in the dark," Brennan explained. He wheeled himself closer, reached a hand to me. I reluctantly took it and felt the same buzz of energy as I did with Nan. My hand jerked away fearfully. *Stop! Just Stop!*

"What did you mean by, 'the human world?'" My words were a whisper, unbelieving of the stupidity of what I was asked.

Brennan's azure eyes widened with a warmth I couldn't ignore. "Don't be scared. I'm as much family to you as anyone, kind of like a big brother." His smile widened; he was too damned relaxed about all this.

I looked back to Nan. She nodded her head, indicating all was fine. *Fine?* Alarm bells blared in my head to run. Not so much for fear of danger, but rather fear of a truth I didn't want to face.

"Listen to Brennan, Sophia, please?" she said softly. Esme nodded as well, a hand on Jaz, but attention very much on me.

My mouth was agape, my blood drained to my toes.

"You need something tangible, fair enough. Esme, would you mind?" Brennan inclined his head towards the front door.

"Of course, Hon," Esme groaned as she pulled herself up, winked at me, and ambled over to retrieve a set of crutches that I hadn't noticed leaning against the wall. She passed them to Brennan, who put the brakes on his chair. He dug them into the floorboards, tried to pull himself up, Esme and Nan protectively at his side. Despite my own worries, the nurse in me fired up, and I immediately went to assist as well.

"It's okay, I can manage," he said with a smile and a wink.

"I didn't know you could walk at all, Brennan," I said, astonished.

"I've been in an extended and intensive rehab program, so to speak. I'm just about done with these things." He eyed the crutches and winked again.

"Follow me." Brennan hobbled slowly but steadily to our book cabinet and leaned himself against the fireplace mantle. Only now that he was standing could I appreciate how tall he was. He must have been close to seven feet. Wide and muscular, he steadied himself against the mantle. As he adjusted his footing, his t-shirt sleeve slipped back to reveal an impressive set of white scars circling his biceps. He opened the glass doors and shuffled some books around. He spoke to Nan without looking back. "It's time, Enl'iel. Why don't you slip into something more comfortable?"

I bristled at this unexpected innuendo. Brennan must have seen my expression.

"Hey, get that sweet mind out of the gutter, Princess."

My cheeks burned; I looked anywhere but at him for a moment.

Nan cleared her throat; Esme clapped her hands together.

"About time," Esme sighed, her cheeks broad with a smile.

"Thank the heavens," Nan exclaimed, patting down her clothes. "Oh, my Lord! I'm still in my nightwear!" She gaped at her linen nightie and dashed to her bedroom.

With Esme sitting back down, stroking Jaz's brow, Nan running about in her underwear, and a semi-stranger helping himself through our belongings, I was lost for words.

Esme's eyes weighed heavy upon me. The ticking of the wall clock and Jasmine's slumbering breaths were as loud as a freight train. The air thickened further, pressed in upon my skin. The slam of Nan's bedroom door jolted my focus back to Brennan.

"What are you looking for?"

"Just a second Princess, have to remember which books… ah, yep, that's the spot."

Brennan removed two vintage Encyclopaedia Britannica's that I don't think had been opened in my lifetime. Dust misted from them when he dropped them to the floor, confirming this assumption. I crossed my arms, drummed my fingers, bit my lip. Brennan seemed very at home, considering I'd never known him to visit.

He reached in again and a light seemed to shine back out, then a clicking sound drew me closer to see what he was doing. His arm disappeared deep into the wall cavity. Now apparently, we had Indiana Jones-type hidey-holes in the house. This was just getting more surreal by the minute.

Brennan removed his arm. In his palm sat a key of sorts. It was large, about the length of a ruler, with a round bow. It was very unusual, a kind of three-dimensional coil of metal at its tip.

"Here, hold this, will you?" he passed it to me.

When it hit my palm, it glowed white, then red-hot. I gasped and dropped it. It clattered noisily.

"Hey, that's an antique!" he said. Blood drain from me again.

"Joking… just joking," Brennan laughed, picked it back up and passed it to me again.

"I don't want it. You hold it!" I was afraid of the strange object.

"It won't hurt you, but it will lead you to some answers," he replied. His brows tweaked as he offered it again. I clasped my hands behind my back, shook my head.

"Sophia, take it, dear," Nan was back, and dressed in khaki camouflage pants, a tight white t-shirt, revealing assets I didn't know she had, and some army-style boots.

"Nan!" I gaped.

"Hang on, I'm not quite done." Nan placed her palms against her face. They began to glow. She slowly stroked them back over her face towards her hair. Her whole body shook slightly as she did so. A visible change in the air around her caused the edges of her body to blur, like that freak at the hospital.

"Oh, my God!" I stammered.

Nan had changed her appearance. I mean, seriously freaking changed what she looked like. She went from Helen Mirren to Cate Blanchet in under ten seconds flat. With my eyes bulging, I edged cautiously towards her, reached out hesitantly to her face. She leaned into it. Her skin was smooth and youthful, and very, very real. She wordlessly placed her hand upon mine and kissed my palm.

"What are you?" I asked tentatively.

"I am a mere shadow of what you are."

The hand holding mine had not a crease, nor an age spot. Her short hair now flowed long and white down the length of her back. And her eyes… I was sure they'd been brown, but were now a blue shade more akin to Brennan's. I backed off. Fear wasn't pushing me away, I just needed to stop and stare.

"Enl'iel," Brennan said huskily; his breath hitched. Nan rushed over to him. They embraced — very lovingly. He bent his head and kissed her lips in a way that told me that they were more than just neighbours. My cheeks burned with embarrassment. I averted my eyes from the intimate scene, but curiosity had them snap back.

"I've missed you so much," Nan said in a voice soft and alien to me. She cupped his face, their eyes melded.

"It's been a long time, too long." Brennan kissed her again, slow and lingering. His silvery, shoulder length hair veiled their faces.

"Oh, I love a good 'ol romance," Esme chuckled and clapped as though this was all perfectly normal. Her commentary broke the moment, and they stepped out of their embrace.

I finally found my voice again. "How did you... and I... ah, your name? What did he call you?" My brain and vocabulary were not in sync, "This is, just... whoa... too much!" My palms pressed either side of my nose, half covering my eyes, as though seeing less of the situation would make it easier to process. "I don't know what is going on here!" My attention was hooked on Nan's youthful beauty. I gaped at something that my brain couldn't accept. All the while, Jaz's snoring serenaded this strange moment.

"Don't be afraid, Sophia, it's still me. I'm the same as I ever was, just a little different on the outside. Enl'iel is my real name. Lily was just a nickname. This will all make sense to you soon. It's too much to explain over a matter of minutes. First, we need you to follow us. There is something you must see that will help. Esme dear, will you please make sure Kea follows on after she has secured Ben?" Nan still hugged into Brennan's side; their arms clung tight.

"Don't you worry. I'll sit here by this young one and wait," Esme answered as she patted Jaz's arm again.

"What do you mean, 'secure' Ben?" I questioned.

"Sophia, Ben is not like us. He may have seen some things that he should not have, despite what he has indicated. Kea is like us, and she is just going to make sure both he and Jasmine are safe from their memories, which in turn will ensure their future safety. Knowledge of what you don't understand can be very dangerous."

Like us? She seemed to be defining us as something different from others. But in what way? I'd always known I'd a sixth sense for healing, like her, but how did that qualify me to be part of an us-and-them scenario? Then again, after what I'd witnessed, there was definitely another kind of something out there. What I knew as normal and real was now a train wreck smouldering in front of me.

"Will Ben be okay? Are you sure he and Jaz will be safe?" I asked, not really understanding what they needed to be protected from.

Nan released Brennan, took my hands in hers, her thumbs circled over my skin. She contemplated me with furrowed brows. As Nan spoke, I listened, but her voice seemed far away, like she was here and I was not.

"My responsibility for a very long time has been to protect you." Nan ran a hand down my cheek, leaving the skin buzzing. "When Ben and Jasmine came along, I brought them into that safety net as well. I will always do whatever I can to protect them, Sophia. Right now, your safety is more important than anything else in this world — theirs, mine, anyone, and that is not said lightly." She then gestured that we should head out the back door.

"Come, follow me. It's time for you to know who you are." Nan took my hand again and led me from the room. I glanced back to Jaz once, twice, before we disappeared into the kitchen.

Our hands glowed in each other's. I stole glances at her, trying to understand what I was seeing. My pulse raced in tune with Nan's, which I could feel through her palm. My senses felt too keen, everything too loud. Nan's pants grated like sandpaper as she walked, the smell of over steeped tea too pungent. My skin was hot and unbearable. The growl of a strange, desperate hunger churned in my gut. Each sensation evidence of something new and surreal.

Confusion and curiosity fused into a pull that was overpowering fear, so I didn't resist it. I let her lead me from the house, something primal pushed me forward.

As we stepped into the warm sunshine, the swing of Brennan's body between the gentle thuds of his crutches sounded behind us. Leaves crunched; birds set flight from nearby trees. Shadow appeared, keeping a protective watch over me. His soft fur rubbed against my legs as we made our way down the garden path.

Nan made a bee-line down the back cobbled stairs, towards the old shed.

"We're not going in there, are we?" I asked, alarmed.

"Of course, dear. Much of what you need to know lays within those walls." She gestured straight to the horrid greying cube.

"No, it's spiders that lay within!" I responded. It seemed a ridiculous thing to worry about in the moment, considering everything else that was going on.

"They will leave momentarily." Nan giggled to herself. "I am sorry, my darling, but I deliberately left them there quite specifically to keep you out. I knew you would never voluntarily go in there that way."

Nice! I thought. Twenty years of feeling the creeps walking past that thing was all her doing.

Nan placed her hands upon the side wall of the shed. Her hands lit, and she simply said, "Thank you." Every hair on my body stood on end as the scurrying of thousands of hairy little legs vibrated en-mass, like an army marching off to battle. I stumbled back and bumped into Brennan in my haste to get out of the way.

He put a reassuring arm around me. "Not a fan myself, but don't share that. I've got a reputation to maintain," he whispered, hugged me a little tighter. He felt strangely and suddenly very familiar, like Cael.

I edged closer to him, eyes squeezed almost shut as thousands of hairy, eight-legged fiends emerge and swarmed their way into the surrounding forest.

Nan pushed open the shed door. "There we are, nothing but rusty tools and dust now. Come on, dear," she said brightly, as though it were a flock of fairies that had just flown by.

Brennan ushered me through the door. My body jerked forward unwillingly, ducking my head and checking for any stragglers as we left sunlight for shadow.

The inside was thick with an earthy, mouldy odour. Nan pushed aside an old workbench with a physical strength I never knew she had. She grabbed a heavy broom from a collection of tools in a corner and swept the floor firmly, revealing a wooden door in the dirt. It seemed as large as a regular door, but was clearly ancient. The original colour of the wood faded grey; divots gouged into the slats. Nan dusted the edge to reveal a large keyhole. There was no apparent handle with which to pull it open. Curiosity urged me closer; there was a faded carving in the middle. It looked like a word. I kneeled and brushed off some remaining dirt, revealing the word Biblionia. The script was old, with an elegant hand to it. My fingers grazed the letters. The word meant something to me — I could feel it intrinsically. My face burned once more.

"It's a dialect of an ancient language akin to Greek, Sophia. It means library. It's a safe place for us. Well now…" she tut-tutted as she swept away one last layer of dirt. "It hasn't been used in such a long while though." Nan wriggled her fingers at Brennan. He dangled the strange key at me again.

"I need you to take *that* key and unlock *this* door. I know you all too well, and you will only come to understand who you are by cold, hard evidence. I know you can feel a power growing within you. Use it to open the door." Her smile was warm, sympathy softened her eyes as she urged me to take the key.

She was right, of course. I could only accept whatever this was with facts, not faith. The only real faith I'd ever had was in her. It was Nan who'd shown me my healing abilities by demonstrating her own. I'd never have believed it possible otherwise. I needed to see, hear, and feel cold, hard evidence. Blind faith was not natural to me.

This strange door at my feet in an old unused shed was going to open a new world, away from the illusion of the life I'd been living. It was terrifying, but as I peered into her gentle eyes, I knew in my heart Nan would never allow me to be hurt. So, despite my innate desire to run, despite the tremble that emanated from my very centre, I reached for the key.

"This will lead you to answers to the questions you never even knew to ask," Brennan said.

The cool metal fell into my hand. I flinched, but held tight. The key glowed white, then red hot, but it did not hurt. I turned it over twice, then held it for a moment with my eyes closed.

Deep breath in, slow breath out, repeat.

The key had a vibrating energy, a tune like a song, a language I was yet to learn. My fingers trembled, yet curiosity curled them tighter around it.

"What is this made of?"

"An ancient and rare metal," Brennan replied.

The key was unusually heavy, the metal smooth, the bow perfectly round.

"I just slot it in?"

Nan and Brennan nodded in unison, so I knelt down and let the weight of it slip it into the keyhole. I breathed deep, bit my lip, closed my eyes and turned it clockwise. As I wondered how I was going to open a door with no handle, the door vibrated. I fell away, shielded my face, peeked between my fingers as the wood shimmered. The door undulated like a liquid.

"What the… is that right?" I crawled forward on hand and knee.

"Yes, dear. It's perfectly normal. Just wait a moment longer."

"Normal? Nothing is normal right now!" I mumbled, more to myself as the door faded into a hazy, almost transparent mist.

There was a dull and deep rumble underfoot, like an earthquake's aftershock. Two blinding flashes, first white then red, dazzled the shed. When the glare subsided, there was no door left at all. A hole gaped in the floor. I inched back as a wave of vertigo struck.

"Well done, Sophia, well done. Seeing is believing. Look what you have done!" Nan clapped and pointed to the black eye in the ground.

"Now, you just need to reach your hand inside Sophia. Use your energy as if you were healing someone. Move some positive light into the darkness," she instructed, as though it was a perfectly logical next step.

I was never one to believe that it was smart to put one's hand into an unknown hole. "Can't you do that?" I whispered as I gazed into the blackness.

"Sophia, you need to exercise your power. This is just the beginning. Don't be afraid," she purred like a mother cat, gently caressing my hair.

"You must learn about yourself through your own power. Go on now, imagine that you have a patient in front of you. How would you heal them?"

As her words sunk in, a breath of cool air whistled from the void. Something was down there and curiosity reared its annoying head yet again. Hesitantly, I knelt a little closer to the edge. Small clumps of earth and stone crumble away, tumbled into the nothingness. No sound came from the rubble hitting a base, so this was clearly not a hole dug by a garden shovel. I looked back at them both, and two reassuring nods urged me on as I clung at the frosty edges of earth.

Eyes closed; I forced my arm down. I felt for the surrounding power, searched for the tingle that snaked through my belly and sparked along my spine when I connected to the Earth's energy. Grasping for anything and everything that was light and positive, I willed it downward through my right hand. I flinched, groaned with the burn. It was more difficult than usual; fear clouded my mind, and a strange pain cramped my fingers. I had never felt pain before and it scared me. I pulled away, looked for injury that was not there, took a breath and plowed my hand back down.

A now resident agony had my teeth grind, sweat spring upon my skin. An intense energy pulsing from Brennan distracted my attention. It was immensely strong, like someone tapping on the back of my head. It clouded my mind. I huffed and fell back again.

"Come on, Soph, just relax. You can do this, Princess," he said.

I glowered at him. "Easy for you to say. I don't know what the hell I'm doing or why?" I rubbed my temples, my fingers slipped on the sweat.

"I know… it's not easy. Just try, one more time," he urged more gently.

I wiped my face with my hands. So hot… they were so very hot.

Deep breath in, slow breath out. Repeat.

What Jaz and Cael had been through lit a fire in me. Keeping Ben safe and by my side had me stretching my fingers out, ready to try once more. If I could find some answers for them through all this, then I damn well was going to gather as much strength as I could. I would survive, I would… I had to help them.

My mouth dried; I took a deep breath. My chest ached. The thrumming in my head banged harder, the sting in my spine more ferocious than ever. Eyes squeezed shut, arm reaching deep into the void, I sought an elemental power few could.

A familiar buzz tickled my fingertips. The Earth's energy sank beneath my skin. I sucked it in, metaphorically, as though one would draw fluid up a straw. I let the power course through me, along every vein, across each nerve synapse. Then I took a breath and set it free, flushing it back out of my hand.

My body flung back with a powerful jolt. Nan helped me up, dusted me off. She peered over my shoulder and smiled, squeezed my arms gently.

"Look what you have done, Sophia." She pointed to the ground.

The void was gone. A phosphorescent tunnel in its place, a spiral staircase curved endlessly down into an unknown place. The walls inside sparkled; dark, shiny stone pin-pricked with golden flecks, reminiscent of space. It looked like a mirage, an unnatural movement, like looking through water.

"Wow!" I breathed.

Nan's arms slipped around my waist. She whispered into my ear.

"Well done, Sophia. You are growing ever more powerful by the minute. You are indeed Quickening. Follow me." She moved toward the stairs, waved me along.

"I'm what?"

"Call me Enl'iel, dear. I am no more your Nan than you are mine. The Quickening is the jumpstart Cael most likely ignited within you when you were exposed to the threat of that beast at the hospital."

"Is that thing gone?" I asked, terror rippled along my skin.

"Try not to worry, for now you are safe here with us. Let's get going. I'll explain it all when we are in the library's safety."

This was far from reassuring.

"For now..." I mumbled, but she didn't hear.

Nan... Enl'iel descended first, reaching out for me to follow, but I hesitated.

"Hang on, how are you going to get down, Brennan? With your crutches?"

"Oh, don't worry, Soph. I've been working on another form of crutch." He threw his crutches to the ground with a thud and leaned heavily onto the edges of an old workbench. His knuckles white with the effort.

"Brennan?" I gasped.

"Are you sure you're ready to try this?" asked Enl'iel. It was going to take time to get used to that name.

"Only been practicing every day for half a millennium!" he puffed through gritted teeth and effort.

That had to be a joke.

"Stand back with Enl'iel, Soph. This could get a little outta hand," he said as his body trembled.

My skin reacted; it tingled, every hair on end as searing heat punched the air. It rolled off a now-breathless Brennan. With one hand leaning heavily on the bench, he ripped his shirt, shredding it to pieces in a mad rush to remove it. His legs held firm, just enough to keep him upright as he struggled away at whatever he was going through. His golden skin glowed from within, as if someone had dusted him with gold powder. He pulsed brighter with each passing second.

I pressed on my temples; my head felt like balls were bouncing inside it. There was a rhythmic strum in the air, it vibrated through the floor. Some kind of light spluttered from Brennan's back. It flashed on and off, sporadically, like sparklers firing up and dying repeatedly. Flashing? I thought to myself. All of those flashes I'd seen coming from his home over the years? More unspoken questions tugged at me.

He groaned a little. I let go of Enl'iel's hand to help him somehow, but faltered as he warned me away.

"Stand back. You'll get hurt if you get too close." His breath was ragged, his chest heaved.

I backed up to Enl'iel. We descended the first couple of steps of the passageway. Concern pinched her face, but Enl'iel didn't intervene. Her fingers worked the charm on her necklace.

A vibration rumbled deeper underfoot, the windows rattled, and the shed whited out. I flinched as Brennan's back lit up like a nuke. I shielded my eyes from the stark light. Enl'iel stared lovingly, unaffected by the glare. Her mouth was open, a blush of excitement stained her cheeks.

Brennan groaned, his head flopped back, arms flung wide, his fingers stretched; trembling. I clung to Enl'iel's arm. He groaned louder, lifted his head, and rose into the air. Brennan was literally suspended in the air... off the ground. He hung there motionless, back to us.

Mouth dry, gawping, I was speechless. I wanted to ask Enl'iel what was going on, but words stuck in my chest whilst she seemed nothing short of enraptured.

"Love of my soul," she whispered. Enl'iel too, now shimmered in a soft light. I didn't know where to look now, but Brennan, who groaned a third time, drew me back.

His body trembled; his spine ruptured with the same inflammatory pattern as mine. Light emanated from these raised welts. No longer sparks, but a soft and warm glow. Like the gills of a fish, it pulsed out of small slits of skin. It was ethereal. It was beautiful. It was freaking me out, yet I edged forward, back up the steps. He had a magnetic pull that I couldn't resist. Mesmerised, looking up at him and barely able to breathe, I brushed my fingers gently through the light bathing his back. A rush of visions surged through my mind, visions that spoke a single word: family.

He's like me — I'm like him! What the hell is he, and what the hell am I?

Brennan turned around at my touch; he was a stunning sight to behold. Soft white light glowed behind him. It arced up and outward behind his back. His blonde hair was now a cool white, but the real spectacle was his eyes. Still blue, but his irises moved, they rotated. Unearthly, glittering opalescent gems.

I shuddered when Enl'iel whispered softly behind me.

"Behold this sight, my dear Sophia. This is a great Watcher of A'vean, your kindred and your protector." I heard the words, didn't comprehend them at all. I felt fuzzy in the head, wondered if it all was a dream. I wanted to reach for him, to see if it was real, but then Enl'iel's hand slid from my shoulder; her tone abruptly returned to her no-nonsense self.

"Enough showing off, Brennan!" she scolded him as though this display was not in the slightest bit extraordinary.

"Ahhh. By the Throne, this feels good!" Brennan stretched each limb, cracked his neck, flexed his muscles, and that light undulated, mesmerisingly behind him. A smile spreading across his face.

"Five hundred long years I've waited for this." He flexed all of his limbs again. The veins in his right arm were rivers of white light, but it was his face that had my attention. He bore the same birthmark as me across his right eye and cheek, and it glowed. My fingers slid across my own. It was warm and sore, and just like his. A disbelieving fog held me in its grasp.

The light behind him moved. It waved back and forth like wings. His sparkling eyes hooked on mine, and he smiled again. He glided smoothly over and pointed to the stairwell.

"After you, Princess."

I looked down into the gaping hole. The blackness was a magnet that wanted to swallow me whole. Enl'iel's smiling face looked up at me with encouragement. Her fingers curled warmly and reassuringly around mine. We descended to where and what; I hadn't a clue.

124

Chapter Fourteen

There was an uneasy quiet about the house in the minutes since Enl'iel and the others left for the library. Esme was comfortable in an old Louis XIV chair. It needed a good refurbishment, but she liked the well-worn dip in the seat that her padded behind sunk nicely into. She sighed, tapped her fingers on the arms. Esme was feeling restless—the air about her wasn't right. The hairs on her neck had alerted her before the air took a strange perfume to it.

Esme was wise enough to know not to ignore these signs. She pulled her brown bag closer to her feet; it was never far from her reach. Digging around inside, she found what she was looking for. She held a thick sheaf of sage, strapped together with a length of brown twine. A sprinkling of cedar wood shavings and it was ready. She already had some lavender hanging above every doorway. The spiritual presence she felt was heavy and wicked, just like the night before. A few repellent aromas might settle it down until the others returned, she told herself. Esme was merely a human with a deep sixth sense; she could no more control a Daimon than a hurricane. She licked her lips, tasted the salt of fear creeping in.

"Oh, for the love of, where are the matches?" She rustled through her bag some more. "Always forgettin' somethin'!" Esme spoke to no one but herself. Easing her old bones out of the chair, she padded heavily to the kitchen, humming to herself to break the thick tension. Picking up a pack of matches from the windowsill, she felt the fluffy caresses of Pumpkin around her ankles, purring like a jackhammer.

"You looking for a snack, eh? Let me see." She opened the refrigerator. "Here you go, a little slice of cheese. Mmmm, don't you go telling Sophia, then. I'll be in trouble for fattening you up too much again. He he!" She laughed to herself, rubbed Pumpkin's head as he ate.

Nature sung in Esme's veins, it drove her life. The natural world had no agenda. Trees, animals… they held no lies or pretences. They gave you what they had honestly and asked for nothing more than a snack and a rub on the belly in return.

People, well, they troubled Esme. Humans were so entrapped in what they thought they wanted that they weaved webs of deception that led to nothing good. She trusted nature, but she always maintained her guard with people. Their layers of falsity made them vulnerable to the spirits, both good and bad. Like lambs to the slaughter, they were.

As Esme plopped back down with a rather unladylike thump, Jasmine stirred.

"Hmmm." *That's not right. Enl'iel's power should have kept Jaz out cold a while longer,* Esme thought. The floor creaked, a breeze curled around her ankles. Esme edged forwards on the chair, and set about lighting the sage to cleanse the room sooner rather than later.

Yet, each strike of a match resulted in nothing but a burnt stick and no flame. There were only a dozen matches left in the package. She kept striking, with no success. Pumpkin ran through her legs, hissed, and disappeared from sight.

Her upper lip glistened, sweat ran down her cheeks.

"Enl'iel, please hurry," she whispered, eyes wide, aware of every corner, every shadow. With the last match left, her hands trembled almost uncontrollably. She took a breath and carefully struck the match.

"Oh…thank goodness." Esme sighed with relief. A flame illuminated her fingers, and she lowered it to the sage. As distinct as if someone were right by her side, she felt the blow of an icy breath. The flame doused before it caught light on the sage. Esme jumped in her seat, dropped the sage to the floor, and clasped the arms of the chair. Wide-eyed, she looked around the room.

"You go leave us alone, you hear? You're not welcome in this home. Go! Get out, get away from here!" Esme felt light-headed and breathless. Her lips trembled, but she sniffed the fear away and rose to check if Jasmine was safe.

She rested the back of her hand on Jasmine's brow, her skin now warm and pink, but a fresh drop of blood trickled from her left eye.

"Hmmm…" Esme picked up a damp cloth from the tea table nearby and dabbed it away.

"You leave her alone, you evil beasts. Go back to where you belong. Pick on somethin' your own size. She's no help to you." Esme dropped the cloth, felt a coldness cling to her shoulders, run down her neck.

"Oh Jesus, Mary and Joseph, protect us," she spluttered, drawing a half-hearted sign of the cross over her chest. Although she was raised a Christian, she had not practiced the faith for decades. However, in moments of extreme fear, she'd sometimes revert to a quick, panicked prayer out of habit.

Jasmine began mumbling incoherently in her sleep. Her eyes twitched rapidly. She ground her teeth, and it further set Esme's nerves on edge. While tucking the blanket more securely around Jasmine's shoulders, the cat reappeared on the back of the sofa. Pumpkin growled and hissed, his hackles raised, ears flat. He spat towards Jasmine; his paw raised threateningly with claws aimed at her.

Another movement caught Esme after she waved him away.

Jasmine's head lolled towards the cat. She groaned. The cat jumped suddenly, screeching as it went flying from the sofa and up the stairs in a blur of ginger.

"Ooh, this isn't good, girl. You hang on there with me. I know it's near you. Don't let it in, please don't let it in? You're strong. I know you've been through a lot in your life. You be strong for me now, eh? I could do with a little help right about now. Old Esme is way outta depth here!" She looked about desperately, hoping for signs that anyone had returned. But it was just her, Jasmine and something else.

Esme pulled the chair closer to Jasmine, sat back down and reached forwards to dab Jasmine's eye again, as much to comfort herself as the girl. Jasmine rolled her head back towards Esme with an unnatural flop. The old woman jumped in shock; pain suddenly racked her body. Esme tried to stand, but her knees gave way and she slipped to the floor. She clutched her heart, pain seared down her arm. Her breath was shallow, lungs unable to inflate. Her skin tingled as oxygen left her. Esme heaved herself onto her hands and knees and unwillingly made eye contact with the face staring back at her.

Jasmine, still as a corpse, silent and tucked in snugly, was glaring at Esme with eyes as black as tar.

"You—leh—her—alo," was all the kindly old woman could mutter.

Esme knew it was the same spirit she'd felt near Sophia the night before. It was right in front of her, attached to Jasmine, and it was murdering her in cold blood.

Chapter Fifteen

I moved in a velvety, dreamlike state. Slow and fluid, one step at a time. Right, left, then right again. I left the old me behind as I descended into the earth, transforming into a girl that I didn't yet know. Hands trailing along the jagged walls, my entire body tingled, it hummed within.

The steep abyss teased vertigo every time I looked down. There was no railing to grasp onto, so I dug my hands into any outcropping of wall to keep steady. I felt sure I was going to tumble forward to my death at any moment. This was clearly no problem for the guy flapping behind me. That transformation of Brennan experience was filed away as yet another thing I would ask about later, when I knew what exactly to ask.

The darkness below buzzed with energy that plucked at my skin. Every so often, Enl'iel placed a hand upon the wall ahead and it would illuminate. She looked back each time with an encouraging smile. My apprehension must have been evident in my snail's pace progression.

"Keep up, Sophia. We are nearly there."

"I'm right behind you," I answered.

"Move it along, ladies. It's a little cramped back here," added Brennan.

It was in this twilight glow that I first noticed Enl'iel too, had a swirling white trail at the edge of her right eye. It was much smaller than mine. It glowed when she smiled at me. How had she hidden that from me?

Eventually, both feet hit solid ground. I sighed with relief.

An earthen opening arched overhead. Glittery stone columns preceded a set of golden gates that would be at home in any gothic cathedral. A deep blackness lay beyond the metal bars, and I felt pulled towards it and it made absolutely no sense. I bit my lip, laced my fingers in and out, felt a jitteriness under my skin. A cool, earthy breeze wafted through from beyond the bars. A heavy silence owned the air, no evidence of what could be there.

"Sophia, would you use the key again?" Enl'iel pointed ahead. She dropped the key back into my hand. My fingers trembled, despite the fusion of excitement and fear snaking through my insides. With slightly more effort than before, the key turned in the lock with a metallic crunch, as though it had not been opened for many years. I looked backed to Enl'iel before I hesitantly pushed the gate. The gate was jammed, and all three of us had to heave it open.

"Where are we, Na… Enl'iel?' I asked.

"We are entering The Library of Antiquity. There are only four sanctuaries left. They are gathering places, learning institutions, homes, and safe havens for us. Places where we cannot be detected by unpleasant creatures, such as the kind you saw at the hospital."

For us… who or what was 'us'

Brennan's light wings ate the darkness. Enl'iel entered, but I hesitated.

"It's okay Princess, nothing nasty down here," Brennan said, wriggling his hands for me to follow.

Thank God for that, I thought. "Shouldn't we bring Ben and Jasmine here? They saw that thing. Aren't they in danger?"

"If Kea can work her magic, they will be just fine. Trust in us, Sophia. Just as you are going to have to trust in yourself," Enl'iel answered cryptically.

How could I trust in myself? I couldn't trust that what I was seeing and doing was not some form of elaborate delusion. Perhaps I was still in the hospital after my run in with the patient gurney? Perhaps I'd been given potent drugs that were sending my trippy while I recovered? It was easier to believe, but I knew it was just wishful thinking at this point. I could taste the staleness of subterranean air, smell earthy minerals, feel the strange buzz under my skin… and of course, I couldn't ignore the winged neighbour flying just ahead.

We made our way along the length of a short, high-ceilinged corridor, whose crystalline walls captured the glow of Brennan. Highly polished stones tiled the floor. They seemed new, never walked on, yet the place had an impressively ancient feeling to it.

We came upon a smaller metal gate. It opened with a light push from Enl'iel.

I halted; my hands grazed its bars. They were warm and made of gold. It hummed under my touch. I released it, inspecting my still-tingly fingers that seemed unharmed.

"Part of the security system," Brennan said. He was still unsettling me with the hovering thing. "Gold is a powerful conductor. We use it to repel unwelcome visitors."

"How does it work?"

"I'm so glad you asked, Princess." Brennan cracked his knuckles, stretched his arms over his head as though limbering up. "Let's pretend your friendly doctor from the hospital followed us down here." He winked; a gleam of excitement brightened his eyes.

"What? He could… I mean… is it going to come back for us?" I backed up, slamming my tender back into the wall behind me, fingers digging into the rock.

"Brennan, look what you've done, trying to show off!" Enl'iel rubbed my shoulder. "No, Sophia, that evil creature does not know where this place is — none of them do. Brennan's security system has never been used to do anything other than to amuse himself!" Enl'iel assured me and clucked her tongue at him.

"Sorry, Soph. She's right, but awfully boring. C'mon Enl'iel, let me show her a little fun." He pouted at her with puppy dog eyes.

"You'll do it anyway," Enl'iel sighed, she waved her hand at him. "Go on."

"It's like you know me." He blew her a kiss.

"So, Princess, just in case you want to know how to get rid of a door-to-door salesman, watch this."

He aimed his right hand towards the golden metal, a brief burst of lightning shot out from his palm. As it made contact, every bar on the gate seemed to absorb the energy with a sucking sound. It hummed like a million bees, then sent a massive shockwave of white light bursting through the other side, down the length of the corridor towards the stairs. If someone was on the opposite side of that gate, it would be an instant cremation.

"Impressive?" He grinned; eyebrows arched.

He was like a big kid playing with his toys. "Wait 'til you see our weapons room in the UK. It's even better!"

"Enough of that now, we are not here to play the fool," Enl'iel glared at him, with a wink and a smile at the end.

"Come, Sophia. Join us in our beautiful sanctuary." Enl'iel pulled me gently alongside her.

I gave Brennan a quick thumbs up for his trick; a massive smile spread across his face. I smiled too, despite the situation, despite the cold hard fear that crushed me.

We entered a dimly lit, cavernous room. At a guess, it was the size of a football stadium, but it was hard to tell. The echo of our footsteps seemed to bounce back from quite a distance away. Running water trickled far off in the pitch darkness. The roof was so high it was nothing more than another inky void.

Brennan gave me a gentle prod from behind

"Don't be scared. Be amazed." he fanned his light wings out, drenching the immediate surrounds.

A multi-levelled room emerged from the shadows. The further we walked; the darkness evaporated where it was lit more brightly with strange candles along the walls. Ornate staircases connected the three storeys. On the second level were row upon row of neat, diamond-shaped storage spaces, crammed with books and what looked like scrolls of paper. A handful of white lights dashed among them, stopping and hovering for a time, and then darting off to another section.

"What the…?" Mouth was agape again; I watched the little lights dash like bees in a hive.

"They are the Keepers of Knowledge. They collect, document, and protect both our history and the history of humanity," Enl'iel explained. They seemed so familiar.

Like my Fairies!

Incredible murals decorated the walls. Mosaics that twinkled, multicoloured starry artworks. I left Enl'iel's side, ran my fingers along the bottom of one, quickly realising that they were made of rough-hewn gemstones. Diamonds, quartz, rubies, lapis, and emeralds — an Aladdin's cave of wealth, woven into the fabric of earthen walls as masterpieces.

I was awestruck. All manner of creature glistened with life. Birds, land animals, sea creatures, and people, too. In some images, the people looked like they were interacting with huge, ethereal beings surrounded by light… they looked exactly like Brennan.

"Incredible!" I whispered.

"This is your story, Soph," said Brennan. "The documents contained within these walls, and the murals, tell of our long history. They evolve and change as we do."

"My story?"

"Yes, Soph. This place will answer many of your questions," he said.

"Who am I?" I whispered.

Enl'iel threaded her arm through mine, drew me close. "Brennan, would you be so kind?" She waved her arm around, indicating the general darkness surrounding us.

He elevated higher with the powerful force of light emanating behind him. It seemed to extend further out of his body the higher he rose. His square jawline set firm in concentration; Brennan raised his arms. Orbs of white, pulsing light appeared magically upon each palm.

He clapped his hands together; the cavernous space echoed like thunder. Light sizzled and flickered between his palms; he seemed to mould something. He then threw this mass of energy above his head.

Fireworks lit up the ceiling, revealing a gargantuan rocky cavern. The light ball he released spun and sparked, eventually retracting into a slowly spinning globe, hovering high in the nether reaches of this underground haven; a subterranean sun.

"Not bad for an old timer, wouldn't you say?" Brennan hovered, hands on his hips, nodding smugly to himself with satisfaction.

Enl'iel walked me deeper into the cavern.

"Let me tell you a story," she began.

Chapter Sixteen

The drive to the market was mind-numbing. Trailing around after humans, half-breeds, and hypocrites was so far beneath Nik'ael, that he almost considered it more enticing to face perpetual oblivion. All they did was worry about protecting *her*.

What about him and his kind? Weren't they as worthy of absolution? Had they not suffered an eternity on this forsaken hell-hole for sins long since forgotten? Sins that these same brethren had indulged in? Sins that he himself had never partaken in. He didn't buy it for a minute that they were not as aggrieved as he — they just chose to bide their time differently. When the end came, they would grip the same handle to slit her throat. They, too, would hold the chalice to collect her blood. They were one and the same to him, travelling on different highways towards a mutual destination.

Nik'ael needed to stop this little shopping expedition from returning too soon to the house at the bottom of the hill. His accomplice needed time there, to get the Rogues in place, to be ready. Diversions were needed to secure the information he required, the vital clues he needed to finally get ahead in the game. How could he do this without being detected? Easy. He was a master of cloaking. He had perfected the art of being so close, yet so invisible, that I'el himself would not know he was underfoot.

As the black car crested a hill, leaving the local village behind, it shuddered.

The engine over-revved, sputtered, and ground to a halt. Kea eased it onto the edge of the road.

"Damn, I just had this thing serviced," she said, frustrated.

"Want me to have a look?" asked Ben.

"Sure, are you good with motors?"

"Yeah, not bad. I built my bike."

"Well, dive in, my friend. I'd like to get back with these groceries for your sister."

"There's no way Jaz will eat or drink any of that. She'll throw that green tea, hot and all, right back at you."

"She sure is a prickly one." Kea crossed her arms, watching Ben lift the bonnet. She sighed, "The last twenty-four hours have been pretty hard on her though. Something's off with her. I don't know what she remembers about the time she was missing, but I'm worried. Would she talk to me about it, do you think?"

Ben hooked the bonnet into place. He huffed and reached into the engine.

"Leave her be. She'll talk if she wants to, but it certainly wouldn't be to someone she met five minutes ago. She doesn't know you from a tree stump, so don't try getting all BFF with her!"

Kea quirked a brow at the sourness of his response.

"Only trying to help, Ben."

"Well don't."

The exchange impressed Nik'ael. He loved a good dispute, especially if it led to a fistfight... or even better, bloodshed. Unfortunately, damned Kea had to keep it all too calm. Boring as Hell. Ha, and how true that was!

"What about you? Do you remember much from yesterday?" Kea eased closer to Ben as he leaned deeper into the engine, her glowing hand out of his sight, hovering just behind his head as he was inspecting the oil dipstick.

Nik'ael smiled smugly to himself.

Ben flinched a little before he answered distractedly.

"Besides feeling pissed off at that doc threatening Soph, not much." He moved to the left, edging her away from him. "I'm not interested in a psych session, so back off!" Ben leaned deeper into the engine. Kea smiled to herself and flexed her fingertips.

She was clueless. She thought she had the upper hand. Nik'ael was intoxicated by the power of his subversive interference.

"Spark plugs were too loose. Try it now," Ben said.

Kea slipped back behind the wheel. The car started easily, and they quickly set off for home.

Within minutes, it came to a rolling stop again.

"I thought you knew what you were doing, buddy?"

"I'm not your buddy, and I *do* know what I'm doing!" Ben raked his hand through his hair, "You might have noticed that you don't have a toolbox or anything slightly helpful in the boot, so give me a break!" Ben slammed the door as he got out again. Kea popped the bonnet again.

This little scenario played out another five times as they attempted the drive back to the house. Nik'ael loved every second of it. He'd send a covert burst of negative energy to the engine, Kea and Ben would get out and fiddle under the hood, becoming increasingly annoyed with each other. They'd head off again, but wouldn't you know it — poof — another breakdown. How very, very convenient.

Eventually, they conceded defeat and waited for a roadside tow service. Luckily for Nik'ael, it was going to be a long wait on that winding, forested road. Time was now on his side.

Chapter
Seventeen

The glowing orb that had somehow emerged from Brennan now illuminated an expansive cavern; walls full to brimming with beautiful imagery. The floor was a mosaic of black stones. Diamond encrusted; it twinkled like the constellations of the night sky.

Something in the distance caught my attention. It seemed central to the whole cavern. Like a regal monarch, a large pedestal with a huge green rock atop it. It cast a dull, jade glow. Beyond it were six arched doorways that led to other unknown places. A radiant, golden star watched over the entrance to each dark tunnel.

"Look around you, take it all in," Enl'iel said with a touch of awe.

"Who made this place? It's incredible." My voice was still a whisper.

"Let's start at the beginning, shall we?" Enl'iel pointed up towards the east wall, towards a triangular formation of stars against the velvety darkness. The star at the peak was large. Surrounded by licks of fire. Within it was an iridescent blue eye, with hints of the entire colour spectrum weaving throughout it. Six smaller stars were underneath. A pyramid of stars that broadened towards the base, with the stars became smaller and more numerous. Hundreds more half stars edged the base of the wall.

"This is a depiction of the Beginning. These stars represent the collective inhabitants of a world known to us — and no one else — as

A'vean. It is a planet impossibly far away from Earth. A place of immense beauty, rather Earth-like, but exponentially larger. Earth is but a blip on a radar compared to the immensity of A'vean. This is the home of the creators of all life throughout the universes, it is the throne of I'el."

I was about to ask something, but she raised her hand for me to be quiet.

"Humans are the creations of the Council of I'el. The Council is a race of enlightened beings, of pure conscious energy. They take no particular form. They have travelled the universe, creating life where there was none, for years beyond the billions. All life sparked from them shares a piece of their energy — a soul—and that provides a connection to them eternally."

"Are you talking about God and Heaven?" I asked, immediately intrigued.

"Yes and no. Humans think of their creator as a God or Gods who reside in a Heaven. Heaven is clearly a derivative of A'vean, long forgotten and bastardised by humans, mind you. The Creator is in fact more than one being. I'el was the First, the Prime Energy. He — and I'll use *he* for ease of description — is everything and nothing, all at once. Neither male nor female, just a pure force, born from the great singularity that exploded many hundreds of billions of years ago. I'el is the Prime of the Seven, the first of anything in this universe to obtain consciousness. He is the supreme and most powerful of the creators. His word is the final one on all matters. In the beginning, he was alone, so he cast six conscious energies from within himself, each responsible for a different function in the propagation of life across the universes. It is a natural compulsion for him to create life... he has no other objective. Taking life is against his very being, and has only ever been done so under extreme circumstances. You can see him depicted here as the star at the peak of the pyramid." She pointed up, her face blossomed, her voice soft. "The eye represents our infinite connection with nature, the universe, and Him. The six stars below him are his brothers, Earth, Wind, Fire, Water, Light, and Dark."

I didn't realise that my mouth was hanging open until her finger gently lifted my chin.

"What do all the other stars in the pyramid mean? Is there an entire race of these energy-beings?" Something buzzed under my skin; excitement, fear…connection?

"Well, yes, Sophia, there are. They are organised into a system of cascading power and function. I'el being the Prime and most powerful, working all the way down to the bottom, which brings us to who we are."

That tingly feeling you get when you actually know the answer to something, but refuse to admit it to yourself, drew my hairs on end.

One more minute of normality, please?

"We, and that includes you and I, are descendants of the energies of A'vean."

I turned slowly around, absorbing the surrounds.

"I'm an alien?" I whispered to myself.

There was a cough. "Hmm-mmm, ah, do I look like ET?" interjected Brennan.

"No, but if I'm one of them, I'm not human, right? So, then what am I?"

"You're a miracle. An Earth-born angel of A'vean, Soph," Brennan beamed with pride. "You're just like me, but prettier… just!"

His humour was lost on me as memories of the hospital stairwell came flooding back. I flew. Lightning shot out of my body. I flew — I damned-well flew.

I leaned against the wall for a moment. Everything hurt. My body felt suddenly not quite my own. I bent over, rested my hands on my thigh, "What's going on? Why have I never known any of this?" I sunk to a crouch, grabbing my aching, spinning head. Brennan helped me back up. Enl'iel scooped my arm in hers again.

"Come, my love, the pain will ease soon enough." She rubbed my back and I felt instant relief.

"You've not known for your own safety. You will come to understand why. This is a lot to take in, we understand, but the time has come for you to know and embrace your heritage. I wanted to tell you in a more controlled and calm manner, but we have been pushed by circumstance to move forward with an uncomfortable haste, and I am sorry for this. You are very precious, Sophia." Enl'iel hugged me, placing her head on my shoulder for a moment.

Should I feel scared, angry, amazed, or honoured? I didn't understand any of it. My emotions were in warfare with each other. I wanted to feel angry at the deception, but I also needed to understand it all too.

"Why did you call me the Earth-born angel?" I asked as I let my fingers graze along the wall, feeling addictive zaps of power.

"Look at this mural, Princess. I'll get to that to the whole Earth-born thing in a minute," Brennan replied. He pointed at the wall right above me.

"This here shows the Six, descending to Earth, sparking life into what was a violent and harsh world. You see those lifeless-looking people on the ground? That's the moment when they thrust the energy of I'el into primitive man, giving them souls, a kick-start to their evolution, and an eternal connection to A'vean." He paused at some of the images with a nostalgic sparkle to his eye, reminiscing, as though he had been there.

"Early humans were weak and didn't learn well. Normally, there's a strict policy of non-interference. Life must be left to evolve in its own way. However, the Council, and particularly I'el, felt a deep compassion for the struggling race, whose image was a physical clone of their most favoured spiritual form. So, after a lot of debate over thousands of years, they voted on minimal intervention, as the survival of this unique species was at risk. Humans were being picked off by predators, and underutilising the potential they'd been given. To help, I'el sent the Order of Watchers to Earth to protect them and gently guide humans so that they could flourish. I was one of those Watchers, Soph."

I looked at Brennan dubiously. "You're like—an angel?"

"Well, I know I look like one, better actually." He quirked a brow. "I was a warrior Seraph, but I tired of the warring worlds, so I volunteered for the Order. Angels, in fact, are a rank or so above us, we've just been piled into the same club by humans. Can't complain, it's not a bad gig!"

"Brennan!" Enl'iel scoffed.

"Oh, you love it!" He winked at her. She just shook her head. Ignoring his self-loving banter. My mind worked overtime.

"Hang on, how old are you?" I asked, my heart kicked up a notch.

He tapped his lips, looked away in thought.

"Well, if I add in this, take off that, throw in the Dark Ages… hmm, I'd say I'm a spritely fifty thousand years young, give or take a millennium. Don't think I look a day over 5000 though!" His smug humour was getting annoying.

"Now you're just messing with me. This can't be real! That would mean you're immortal!"

"Watchers descend from I'el, so yes, we are indeed immortal. It's kinda cool, but has its drawbacks, particularly if you're injured. We can endure illness and injury for thousands of years, which isn't pretty. Just come through that, as you can see." He pointed to his newly working legs. "I know it's hard to believe, Princess. Last week I was just the guy in the wheelchair across the road. But now I'm recovered. I'm your own personal immortal wingman." His eyes lit up; a smile spread across his face. "I crack myself up — wingman!" He shook his head, musing at his own joke as he flapped his wings at me.

"Brennan! Save your stand-up set for later," Enl'iel scolded.

"Sorry." He winced and urged me along the east wall to another mural. I clung tighter to Enl'iel's arm.

"Energy doesn't disappear, it simply moves from one realm or form to another. Humans and other life forms have souls that move on to different states of being after their mortal death. They have no control over what becomes of their souls. However, if that energy, like you and I, has a higher level of consciousness, then it is perpetually self-determined — effectively, immortal." Brennan had a perfectly matter-of-fact expression, as though this was all too boringly normal.

Words failed to come to my mind. I felt wide-eyed like a child, as though listening to the most riveting bedtime story of all time. It actually *was* the most riveting story of all time.

Brennan's light wings moved, pushing him alongside Enl'iel and I.

"We arrived to guide humankind in whispers and dreams, to protect them from themselves and the wild world they barely survived in. Because of their frailty and suspicious nature, we assumed human form. Humans can't look at us in our true form and survive."

"Why?" I asked.

"They spontaneously combust from the intensity of us." He shook his head at an unpleasant memory. "Learned that the hard way, unfortunately."

"Oh God! That's awful!" I pressed my hand to my mouth, trying not to imagine it. "So, you disguised yourself so humans didn't catch on fire?"

"Yep. Even a small glimpse could blind someone instantly — it was no way to make friends. So, we transformed ourselves to look and feel like humans. Most of us kind of like these fleshy costumes." He smiled, plucked at the skin on his arm. "Been fun taking on various sizes, shapes, and colours." He pointed high on a mural. "See, up there, we're those streaks of light cascading over the Earth, the ones with the rather creepy looking faces. The artistic licence is a little loose. Hmm!" He frowned.

Comet-like streaks were indeed cascading across the rocky scene. Only because Brennan pointed it out, did I realise that they all had faces.

My fingers drummed on my thighs; I bit my lip, mind racing.

"So, you're immortal, and you can change form!" I couldn't believe I was going along with this as I did the mental math, "So, why have you been a paraplegic ever since I met you?"

"Ahh." He waved the question away, "A particularly nasty fight. Got myself a really good beating — nearly killed my body." He patted his chest. "It's taken me forever to heal. After our initial transmutation to a human form, we can't acquire a new body if the old one is ruined. We need to look after our bodies carefully. If they're injured, we can heal to a certain point. However, if they're irrevocably damaged, we return to our original form. We aren't magicians!" He shook his head at me as if it was perfectly obvious.

"What happens then?"

"We ascend to the Sanctuary of Souls. I wasn't ready for retirement when this happened, so I've been healing myself for five hundred years or so. The Middle Ages were nasty times. Daimon were bolder, one on every street corner when humans were obsessed with Hell and such. Fun times, Princess," he sighed, closed his eyes a moment as though reminiscing.

"Okay," I drawled.

Enl'iel moved me on to the next mural as I tried to digest this information. What was a Daimon? I wasn't sure I really wanted to know.

"What can you make of this image, Sophia?" asked Enl'iel.

I didn't answer for a moment as I caught myself looking at her youthful complexion again. Her lineless face was a vision of immense beauty. Long white hair nestled around her shoulders and shone like diamonds.

Dragging my attention from her, I looked at the mural.

"Looks like people having a party. There's food, and I think wine, and, oh — um, some of them look like they are…"

"Intimate?"

Heat flooded my cheeks.

"What do you notice about the couples?" She prompted.

I bit my nails; the right words were hard to extract when I felt like I might combust myself from the embarrassment.

"Um," I pressed my hands over my mouth.

"I'm not ah…oh!" My hands fell away. It dawned on me exactly what was happening. "It's humans and…." Some of the lovers were glowing. "You and they—?" I stopped.

Neither of them spoke.

"You're like, the Fallen Angels from the Bible? You fell in love with humans, and were thrown out of Heaven?" My jaw dropped.

"Well," Brennan scoffed. "It wasn't as simple and debase as that, but yes, guilty as charged." He raised his hands up in mock defence, a coy grin plastered across his face. Clearly, the poised, perfect beings sold by religious institutions missed the part where they could act like irreverent class clowns.

Enl'iel waggled a finger at him. His expression sobered.

"It was a bad thing, Sophia. It has led to much suffering and affected the Order of Watchers' ability to return home. It changed the course of human history forever, and not for the better. You should not be so flippant, Brennan. You're a part of this mess."

"You're right, of course, apologies," he responded, a more serious note in his tone for a moment, then he reverted back to the clown.

He pulled Enl'iel away from me into a spin and an embrace, kissing her passionately on the lips.

"But, if we hadn't partied, I would never have found you, and that would be a Shakespearean tragedy of epic proportions!" He leaned in and kissed her again. The mark on her face glowed.

"Yes, well…" Enl'iel blushed like a teenager, self-consciously straightening her top as she pulled herself from his arms. "Let's keep the pace going Romeo, we must return topside shortly. I have so much to show you, Sophia. We can discuss the more colourful history later," Enl'iel cleared her throat, pulled herself together.

I could barely suppress a smile.

"Let's move on, shall we?" Enl'iel pointed to the next mural. It depicted Watchers cowering on the ground below a bright light with a fiery eye within it. They were in front of a huge, glowing doorway. They appeared to be reaching towards it, trying to get through.

Brennan continued the narration, "That's the day the portal to A'vean closed indefinitely to us. With that connection severed, we were stripped of a ton of power. Our minds were instantly erased of immense chunks of our universal knowledge as punishment, including our native language. Only small portions of it remained. We've managed to salvage what we remembered by teaching it to the Mycenaeans. They were the most receptive at the time. Modern Greek is the closest thing we have to our own language now. This is why you'll notice many references or adaptations of a Greek-like culture in our everyday life and history."

My skin buzzed, something tapped in the back of my mind as though some deep, locked away part of me somehow knew this.

Brennan hovered at another mural; a darker, more sinister energy emanated from it. I didn't want to get too close. He tapped the wall.

"These are our enemies — your enemies, Princess. The Unseen." Brennan rested a hand on my shoulder. It was warm, reassuring. "They are not, and never will be on your side." His fingers squeezed my shoulder and he let go. "You'll hear them referred to as the Satans as well; that's a more familiar name to you, I imagine?"

I nodded, "Why so many names? What have they done?"

He huffed. Enl'iel's body tensed.

"They behaved like a race of vicious beings from Satanos, a planet long ago destroyed due the violence of its inhabitants. Satan was picked up liberally by humans and stuck. We refer to them as 'The Unseen' because they dwell in shadow, rarely seen, but always causing havoc. When we were exiled from A'vean…" He pointed one at a time to shadowed figures in the mural, "…These five brothers of ours were so enraged that they split from us. Over time, they've enlisted many more of us, those fed up with exile. The Unseen vowed to cause carnage to humans as punishment to the Council for cutting them off. They didn't believe we deserved such a blanket banishment, and perhaps we didn't, but who am I to judge that?"

"What exactly have they done?" I asked. An instinctive revulsion gnawed at my gut.

"Every war, every major disaster in human history, has been initiated or fuelled in some way by the Unseen and their pack of devils. They've stolen from humans the memories of their origins by mimicking Gods. This action alone thrust humanity into religious wars and power struggles for millennia. They get a smug satisfaction from the confusion and misery they cause," he explained. The warmth of his face faded as though he personally were at fault.

"So where do I fit into all of this? Are you a Watcher, too?" I asked Enl'iel.

She squeezed my arm, hugged into me.

"No, dear. I'm Eudaimonian, a hybrid of a Watcher and a human. Some of us are born of two Eudaimonians, or of Watchers and Eudaimonians. Rarely, since the great fall, have Watchers mated with humans. Those who do are shunned by the Council of Eloi — they are our elders who try to keep us all on a righteous path. The same cannot be said for the Unseen, who interfere to this very day with humans in ways they should not. The Christian Bible calls us Nephilim, and we have been wrongly portrayed as evil. Eudaimonians may have all or none of the powers that a Watcher has. Those like myself who inherit many powers can live a very long time. Others might live a life as short as any human. Those who have the minor powers of clairvoyance and such, like Esme, are more common than those like me. Generally, though, they would never know of their true heritage, such is the weakness of their lineage. The stronger the bloodline we have to a Watcher, the more similar we are. Before you ask, I am not as old as Brennan. My mother was human, a beautiful, kind woman from rural England. I was born in Tewkesbury in the year 1784."

I did a quick mental calculation and felt a little faint. "You're over two hundred years old?"

"Yes, dear."

"And still looks twenty-one, don't you think, Princess?"

"Are you ever serious?" I snapped.

"No sense of humour, chill Princess!" Brennan pretended to look at something in the distance. I scowled at him, considered all he'd just divulged, and instantly flushed with guilt.

"Sorry Brennan."

"All good, I'd be the same if I suddenly found out I was a human!"

I rolled my eyes at him. I looked back to Enl'iel.

"So, if you said Watchers didn't breed with humans for thousands of years, then how are you here?" I bit my lip as the obvious immediately registered.

Her arm slipped from mine; her cheeks stained with annoyance.

"No more talk of this now." She pushed me along. It was crystal clear that this topic was off limits, at least for now.

"Now," Enl'iel continued as though nothing had happened. "Before the great flood twelve thousand years ago, I'el took aside a human he felt great admiration for, due to his unwavering diligence and devotion to whom this human believed to be his creator. A man of peace, humble and generous in a savage world. I'el respected this deeply. Enoch is the only human to have been in the presence of I'el. He took him from the Earth, taught him the mysteries of the universe, and warned him of things that would come to pass. Most importantly, he gave Enoch a very important gift, the gift of salvation — for us and for humankind. Enoch became a prophet and could see into the future. He wrote it all down and shared it with only one other. He left snippets with our most ancient ancestors as clues, with the strictest of instructions that none but the Earth-born angel should decipher his messages to reopen the last portal to A'vean. You, my dear, are the key to finding and unlocking the mysteries of Enoch. Enoch wrote of these in our long lost A'vean language, said to only be decipherable by you."

I pinched my leg… I was still awake.

Enl'iel took over the tour, pointed to a new mural.

"You will see up there the archangel Uriel carrying Enoch back to Earth. Enoch returned with the prophecy that you would be created when the line of your heritage had once again merged into purity. Clues about who you would be have been dangled for us for thousands of years. Visions have been received, but only by the most trusted. These walls are brimming with snippets we have gathered that can only be sewn together at the right time, by the right person. Now is that time. Hidden around the Earth are the pieces to the greatest puzzle of all time. You alone have the ability to help the Watchers read Enoch's words and find the answers to opening the Gate of A'vean." Enl'iel maintained a serene calm, whilst I was stunned by the gravity of what she just said. Creators, angels, watchers, saviours.

"How do you *know* that I am this person?"

"Upon your birth, there were signs prophesied by Enoch as passed down by the leader of the Eloi council, Gedz'iel. He received visions from I'el. In the past, there were many hopeful births, but yours was the first to show each and every sign. On the night of your birth, our enemies rallied in full force — such was the power emitted by your arrival. Your first cry was felt in every corner of every dimension. The movement of the Unseen proved to us without doubt that you were the one. You drew them out of every hidden realm that they cower in."

Fear pricked my skin, replacing the wonder with a need to run, to hide, to unhear all I'd just heard.

Enl'iel rubbed my arm. The warmth returned to her and it seemed to sink into my skin, alleviating the horror clawing to get out.

She drew me towards a large mural that was clearly the Great Flood, ark and all. The only thing I noticed in this scene was a downcast-looking figure, hovering over an ocean brimming with bodies. Head in his hands, he appeared to be weeping, his sorrow added to the flood. His image moved me. I felt an instant and deep sadness at this sight.

There was a dark shadow lurking behind him.

"Who's this?" I asked.

"The one and only Eudaimonian who was drawn into the clutches of the Unseen. His name is lost to history, but not his story," she said.

"What happened to him?"

"He was almost as powerful as a Watcher, it is told. He oversaw a thriving village, caring for and protecting humans and Eudaimonians alike. The day the rains began to fall, he came home to find his entire village slaughtered, including his wife."

"Oh my God!" I gasped, "By who?"

"Archangels, I'm afraid. They attempted to cull the half-breeds to limit their survival on Earth. Only humans were meant to survive the great flood. An attempt to allow humanity to start again, pure and unsullied." Enl'iel's voice was low; it was clear she didn't support this tragedy.

"He was betrayed by his own kind?" Sadness veiled me. To be betrayed by your own; I couldn't imagine it.

"It was a dark time, Princess. But, he had us, he just chose the wrong path, bloody fool!"

I wanted to know more about this poor Eudaimonian, but I was moved quickly away. I itched to look back at him, to understand his pain... to help.

I however, found myself staring at a mural of a woman reclining on a bed, surrounded by glowing beings. Swaddled in her arms was a baby. A light beamed from the baby; a starburst exploded where this light hit the night sky. The entire scene rested upon a backdrop of rubies. The gems swirled around, enveloping the mother and child in the same shape as my birthmark. I touched my face in silent recognition. A pattern of concentric circles sat below the bed. At the foot of the bed, there was a sorrowful man. The mother was also weeping. That seemed strange. The birth of a child should be joyful.

"Who's the baby?" I felt drawn to this one, ran my fingers under the mother. Something shifted; I wanted to immerse myself in the image.

"This, my dear Sophia, is the day you were born," Enl'iel said quietly. "It was a day that allowed only brief joy. Unfortunately, your birth put you in immediate danger."

My attention hooked upon the mother I'd never known. Tears welled in my lashes. *What happened to you?*

Enl'iel let me linger a moment longer before drawing me away, despite every cell of me wanting to stay, to look at my mother; to know her. The tears spilled, Enl'iel passed a handkerchief, and I dabbed my face dry, but felt a million more unshed.

I forced myself onwards, grudgingly dragging my eyes away. This new mural was a young girl with long, white hair and eyes equally white. She was surrounded by white comets of light. Outside of this barrier of light were shadowy arms, reaching out of nothingness, grabbing for her.

"This is me, isn't it?"

"Yes, dear. You've been hunted your entire life. You've been in constant danger, more so when you were younger. There has always been an army of scouts nearby you, keeping watch. If you think about it, you will remember them. Their presence is embedded in your subconscious. Did you not see one this past June?"

"You know about the attack at the club?" I asked, incredulous.

"I know all of your movements. That was our beautiful Cael who intervened when that Rogue attacked you."

I remembered that flash of light as I was running to the door. Something had knocked my attacker to the ground. Cael — poor, poor Cael. "He saved my life. I need to go to him, try to help him." Guilt plagued me as I thought of him suffering alone in the hospital.

"Cael will be fine with time. He has already been moved to a safe place. We never leave a soldier behind."

At that moment, a shudder rumbled underfoot. I stumbled into the wall before steadying myself. Brennan and Enl'iel looked up sharply to one another.

"Sophia, you're safe here, but we need to return to the house. Promise us you will stay *right* here. Nothing can harm you in the library. The Keepers will be here for company and protection," Enl'iel instructed, her face solemn.

"What's going on?" Nerves tugged my voice.

"We'll be back shortly, Princess. No time to explain right now, just stay put." Brennan placed his hand to the right side of his face, closed his eyes, and disappeared in a flash of light. I fell back into the wall, mouth slackened, speechless.

"You will learn that little trick too, before you know it." Enl'iel smiled, but it was fear that coloured her eyes. "Please promise me you will stay here?"

"Okay," I relented, as she too disappeared in the same surreal flash of light.

Chapter
Eighteen

Alone underground, I could have been the only person left in existence; such was the feeling of relative silence and solitude in the Library of Antiquity. Apart from those little orbs busying themselves on the levels above, I was very alone. I dared myself not to wonder what Enl'iel and Brennan rushed away for; I didn't think I could take any more surprises for one day.

My mind reeled. There was just too much to comprehend. Instead of trying to make sense of the unreal, I used the opportunity to look closer around the cavern. It was either that, or curl up in a ball and cry. I chose the former, deciding to undertake a baptism of fire into this new existence.

I returned to the depiction of my birth again, pulled almost instinctually towards it. As I stared up at the bereft woman, I wondered with mixed emotions, who and where were my parents? My entire life I'd been told that I had been taken in by Nan because my parents couldn't care for me. Jaz suggested more than once that they were probably weirdos like hers, but now, who knew what or where they were. Did they know about me? Did they care?

Were they even alive?

There was another shudder underfoot. I swayed for balance. The little glowing Keepers responded quickly, taking on a frenzied state, buzzing frantically along the upper levels. A veil of darkness descended over the shelves they monitored. It drew down like a curtain. I coughed as the unsettled dust swirled in the air. Everything suddenly felt very wrong. The ache I'd forgotten about reignited in my back and head. The veins along my arms burned like poison ran through them. I rubbed them, trying to calm the discomfort. An intuitive fear exacerbated the pain.

To distract myself, I studied the fall of the Watchers more deeply. Cowering from the heavens, they shielded their faces from the wrath of their creator. One stood out, a lone figure who was not cowering. This aura-shrouded Watcher was pulling at something from a hand reaching out from the ground. There was a circular object and a cylinder in his hand. The blackened hand arising from the earth was grasping at it. The hand was clawed, and seemed to be trying to steal whatever the Watcher was holding onto. Unfortunately, the detail of the design was not clear enough to make out what this tug of war was about.

While I was intently studying this scene, I heard a whisper behind me. I spun around, breath hitching up a notch. Of course, I was alone. Even the Keepers had disappeared with the last rumble. I wished they would come back. Their light and hum had been strangely comforting. I turned back to the mosaic, but again, another whisper. No, it was more than one whisper. Turning nervously, I stared into the farthest reaches of the cavern. A spring of sweat ran down my neck. I searched for the source of the voices. Nothing. A hum buzzed in the atmosphere as I once more noticed the massive stone in the middle of the cavern. Eyes searching constantly as I moved, I was drawn to this stone, like a bee to a spring flower.

Nearing the stone, I could more fully appreciate the magnitude of its size. The jade-coloured chunk of opaque rock dwarfed me by meters. It was the shape of Lady Liberty's flame. I guessed that its circumference would take at least three or four average peoples' arm lengths to stretch around it. The whispers were nearby now, so I walked around the rock, sure I would find someone. Nobody was there. Curiosity eclipsed fear.

It rested upon an engraved pedestal. An iridescent blue opal inlaid in the middle of symbols the exact same design as the birthmark I wore. More of the birthmark-like swirls trailed down the supporting column. At the bottom, concentric circles rounded the base. This symbolism was completely foreign to me. I found myself tracing the shape. A strange but pleasant tingle ran along my fingers. They trailed upwards to the stone, and for no particular reason, I placed my palm flat on it. I jerked back in surprise. The second my hand made contact; my head erupted with a million whispers. I leaned in, touched it again, closed my eyes. Yes, the whispers were coming from it. I couldn't understand anything, but they were calm, soothing sounds. It sounded like having the radio tuned into every station at once. I pressed my ear to the stone. The voices flooded my mind, replaced uncertainty with happiness, like being lost and then found. My physical pain was momentarily silenced by an energy that stirred something deep in my subconscious.

The floor shook again. This time it was followed by a clap of thunder that thrummed through my bones. Sweat beaded on my lip. I tasted fresh fear. My palm was no longer in contact with the rock, yet I still heard voices — desperate voices, screaming for help. I grasped my head, my eyes shut tight as they pierced through my mind. They were as clear as if they were right in front of me.

Jaz and Ben; they were the ones screaming. They were in trouble. Jaz was up there, Ben and Enl'iel, too. They were all I had in this world, and they were up there without me. So, as most stupid people in scary movies do, I did the exact opposite of what I was told. I ran for the golden gate, took the stairs two by two, swatting at the Keepers buzzing in my face who had re-appeared suddenly, seemingly trying to stop me from leaving. My determination outgunned their efforts, though my thighs burned and my chest tightened all the way up. When the shed door slammed behind me, I immediately knew why I was told to stay where I was. Something whispered in the shadows of my mind, and it wasn't an answer to what was going on.

Awaken

The sky was heavy with billowing, dark clouds. A stinking fog blanketed the ground at knee height. The air temperature had dropped unnaturally low for summer. My skin prickled with the coolness; my heart thrashed in my chest. I snuck behind the stone embankment that separated the rest of the property from the back garden. I climbed the mossy stones carefully. As a child, I'd played endlessly on this wall, but right now, with my bare feet, it was nearly impossible to get a foot or finger hold to hoist myself up by. After as many slips as successes, my eyes finally peeked over the top row of stacked rock.

The sky darkened to an eerie black, whilst my home was alight with flashes of blinding light. Smoke snaked through every crack and crevice, curling up into the thickening darkness. Much of the pine cladding was scorched, yet no flames were visible. The corrugated roof was peeled back like a tin of beans. A stench that bordered on putrid replaced the normally sweet bush aromas.

Screeching, thumping, clashing, crashing. A body flung through splintering glass out of my bedroom window. It fell with a sickening thud. My eyes were wide with shock. I held my breath, too scared to make a sound. Hand on my mouth, caging in a scream, I slipped back off the wall. My vision blurred at the edges. I rubbed at my eyes. *My contacts must need changing*, I thought. This was no time to have poor vision. If ever a girl needed to see what was going on, it was now.

I crept around to the stairs that led toward the lavender hedge, aware of the heavy sound of my breaths. It took all my courage to push myself to crawl up those six steps. Flattened to the ground, I shimmied up like a lizard. Pushing a peek hole through the lavender, I saw a body laying a few metres away from me. The body was spreadeagled, with arms and legs askew in nauseating, awkward angles. The figure, clad in a gaping hospital gown — to my utter shock — stood straight back up. It attempted to straighten its clearly broken neck. The head flopped sickeningly back onto its left shoulder as it hobbled towards the house. There was a morgue toe-tag on its left foot as it dragged that mangled leg along the ground. Ripping the wire door from the hinges, it disappeared into the kitchen.

I shrunk down into a tight ball behind the hedge, horrified. My heart raced so fast; I could barely think. Consciousness wanted to slip away. It was nearly impossible to panic in silence. I rubbed my hands over and over to quell their shake. *What was happening to my family and friends in there? What the hell was that thing?* I gripped my face, as though hiding the sight of this unreal scene would make it stop. Black spots peppered my vision. My eyes burned as intensely as my back, like standing too close to a bonfire. After a life of perfect health, I struggled with the agony. Pain was what I cured, not felt.

I plucked gently at my eyes, removing the contacts and threw them to the ground. The sudden glare was intense, but my eyes felt slightly better as soon as the brown-tinted lenses were out. Within seconds, my sight was clearing. It was surreal. Severely vision impaired all my life, now I could see perfectly well. I gently rubbed them and looked up at the sky. Through the overhead yellow wattle blossoms, the ominous clouds were crisp and three-dimensional. I could have plucked one down. Small snatches of azure sky hinted through cracks in the dark mass. A bird of prey circled high above a potential victim. The subtle brown hues of its feathers were crystal clear. The whisper returned.

Awaken

An explosion erupted within the house, jolting me into a defensive crouch, my head strategically below the hedge. Even the bees had disappeared, and the birds had dulled their tunes. The chaos within my home sounded distant through my panicked breathing. Peeking through the hedge, there was another explosion, and that same deranged body flew out through the kitchen window amongst a hail of wood and glass. It writhed on the ground, flames licked the flesh from it, but it continued to struggle back towards the house. At the base of the porch steps, it reached out a skeletal hand, grasping for the balustrade. It suddenly collapsed into a pile of glowing ash. A plume of black smoke coiled from it; an unearthly howl pierced the air.

Awaken

Against my better instincts, I commando-crawled cautiously along the ground towards the house, under the protection of the lavender.

The smell of the purple buds was the only thing that felt familiar. The coarse stone path scraped into my skin; my dress now shredded to ribbons. My fingernails ripped and started bleeding. My plan was to get just close enough to listen to what was going on in there. From that point, I had no plan.

Awaken

This apparently was all about me, though the reasons still remained unclear, frustratingly unclear. Something wanted me in that hospital, and Cael was attacked after taking me out that night. Was the dream of the fighting creatures in the hospital meant to be a warning? The coincidence of seeing the circular imprint upon his palm in that vision and then all around the cavern was not lost on me. People had been laying their lives on the line to protect me from an unseen enemy for my whole life. I couldn't just lay there and let my loved ones suffer for me. Despite this, my basest instincts screamed at me to run. It was against this natural urge that I fought within myself to push forward. Whilst trying to bolster my bravado, voices shouted inaudible threats, monstrous screams plunged my courage. Another tremendous boom scared the last of the birds from the trees. Two streaks of luminescent light arced into the sky, dissolving into the thunderous clouds.

An unsettling silence descended after that. I froze, listening, shaking. Not a sound came; the house and surrounding forest were dead silent. As I lay on my belly, holding my breath and shrouded from view, my blood ran ice cold and my skin crawled. A faint shadow appeared on the ground behind me. Gurgled, rapid panting accompanied this shadow. I flipped over in an instant, only to be met with another body in a white gown, glaring down at me with glazed, black eyes. Frothy green drool dribbled down its chin. It was a woman, at least it had been, until recently. Unfortunately, I'd seen plenty of dead bodies as a nurse, and this was no living person. Pasty skin, white lips, and an odour that was all too familiar — cadaver.

Awaken

She reached down, her bones cracking. She dug filthy, jagged nails into my ankle with a vice-like grip. A screamed punched from me. The cold of her touch was horrifying. Her grip slipped deeper into my flesh. My body went numb as she dragged me towards the house. She lumbered with ease as I kicked and screamed. Hy hands raked through the grass and rubble of the path, ripping back my nails to the skin, leaving tiny, bloody trails behind. Where was that lightning power when I needed it?

Awaken

I grasped for anything in my reach to defend myself. As I tried to pull at chunks of the woody lavender for support, my arms were pricked and sliced. Just short of the stairs, near that pile of sulphurous ash, I got hold of a fallen tree branch, flipped, swung and struck at this thing with all of my strength. I missed. It pulled me further, bruising my body along the stony path.

Awaken

I listened to the whisper this time.

Anger and fear melded as one emotion. Survival mode kicked into overdrive, and I was acting on autopilot. As this feeling permeated through my body, something snapped within me. The veins in my arms glowed white, a simmering energy pulsed through my muscles. My fingers curled tighter around that branch, it heated under my skin. With one huge thrust forward, I knocked her grip from my feet as I rammed the branch forward. It pierced upwards into her livid, bloodless back. She turned on me. A deep, animal growl rumbled over her foul lips, and more putrid fluid drizzled from her mouth. She yanked the tip of the wood out of her torso without a flinch, a gaping hole left in its wake. The stench of burnt flesh permeated the air. I quickly scrambled to my feet, backing away towards the hedge again in a crouch. Regaining my grip on the wooden weapon, I swung furiously, making contact numerous times, but not enough to stop her attack.

Mid-swing, she managed a forceful fist into my face that knocked me backwards. I was momentarily dazed from the blow. She was grabbing for my legs again when a loud thwack sound caught my attention. Her head sailed silently from her body. It landed right next to me, bouncing once before rolling to a gruesome stop. Lifeless black eyes glared at me. The mouth gaped in shock for a moment, then went slack. The headless body fell to its knees but continued to move, clawing along the ground for a moment before going limp and disintegrating into another pile of ash.

Revolted, I jumped back, ready to run, and accidentally kicked the severed head with my bare foot, before it, too, disintegrated. My skin crawled, bile licked at my throat and I slipped back to the ground. My stomach heaved itself of its contents.

"Ugh…When you're finished…"

My head snapped up; a familiar face looked down at me.

"This is some crazy shit, Soph. Don't tell me I never have your back!"

Chapter Nineteen

Jaz's blood-tinged eyes were wide with the high of an adrenaline rush. She held a large shovel dripping with black fluid.

"We've gotta get out of here!" she whispered through gritted teeth. She glanced all around for the next threat, like prey in a lion's den.

There was a sharp glare around her, I shielded my eyes, gathered some strength to move... my head pounded from the blow from that thing that now sizzled like a fire pit.

Pushing up on hands and knees, I edged closer to Jaz.

"Are… are you alright?" I coughed, my mouth tasted of ash, my stomach threatened to release again. I waved her over, pointed down to the lavender hedge.

Blood coated my tongue and mingled with the acid lapping in my throat. I shuffled deeper into the shade of the lavender to hide from the monsters and the glare that pained my newly acute vision.

"Let's redefine 'okay', but for the moment, yes, I'm okay." She squished down next to me. Jaz shivered deeply as she surveyed the surrounds again, then hugged me tight.

There was a sudden bang from inside the house, making us both startle. Jaz threw the shovel aside and fell into the hedge. We sat in terrified silence.

"Soph…" Jaz's eyes were wide; she clutched my hand. She seemed about to say something else, but her mouth fell open. "What the…?"

Jaz pressed an unsteady hand to my face, tilted my head left and right. "What the actual hell?" she whispered slowly. She leaned closer to me, squinted, touched my right cheek, looked deep into my eyes.

"What? What is it?" I felt my skin. It was hot, my hand came away clean… no blood, no injury. My pulse raced at the sight of shock paling her face.

"Oh my God!" she whispered again.

I shrunk back, averting her gaze and touch.

"Soph, what's happening to you?"

"What do you mean?" I blinked rapidly, covering my face with my palm, scared of the answer. My head throbbed too loud.

"Your face, it's… and your eyes! Fuck… Soph your eyes, they're bright blue, and…" She rubbed her own green eyes as if to sharpen her sight, then looked closely into mine again, "Soph, your eyes are sparkling!"

I pressed both hands weakly to my temples. "I don't know what's happing to me. My body feels like it's turning inside out," I whispered back.

"Do you know that your face is glowing? Your cheek… you've got, I don't know, it looks like a tattoo."

"I'm scared." I covered my face with both hands and cried a few of the backed-up tears that begged to emerge. "I don't know how to explain what's happening!" Jaz's hand slipped over mine again.

"When I said one day you'd shine, I wasn't expecting it to be literal," she laughed nervously, then peeked over the hedge, checking for danger again. We both smiled awkwardly at that. Jaz could make a joke out of anything. Despite her darkness, she was the brightest person I knew.

I wiped my tears away and sniffed, "I can't believe you were in there." I indicated towards the house. "What's going? I think Enl… err… Nan and Brennan are in there. Did you see them?" It was still and quiet now. The air felt lifeless, the bush too scared to tweet or rustle. Perhaps everything, whatever it was, had settled down.

"I don't know what the fuck is going on. I woke up underneath the couch with a killer migraine. There were a bunch of people shouting threats at each other. I saw some strange stuff, enough to make me wish I were in a coma, dreaming it. There were more of those things." She pointed with a shaky hand to the ashy remains nearby. "They were attacking a woman I've never seen before, and your neighbour… what's his name?"

"Brennan."

"Ah, yeah… he was ah… floating." Jaz paused as though expecting me to laugh. When I didn't, she continued, "No shit, Soph, he was zooming around throwing bloody Zeus-like bolts out of his hand!" Her pupils dilated as she recounted this with increasing fervour, "I was trying to sneak out when one of those things grabbed me. The woman zapped it into a bloody fireball and told me to run for the shed and not look back. I didn't need convincing. I was hiding around the side of it when I saw that one sneak up on you. I would have run for the hills otherwise… but I couldn't leave you."

I hugged her tight, "You saved my life, Jaz."

"Do you think we should go in? It's been quiet for a while now. I'm pretty sure Nan's in there. I need to know she's safe."

"No friggin' way! We absolutely don't go back in that hellhole, not ever. I didn't see her in there, not that I was looking for anything other than an escape route." She smacked the ground, rolled her eyes. "Damn-it Soph, we're going to have to check for her, aren't we?"

I nodded slowly.

"I don't want to, but I can't leave Nan behind. Besides, I don't know what the hell to do without her!"

"Fuck!" Jaz balled her fists, then her attention fell back to the shovel. "Wouldn't mind taking a shovel to another one of those things that attacked me in the hospital," she laughed nervously.

"You remember what happened to you?"

"Not goin' there, sister! Take this." She passed the shovel to me as she sniffed back rare tears and pointed to a set of garden tools leaning against the back of the house. "I'll get that rake. If we're going to die, I'm taking one of those fuckers with me." We looked at each other, seeing who would cave first. We didn't, clasped hands and nodded in silent agreement. I was terrified. Jaz's visibly shaking body told me she was too.

As we made to move, a massive explosion resounded from within the house. We fell back, the ground vibrated, hot air blew back at us. Another creature flew up and out of the roof, evaporating into dust as it hit the open air. We grasped hands tighter, were about to run for it, when Jaz was ripped away through the thick lavender. I was dragged immediately after as something powerful grabbed me from behind. I screamed, struggling fiercely, trying to twist away. I lost the shovel, having only my bare, weapon-less hands to claw at it. Jaz swore with every foul word imaginable. I would have too, if only I could have found the spare breath, but my desperate screams were exhaustive. I'd lost my footing, and whatever it was, dragged me mercilessly across the ground, bumping me up the steps and into the house.

It was silent inside, other than the struggles that we were making for escape. My body was carelessly banged through the doorway and yanked into a totally trashed living room. Still in the grip of some stinking creature, the destruction of my home seemed to sap the last of me.

The curtains were ripped and partially drawn, which struck a creepy afternoon shadow across the room. Piles of ash dotted the floor. I think I was dragged through one, putrid dust caked into fresh blood streaming down my arms. Part of today's newspaper was scattered across the floor. The headline faced up. *Morgue raided; bodies stolen!*

"Can I put this thing down now?" asked a guttural voice. "It's going to make me puke. Ugh, it's covered in that purple stuff." The vile creature retched over the top of me. A splash of bloody fluid hit the ground near me, making me want to repeat the gesture.

"Drop it there," a fluid, male voice responded.

I was tossed to the ground like a piece of garbage.

I slowly hoisted myself up onto my hands and knees, two chubby feet in pink slippers in my immediate line of sight. A familiar floral kaftan greeted me next. As I hesitantly raised my eyes, I collapsed in shock. Esme grimaced down at me; a sickening bloodied grin. Her once soft face was pocked with missing chunks of flesh. Deep blue veins strained through her skin like writhing snakes. The depth of blackness in her eyes was never-ending.

"Don't look so sad, petal, it's me… only better!" she laughed, evil dripped from her scratchy cackle. It wasn't her voice at all; it sounded male, and it was terrifying.

"What have you done to Esme?" My voice cracked through a scream. I didn't know who or what I was talking to. I scuttled away until I hit the upturned sofa.

"If you hadn't caused such an ordeal at the hospital, I wouldn't have needed to go to so much effort today. But as luck would have it, we've driven away your pathetic band of soldiers for a while." The evil smile widened. "Lucky me, I have you all to myself!" She, or it, laughed and banged a glowing, forked weapon on the floor.

Horror drained the blood from me. The voice spilling from what used to be my beautiful Esme held me in place. Was this really happening?

"Thank you, my dear," Esme…It, nodded towards Jaz, who was upside down, hanging by her feet in the grip of the other creature. "You were a very agreeable hibernation vessel for my soldiers, though far too foul-mouthed. Modern ladies really are quite unsavoury these days, don't you think?" It cocked an eyebrow at me as though I'd give a damn about what it said. "I prefer a Victorian woman, well groomed, finely mannered, and *very* obedient. Much easier to deal with — in all activities." A sick laugh followed that disturbing innuendo.

"What the hell are you talking about, you mother fu…?" Jaz was kicked unconscious by the monster holding her. I screamed as blood trickled slowly from her temple.

"She is hard to warm to. I might feed her to the Rogues, they do love fresh blood."

If cruelty were a species, it was standing before me incarnate.

"What do you want with me, whoever or whatever the hell you are? Leave my family alone! Do what you want with me, just don't hurt them!" My bravery was forced, but I meant what I said.

"Your heart really is your weakness. What a divinely poetic weapon to use. She'll live, but only after we've taken that little trip I offered you yesterday. What do you say? You are a very special girl, Soph'ael."

"What did you call me?"

"Of course, they've told you nothing." The deepening voice chuckled. "Makes you all the easier to manage. Soph'ael is your true name, the Earth-born saviour... blah, blah, blah." It... she... waved the comment off. "The healer of nature, the one who shall return us to our home and deliver us the retribution for which we are owed... blah, blah, blah. You get the picture?" Esme hoisted me up with a superhuman strength in one hand. I dangled painfully by one arm, high above her head. The odour of decomposition emanated from her; I gagged. Pain and terror consumed me. There was no energy to escape — not that I even thought it was possible. Instead, I just hung there as she glared at me. I matched the stare with a false sense of defiance.

"Whatever you think you're doing, it won't happen." I had no idea what I was saying, but I had to say something.

She merely laughed. "You truly do not know, do you?" She looked away and sighed. With a flick of her wrist, a swirling vortex of fire erupted on the floor beneath me. My feet burned. I tried to curl them from the lick of the flame. There was also a heat boiling inside me, a heat that felt different, felt good. I concentrated on it, blindly willing it forward. Believing that I might have some control over this power thing, I desperately urged it out of me.

"Uh-uh, don't try it. One wrong move from you, and her head will be ripped from her shoulders." What had been Esme, pointed me towards Jaz, who was now upright, unconscious, held by her hair alone.

"Okay, okay!" I let the feeling fade in defeat.

"Smart girl."

The growing, fiery hole crackled louder. A thick blackness formed in its centre.

I was convinced this moment marked the end of my life.

Chapter
Twenty

This day was progressing so much better than Nik'ael had hoped. Separating her and those fools was far too easy. They had always underestimated the power of his distractions. This battle was a superfluous fight used to draw them away, to have her alone, defenceless, so that he could assess her progress. It was more than his ignorant brothers could possibly manage.

A little voice mimicking, and she was putty in his hands. Her innocence and ignorance were profound. She was far from ready, though, too easily drawn from wherever their safe haven was. The sheep, as he liked to call them, had learned nothing over the past thousand or so years. They followed their hearts, not their brains — somewhat like his brothers. These do-good Watchers had no dignity in his eyes. It was further proof that they were not as worthy to return to face off with I'el. They would probably roll over at his feet like the dogs they were. Yet, their ability to hide was somewhat admirable. The sanctuaries they hid away in frustrated him to no end. To his knowledge, none of his brothers or lackeys had ever been able to infiltrate these secret places. If they had, this war would have been won long ago. With his skills, Nik'ael should have been able to hunt at least one sanctuary down, but they outmanoeuvred him at every turn. He was a master of subduing his presence. But still, he was detected each and every time he got close to their damned Seraph-trained militia. They'd bred far and wide, and had eyes everywhere.

As always, Nik'ael didn't involve himself personally in petty altercations such as the scene playing out in the small house on the mountain. He stood quietly back and observed as Belial and the Rogues did his dirty work. Take a rancid soul, plus a fresh corpse, and he had the almost perfect soldier. They were a handy, disposable army. Dark human souls were desperate for something to cling to, an alternative to utter oblivion. They had no place to rest in the Middle Realm, being such as they were. With no afterlife to move on to, they became prisoners of the Empyrean dimension. They were the worst sinners of their species, hunted and tormented by bored Daimon for sport. You can't die when you're already dead, so the constant do-overs of different ways to die were unbearable for them. They could feel pain and fear, but never the release that death should provide.

This cannon fodder infantry was promised something better than eternal suffering. They had no real choice. Again, fools, as were all humans, they did their job and were blasted away anyway, which is what these dregs of creation deserved. Nik'ael may be many things, but even he could not atone for the souls of child killers and abusers, wife beaters, and the like. They were cowards, and he despised cowards. He used these pieces of filth at his will and gave them nothing in return. It was the absolution that they deserved.

The irony of humanity was that they didn't need the Unseen to guide them into destruction. For an eternity the Daimon had dabbled in human affairs, interfering and provoking nuisance and distress for their own amusement. Humans were ironically innately wired to destroy themselves in the name of power, desire, or religion. They were self-evolved devils in their own right. Nik'ael could have just sat back with his brothers from afar with a box of popcorn and watched the apocalyptic movie play out before their eyes. But it was the boredom of exile that drove them long after their initial raw hatred had waned.

A few spare Rogues were kept around long term, those who had proved more worth *'alive'* so to speak. Older, more experienced ones were excellent for reconnaissance. They possessed no fear, knew their way around. The difficulty was that they had to be fed, and in modern times, letting them suck a human dry of their blood was getting profoundly more difficult to achieve covertly. Creativity was required to satiate them, usually an errant drunk or murderer on the run. Without a decent feed every month, their corpses seized and desiccated; it was an ugly business. The positive in all of this was that each empty human provided a nice, fresh body for the ever-increasing population of feral human souls banging around in his realm. He grimaced with revulsion at the thought of them.

Today though, with Belial, ever the guard dog on hand, Nik'ael could dispose of them all. He was rather impressed with the feisty girl decapitating that Rogue in the garden. He liked her. She'd make one hell of a Daimon if she could just keep her mouth shut. He'd sent Enl'iel and Brennan off on a wild goose chase just long enough for him to see this plan through. The mere suggestion that Sophia had run off into the forest, chased by Rogues, had them out of there without question. Too damned stupid.

That Kea, though, she'd been a problem. He'd forgotten how strong she was. They'd been friends once, long ago. Friends look out for one another. Well, not always. She'd managed to escape the great deluge unharmed and fled elsewhere. But what did she do to help her kindred? She could have helped him, or at least called for help. They couldn't have fought the Archangels alone, but they could have at least healed as many of their own as they could, and saved them from being washed away. His eyes narrowed in hatred at the thought of her betrayal.

Ben was a handy character to have around. Threatening him was key to Nik'ael's success. Keeping Ben nearby, but in constant danger, left Sophia open to manipulation. She would never let anything happen to Ben. Nik'ael sensed a hint of something more than friendship lingered between them. It was a weakness worth exploiting.

Nik'ael listened whilst Belial talked the talk. He was not trustworthy, not one bit. He couldn't put his finger on it, but there was something about Belial that seemed off. Although, so far, he'd always done what he was told, successful or not.

The time was getting close. Nik'ael's mission had nearly come to the point where he needed it to be. The answers would soon be in his hands.

He studied Soph'ael as Belial held her aloft. A small, distant pull inside him made him falter. She wasn't ready. She was too weak. He… no, she needed more time. For the briefest moment, he wanted to smack Belial to the ground, rip him to pieces for touching her. No one should touch her. She was so innocent. She was his. He shook his head, clenched his fists into tight, painful balls of rage.

Sophia was essential. That was what he was supposed to think.

Chapter
Twenty-One

Dangling over the ever-widening abyss, someone was screaming at me to hang on. My arm felt like it was about to wrench out of the socket, so I listened for that voice to divert my mind from the pain. My eyes squeezed shut; I didn't want to see what was going to happen to me.

The voice was getting louder in my head. *"Don't go, Sophia. Don't let him take you. I'm coming for you,"* it sounded familiar, like Kea's soft, melodic voice.

I opened my eyes just a crack. Esme's grotesque form was still at the end of the arm holding me in the air. She grinned in a sickening way. "Pretty thing, aren't you? Such a shame," she laughed, it was phlegmy and vile.

There was a flash of light, and a blast of energy sizzled through the room. A gush of hot air rushed across me. A thud pounded behind us. Esme turned, dangling me like a rag doll. Her movements were jerky and unnatural, like a puppeteer working a marionette.

"Make a move, and I'll just crush her now. Then we'll all be exiled for eternity." The hate in Esme's possessed voice was palpable.

Kea appeared in a sudden flash of bright light, crouched in a defensive stance. Wings wide, she was ethereal, she was breathtaking. She scanned the room in a nanosecond, taking in the entirety of the scene. Tears fell, my body shuddered with relief.

"Put Soph'ael down, Belial. What have you done to that poor old woman? I can see it's you." Kea's face was grim. "Your actions condemn you, yet I know you do this against your true nature. Why do you continue? You know you're not really one of them. You're their lap dog, less than nothing to them. Re-join us, you can atone for what you've done. Do you forget your past so easily? This is not you; I know it." Kea edged a little closer.

That distraction was all that was necessary for what came next. From the corner of my eye, a shadow emerged from the front bedroom. Something long trailed in its hand.

While this Belial creature was engaged with Kea, a crunch and squelch thudded near my legs. I looked down just as a huge axe head swiftly pierced through the middle of Esme's body, stopping millimetres from my legs. As I fell toward the swirling mass beneath me, Kea swiftly scooped me up in her arms and pulled me aside to safety. She flew at lightning speed. Kea then spun around, fired a blast at the thing holding Jaz. The impact sent it into a scattering ash cloud. The grey matter fluttered to the floor and covered Jaz's still unconscious form.

In the middle of the living room was the writhing form of what was left of my beloved Esme. She looked down in surprise at the sharp blade protruding from her stomach. She pulled it out, its handle still in the frozen grip of Ben's hands; his swollen and battered face splattered with blood. He stumbled back, released the axe's handle. It clattered to the floor. He reached out for a handhold on the window frame and slid slowly down in a heap.

"Bastard human!" Esme screamed at Ben as her body began to shake uncontrollably. Her mouth gaped wide; her head fell backwards. She collapsed to the floor. Whilst writhing in spasms, thick black smoke poured from her mouth, nose, and ears, converging into the figure of the creature from the hospital. He looked as impressive as he did there, but exponentially more deadly. He shook himself out, stretched casually, cracking his knuckles suggestively towards Kea and Ben, as if teasing them for a fight.

"Something is not right. This was not the plan," Belial said to no one in particular. "I'm being toyed with. You," he pointed directly at me and bellowed. "You will have your day before too long, girl. The time is near. I see the change is upon you. There is no escaping your fate, pretty one."

A frenzied gale surged from the hole in the floor. The curtains ripped from the windows, sailing like ghosts around the room. This Belial creature stepped towards the fiery abyss to escape, knowing he had been outmanoeuvred. His backup creatures were now nothing but specks of dust, fluttering around in the air, chasing the curtains. I made a move to grab Esme's body. Belial snapped his head in my direction and viciously kicked her, sending her into oblivion, down through the swirl of fire and darkness.

"No!" I screamed; an unbearable agony tore through me. I crawled closer to the hole, reaching into the flames, but Kea swiftly pulled me back to safety behind her. She held me close, trying to soothe what was inconsolable. I cried for my beautiful spirit-mother and slid out of Kea's grasp to the floor. All I could do was curl up in a ball like a baby. Tears blurred my burning eyes. I hid from the hellish scene in front of me, covering my face with bloody, shaking hands.

Belial laughed vindictively, "See you very soon, Soph'ael. I promise it won't be long. Tick tock, tick tock." Through the gaps of my fingers, I saw him launch feet first into the hole. It swallowed him up and extinguished itself with an ear-piercing crack, leaving nothing but a scorch mark on the floorboards.

Popping sounds and heat filled the room within seconds of this, and I knew without looking up that Enl'iel and Brennan had returned. In the muffled background of my sobs, Kea explained what had happened. I felt the weight of their footsteps draw near.

"Sophia, are you alright?" I ignored Enl'iel.

"You weren't meant to see any of that. I'm so sorry, Princess." Brennan rubbed my back gently. I shook him off.

I couldn't look at them — any of them. I couldn't even move. How much pain could one heart take? Every beat sent emotional and physical agony through to my very core. Every atom ached with loss. I could have drowned in the grief. After a while of hearing their frantic murmurings, I realised I wasn't alone in this. I had more that could be taken from me; more love, more happiness, more lives. Curled up in a foetal position, I resolved to not lose another person that I loved. The fingers that were cocooning my face became rigid with anger. I let them slowly curl into tight, burning fists.

I lay there for a while longer, allowing the ball of fire that was building in my gut to grow. Where sadness had enveloped me, a new strength began to rise. I calmed my breathing to a slow and deep rhythm, letting this feeling unfurl its tendrils and spread under my skin. I pushed onto my hands and knees, barely aware of someone calling my name. With my head bowed and eyes shut, I ceased to resist. No longer did I bite back against the turmoil. I relaxed with a deep, calming breath.

Awaken

"Don't be scared my sweet girl, I'm here, you are safe," Enl'iel's presence soothed me, while my body screamed from within.

"I…help… please…" I couldn't catch a breath.

"Kea, call for Koi. We will need him as soon as he can get here," Enl'iel sounded far away.

I thought I heard Ben call my name, but it was Brennan's alarming comment that was the clearest.

"She's Quickening, give her space." Brennan's presence felt nearer. "It's okay, Soph, let it happen. Let go. You'll be okay, I promise, Princess."

I drew a breath, impossibly deep, opened my eyes wide and without warning, let out a primal scream. Light poured from my mouth. The force thrust me back on my heels, my arms flung wide. My scream seemed to go on forever. There was a connection to something in the air surrounding me, like plugging myself into a socket. Something crackled across my skin. A million energies passed through me. Countless ghostly faces came in flashes. They were strangers, and yet, they were somehow familiar.

Then I saw Him. I'el's eyes were a swirling galaxy of every colour, and they looked deep into mine. An indescribable beauty, yet not of flesh, but of love. I knew Him, and He knew me. I tried to call out His name, to beg for help, but I was mute, and He was gone.

The pain took over. I screamed as my entire body lit up seemingly from within. Acid poured through every artery, pumped through every vein. My spine cracked and crunched as it changed and contorted. My will to resist, my understanding of normality was no longer in my repertoire. My body thrust forwards as an immense burst of energy erupted from within. It was like electrocution in reverse. *I* was sending out the impulses. Each beat of my heart thundered in my head. Heat poured from my spine as a bright light enveloped me, forcing me to fall forward to the floor again — spent.

I forced myself back up, mesmerised by the veins that glowed iridescent under my skin. Their light pulsed in tune with my heartbeat. Each thrum lit up the vessels like rivers of white light. My limbs felt heavy. My hands seemed foreign. The wounds on them healed over, the drying blood crusted in the grooves sparkled. Specks of light swirled within the crimson detritus. I frowned, so very confused, trying to make sense of what I was seeing.

The pain slowly dissipated, replaced by something else. My back now tingled in a more pleasant way, like having a warm blanket thrown across cool skin. My body felt lighter, almost weightless. My head no longer ached, and the sting seemed gone from my eyes. A new sensation dawned upon me, and it felt like I had an extra set of arms. I could feel myself waving these things, but they weren't exactly arms. I wanted to move them, but they felt stiff, as though they'd not been used for a long time. I waved them about. My entire body shifted along the floor. Surprised, I moved them harder. I travelled further along the floor. I had no idea what I was doing or why, but knew in my bones that I needed to do this. I put as much effort into the movement as I could muster. Suddenly, my legs no longer felt the floor. I looked down at my dangling feet as I rose into the air. Breath punched from my chest, then rushed back in.

Light pulsed behind me in tune with my heartbeat, keeping me steady and aloft. My new arms were wings of light that I seemed to have control of. I could make them move back and forth at will. I realised in that moment that I felt right, and that before this, I had actually never been normal, never right felt at all. The pain ebbed away completely, replaced by warmth and strength. My body was telling me who and what I was.

On that day, I was reborn.

Chapter Twenty-Two

Five faces looked up at me. Three wore smiles, and two were visions of dumbstruck shock. Suddenly self-conscious, I faltered, and like a toddler losing her balance, I tumbled to the ground with an ungraceful thud.

"Take Ben and Jasmine underground. They are no longer safe here," Enl'iel spoke with urgency as both she and Brennan rushed to my side.

"Done," responded Kea. "All right, guys, come with me. You need to hang with us for a while." She reached for Jaz and Ben.

From behind the protective arms of Brennan and Enl'iel, I noticed Jaz speechless for the first time ever. Her bloodied face was a picture of disbelief. Ben stared at me with incredulity. His emerald eyes burned intensely amid bruising and swelling.

They both wordlessly followed Kea towards the back door of our destroyed home, casting a few wary glances back at me as they went.

Enl'iel helped me to my feet. "How are you feeling?" she asked quietly and placed a kiss upon my still fiery cheek.

"Um…" I had to think about the answer for a moment. I inspected my trembling hands, arms, and legs… all normal and present. Everything seemed intact. I hesitantly patted myself down, feeling for something, anything, out of place. The wing things seemed gone; my skin looked… like skin. Had it been a hallucination? Everything was checked off my 'not about to imminently die list.' Everything seemed okay, but there was something deep inside that felt very different. "I'm exhausted… uh, kinda freaked out. What's crazy though is that I seem to feel okay." My voice was thready, tears pricked the back of my eyes.

"Perfect. That is how you should feel. No more pain. You are exactly how you were always meant to be," she soothed.

"What happened to me? Exactly *what* am I?" My words were thicker, emotion rasping them once more. I knew the answer, but I needed to hear it spoken out loud.

I looked to Enl'iel, but Brennan responded instead. "You are bigger and better than both of us, Soph. You've just been through one hell of a metamorphosis. You've just transformed into a High Angel of the Kingdom of A'vean. You're the living proof of Enoch's prophecy. This makes you incredibly unique and ridiculously powerful. I'm slightly jealous, actually." He quirked a brow, nodding as he appraised me.

His familiar wink and irreverent attitude tugged a whisper of a smile from me, despite everything.

"We were interrupted in the middle of trying to tell you this. You were always going to go through this change on your twenty-first birthday. However, you've unknowingly been in the presence of increasing and imminent danger. It appears Cael sent you into a Quickening to bring you to maturity more rapidly, for your own safety. Right now, though, we're going to get us all to safety. We've plenty of time to discuss specifics. Hold on, dear, we are going to take a different route back underground," Enl'iel said cryptically.

I was too mentally tired to ask any more questions.

In my exhausted silence, they encircled me. Brennan released his wings to envelop us. They both touched a hand to their faces, which lit up like New York City at Christmas time. Before I could register much more, I was sucked backwards.

There was no sense of being present in my body as darkness and wind whipped by. At first there appeared pinpricks of light. Then, they became bigger, brighter, and denser, as though I was thrown into deep space, rolling through the Milky Way. It was neither warm nor cold. I sensed Brennan and Enl'iel nearby, but couldn't communicate with them.

I was moving fast, yet everything around me seemed to move slowly. The world was paradoxical in this dimension. The sensation of falling overwhelmed me, and it took a few moments before I realised that my feet had safely planted themselves back onto solid ground. Two warm bodies stood on either side of me, holding me up.

I opened my eyes. Enl'iel and Brennan kept hold of my hands to keep me upright until my balance kicked in. We were back underground. The Keepers buzzed frantically around me; it felt as though they were checking me out to make sure that I was okay.

I was about to speak when Enl'iel chided me first.

"What part of 'stay here' did you not understand, Sophia?"

I was being reprimanded? My jaw clenched; I held my tongue.

"I specifically asked you to stay here! Do you realise why now? You could have not only got yourself but others killed! You must listen to us, Sophia. You are a fish out of water, and you cannot possibly know how to protect yourself!"

"Ben and Jaz were screaming for me. I couldn't just hide down here and save my own skin while others were in trouble. How was I supposed to have any clue about what was about to happen?"

She glared at me; anger faded quickly from her eyes. Concern and possibly regret flickered across her face.

"Your compassion will be your undoing, young lady."

"Enl'iel…" Brennan tried to intervene, but she put up a hand to silence him.

"Saving your own skin is *exactly* what you need to do. That was Daimon trickery. You were fooled by a Daimon, and a strong one, too. You have grown up human, which means you have yet to be taught the nuances of detecting Daimon interference. Even I can be fooled, and I'm very skilled in this subject. It must have been mimicking their voices to lure you out. Clearly, this Daimon is familiar with your weakness for helping others. It means you've had one watching you for some time now." She nodded, assured of her assessment.

An immediate feeling of violation rolled through me. I was being stalked? I hugged my arms around myself in an attempt to soothe a new wave of fear and anger. I knew something had been outside Miss Marple's the other day. Was that it?

"Now," interrupted a new voice, along with the sound of clapping hands. "Where is this student of mine, and what kind of mess do I need to fix?"

My eyes were immediately drawn to a huge, muscular man descending one of the ornate metal staircases. His chest was heavy with silvery scars. Flaxen skin flashed underneath a white, karate-style Gi. Power oozed from him.

Large hands clasped firmly around mine. More silver scars struck across his knuckles. He drew my hands to his lips and placed a light kiss upon each one. I flushed scarlet.

His face was a perfect balance of smooth Asian beauty. Behind a swirling white mark like my own across his cheek, intoxicating blue eyes sparkled at me, while thick, cropped white hair set him apart. He stood back and bowed before me.

"It is a supreme honour to meet you. I am Koi, your kindred and your teacher," he said in the slightest of Japanese accents, but there was a mix of a few influences. His voice was deep and arresting.

Both Enl'iel and Brennan leaned forward, each pressed their right cheek gently upon Koi's in greeting. A slight glow passed between them.

"Good to see you, Koi. Kea was quick to get in touch with you," Enl'iel hugged him firmly.

"I was already here, waiting. This one called me." He pointed to me. I shrugged, "I…um…"

"You called me through the Zythros Stone, didn't you?" Koi asked.

"Um, the what?"

"Did you touch that stone over there?" Enl'iel pointed to the huge central stone that seemed to whisper.

Instantly feeling like a kid caught touching something I shouldn't have, I meekly nodded, "Sorry, I couldn't help it. I felt drawn to it."

Koi laughed heartily, "You are an innocent, aren't you? I heard your thoughts when you touched it, and I knew that if you were down here, then it was time for me to come."

I must have looked as confused and exhausted as I felt, because Enl'iel pulled me close. "Let's get you some food and rest. Too much to take in for one day. That transference has sapped the last of your strength. I'm sorry you were put through that before you were physically ready, but it was a matter of urgency, I'm afraid."

I realised just how tired and starving I really was. My stomach growled instantly at the thought of food. I hadn't eaten since yesterday.

"I have something small prepared for you," Koi spoke up as though reading my thoughts. "Follow me." He waved me on.

We entered a tunnel on the east side and as we walked, the same crystalline lighting instantly illuminated the passage. It was as though the earth intrinsically responded to our presence. There were many rooms along the tunnel, each with a white wooden door.

We came to a stop in front of one of these doors. Koi opened it for me.

"After you," he said.

I entered a small room, as cosy as any bedroom. A small camp-style bed on one side, a knitted throw neatly tucked over it. Nan… Enl'iel had been expecting me for some time, by the look of it. Despite myself, I giggled.

"What is it?" Enl'iel asked.

I pointed to the throw. She could get a little defensive about her hobby. "Well, I've had a lot of years to keep myself occupied, young lady!" She pretended to look offended.

"It's lovely… it's a piece of normal in a whole lot of freaky." I gave her a hug, one that I think she needed. She squeezed tight and let it linger.

"This will all make sense soon, Sophia. Right now, we are in emergency mode, and unfortunately, a lot of your questions will need to wait until we have you as safe as possible. Please trust in me?" Enl'iel's eyes moistened.

I responded with another hug.

"Make yourself comfortable now," she said.

There was a small table with a water decanter, and what looked like a shower cubicle. On the table was a steaming bowl of something, which had my mouth instantly watering.

"It's my very own miso soup. I added extra vegetables, the way you like it. I hope you enjoy it." Koi gestured with a bow and an outstretched arm for me to take a seat on the bed.

I almost ran to the table. The hot, savoury liquid was incredible. My senses seemed heightened; a mouthful of spice punched my taste buds. I groaned with pleasure as I practically inhaled it.

The three of them talked amongst themselves while I devoured the meal. It was finished off with some sweet coconut rice. I sat back, exhaustion now an anaesthetic swirling through my veins. My head felt encased in a ball of cotton as everything sounded distant and muffled.

"I need to sleep." I leaned back on the pillow, suddenly lightheaded; visions of the day's events crowding my mind for attention. It was all too much. I heard my intoxicated voice say a few goodnights as I helped myself into the comfy cot. I didn't notice them leave, just someone tucking me in and placing a kiss on my head.

Chapter
Twenty-Three

My eyes opened to find Ben sitting by the bed, head in his hands. A dreamless sleep had finally allowed my body to get some decent rest. Before I'd opened my eyes though, I'd felt the presence of someone, the scent of spice and ash that was all too familiar.

"Ben?"

He looked up, distress washed through a pained expression. His battered face was a sorry reminder of what he'd been through, and all because he was associated with me. I felt the sharp bite of guilt gnaw at me.

"Look at your poor face." My voice caught as I reached out to touch the wounds, but he flinched sharply back. I felt a momentary hurt.

"I'm okay, Soph." His voice was thin and haunted; guarded. "What about you? Are you alright?"

What should I say? *Hey I'm fine, and by the way, apparently, I'm an angel and I'm here to save the world or something!* Awkward, surreal and embarrassed were all fair descriptions of my feelings. I leaned up on my elbow, pulling the bedcovers with me.

"I think I'm okay. Physically, that is. I don't think I can string the right words together to describe what's going on in my head right now, though. What happened yesterday, what I saw, and what I did…" I let that last thought trail into nothing. I couldn't look him in the face. I felt so uncomfortable. Picking at my fingernails was suddenly a very interesting distraction.

"You mean when you flew in the air and shot lightning bolts from your body?" He finished for me; his tone was strange. Our eyes couldn't meet for more than a quick glance. Ben focused on the floor and worked at a thread sticking out of his jeans. I examined every fingernail thoroughly. The edge to his voice and demeanour made me feel as though I'd offended him somehow.

"Well… yeah." I was stumped as to what I could really say, so I sat up and forced myself to look at him. He looked up too. My friend, who I adored, felt very much a stranger. My back and head began aching again, and nausea nagged at me with a sudden viciousness. I swallowed it down and took his hand in mine.

"You saved my life yesterday." I put my other hand on top and gripped firmer, as though I needed him to know I didn't want to let go, to lose him; that I was still me.

He remained silent as our hands warmed in each other's. He quietly regarded me, unblinking, and scanned every inch of my face with what seemed to be conflict.

"You stopped that… thing from taking me. Thank you," I said as I recalled that the creature used to be Esme. I choked back a quiet gasp of grief at the thought.

"I murdered. For you…" Ben's voice trailed off; he pushed my hands away. He looked away, then back to me and said with a surprising conviction, "I'd do it again… for you."

"Oh Ben!" My lips quivered. *What have I done?* Love and fear and confusion rolled through me as he sat hunched over again, roughly raking his hair.

"I'm sorry. I'm so sorry that you and Jaz have been dragged into this madness, whatever it is. I'm sorry you've been forced to do such a horrible thing. And look at you…" I tried to reach for him again, but he flinched. "You're injured because of me. If I could've protected you both from it, I would have. I had no idea about any of this. I can't even begin to explain any of it to you — I barely know what's going on myself. I was happy just being me. This is all happening to me. I'm not choosing to do it. I promise I'll do whatever it takes to make things right, and to keep you safe." I looked to him for reassurance, but found none.

He remained stony faced, looking at me again as though he was trying to peel back the layers to find an alternate truth. It was unnerving. It was so un-Ben.

I broke the tension by diverting the focus from me, "Is Jaz okay?"

"She's fine. Still sleeping it all off."

My relief at hearing this was overshadowed by his curt tone. He was so confusing. He looked at me with an intensity that appeared to be a war of love and disdain. His voice was cool and distant. He was hurting, and I was the reason.

"And you? You must be in so much pain. Your face is so swollen!" This time when I reached out, he let me touch him. I sat up straight on the edge of the bed to get a closer look at his injuries. He was badly bruised over his cheekbones, with one of his eyes swollen half-shut. The bruising was an angry shade of deep purple. Our faces were mere inches apart now. I could feel his breath on my skin. It sent chills through me. Those emerald eyes were too intense to bear.

My fingers gently traced the edges of the bruising along his cheek and jaw. He didn't resist, but I could feel his tension. His bottom lip was swollen as well and split in the middle. Dried blood crusted around the wound. I lightly grazed my thumb across it. We both drew in a breath at the same time, and our eyes hooked. I felt so immensely drawn towards him in that very moment. I pulled my hand away, but he grabbed it back and placed my palm flat against his cheek. He leaned into it and closed his eyes, pressing his hand over mine. He took in a slow, deep breath, as though he was savouring this moment. I felt faint from the rush of my pulse. Electric zaps ripped up and down my arm from the point where our skin was in contact. We sat in silence like this for a few, all too short seconds. He was the one to break the moment as he sat back and took his hand from mine.

I placed my left hand on his other cheek and whispere, "Please, let me heal you." I didn't bother trying to explain what I meant by it.

There was turmoil again in his eyes when he looked up. He nodded with the smallest inclination of his head, not questioning my request. I was surprised that he acquiesced, he didn't know what I was capable of. I'd never revealed my healing craft to him before.

"Take a deep breath in and let it out slowly. Let yourself relax. I won't hurt you, I promise." Ben did as I said. His pained eyes didn't leave mine. I pushed his ebony hair out of the way and spread my fingers gently across his skin. My stomach lurched again.

Deep breath in, deep breath out, repeat.

I concentrated on the negative energy flowing through him. It was abundant, as though his injuries were more than skin deep. His skin was soft and warm, and the connection sent a thrill through me. *I don't want to let you go.* His pulse quickened, in sync with mine. Suddenly extremely self-conscious, I looked away for a moment at the floating orb in the corner by the door and took in another deep, calming breath. *You can do this.* The jelly-like feeling in my stomach was easing. The strangeness of his proximity was highly distracting, however.

I turned back to him with determination. I pulled at the strong negative field within the cuts, scrapes, and swelling, drawing it out, and pulled it towards myself. The nausea in me lurched again. I felt as though I might be sick. I had to swallow calmly through yet another slow breath and put it out of my mind. It wasn't easy. There was deep suffering within this boy. Guilt rippled through me. I should have known that he was hurting. He was my life-long friend.

With a renewed compassion, I ignored all that my body was throwing at me. My fingertips tingled sharply as the attraction of the positive and negative energies collided between us. He tensed as the veins in my arms began to glow. I glanced at him as I repositioned my hands. His breaths were coming short and sharp through flared nostrils. I felt anxious and under pressure from his heavy, nervous stare. Heat emanated from my right temple. The current of power surging from me cast a glow of white against his face, giving him an ethereal radiance.

The negative current sucked into my hands and was replaced by the warmth of the positive infusing from me back through his skin. He drew a surprised breath in, groaned as the surge sunk beneath his flesh. His head fell back with the effect. As the last of the heat left my fingertips, I bowed my head in exhaustion. The glow in them dulled and the transfer ebbed from a burn to a tingle, then dissipated into nothing. I felt overwhelmed physically by this healing. It wasn't unusual to feel tired after a healing session, yet this time it was much more intense. As I raised my head, I found him staring intently at me. The green of his eyes had deepened with unshed tears. He gently prodded at his face.

Ben's face had reformed to its previous arresting angles; he was healed. He was perfect. His skin was once more unmarred and perfectly Ben, right down to the scar along his jaw. I wiped away a warm tear that had trickled down his cheek. His bottom lip trembled. His jaw feathered as he fought the emotion that was still torturing him. He reached over and traced the lines of my birthmark. His breathing was increasingly unsteady, and mine stopped altogether. As his fingertips lightly glided along the swirling lines, the act felt as intimate as any touch could. His skin barely grazed mine, yet it sent ripples of emotion through me. If his gaze were any heavier, my heart might cease to beat. I couldn't tell or didn't want to know if it was fear, confusion, or something more. I wanted it to be something more.

He withdrew his hand suddenly and with such a speed that it was as though he'd been stung. He grasped both of my wrists, never once taking his eyes from mine. I thought he was going to say something. He opened his mouth a number of times, but then thought better of it. This exchange seemed to hang in the air, breathtakingly uncomfortable. He sighed deeply as he laid my hands back on my lap. He stood. The corded muscles of his arms were tight, veins twirled along them like blue rivers; he clenched his fists. Ben looked down at me, his expression dark.

"Why couldn't you just be normal?" he left the room without another word.

I felt like a gutted fish.

Chapter
Twenty-Four

It tortured Nik'ael to see her like that with Ben. She loved Ben. He felt it, even if Sophia couldn't acknowledge it. Ben loved her too, and had done so for many years, but he was weak and stupid, destined for a bad end. That stupid boy had suffered through the solitude of unrequited passion for years. Nik'ael watched in the shadows as Ben kept a platonic distance deliberately to hide his true feelings.

Finally, Nik'ael had been the one to penetrate into one of their hidden sanctuaries. Yet the pleasure he received from his victory was overshadowed by the complexity of emotion striking through his dark heart. He was once a peacemaker, a protector, and a lover. But for thousands of years, he was a hater, vengeful, and at times, cruel. Now, just when he neared the culmination of his mission, doubt plagued him. His energy rhythm was out of sync. Hiding in these tunnels was not helping things, either. He could feel the effects of the repellents they used to protect this place. It sapped his strength. The chromious-lined ceiling was an osmotic force, sucking the life from him. Sneaking around in the darkness, watching her, was becoming insufferable already.

Knocking Ben around had been a great release of his frustration. Feeling his power inflict damage across Ben's body was healing for him, in a way. His thoughts had been realigned, and his vigour renewed. But now, she'd healed him. Despite her own pain, she had put Ben before herself as she had always done. Her compassion and strength, her self-deprecation, gnawed at the distant him, the one that would have scooped her up in his arms and taken her away, protected her, loved her.

He screamed silently in his mind as he smashed his fist into the rock wall. He felt the bones break. The pain was a balm, not a burden.

He clawed his head with his good hand. Why was he doubting everything? Why now? Yesterday, he'd been on a high as he lorded over the destruction at her house. He hated her… he *had* to hate her. It was his mission to hate her. Yet at every instance, her every selfless move tugged at him mercilessly.

Finally, Nik'ael bolstered himself up. He had to get out for a while. He must stay away as much as possible and manage this from afar. He needed his vengeance, not just for himself, but for Neren'iel. Guilt swirled like a storm through him again as he touched his bracelet. She would never forgive him. He knew it. But he had to do it anyway.

Blood trickled down his wrist. He wiped it carelessly away on his pants. The explosive pain was now an annoyance. He ran his other hand across the broken one and winced as he felt the bones knit back together. He left one small bone unhealed. One piece of him would remain broken, so that the pain of each movement would remind him of the pain he and his loved ones had suffered. It would keep him focused. At least that's what he told himself. He would take his leave for a while to think. He would be back soon. The proximity of her was just too much. He blinked out without taking the chance to hesitate.

Chapter
Twenty-Five

Grief engulfed me. My fingers gripping the edges of the cot. I felt like I'd just lost something that I didn't realise I'd had. Tears blurred the wall I was staring at. Utter misery had swept through me since Ben had sideswiped me with that parting insult. I didn't understand his anger towards me. I could accept shock and fear at what had occurred over the past twenty-four hours, but this angry Ben was not what I would have expected at all. He was usually the first to jump to my defence, to protect me. It didn't make sense. Perhaps he felt he needed protecting from me?

The light of the floating orb brightened the underground room more intensely at that moment, as though trying to catch my attention. Its surreal presence distracted me from my thoughts long enough to force my attention to the room around me. I ran a hand through my hair, looked around the little space, noticing a bowl of fruit and a booklet on the table by the bed, a handwritten note on top.

Sophia,

When you wake, feel free to use the shower. It is a thermal spring, enjoy. I have left you a change of clothes on the chair, and there is a backpack of belongings for you. I will be in shortly to collect you.

XOXO Enliel

The booklet was a passport. The small blue document had my photo and details inside. I'd never had a passport. Who knows how she got this one? Clearly, we were going overseas, but to where? Were they even going to ask me if I wanted to leave? Who knew what was coming next? Anything was possible. The impossible was, in fact, happening. Despite still feeling raw about Ben, I knew that my assaulted body would drink in a shower. I found some toiletries, along with black cargo pants, a white t-shirt, and a black zip-up hoodie.

The shower cubicle was merely the rock walls and stone floor with a drain fashioned below them. I pushed the silver flip faucet sideways, and steaming water immediately flowed overhead. Earthy, mineral smells punctuated the air. The temperature was perfect. I leaned under the hot stream and relaxed.

Too much, too soon. That's all that I could think. My emotions were fighting against the tidal wave of change engulfing me so quickly that I could not catch a breath. I quelled a panic attack with some calming breaths and focused on scrubbing my hair squeaky clean. A million thoughts raced through my mind. It was hard to focus on one long enough to find an answer or logic to any of them.

What was to become of me from here? Was I going to die? Could I even die? Is everything I've ever known completely wrong? Is there a Heaven? What happens when people die if there's no Heaven? Who were my parents? Where are they?

I shook my head with utter confusion and immersed my face under the steam in an attempt to wash away the conflict. I massaged my temples and sighed out loud to myself, "God, help me… or whoever you are."

The warm water felt strange as it flowed down my back. I reached around and prodded at my re-designed spine. Knobbly prominences protruded from under my skin. I could just feel the soft leaflets of skin that surrounded them. It was bizarre. It was like I was touching a stranger, yet feeling the sensation myself. I wasn't sure I could come to terms yet with this within the period of a single day. My physical appearance had changed so dramatically. Like a science fiction movie,

I'd morphed somehow from Sophia Woodville, average twenty-year old girl with poor eyesight and a fear of spiders, to a lightning-throwing, flying being, with swirly blue eyes that could track an ant from outer space. It was all too unbelievable, but there it was.

After dressing and finding a rather handsome pair of Doc Martins to wear, I looked for a mirror to brush my hair. There wasn't one, but there was a brush and a hair clip near the passport. After putting my hair up, I glanced down at myself. I looked about ready for boot camp. It was a mirror image of what Enl'iel had been wearing after she morphed out of dear old Nan. The memory still messed with my sense of reality.

As though she knew she was in my thoughts, there was a light knock at the door. Enl'iel entered.

"Good morning, Sophia. Did you sleep well?"

"Yes, thanks," I answered, kind of blandly.

She sat on the cot and gestured for me to do the same. She picked up the brush. "May I brush your hair?"

"If you'd like." I pulled the clip back out of my hair. As a child, she brushed my hair every night. A perfect hundred strokes before I went to sleep.

She spoke as she brushed.

"This is an impossibly difficult situation, Sophia. I'm so sorry that all that has come to pass over the past few days has assaulted, frightened, and shocked you. It should have been a gradual and controlled unveiling of information and disclosure, but it has turned into a chaotic avalanche.

I let her continue, not disagreeing with her assessment.

"Upon your twenty-first birthday, on December 31st, you would have entered this change naturally, and I was just recently preparing to reveal it all to you. Unfortunately, it has been thrust all too forcefully upon you and all of us. I would have informed you and eased you into the truth of your heritage more softly. You would have been trained carefully, over time. Now that option has been taken from us by those who wish to destroy, rather than work with us. The coming days and weeks are going to be confronting and challenging for you, dear, but I am and have always been your guide and protector. I will be with you, among others, to teach you and prepare you for what is to come."

"What exactly is to come? I've heard about opening up A'vean so everyone can return. What does it all mean, and why does it have to be me?"

"As I've begun to explain previously, Enoch received instructions from I'el, about how the gateway to A'vean could be re-opened to those who had lost favour. Those fallen ones being your ancestors who were the protectors of humans. Do you recall this?"

"Yes, the fall of the angels."

Enl'iel brushed a little firmer.

"Well, as the story was handed down through the generations, Enoch prophesied that at an undetermined time, there would be the birth of a descendant of A'vean on Earth that matched the level of purity in which such beings were first created. It would be then that the gates of A'vean could be re-opened by that pure angel alone. We were told that the prophecies, as handed down by Enoch through his hidden writings, are meant to provide the clues to what this angel must do to achieve this goal. The clues will lead them alone to the gates on Earth—and eventually open them so that those who wish to reunite with their homeland may do so. All human souls of measurable worth may also be released from the limbo of the Middle Realm and return to their origin."

My fingers laced and unlaced.

"So, I have to go find some old books or something?"

"You must find and follow the writings of Enoch, which have been preserved for you and you alone to decipher."

My knees bounced; my fingers locked. A deep unease setting in.

"If you know that there are answers written somewhere, why hasn't someone read them before now?"

"Only the Earth-born angel's eyes may read the sacred words. No other could comprehend them. They are of our ancient language, and that is buried deep within you." She gently tapped my temple, "None of the exiled can read these words, so there was no point in us trying to do that which we are incapable of. It is the punishment handed down from I'el. The answers have been here all along, scattered in secret places around the Earth. However, if the wrong person were to find them, the risk is that not only will they be unintelligible, the rumour is that the writings will crumble to dust. So, my dear, you are absolutely irreplaceable."

"How will I know if I can do this? That I'm the right person? I'm just— me!"

"The knowledge is within you, that I have no doubt of. You shall not be alone, but you alone must be the one to read the secret scrolls and activate the gate through the purity of your blood," she explained.

I jumped up from the bed, backing up to the wall.

"What do you mean?" My heart raced so hard it pulsed in my lips. What was I now, a sacrificial lamb?

"What are you going to do to me?" I panicked and gripped at the wall behind me. A single tear slid to the corner of my mouth. I could taste my own fear.

"Oh, no! No, no! Oh, I'm so sorry, I've frightened you." Enl'iel approached, her hands held up in defence.

I put my own hand up and screamed, "Stay away from me!"

She backed off immediately. "Oh Sophia, I've chosen my words poorly. What I should have said was that a token of blood is required to unseal the scrolls of prophecy. A drop, my dear, sweet girl, just a drop; a pin-prick. You will not be hurt. I'm sorry I frightened you. We would never allow you to be hurt." Enl'iel's brows arched; her eyes were moist with emotion. "Please believe me, Sophia?"

My body eased a fraction, but I stayed where I was.

"Somehow, I don't at all feel safe."

Enl'iel nodded, her shoulders slumped.

"Indeed, you should feel such caution. It is the Daimon that have got it all wrong. This is why they hunt you. They got wind of snippets of information, thousands of years ago, from Watchers who were lured by them to the dark ways. They have wrongly believed you are meant to be sacrificed in order to open the doorway, despite us trying to convince them otherwise. The Unseen have a bloodlust that prevents them from accepting that it is but a drop of blood that is required. They have accused us of falsifying the truth to deter them."

Enl'iel reached out to me again. My panic began to wane... only a little.

"We've protected you since the day of your birth because we knew who you were, and we loved you. We have not let you out of our sight. They have circled you like vultures for twenty years. You've never been alone. Do you not remember when you were attacked in the city?"

"I will never forget it!" I snapped.

"I told you Cael saved you that night. He has mirrored your movements every time you have left the house, for your entire life."

"The Unseen want to kill me because they have the wrong information, but you will protect me because you know the truth? Either way, I need to be used for someone else's purpose!" I frowned; my fingers drummed my thighs.

"Sophia, I know this is impossibly difficult. But yes, to be blunt, you are the salvation for those wanting redemption, and also for mankind itself. You can reawaken humanity to the truth, provide them peace through a knowledge that has been long lost. This is a huge responsibility. I know it is difficult, but you know deep down that you are capable of this. You have always known you were special. I know you have always wanted to be the girl in the middle of the back row, the one that doesn't get noticed. However, you've been aware of your healing gift for a long time, which tells me that you have also always known that you were actually the girl meant for centre stage."

I rushed away from the wall. Poured a glass of water, my throat was parched.

"You may be right, but it doesn't mean I want it. I knew I was different. I know that's why you didn't let me go to school until I was old enough to colour my hair and wear contacts. I knew I was completely weird to look at with pale hair and eyes." Memories flooded back of me begging to go to school, but Nan insisting I had to wait, that the children wouldn't understand my appearance and would be unkind to me. I was basically blind until the age of seven. When I was eleven, she taught me to wear contacts. Once I could wear them comfortably, I was allowed to go to school. It dawned on me then how abnormal my childhood had actually been. Now I knew why. I was a freak who had to be hidden from the world until I could be appropriately disguised.

Enl'iel was close by me now. I didn't flinch when she gently took my hand. The small swirls about her right eye glowed faintly. A calming warmth flowed through me. She was safe, I knew that in my heart.

"Enough for now, my dear. We have a lot to get through today. You are a strong girl, Sophia. You can rise up to this, and you will do so with all of your kindred behind you. Now, let's eat. Many people have gathered to meet you. We will talk some more later. Too much is crowding that head of yours already. Just know that you are safe and loved, and we will all protect you."

I nodded. She opened the white door.

I followed Enl'iel through the glistening tunnel towards the light pouring in from the main cavern. I wondered which door Jaz and Ben were behind. Had I lost them?

When I entered the main cavern, many people were now present. I hesitated in the archway, wary to walk through such a crowd. Some milled around the green stone, while others huddled in groups chatting, drinking from long flutes, nibbling from large platters. Energy flowed powerfully through the room. The heightened elemental power snaked through the air, tendrils of light like the Aurora Borealis.

Some of the people flapped their light wings, like one would use hand gestures in conversation. Others were more subdued. I noticed that they all wore variations of white clothing that allowed their wings to move freely. I stepped into the room hesitantly, and as though a siren went off, everyone turned to face me. I nearly died of embarrassment. Women and men all glared at me with awed surprise, as though looking upon something mythical. No matter their skin tone or size, they all bore the same white hair and piercing blue eyes.

"Sophia!" called Koi. He rushed from behind the jade stone and was the only familiar face.

"You're up! This is excellent." He placed a comforting hand on my shoulder. "How are you feeling? I understand you must be most exhausted, physically and emotionally?" Koi looked at me questioningly with a genuine concern in his bright eyes.

I glanced back towards Enl'iel.

"Sophia has just received some deeper insight into her purpose."

"That's an understatement," I mumbled.

"Oh, I see," Koi crooked a brow. "That calls for some decent tea and breakfast, then." He directed me beyond the whispering stone to a small outcropping of rock, where a cloth had been draped with a tea setting and fruit platter. He poured me a dark brew and dropped in a large lump of sugar. I didn't even need to ask, he sensed that I needed it. I sat and took the hot cup, drinking it thankfully. I ate a few strawberries before I spoke, trying not to notice all the staring faces behind me.

"I found a passport by the bed." I poured some more tea.

"This afternoon you will fly to London. We're retreating to our main Sanctuary in Strensham to train you in safety, among other things, before we start your quest."

"Quest? Is this what Enl'iel was referring to?"

"Yes, Sophia, it is." He took my empty cup from me with a warm smile. "Come, let us talk."

We walked towards the south wall of the cavern where new murals awaited. A hundred eyes were focused on me. People parted the way, bowing politely as I passed. It made me very uncomfortable. This is just me, guys. I'm lazy, I throw phones, and I live in a room that's a pigsty! Well, I used to.

"Look up, tell me what you see," Koi said, ignoring the others as though they weren't there.

I studied the wall and sucked in a shocked breath. There must be a point at which the constant barrage of insults to reality would render me numb. I wished for this sooner rather than later. There, high upon the wall, were depictions that were clearly of me in the present. My rainbow hair glistened in gemstone form. In another image, I was riding Grey. I was there leaning over a person in bed, laying my hands on them, healing them. I was there shielding my eyes from an outstretched hand with a picture of a concentric circle on the palm. I was standing over the horned Daimon that murdered Esme as he retreated down a hole in the ground. A white aura surrounded my body in every picture.

Lastly, I could see myself floating in the air, surrounded by wings of light, reaching outward. It was confronting and frankly, I felt embarrassed, again. Dead bodies lay at my feet in this image. They appeared to be gnarled and grisly, with leathered skin and claws for hands. I concluded they must be the bad guys. I held in one hand a cylinder, and in the other, a large disk. Behind me shone an iridescent, blue oval eye. I was sure all these murals weren't there yesterday. It slowly dawned on me as I scanned the wall that in each picture, there was also a shadow behind me.

"What is all this?" I asked as a little Keeper zoomed around me, tickling at my hair.

"This, Sophia, is a brief reflection of your life up to this point. Does it seem familiar?" Koi cocked an eyebrow in question.

"Yes… and that there," I pointed to where I faced off the creature in my house. "That's what happened yesterday! How can that be?" Before he responded, I noticed the last picture of me again. My hair was pure white in it. Instantly, I reached around behind my neck. My hand held onto a thick lock of white, not a hint of pink or blue.

"Oh my God!"

"Worry not. This is just an effect of the Awakening you went through. The power that courses through you and all of us whitens our hair. In time, you will learn the art of camouflage, if that is what you wish." Koi chuckled to himself, "You are the most powerful being in this world, and you are shocked by your hair!" He laughed more heartily.

I looked at him questioningly. Hair colour was not the issue, so much as it was more a revelation. Seeing my image on the wall, and then physically acknowledging the change in myself, was shocking. Everything was shocking.

"I've offended you. Forgive me." He bowed, clasping my hands in his.

"No, it's fine. I know you were just joking. It's just that so much is going on… it's just too much at once."

"Yes, it is, but you are not alone. That is why I'm here. I will guide you, teach you our ways, and help you harness the power that lurks just under your skin. Once you can control that with ease, you will feel emotionally in control as well." Koi spoke so wisely, yet looked so young. The youthful appearance of all of these new people didn't gel at all with their intensity and apparent longevity.

"How did these murals appear? They weren't here yesterday," I asked as the Keeper buzzed more excitedly about me.

"Ah, that is a story of pure amazement. However, I shall save that story for another time. Now, let's finish our first meal and get you ready for the Unsealing."

"What's that?" I shoved more strawberries in my mouth.

"I shall defer that answer to the lovely Enl'iel." He bowed and stood back as Enl'iel returned with a plate of pastries. I took two without thought; my hunger was immense.

"Sit with me a while, Sophia. Share first meal with me. Afterwards, you will unseal the Scroll Chamber."

Chapter
Twenty-Six

Yeqon smirked with grim satisfaction as he looked down upon the deeply slumbering young man. His captive's breathing was rhythmic and calm. Yeqon was in total control, just the way he liked it. The sounds of fire crackling in the blackened hearth interrupted an otherwise dead silence. The time was near for his coming of age. After this, he would be less a burden and more an asset. He had been stubborn to train. Defiance ran through him like a life force, yet he had grown into a powerful and obedient servant — in the end.

Yeqon rested upon a stone bench near the head of the bed. He stretched out his long legs and crossed them at his ankles. Orange light from the hearth licked across his knee-high boots. He could not lean back comfortably, his horns gouged into the wall behind him. He was seriously getting tired of these things. They were amusing centuries ago, especially for scaring the life out of religious zealots and the ignoramuses he had the misfortune of meeting. On the rare occasion that he chose to leave this realm these days, they sorely disappointed his vindictive nature. Modern man was too informed, and surprisingly now grew rather partial to a little Daimon worship. Toying with them was no fun when they believed you were just a great Halloween costume, or the living deity of their offbeat cult.

As he contemplated removing his horns, the door to the bedchamber creaked open, making the sleeping boy stir. Yeqon placed a large palm across the boy's brow, sending his brain back into the waves of a deep, delta sleep.

"Your Grace," Nik'ael entered, bowing deeply.

"How goes your mission? Belial informs me that she has Awakened." Yeqon looked Nik'ael up and down, surveying him for any signs of betrayal. Belial had bored him to death through a tirade of complaints about being uninformed about all of their plans. Nik'ael's plans, as it turned out. Belial was none too impressed with the events in the house on the mountain, thinking he'd failed again. Belial was an unwilling but powerful pawn who wanted to be a king. It made him wonder why Nik'ael worked around Belial and not with him on this occasion.

"It is proceeding well. She has indeed awakened, but she is weak and immensely ignorant," Nik'ael responded, fidgeting obsessively with his bracelet in a way that annoyed Yeqon. "I am pleased to inform you that I have finally penetrated one of their sanctuaries. I believe I am within the grasp of all that we need."

"Excellent, bring her to us immediately," commanded Yeqon. He stood tall and foreboding. He rubbed his hands together with anticipation.

"Forgive me, but I think it may be best to leave her with them a little longer. I do not believe she will be able to access the prophetic writings outside of their watch. She is green and nervous. She knows nothing of her heritage, and has no knowledge of what it is she would be looking for. They know many pieces of the puzzle already. She will learn from them what we do not know, and then we can take her, strong and knowledgeable, but sensitive to our persuasive ways. I know her, after all these years. I believe her energy will be too unstable if we were to force her to search under duress." Nik'ael bowed and took a protective step backwards as he dared to speak so boldly.

Yeqon stood taller, a menacing expression glimmered across his rugged face. His dark eyes glistened with intellect. "You presume to question my authority, boy? My understanding of the situation? How long have I dwelled among the worlds? I am of the first incarnation. I am spawn of the first six. You… you are a nothing, born from human garbage." Yeqon spat the words like venom. Nik'ael shrank back, cowering slightly. Yeqon revelled in biting hard at others. He swelled with power when others feared him.

"Please, Lord Yeqon, I mean no disrespect. I honour your great wisdom and longevity. Your lineage to I'el precedes you." Nik'ael bowed more deeply again. "However, we have but one chance to use her. If we destroy her in our haste, we will be lost eternally, with no key or knowledge or power upon which to use it. We have awaited this moment for so long. I humbly suggest that we let them use their energies to prepare her and build her up to her strongest potential. When we do take her, she will be malleable, knowledgeable, yet still breakable. We need her physically and intellectually strong, not emotionally." Nik'ael bowed in submission again.

Yeqon paced back and forth, kicking up dust as his eyes darted between the sleeping boy and Nik'ael. His patience was thin and his temper frail. The pressure from the others grew with every passing day. He did not want to seem weak. Yet, this loyal servant spoke some truth. If they were to accidentally destroy her in their haste, that would mean certain annihilation for them all. All hope would be lost, and his driving force was nothing but vengeance. He would have it, and he would have it at any cost, even his pride.

Of all his kindred, Nik'ael was the only one ever able to get close enough to discovering the secrets of the Watchers and Eudaimonians. He was impressed and irked at the same time that a half-cast had done what he could not. Nik'ael was the first to detect the birth of the Earthborn, and his skills at camouflage were unsurpassed. He was able to get closer than any of them ever had without detection. Nik'ael's power was unheard of. His sire had been strong, his mother also of great lineage. Part Watcher and Eudaimonian of the first commission to Earth made him more powerful than even the boy himself understood. That was knowledge he would never share with Nik'ael, lest he think he was an equal of the Five. Yeqon knew though, that he should at least consider his opinion.

"I will speak of this to my brothers. If they concur, then we shall wait. Until then, stay as close as you can. By any means, discover the place of the scriptures. We need them as well as her. The very moment she is of sound condition, you shall personally deliver her to me, at my feet, where she shall bow to me and beg for her life." Yeqon cast a glance back at the boy.

"Much as he did," Yeqon said with a slight chuckle.

"As you wish. May I ask how the boy fares?" Nik'ael inquired.

"He does what he is told. That's is all that is required of him." Yeqon brushed off any further discussion about the slumbering boy by turning his back on Nik'ael and walking back to his seat. He picked up a flute roughly hewn from a leg bone and drank the draught within. He belched with satisfaction. Looking back at his kinsman standing by the door, Yeqon scowled. "You trouble me. There is conflict in your aura. Do you suffer a faltering in your loyalties?" He raised his eyebrows questioningly, daring Nik'ael to answer incorrectly.

"I am un-yielding in my loyalty. Have I not served you since the deluge with the utmost conviction? I betray only myself in that I am weary. I long to be rid of this wretched existence. I yearn to draw the force out of those who have cast us aside and murdered our families. Anger boils beneath my skin like an inferno." Nik'ael bowed once more.

"Be gone then. Go chase down this wench. I too am weary of this forsaken situation. Remove all obstacles, be they human or A'vean. Let blood run free and plentiful, let it drown the Earth. All the more for the Rogues to feast upon." Yeqon let out a deep, rumbling laugh.

"Get out!" Yeqon shot a blast of black smoke from his left hand. It landed just short of Nik'ael's feet, making him jump backwards.

Yeqon was alone again in the room as the door creaked closed. The sound of sleep filled the silence. The boy rested peacefully beside him.

"I will have pleasure killing you one day, boy. Great pleasure."

Twenty-Seven

I waited with Enl'iel by the large stone that I now knew to be called the Zythros stone. Its name translated to Whispering Stone, like an angelic internet. All you had to do was place a hand on it and you could communicate with any Watcher or Eudaimonian anywhere on the planet. Enl'iel had just done this whilst waiting for this Unsealing ceremony.

"Today you will perform an ancient and long-awaited ritual. Only you have the ability to perform the ancient and long-awaited ritual, though again, you will not be alone. We will guide you. The first scripture of Enoch lies somewhere beneath the library, long ago interred for safety by the archangel Uriel. Just now, I have called upon His Grace, Gedz'iel. He is a Watcher who did not fall foul of I'el, but chose to stay among us to protect and guide those who were left behind after the great fall. We admire him for his compassion and sacrifice. For his great service, Enoch and Uriel took him into their council and shared enough with him that he may guide the Earth-born angel on her quest whenever she should arrive."

Panic was banging at the door of my mind again.

"I don't know if I can do this Nan…sorry, Enl'iel. See, I can't even remember your name!" I face palmed with frustration.

"Hush, you are too harsh with yourself. Take a breath and relax, we are all here to help."

"But what if it's just not me? Can't this wait a couple of days so that I can get my head around what's happening?"

Until two days ago, I was ordinary, average. I'd never even finished a crossword, let alone solved a puzzle that could determine the fate of a whole race. Self-doubt eroded my courage with each passing minute.

"Sophia, our hand is forced. We do not have the luxury of time to ease you into this. I'm sorry for that. You do, however, have the answers coursing through you. You have nothing to doubt. Draw strength from me, Sophia, as you can from us all," she soothed me with her familiar voice and soft eyes. Still, this was immense, and my faith in myself was not.

"I haven't seen Jaz yet, is she okay? I saw Ben this morning, but I haven't seen her? If I have to do this thing now, can she come with me at least?"

"They are both perfectly fine. However, they cannot be here for the Unsealing, as it leaves them open to subversion. The less they know and see, the better. Our enemies could torture or possess them to gain our secret knowledge, which would lead them straight to us. Poor Jasmine has already suffered such a violation. They are comfortable and safe for now. You will see them at the airport when we leave for London." Enl'iel seemed distracted as she spoke and searched impatiently around the room for someone. I wondered if Jaz was as offended by what I'd become as Ben apparently was. I couldn't handle being shut out by both of them. If ever I needed her wisecracking, crass attitude, it was now. She could break the intensity and fear that I wore like a heavy cloak with one lash of her tongue.

"Why do we have to catch a plane? Can't we do that thing you did before and teleport, or whatever you call it?" I asked.

"Oh, no! Goodness! That was for an emergency only. Your body is too weak to do that again and over such a distance. It could render you unconscious for months. It would certainly kill Jasmine and Ben. Human bodies cannot transfer like ours. "Sadly, we have also learned that the hard way," she explained. I grimaced at the unpleasant thought as Enl'iel nodded knowingly at me, her expression sympathetic to me naivety.

A general murmur of excitement broke through the crowd at that moment. Up ahead, people bowed and parted as they had done with me. Who could this be?

A crewcut of white hair emerged above the others. Being generally very tall people, that I could see the approaching person's head above the crowd meant he was a Goliath in height. I felt that familiar rush and tingle run through me, just like when I was surrounded by those who were like me—good and bad. This person was incredibly strong, as though a powerful energy surge had entered the room. I shook the pins and needles from my arms.

"Excellent. They have returned. Sophia, you are about to meet Gedz'iel. He will guide you through the Unsealing," Enl'iel whispered in my ear.

The crowd directly in front of me parted, revealing Kea and Brennan, who both winked at me as they stood aside. In silent splendour stood Gedz'iel, muscles like mountain ranges under the bare, golden skin of his chest. All he wore were loose white pants. He took my breath away, not only from physical attraction, but because his sheer presence seemed to fill every corner of the room. He had an aura of superiority that made me feel small and insignificant. All without saying a word, just by being present.

His wings emanated a hum that echoed throughout the cavern. His face carried the stoic expression of a regal king, yet it was not warm, nor pleased to see me. The excitement that bubbled underneath my skin died a quick death when he spoke.

"This is she?" With his arms clasped behind him, Gedz'iel looked me up and down, his face devoid of emotion.

"She is small and weak. Are you sure this is the One?" He addressed Enl'iel as I burned with the humiliation of being inspected like livestock.

She bowed to him, "Welcome, Gedz'iel. Your presence honours us. I assure you that Sophia, also known as Soph'ael, daughter of Sarun'iel and Rik'ael, is indeed the Earth-born. Upon her birth, all the prophesied signs were present. She has not transitioned through the Right of Sevens, and her markings are such that she could be no other. She has been ceaselessly hunted from the moment she drew her first breath. Almost unheard of, she awakened through a Quickening just this evening past. Soph'ael appears to possess every gift that a native of A'vean would have, something a hybrid could never achieve. I defer to your assessment." Enl'iel bowed again.

As she said this, Enl'iel spoke to me in my mind. *Do not fear Gedz'iel, dear, he will not harm you.* All I could focus on were the names she spoke. My parents' names. I had never heard them before. Did that mean they were alive? My head swooned from the surprise, and I staggered a little, but managed to right myself.

"Are you ill, child? You seem unable to stand. Come, let me look at you," Gedz'iel's deep voice commanded, rather than requested.

I tentatively took the few paces to him, only with an encouraging push from Enl'iel. His size intimidated me, even though I had never been particularly vertically challenged. His eyes mesmerised me immediately. Not only did they glisten with that familiar bright, sparkly blue that we all appeared to share, but his irises actually swirled with constant movement. Pink, yellow, and green flickered in and out from the black circle of his pupil, and it was almost impossible for me to take my eyes from his.

He reached out to me and placed a hand on either side of my face. I reeled backwards, instantly blinded by an intense light and burning heat. It felt like only a second had passed, and it was over. Yet when I opened my eyes, I was surprised to find myself floating in the air with the sound of shocked voices beneath me. I looked down to find Gedz'iel flat out on the ground, unconscious.

As had happened before, I fell to the ground in shock, having no control over this flying business. Enl'iel gathered me up as Brennan and Kea attended to the quickly rousing Gedz'iel.

"What have I done?" I asked, horrified. It was clear by the way everyone was looking at me that I was somehow responsible for the collapsed Watcher.

Through the excited background chatter, Brennan called to me, "Well, that's one hell of a way to prove who you are, Soph!"

"What did I do?" I asked again, looking at Enl'iel, whose face was trying to mask a smile of vindication as Gedz'iel stood up, looking markedly more annoyed.

"You rendered him unconscious when he tried to read your aura. You defended yourself in reflex, just like yesterday. Your strength has shone right through." She squeezed my shoulders for assurance that this was a positive thing.

My attention was still only on the massive figure who again loomed over me.

"Your manners are sorely lacking in proper protocol. I see your human upbringing has left you ignorant of our customs. May I suggest that next time you are addressing a superior, you refrain from attacking him?" Gedz'iel's expression had not changed, and it bordered somewhere between serious and deadly.

"Please forg…"

"Silence, young one, you need not apologise. You have caused neither offense nor injury. Your outburst has, however, has shown me first-hand the power that runs through you. No one else could overcome me with such speed and vigour as you have done. I see in your eyes that you bear the mark of I'el. Only a pure, full-spirited energy descended directly from the Prime Creator could exhibit such intensity in their mortal eyes at such a young age. The power of E'lan, the universal energy, shines deep within them already."

I recalled that name, E'lan, from my distant memories as the word Nan had used to describe the energy that was the foundation of our healing ability. Small fragments of my past were standing out as the red flags of who I really was. Gedz'iel gently turned me to face the silent crowd. A sea of expectant faces.

"Look at the way this legacy of I'el yearns to reveal itself. Soon her eyes shall turn, as do his." Gedz'iel almost smiled as he looked around the cavern, gently turning my chin this way and that, exhibiting my apparent amazingness. As he released me, I touched my eyes in wonder. I assumed he was referring to the freaky, sparkling blue. The socially unacceptable milky hue seemed a mere unpleasant memory now.

Gedz'iel seemed to rise taller, his wings extending further and his arms wide in gesture.

"Behold, my kindred, the Earth-born angel of A'vean stands before us. Finally, you are rewarded for your loyalty and patience. Only in your good deeds could this child be offered to you as salvation. Only in your repentance and abstinence from further temptation would I'el allow her to grace the Earth. We must all rise to this and pledge upon our very souls to protect and honour her, so that she may achieve her purpose and therefore, your chance to once more attain the rapture of A'vean. Both Watchers and Eudaimonians, you are all bound by blood and spirit to follow that path set forth by Enoch through the word of the mighty I'el. We shall guide Soph'ael and fend off the threat of the Unseen at all costs, so that she may succeed in her quest." He paused momentarily, assessing the enamoured silent faces.

"For those of you who may be tempted, hear me and fear me now. If you, as others have, fall victim to the pleas and temptations of the Unseen, and in any way interfere with or place the Soph'ael in peril, you shall suffer immediate and severe consequences. Be wary, my brothers and sisters, as the Unseen and their foul minions are more cunning than ever at manipulation and false promises. I sense even now that one is all too near us. Be on your guard. Do not let your weariness or desperation allow you to fall victim to them. The truth lies here." Gedz'iel pointed to me, and I took a step back, overwhelmed.

"Who among you recalls the fate of Mal'ael?" Gedz'iel turned his broad shoulders to face a distant wall and threw a ball of light towards a darkened corner. The orb hung high in the air and highlighted a horrific scene. Gedz'iel, whose hand was delved into the prostrate man's chest, pressed down on the Watcher in a fearsome manner. The scene next to him showed Gedz'iel with a long, twisting snake of light hanging from his fist, as the dead corpse of the Watcher lay below.

"Mal'ael, once a strong and wise soldier, fell victim to the seduction of Anjou'elle. His alliance under her spell caused the destruction of much human life and allowed the Unseen to infiltrate the safe haven of Derinkuyu after the great flood. He paid for this with the annihilation of his soul. This is now the most critical time. You choose to fight with us, or you choose Mal'ael's fate!" He bellowed the last of this vignette across the expansive space. The room was pin-drop silent as he looked around at every face, satisfied that his message had been well absorbed. "Now, Bren'ael, my old friend, where is the chromious key?" he asked.

I remained in a state of complicit silence. I had nothing to contribute to the unfolding situation other than dumbstruck awe. I didn't know the questions to ask about a scenario that made no sense, so I stood in quiet wonder and simply watched. Brennan seemed to cringe as he was called forward by his apparent true name. He quickly brushed it off, though, and from a brown satchel he produced the key I'd used to unlock the door in the floor of the shed. He handed it to Gedz'iel, who turned back to me.

"Soph'ael, daughter of Sarun'iel and Rik'ael, child of I'el, born of mortal flesh in purity and perfection; behold."

I thought he was about to pass it to me as he bent forward. However, instead, he began to push the ends of the key together, crushing it in on itself. His palms lit up, as was so commonplace around here. The key glowed white as he pushed it, squashing it slowly in upon itself. Buzzing and hissing crackled between his hands with the force and energy he was exerting. The room remained silent, other than the sound of some falling rubble in the distance. Distracted by this, I looked up, and with my dramatically improved eyesight, I glimpsed two faces peering out from around one of the furthest tunnels. It was Ben and Jaz. They weren't meant to be seeing this, for their own safety, but I wasn't about to let anyone know that they were there, so I quickly averted my eyes back to Gedz'iel, just as both of his hands moved flat against each other.

"Soph'ael, this is the key to the Prime Scroll Chamber. Take it and begin your journey, our journey." Gedz'iel handed me the metal object with a reverence that further embarrassed me. In my hands was not the large swirling key I'd used before, but a platinum disc that was identical to the concentric circles that were repeated throughout this cavern, the same as Cael had shown me in the vision.

I was about ask what I had to do when the disc burned, and I was hit with sudden and vivid visions. Rapid flashes of symbols, stones, light, and dark. Images of engravings and blood dripping down rocky walls. I should have been frightened, but I wasn't. What I felt was an enlightenment. My eyes flew open. I knew what I had to do. Clarity just descended upon me. I just somehow knew exactly what I needed to do right then and there.

I turned and walked to the Zythros stone. I paced slowly around its circumference, inspecting it. When I found what I was looking for, I stopped. I glanced up to see Enl'iel nod in support, that I was doing the right thing.

Deep breath in, deep breath out, repeat.

One of the concentric circle engravings was larger than the others and had just the slightest depression in it. I turned the circle over in my hands, rubbing my fingers lightly across the circular pattern, and then, without hesitation, pressed it up against the rock. It fit snuggly into the space. I watched and waited. I looked behind me at all the expectant faces. Every pair of eyes glued to me with anticipation, as if their horse was meters away from the finish line in a one-horse race, and they had all placed their bets on me.

I looked back at the disc and contemplated it for a moment. As though a magnetic pull existed between it and me, I reached forward and pushed the circle against the stone. My hand instantly lit up. The pressure of my skin on the disc caused it to glow insanely bright. A rumble of grinding stone vibrated underfoot, and a slight tremor unsettled the floor. Energy flowed back and forth through the disc, myself, and the now glowing and pulsating Zythros stone. Voices filled my head, urging me on, welcoming me, but also warning me of danger. I pushed harder at the disc, and the entire stone monument heaved forward. The disc sunk away deep into the pedestal, and the Zythros stone ground noisily away from my feet. As it slowly revealed an opening in the floor, the stones underneath slid in and out to create a staircase. The echo of grinding stones bounced back through the cavern as they continued to move and clunk into place in the deep darkness. As the rumbling ceased and the Zythros stone stood still once more, I looked down at the staircase that disappeared into pitch darkness.

Another dark hole in the ground. Fabulous!

Chapter
Twenty-Eight

Suffice to say, I was not impressed with going down another dark hole, but something strangely innate told me it was safe to do so, here at least.

Gedz'iel threw a light orb down the stairwell to illuminate the way, and I followed as he took the lead. I was secretly looking forward to learning how to throw out one of those babies; it seemed like a pretty handy skill. I glanced back briefly at Enl'iel. Uneasiness caused my entire body to shiver. She urged me on with a smile, yet her eyes, warm and comforting, spoke of a motherly concern.

I followed Gedz'iel. Enl'iel, Kea, Koi, and Brennan came next, along with a handful of the little Keepers. Everyone's excitement ignited the air. I glanced back at the group. Brennan winked every time he caught me looking back, always quick with a broad smile.

Dripping water and mouldy, wet earth were an unwelcome assault to the senses as we descended the steps. The air was freezing, yet it didn't seem to bother my now permanently fiery skin. The way ahead was lit by Gedz'iel's powerful glow. His wings never dulled, yet the walls stayed dark and dirty, unlike the bright tunnel that led us to the main cavern of the library. It wasn't pretty down here; the energy far less inviting.

Gedz'iel didn't speak, as we followed on silently. I focused on the drip of underground water, the hum of his wings and the sound of his loose pants flapping against his ankles as he walked. I dared to think of something to say, but no words were brave enough to tease my mouth open. The stairs wound down steeper until there was a gap where some had crumbled away. We jumped across the small crevasse, rock tumbled away deep into the earth, never hitting a bottom. *What the hell am I doing? I'm not Lara Croft!*

The stairwell was a tight squeeze, which I found ironic, as we were all so tall. It seemed an understated hiding space to access when it was meant for us… for me. It had more of a Hobbit feel to it. I picked out clumps of dirt from my hair as it fell sporadically from the unsupported roof. Thankfully, the stairs levelled out quickly and finished in a small chamber carved out of a vertical sheet of rock. There was little effort put into this place, other than roughly hewn indentations in the walls where hundreds of small orbs burned away the darkness, the musty air now rich with lavender and cedar.

The floor was muddy and unpleasant underfoot. Numerous roughly engraved writings were also covering the centre of the wall. The lettering initially looked completely unintelligible to me. A mish-mash of symbols that appeared a hybrid of Greek and Arabic, with swirls and dots here and there, nothing akin to the English language. Gedz'iel spoke for the first time, dulling his light as he did so.

"Soph'ael, can you read the inscription?"

I stepped forward in the dim light and peered closely at the unfamiliar characters. It seemed to be a passage, perhaps a prayer, I wasn't certain. The passage was set into three stanzas, with three lines in each. Initially, panic set in, as it looked like gibberish. Sweat slid down my neck, my nerves rattled. I looked back at the three of them for help.

"Young one, do not panic. Do not doubt. Look with your spirit, not with your eyes." Gedz'iel encouraged me with his first hint of kindness.

I refocused on the wall, tracing my fingers over every grainy character. The rocky interface was cool, but my fingers burned and glowed as they touched each engraving. I stood back and looked again from afar. Something inside me told me to close my eyes, to look no more at the words. I did as my instinct instructed.

After a few nervous moments, something happened. The sounds and smells of the cave dwindled away into nothingness. The blackness behind my eyelids was replaced with an ever-brightening light. My heart fluttered with excitement.

In my mind's eye, there was an elderly man dressed in a Biblical style linen tunic, seated upon a rock. He leaned earnestly over a parchment, writing with a stick fashioned into a quill. He dipped it methodically into an inkwell.

The man looked up at me and smiled. "Welcome, dear child. I have awaited your arrival a long while."

He then picked up the parchment he'd been labouring over and turned it around, holding it up for me to see.

"Read," he instructed.

I looked at the words, and in an instant, they were clear to me, as though they were written in English. With my eyes shut tight in concentration, I recounted them out loud from the vision I was seeing,

"Ten by seven years thereafter, the East is reborn through death.

Mine words shall guide thee.

Thy blood shall wash upon this wall.

Caress thy palm with crystal blade.

The fifth element shall fill with thy flowing spirit.

And the mysteries of I'el shall be revealed.

North, South, East, West.

Thy light within shall guide the way.

Great child of I'el, beware thy heart."

I opened my eyes with a start as I finished speaking. I turned to everyone.

"Did you hear that? Did I make sense?"

"Not to me. It sounded like A'vean, but I couldn't quite get it. It's been a long time since I've heard it in its pure form. The old neurons just don't seem to jiggy-up with the old language these days. It's like trying to watch T.V through static. Damn!" said Brennan as he tapped his temple, his face a picture of frustration.

"Same here," Kea added.

"What do you mean? I saw it in English in my mind and read it aloud, didn't I?"

"Soph, you spoke in another language. You spoke the lost language," Brennan responded, looking rather proud.

Gedz'iel interjected, "Soph'ael, you have spoken the true language of A'vean, inscribed by Enoch, as taught to him by I'el. Only you, at this time, can understand and speak this tongue, as we remain blocked from the universal connection. Only you possess the elemental ability to channel our ancient words. Please, will you repeat it in English? Trust yourself, it will come naturally." His eyes warmed with encouragement as he nodded for me to reveal the meaning.

There was no point in allowing myself to be shocked by this. It was a waste of effort in this upside-down world of mine. I looked to the wall and repeated the words, concentrating hard to make sure it came out exactly as I had said it just moments before. I repeated it twice more, slowly, so they all could think about it. After a few minutes of silence, Enl'iel spoke up.

"I believe it refers to the time in which Sophia was meant to reach the scroll. The year she awakened. If we go by today, 2014, then it is certainly accurate. Ten by seven years ago, I assume refers to seventy years ago, and the rebirth of the East. What happened seventy years ago to the East? The end of the human World War Two. Japan was decimated in 1945 by the Hiroshima and Nagasaki bombings. This is a country that indeed has been reborn into a modern and peaceful region," she explained as she inclined her head towards Koi, who nodded in response.

"Indeed, my Earth-bound homeland was re-birthed," Koi acknowledged.

"It has also long been known that you are to offer a small token of blood as assurance of your lineage. Ignore that washing the wall in blood rubbish. Enoch clearly was overdramatizing!" Enl'iel furrowed her brows in thought. "It's how and where you place this token that we must ascertain," she concluded, as Gedz'iel gave her a nod of approval. I was kind of impressed with her flippant rebuke of Enoch's poetic licence.

I further studied the chamber along with everyone else. The inscription I had just read out was the only thing of interest, other than being surrounded by hundreds of repetitive symbols gouged into the rock. Nothing jumped out and said, *deposit blood sample here and press enter.* That would have been so much easier.

Gedz'iel spoke, "Young one, the answers are right in front of you. Invisible, yet in plain sight. We must consider Enoch's words carefully, as they will hold the clues for what is required of you." It struck me that he spoke so formally, like he was from a different time. Like Koi, his accent was hard to pin down. Perhaps a slight Middle Eastern lilt, but I couldn't be sure.

I looked back to the wall. "Could you guys please help me? I'm not even sure where to begin." A room full of nods reassured me.

We studied the wall for a time. Each of us mulled over this and that, offering, then retracting suggestions. We prodded and poked at the engravings. Symmetrical decorations adorned the wall around the script, with all the symbols reflecting each other. Circles and diamond shapes with swirling curls, like raging waves, swept across the bottom of the wall. Some symbols were faint, while others had been hewn deeper into the rock. The wall glistened with dampness. Or was that something else?

"I need some light. Can I pick up one of those things?" I pointed to the orbs.

"Indeed," Gedz'iel said and immediately passed one to me. He rested it carefully on my palm. It tickled like a warm feather. I held it aloft, stepped forwards. I noticed the tiniest glimpse of gemstones embedded within the rock. Hints of glistening gems winked when the light fell across them at just the right angle.

"If I could get a little more light, I could see better. This is too dull." I looked expectantly towards them all, hoped for one of them to flip on their switches.

"First lesson, Soph'ael, is to cast your own aura out to light your way," Gedz'iel instructed. "Does the great passage not say to let the light shine from within? I believe Enoch has instructed you to reveal your aura to light the way forward."

"I was kind of hoping you guys could help with that. I'd love to light up on demand, but I have no clue how that works. Apparently, it just likes to randomly surprise me!"

"Despite your sorry lack of upbringing Soph'ael, it is as natural as drawing a breath to cast an aura," he responded, followed by a muted tut-tutting from an offended Enl'iel behind me.

"How? I don't understand how?"

"You heal?" Gedz'iel asked.

"Yes."

"Then you know how to draw and repel energy. It is the same with an aura. As you repel energy, it opens up space in the particulate matter around you, and your true form can emerge… your aura. Until recently, you have performed a mere trick with your hands. Now, you are truly one of us. You must and you will rise to who you are. You will learn to utilise this new power with your entire body. Even I can feel the energy coursing through you. Harness that strength Soph'ael."

I felt small, weak, and so was my voice.

"I understand what you're saying. I feel more connected to the elements than before, but I just don't know how to control anything. It's not like you've given me much of a chance to learn," I grumbled in annoyance.

Gedz'iel's expression turned to one of barely masked impatience. My stomach churned. He was pissed, and I really didn't like the idea of someone like that cracking it with me. Note to self… keep whinging to a minimum and preferably not in front the head honcho of the Watchers!

"Can you help me a little more… please?"

Gedz'iel nodded.

"When we heal, in our mind's eye, we see energy flow in and out. We focus on our hands until we allow the release of that energy. It is not difficult. It is the same concept Soph'ael, just focusing on your entire form instead of merely your hands." He'd taken a step closer, looming over me in a way that made me feel small and insignificant.

"Enl'iel?" I looked at her for even the smallest clue. His mere proximity overwhelmed me. I knew he was trying to help, but his demeanour clouded my mind to the point that I couldn't think straight.

"Take your time Sophia, listen to your instincts. You know what to do. Don't be frightened," Enl'iel answered. She really was taking a back seat and throwing me to the lions. I felt justifiably crappy at her, too. Gedz'iel grabbed my shoulders, turning my attention back to him. I looked up into his eyes. There was a softness in them, concern perhaps, but his expression was still cool and hard.

"You have unfurled your pterugia three times now. Perhaps if you do this, it will assist you. The sensation is the same and your aura will emerge along with them as a natural consequence. Now, release your pterugia," Gedz'iel said and took a step back, arms folded, with an expectant look on his face.

"Um… unfurl my what?"

"They're the flappy things, Princess. Your wings," Brennan whispered.

"Oh, right, pterugia. Okay. I have no idea how to do that!" I threw my hands in the air in defeat. Good one Soph! In one minute flat, I'd already broken my previous promise to myself to not complain in front of said scary Watcher. I kicked myself on the inside.

Gedz'iel snapped, "Has she been taught nothing of her heritage?" His mark glowed as muscles flexed impatiently across his chest.

"Your Grace…" Enl'iel began, but he interrupted her as he quickly calmed down. He put his palm up to silence her. His expression softened from annoyance to contemplation.

"No. My expectations are unreasonable. No more could be expected of her. Take no offence, Enl'iel. You have carried your cause well. Perhaps I'm too intimidating for the girl. Ke'arel, you help the young learn when they emerge from stasis. Help Soph'ael," he ordered.

"With honour," Kea replied with a bow.

"Soph, you can to do this. Piece of cake." Kea stood in front of me with her hands on my shoulders. She winked at me, just like Brennan had.

"Close your eyes. I want to you to pretend that you are about to do a healing. Close your mind to everything but the buzz and heat in your back, not your hands. Concentrate on that energy swirling through your gut, trying to get out."

I did this easily, as it was what I always felt before I did a healing, apart from the weird back sensation. The second my eyes closed, the tickle and burn in my spine eclipsed all else and my stomach churned.

"Okay." I nodded, "Now what?"

"Now, imagine that energy wanting to burst out of you, and, like a raging waterfall, let it go. Let it run and spread far and wide down your back and out of your body. Picture pure white light. The more you think of it, the more your mind and spirit connect. Before long, that connection will become so strong that it will be a reflex, just like breathing."

I concentrated on her words. There was a lot riding on me here, so it wasn't easy to be calm and stay focused.

Deep breath in, deep breath out, repeat.

I pictured that warm, white light that came so easily to my hands, travelling up my arms and down into my spine. Remembering how threats had triggered my other supernatural episodes, I thought of Ben and Jaz and how I wanted to protect them. This fanned a small fire of rage which smouldered in the pit of my stomach. I thought of Esme and that fire burned brighter. My body responded with an instant temperature spike, my spine tingled and tensed. Sweat drizzled down my temples. I wanted to stretch. I felt balled up, like a knot. Like letting a rubber band snap, that pent-up energy suddenly released itself from my spine and I willed it to relax and melt away. As I did so, my entire body burned like a furnace. I could feel a shift occur within me.

"Yes! Yes, that's it, Soph. You did it, you're a natural!" Kea cheered.

I opened my eyes to find the room ablaze with a bright bioluminescence. I looked down at myself to see a soft light emanating from my skin. The pulse points on my wrists rhythmically threw out a hypnotic glow. Every corner of the room was revealed from the darkness, like a sports stadium lit up at night. Everyone was bathed in this soft light, and their facial markings seemed to glow with camaraderie. I turned my head side to side and saw on both sides of me large wings of light gently encasing my shoulders. It made me feel huge and powerful. I felt that same urge to move them as I had yesterday, and so I did. It wasn't the best idea, as they propelled me forward with such a sudden lurch that I was flung straight into Gedz'iel, who caught me in his massive arms.

"Hmm, some instruction is required here, I believe," he said this with the hint of an amused smile. "Refrain from exercising your pterugia for now. Still yourself, and use their light to guide you. You learn quickly though, well done. I am pleased. Your aura is strong." He propped me back on my feet, and faced me towards the wall. *Well done me.*

"That'll teach you for showing off!" Brennan quipped.

"There's a time and a place, you know!" I glared at him.

"My bad." Brennan shrugged.

I returned my attention to the wall. I felt all too well the pressure to figure out this puzzle and was now slightly giddy with the sudden light show my body was putting on. I examined the rocky edifice for a long while. All the symbols popped out at me, but then just blurred into meaningless indentations. My confidence waned after many long minutes of intense study, and my eyes tired, forcing my vision into a trance-like stare. It was surprisingly this brief state of absence that did it. My eyes glazed over, the light blaring off me cast a shadow across the wall in such a way that it revealed a hidden cross-like formation within the symbols.

The words of Enoch were centred in the middle of this previously hidden cross. The twinkling of gemstones was evident only in certain shapes, and they lit the way, delineating the cross as though a guiding path to what I was seeking. Only the light cast from me brought out this ethereal quality, showing me where I should look next.

The cross was comprised of the same repetitive pattern of symbols. Diamonds, with five squares inside them. The only significant difference was that at the end of each bar of the cross, on the point, the symbol was slightly larger. It reminded me of the face of a compass.

A compass!

"Can you guys see what I see?" I asked, awestruck at the sparkling vision.

"Yes, Soph'ael, they are illuminated through you. The Earth speaks to us through your light," answered Gedz'iel.

"It kinda looks like a compass to me," I said.

"Soph, you're a genius! North, South, East, and West, the directions that were hinted at in the passage. It's a freaking compass!" Brennan exclaimed as he slapped me across the back like I'd just scored a goal on the field.

"But how does this help? If it's telling us which way to go, it doesn't make any sense. We can't go in any of these directions unless we head back up!" I was stumped.

"Perhaps it pertains to the location of something within this chamber?" Enl'iel asked.

I thought about it further. Gedz'iel ran his hand across the symbols hopefully.

"Hmmm, I wonder..." Gedz'iel said.

"What do you see, your Grace?" Koi leaned in closer.

"We are in the southern lands." Gedz'iel knelt and inspected the bottom symbol of the vertical bar. The light and shadows cast across his muscular back revealed silvery scars etched up and down his spine. I wondered how he got those.

"I believe this is where we should focus." He gestured for me to look as I quickly averted my gaze from his back.

The rough-hewn symbol initially didn't look any more interesting than the others. Gedz'iel probed at it with his fingers, running them along its ridges and indentations, and finally over the cracked rock surrounding it. The gems sparkled under his touch, but nothing more interesting than that appeared.

"May I?" I asked, not sure if I should touch it also.

"Do as your spirit wills you. I am a mere guide for you." Gedz'iel stood up and backed away.

I knelt as he had and reached out, touching the symbols above the bottom one first. They glowed, heated, and emitted a small vibration. I let my hand run down to the bottom diamond and repeated the same tactile exploration. For a moment, it just vibrated as the others had. Then, without warning, the five small squares within it glowed white and bright, as though lights had turned on from within the rock.

"Look, do you see this?" I blurted out excitedly to no one in particular.

I could feel the anxious energies behind me. A magnetic force seemed to draw my hand towards the symbol again. With a suddenness that I was clearly not prepared for, this force sucked my fingers to the wall. I had no time to resist. It pulled each finger awkwardly onto the five square pattern, as though they were pressing all the keys on a keypad at once.

A massive jolt fired up my arm, forcing my head to fly backwards with the kickback. It would have thrown me to the ground, but for the fact that my fingers seemed glued to the wall.

"By the Great I'el, I believe she is opening the chamber!" Gedz'iel exclaimed.

"Help me! God, what do I do?" I screamed as I pulled wildly at my wrist. My hand was stuck firm.

The vibration shot through the entire room, rumbling the floor underneath me. Dirt rained.

Enl'iel knelt by my side, shielding me from the debris. "Do not fear, you will not be harmed. Breathe calmly. I believe the elements are identifying you as the true Earth-born angel." She rubbed my static-filled hair, soothed me in a moment that I was sure had no standard textbook approach for reassurance.

"What if it doesn't… recognise me?" I groaned, still struggling for freedom.

"Oh, it will, dear. It surely will!" Enl'iel soothed.

Clearly lacking human tact, Gedz'iel also answered my question in a matter-of-fact tone, "It will disintegrate an imposter."

"Oh, fabulous!" I pulled harder at my hand. Extreme panic set in. At the peak of my fear, I suddenly rolled backwards, released from the wall as an arc of lightning shot through the room. Everyone, including Gedz'iel, ducked as it bounced around the space and disappeared back through the centre of the cross with a cracking explosion. As I lay coughing on the dusty floor, any thoughts of seeing if I was injured were overrun by what happened next.

Chapter
Twenty-Nine

The wall rumbled. The bottom symbol that had held me hostage began to move, sinking slowly back into the rock face. All the other symbols making up the cross pattern did the same with a dragging, stone on stone grind. Gasps of blessings to I'el were whispered behind me. I couldn't take my eyes from the sight, but I did scuttle backwards, not knowing what might happen next.

Once all of the symbols had receded, a dark cross-shaped opening ominously glared back. I stood up cautiously to take a closer look, keeping what I hoped was a safe distance. The light from my wings was like high-beams, yet the recess must have been deep. All I could see was a black void. We all approached it, another rumble shook the floor, we paused. More stone grinding followed, and then, one by one, every other symbol on the wall rapidly collapsed in on itself, like a block puzzle falling to pieces. Dust blew back at us through the deafening noise.

In the aftermath of the explosive rock fall, I found that we'd all managed to huddle together, with Gedz'iel surrounding us all protectively with his expansive wings. As the last of the dust haze settled, a soft wind whistled through from the now much larger opening.

"Oh, my God!" My skin tingled; my pulse pounded. A thrill ran hot and cold through me. I moved carefully amongst the rubble, inching my way to the opening, and grasped the craggy edge.

The breeze was stale... dry and ancient.

"Indiana Jones couldn't have done any better," Brennan joked.

"Just call me Tomb Raider," I laughed, remembering my earlier thoughts about entering a strange hole in the ground.

"This is no time for humour. We are at the crux of a momentous occasion for the children of A'vean. Appreciation for the reverence of this moment and this place should be heeded. You should know better, Bren'ael. You are an ancient and should appreciate the customs of your people with more respect," Gedz'iel's tone was scathing.

Ouch. I cringed inwardly for Brennan.

"Forgive me, Gedz'iel. My years have been long in the human world. I have acquired many of their appalling habits." He bowed respectfully, but his smirk of amusement was barely hidden.

"I'm sorry." I couldn't quite meet Gedz'iel's eyes. I dared not smile, despite desperately wanting to.

"There is a time for enjoying the comforts of human frivolity. Now is not one of them." He turned away, dismissing us both. "Follow me." Gedz'iel stepped through the gaping black hole and disappeared. We moved quickly. Brennan went ahead, then me and Koi, who placed a reassuring hand on my shoulder. Kea and Enl'iel filed in last.

Our auras and wing-lights combined to light the way out as we moved through a tunnel. I noticed that Enl'iel remained in relative darkness. It occurred to me then that she must not have wings. I recalled her telling me that Eudaimonians could have many or none of the Watchers' traits. Perhaps wings were the one thing she was missing?

The musty air clung uncomfortably to my skin as we progressed along. Gems of all kinds glistened along the walls. The floor was hard, packed earth, with crunchy gravel underfoot. Brennan stopped suddenly and put his hand up for me to stop too. Gedz'iel had also halted, staring at a light that had appeared up ahead.

An agonised moan followed, making me jump nearly out of my skin.

"What was that?" I whispered, imagining monsters hiding in the shadows.

"No idea," answered Brennan, concern shadowed his face. "It doesn't sound too inviting."

"Let's continue." Enl'iel gently nudged my back. We proceeded forward, following a cautiously paced Gedz'iel into a new chamber on the left.

We turned the corner to find another orb-lit room. We halted again behind Gedz'iel, who was unmoving as he looked at something in the small space. The moaning intensified. I bristled, wondering what the source of this dreadful sound was.

It abruptly stopped, which seemed even more frightening. Gedz'iel raised a hand to stop us from moving any further. I shifted sideways around Brennan to get a better view.

Hovering in a corner was a ghostly figure with its back to us. Its head was downcast; it was silent, floating gently up and down. It began to flicker like a dying light bulb and then let out a piercing scream. I plugged my ears with my fingers. It then turned, revealing a ghastly pale face with dark, sunken eyes and a black, gaping mouth. It glared at us momentarily, then collapsed into itself, becoming a streak of light, like a shooting star. The light darted out and around Gedz'iel; he did not move or make a sound. It zipped up and down around him, shrieking wildly. Shockingly, it pushed itself right through his chest, emerging from his back. He grabbed at his heart, dropped to his knees, and moaned. Despite myself and the poltergeist thing, I moved to help him, but Brennan held me back with a shake of his head. Gedz'iel put up a hand to stop any interference and seemed to recover quickly, gathering himself up onto his feet again. The spectre turned its attention to us and sped rapidly around us, screaming a terrifying squeal. It corralled us in an ever-tightening circle. Curses of warning were yelled in our faces as we gathered our backs together, not wanting to take attention away from the frightful thing. Horrific images of mangled faces popped in and out of the spectre. It seemed to be trying to terrify us. It succeeded with me, while the others were cautious but unaffected.

Kea spoke to it softly, "Oh no, you poor, poor thing." It stopped the circling instantly at that and hovered over her head. Rainbow streaks of light emerged from within it. Then it snapped back into a tight, floating orb. A new shape emerged fluidly from the orb, elongating vertically and filling out into a translucent human form. Her wings ebbed slowly as she floated silently in front of us. Long, pale hair flowed over white robes punctuated by a silver and gold armoured breastplate. She wore similar wristbands and an impressive sword on her side. She looked every bit a Grecian goddess of war.

"This is Andr'eal. She has guarded this place from the time of Enoch," Gedz'iel said quietly as he reached a hand to her.

"Be still, my love. Come, the pain is over," he soothed. His face was an unexpected picture of longing. His breath hitched; his face flushed with emotion. Andr'eal regarded him with beautiful but disbelieving blue eyes. He didn't remove his gaze from her as he continued to speak to us.

"Her penance for repeated liaising with humans, teaching them elemental magic, was to either banishment to the Unseen Realm, or to stand sentry guard of the Prime Scroll chamber. She chose this; perhaps a greater punishment." His voice was thick as she glided cautiously forward and took Gedz'iel's hands in hers.

My heart ached for her. In her human visage, she looked a pitiful soul. Beauty and grace glowed through her, yet utter desolation emanated from within, almost as tangible as if she were flesh and blood. She was as wounded as anyone could ever be.

She spoke in a haunting voice as she gazed up at Gedz'iel, "Husband, I beg thee to free me from this confinement. Look about you, I have protected this place well. Nothing has passed by me; the great words remain secure."

I think we all jolted with surprise at her revelation. She was Gedz'iel's wife!

She spoke again. "I feel her presence." Andr'eal searched us all, then drifted to me. She tilted her head, inspected me with a pained smile. "The Earth-born is finally here?" She ran her spectral hand across my cheek, leaving a chill on the skin. "Welcome, saviour of the children of A'vean." She kneeled before me and begged, "Please grant me release?" I looked to Gedz'iel. I didn't know what to say.

"Beloved, you have suffered greatly. I have suffered with you… your absence has been a torture." His voice faltered; tears streamed silently down his dignified face. "I see you have fought well." He moved towards her again and as he did so, he kicked at something on the ground with his bare foot. A skull rolled to a stop just short of my feet. I realised with disgust that it was not gravel that we had been trampling on, but bones, thousands of them.

"Come," Gedz'iel said.

Andr'eal glided back to him and they embraced. I could see that he didn't want to let her go as she pulled away and returned to me.

"I am at your service." She bowed.

"Please, don't do that, and just call me Sophia." I felt that familiar flame of embarrassment heat my cheeks with the over-the-top attention.

She inclined her head in acknowledgement. "I have fought the Daimon to preserve the scroll for you, Sophia. I hope I have pleased you."

"You've fought here all on your own?" I asked, "I thought this place was unknown?"

"It was, but there have been some among the kindred who have turned to the Unseen and other enemies just as vile. We have been betrayed. Look about you, I have been forced under duress to annihilate my own people." She pointed to what I had thought were more crystals by the base of the walls, but realised that they were parts of skeletal remains.

"Oh my God!" I knelt by one. The site was grisly, yet I felt drawn to run my hand along the smooth clear skeleton. Enl'iel knelt next to me.

"When a Watcher or powerful Eudaimonian ascends, they leave a diamond skeleton behind. The particles of carbon in human flesh, over thousands of years, eventually fuse, like coal under great pressure, into remains such as this," Enl'iel explained.

"How did they get down here? We had to go through all that back there just to get in here. I thought I was the only one who could access this place?" I turned back, speaking to the forlorn figure huddling into Gedz'iel's side again.

"They tunnelled through the walls, sniffing out anything that could be us. The Rogues and the Afflicted, they have blasted through many a time. The Rogues clawed through with their rotting fingers. You must hunt down the betrayers." Andr'eal pointed to the many greying bone fragments scattered around. Gedz'iel growled like a wild animal.

"Traitors!" Gedz'iel mumbled.

"I have patched the walls at least once a century until this one just passed. Not one attacker has succeeded in escape to tell the tale of what lay within my prison. I have not faced an intrusion in 150 years, although I believe my sense of time has somewhat faded."

"Who are the Afflicted?" I asked, inwardly wincing as she called this place her prison.

"You are indeed blessed if you are yet to meet an Afflicted being. They are the Flourishing ones who have fallen victim to the heinous effects of Thanratos." Andr'eal bowed again as she addressed me.

"What's that?" I asked.

"Dearest Sophia, it is the powdered bones of the mortal remains of a Watcher. The Afflicted ingest this substance to invigorate themselves. It does not bode well for their health, however. They lose their sensibilities and behave like savage beasts, desperate to obtain more and more. Our enemies use this to their advantage and bribe them with Thanratos dust to perform heinous acts. Watchers and Eudaimonians have been hunted to their mortal deaths purely so the enemy could obtain their earthly remains. Thanratos is immensely rare and powerful. I have fought many a battle protecting my own bones from falling into their hands. She pointed to a darkened corner and threw an illuminating orb that lit it up.

I gasped at what I saw. "This is…or was… you?"

"Please?" Andr'eal gestured me towards the grisly corner. Gedz'iel drew a sharp breath at the sight, yet he maintained a dignified silence and stature. Propped up against the wall was a perfectly preserved diamond skeleton. It sparkled like a newly cut gem, a work of art as beautiful as it was disturbing. The ribcage was housed in the same armoured breastplate that she wore in spirit form. Intricate carvings were etched all over it, including that same swirl of our common facial markings.

"This was me. I was badly injured in an encounter a few thousand years ago, and with no one to help heal me, I ascended, but was unable to leave for the Sanctuary of Souls," she replied.

I was horrified. What a dreadful existence. I was learning, that despite their goodwill and intent, the Watchers could be just as brutal as their enemies when threatened. The evidence of her victories sparkled directly underfoot.

I felt physically ill for her inhumane fate, and was immediately determined to get what we came for and set this poor spirit free.

"What do I need to do? Let's get you out of this place," I said, with a rush of determination.

Andr'eal glowed with anticipation, "You have read the scripture henceforth from the entry chamber?"

"Yes, and unfortunately, it seems you need some of my blood?"

"That is so," she answered.

With that, Andr'eal leaned down and snapped off one of her skeletal rib bones with a glass-like crack. She ran it through her palm, lighting it until it glowed lava red. As the glow died down, she opened her pale, translucent palm and offered it up to me. There lying across it was a razor sharp diamond dagger.

Chapter Thirty

I took the sparkling weapon that Andr'eal offered me. It looked more beautiful than dangerous, just like a Daimon. It was still hot, the heat warmed my palm, but left no mark. I turned it over a couple of times, admiring its beauty. I found it was every bit a weapon. The blade was fine and sharp, its ability to maim evident. The handle was heavy and felt surprisingly comfortable in my palm. It was also engraved with words that spiralled neatly around the heavy grip.

Without hesitation I surprised myself as I read them aloud,

"Child of A'vean, a drop by thine own hand shall engage the fifth element."

Andr'eal spoke. "Blood drawn by your hand alone shall see the prophecy fulfilled. By force or vexation, it shall come to naught. But a drop from thy palm upon this stone shall reveal the Prime Scroll." Andr'eal pointed me in the direction of an unassuming, vertical rock protruding from the floor. It had no point of interest, no decoration. It would be something you would walk past, unnoticed. I looked back at the others for reassurance. Their faces were tight with concern. A nod from Enl'iel and Koi encouraged me. Brennan gave me a thumbs up. I turned back to the stone, prodded all around it with my fingertips. Nothing really seemed to point me in any particular direction until I noticed a small indentation on the top. A thin channel ran from its edge and sloped downwards to the floor. There was nothing on the floor of interest. I was confused and mulled over this spot until Andr'eal seemed to understand my confusion as to what to do next. She placed her palm over the indentation and mimicked the action of slicing her hand.

I gulped. The thought was easier than the act. To slice my own flesh deliberately made my belly quiver. Again, resorting to some calming breaths, I closed my eyes for a moment to gather courage. As I did so, I was confronted with the image of Esme being brutalised by Belial, and my anger surged forward. I took a step closer to the rock and, without hesitation, used that anguish for Esme. The blade sliced quickly across the base of my palm. I winced at the sting. I watched with ghoulish fascination as my surprisingly dark and sparkly blood drizzled onto the rock. As the pool of crimson filled the concave space, it began flowing down the channel. Andr'eal then placed her ghostly palm over my bleeding one and instantly cauterised the wound.

"Thank you." I smiled, and returned my attention quickly to the blood flowing smoothly over the stone receptacle. It dribbled down, spilling luxuriously onto the floor.

I gazed at the scene, which seemed to occur in slow motion. The expectation of something magnificent happening made the moment drag out. The soft drips hit the floor, one by one, in the cool silence. As the flow ceased and there was nothing but a congealing mass of my blood on the ground, I began to quietly panic that perhaps I did it wrong, or even that I was not, in fact, the person they were waiting for.

That thought was eradicated with a deep, thunderous boom throughout the chamber. It powdered dust and debris up into my face. I swiped it out of my eyes as a tremendous breeze blew up from apparently nowhere. Bone fragments and rock rose around us. I protected my face with my forearms. Sharp bony projectiles flew around, but then it settled as quickly as it had begun.

The miniature tornado had disturbed the remains on the ground and exposed another diamond pattern carved into the floor beneath the stone receptacle. Within the diamond, sitting in the middle square, was the drying pool of my sparkling blood.

A cracking sound broke the brief silence as the rock split vertically up the middle, then crumbled away noisily to the ground. In its wake lay a long, rectangular box, half-buried in the bone and stone rubble. It was ornate, but tarnished. I knelt, picked it up, polishing it with the sleeve of my hoody. Swirls and concentric circles covered it, and it surprised me with its lightness for its size.

It hummed in my hands. The quickening pulse in my temple seared through my birthmark. A distorted reflection of my face beamed back at me in the few un-tarnished patches where I had just polished. My eyes swirled with colour in its reflection, and the more intensely I looked, the more my irises glowed with colourful bursts in the blue background.

How could this be me? I'm just a normal girl… well, I *was* just a normal girl.

My reverie was cut short by a momentary vision that felt as real as the ground underneath me. A large eye, a single eye, appeared in the reflection, blue and swirling. A supernova-like burst of colour; warm and inviting. A voice entered my mind, deep and soothing, yet commanding.

"Daughter of A'vean, beware. Thy heart is thy strength and thy weakness." In a split second, the image was gone, and I was back to staring at my reflection in the metal box.

Another rumble underfoot, and a rain of rubble pelted my head. Powerful arms grabbed me from behind. "We must go, Soph'ael. The chamber is about to collapse!" Gedz'iel picked me up, the box clutched tightly to my chest. He flew with immense speed back through the passages towards the staircase. I felt my aura dull in his proximity. The safety of his grip seemed to cause my entire body to relax, to where I nearly felt ordinary again — nearly. The walls were crumbling fast, and the deafening sound of grinding and crashing rocks made it impossible to hear where the others were. I hoped they were right behind us. I closed my eyes and wondered what in the world could come next. A familiar voice snuck into my thoughts. *Knew you could do it, Princess.*

Gedz'iel's grip was strong, and his speed had us flying up and out of the hole under the Zythros stone in what felt like seconds. The room remained full of people wearing expressions of great anticipation. Enl'iel was safely in Brennan's arms as they flew out behind us, with Koi and Kea at the rear. The large stone was already moving back over the gaping hole with a slow grind, shutting out the plume of dust spewing up from underneath. I was gently placed to the ground and checked over thoroughly by Enl'iel. My hoody fell to the ground as she turned me around, apparently burned away by my wings. She did a quick creative knot to stop my t-shirt doing the same. Now that could become a problem!

"Well, you seem to be in one piece," Enl'iel said with a relieved sigh. She rubbed gently over the fading white scar on my palm and dusted off my face. "You have done well, dear. Very well. Esme would be so very proud of you." A tear slid down her face as she leaned forward and placed her right cheek to mine, a gesture she had never before afforded me. I'd witnessed it between her and Koi, though. It was like a kiss, warm, reassuring, and full of love. "I love you, dear child. Do not, under any circumstances, believe otherwise," she said.

Arms enveloped me. Brennan hugged me from behind, "You're a star! Seriously, my own brilliance dulls in your presence!"

"Bren'ael, I fear you have been too long in the human world. Your conceit is unbecoming," Gedz'iel said dismissively as he drew my attention to him. "I commend and praise you, Soph'ael." He did the cheek-kiss thing. He then addressed the waiting crowd.

"Dear kindred, the Earth-born has begun a chain reaction that henceforth cannot be undone." A cheer arose as wings emerged and flapped in celebration. "We must leave immediately to protect and train her further before we begin the search for the Kaladai."

I wondered what this new thing was he referred to. I leaned heavily on Enl'iel as I listened and wondered, absolutely spent.

"What's a Kaladai?"

"It is the last of the keys for the great portal to A'vean, Sophia. It is the only thing that will open the gate," she replied. Overwhelmed, I focused on Gedz'iel as he continued.

"Return to your homes to await further instruction. You shall be called upon when the time is nigh. Ready your scouts and prepare for battle. Those who have yet to complete the Right of Sevens must be kept within the sanctuaries. Any human kindred must also be warned and armed well if they wish to join us."

As the crowd dispersed, the Zythros stone began to pulse like the beat of a rhythmic drum.

"Bless the heavens, a Keeper is coming!" Enl'iel exclaimed. Before I had a chance to wonder what they meant, a beam of light shot up from the point on the stone. It hit the roof briefly, then vanished. In its wake was a lonely little orb, a small Keeper. It blinked on and off, hovering above us. A group of Keepers zoomed out from the shadows, circled it, and then whisked it away. It was all over in a matter of seconds.

"Blessed be A'vean," the last of the crowd chorused, before they blinked out in a mass of white, streaking light, heading back to wherever they'd come from.

I was still staring at the Zythros stone.

"That, my dear, is how Keepers are born. When there is sufficient positive energy flowing around a Zythros stone, it generates the life of a Keeper. It is a great joy," Enl'iel explained.

Gedz'iel moved as though to leave, breaking yet another moment of amazement, "I shall return within the week. I must seek counsel with the Eloi. I shall also take Andr'eal to the Sanctuary of Souls. Her confinement is complete. Peace and comfort await her there." Andr'eal was close to his side, lovingly cuddled into him as he stroked her ethereal hair that floated like a halo in the breezeless room. Her translucent arms enveloped his chest.

"Enl'iel, keep Soph'ael well protected until she arrives in the Northern lands. I have Keepers and scouts at the ready to follow you. Jud'ael shall greet you in London," Gedz'iel said. Brennan quietly cursed to himself at the mention of this name. Gedz'iel left us with a warning, "Beware these humans you keep, they are a liability. Keep them under control. Soph'ael, learn your craft through the teachings of Koi, strengthen your body as well as your elemental energy, for at this time you are weak and vulnerable. Most importantly, strengthen your mind. Without self-belief, there is no benefit in physical or elemental strength, as your enemies will exploit any weakness of constitution." With that, he bid us all farewell with the same cheek-on-cheek gesture and disappeared in a blinding streak of light.

Leaning heavily on her arm, I asked Enl'iel, "When are we leaving?"

"Immediately. Koi has prepared appropriate transportation, since you cannot travel safely by transference yet."

She guided me quickly away and up one of the swirling metal staircases leading to the second level. I was agonisingly tired; my legs barely had the energy to make it up each step. As I ascended, I saw the artists responsible for the murals. Buzzing frantically over a spare piece of wall, the little Keepers were drawing out crystalline colours from within the earth, creating a new image. It was no shock now, after everything that already had happened, to see my image revealing itself. A diamond dagger lay in one hand and a bleeding wound spread across my other. It was both surreal and phenomenally impressive.

"Can you explain transference to me?"

"Certainly." Enl'iel's eyes brightened. "It is how we move within the realms of the Earth, utilising portals in the atmosphere. We dissolve into the ether and reappear at the destination of our choice. Before the fall, Watchers could move throughout the entire universe and the Earth. Now we are limited to the realms within the Earth. With practise, you too will be able to do this." She squeezed my hand reassuringly, "But at the moment, your body is still growing and recovering from your awakening. It will take time, but it will come."

Like the impressive light orbs, I thought that would be a pretty cool trick to have up my sleeve.

We quickly arrived at a large wooden door and pushed through it. Kea, Koi, and Brennan were already inside the small room at the base of another staircase. Seated on the floor with a bag on each of their laps were Jaz and Ben. They both glared at me. I felt weighed down by their sombre expressions. My mouth went dry. After what happened with Ben, who knew how Jaz was feeling about me? Self-conscious, I glanced away, feeling the heaviness of their attention.

Koi pointed up the stairs, "A vehicle is waiting to transport you to the airport. A private jet will be ready for take-off. We will be shadowed by scouts—our military, so to speak. You will be safe, Sophia." Koi smiled reassuringly. "Let us depart." He waved everyone up the stairs, and smiled again at me on my way up. "You have done well. I very much look forward to training you." Koi gave my arm a reassured squeeze as he led the way.

I looked back at my best friends as I went up ahead of them.

Had I lost them as I accepted my new destiny?

Chapter
Thirty-One

It was early afternoon as we drove in a limousine, of all things. Where the money was coming from, I couldn't imagine. A private jet, too? Those forty-five minutes were supremely uncomfortable as my friends sat opposite me, wordless and avoiding all eye contact. I picked my nails, closed my eyes, even counted all the red cars that went by. Ben and Jaz's silence was almost unbearable. How inverted my world had become in a few short days.

Finally, we arrived, and it lessened the tension as we were driven directly onto the tarmac like celebrities. Both Ben and Jaz leaned into the windows, eyes wide at a well-dressed crew standing by the jet. They looked every bit like regular people, but as Enl'iel and Koi greeted them, the crew flashed their eyes a bright, sparkling blue, before they returned to average brownish hues. An impressive, covert greeting. I was kind of blown away by this completely awesome trick. It was hard to suppress looking like a gobsmacked kid.

Kea and Brennan ushered Ben and Jaz into their seats, and then we were off within minutes, with none of the fuss that flying commercial entailed. Brennan made his way over to me whilst Enl'iel spoke quietly with my friends.

"Hey, Princess. How are you doing? Big day… big couple of days, huh?" His Aussie accent was suddenly more muted, less discernible.

I contemplated his question as I watched the ground drop away through the tiny window. "I'm… I don't know. It's like I'm being swept up and away on a tidal wave. I can't go back, I realise that, so I suppose I just have to ride it forward… blindly," I leaned back against the beige leather seat, my eyes heavy, "I'm overwhelmed, Brennan." I rubbed my temples, grimacing in an effort to put everything into place.

"Yeah, it's been full on, but it'll all fall into place. Don't you worry Princess. Your million questions will slowly be answered. Just know one thing — I've got your back." He patted the back of my hand.

"I thought my friends did too." I slowly succumbed to sleep. I gazed at the soft white clouds that rolled by like a stormy ocean. The last things I saw before I drifted off were white orbs zipping around the wing in various formations, accompanying us like a military detail.

I awoke to the thud of the wheels hitting the tarmac, the jerk of the brakes jolted me forwards, forcing my eyes wide open. I swivelled around to get my bearings. Something jabbed into my leg as I leaned forward to retrieve my backpack. I fished around in the leg pocket of my cargos to find the sparkling diamond dagger. I frowned, turned it over in my hand, then slipped it back in the pocket. I couldn't recall putting it there.

"We're home, finally. Man, I've missed this place." Brennan unbuckled his belt enthusiastically, looking around with the anticipation of a kid at Disneyland. "I'd much prefer to wing it next time, though, so hurry up and learn to fly, Princess. It's much more convenient." He smiled.

"We're here already?" I asked through a wide yawn. My mouth was dry. I needed a drink, "I thought this must be a stopover!"

Brennan was stretching out his huge frame. His biceps flexed with a jaw-dropping pop. The mysterious scars on his upper arms peeked out from under his sleeve. His legs seemed as strong as though they'd never been injured at all. Strength oozed from his every pore.

"You were playing sleeping beauty for twenty hours straight! Let's go." He leaned down, kissed my forehead before heading for the door. Ben followed, but didn't even look at me. That sinking feeling re-emerged. Jaz at least glanced back at me as she followed them. She half-smiled like she wanted to say something, but then thought better of it. Her eyes were sunken, crescents of exhaustion underneath.

I followed down the stairs with my backpack slung over my shoulder. The Prime Chamber chest within it hummed ever so slightly. I wondered if anyone else was aware of its presence like I was... it felt almost like it was somehow communicating with me. The knife banged back and forth against my leg. I wondered about these mysterious items. The Kaladai, the scroll, and whatever else was coming my way. According to Enl'iel, I couldn't open the scroll until Gedz'iel returned. The mystery would remain a while longer.

In Heathrow, the seven of us passed through customs, passport at the ready. We were waved through with a quick stamp and another flash of sparkling blue eyes by a woman who was all business and no conversation.

"What's with all the eye flashing?" I asked Enl'iel, "Do they all do that?" I wondered if Ben and Jaz had noticed and been even more freaked out.

"It's our private acknowledgement of one another in the human world. We're everywhere. Some are Watchers, but most are Eudaimonian. It's how we navigate covertly around the globe. In all areas, from healthcare, to government, transport, housing and agriculture, you'll find us if you know how to look. We exist this way to stay invisible, as well as to keep our ears to the ground to pick up on fluctuations in Daimon activity. Did you ever once notice that I have never carried a purse, or money?" Enl'iel asked with a coy expression.

"Actually — no! How did we get by in Australia? How did we pay our way?" I inquired, rather surprised at this immensely obvious oversight. I had money from work, but couldn't recall ever once seeing her whip out an ATM card.

"The network, my dear. The network provides all that we need." She smiled an all-knowing smile.

After a long walk through the terminal complex, we reached a bustling taxi rank brimming with compact black cabs. The smell of Christmas scented coffee lured me to a nearby coffee cart. A flash of blue eyes ensued from the barista, and I was sipping an espresso with a hint of cinnamon in seconds. I blew the hot liquid; the steam curled back and warmed my lips. I immediately loved this network.

The cool, wintery air and hot coffee quickly pushed away the last wisps of sleep. A light drizzle fell as another limousine was loaded with the few bags we'd brought along with us.

"You guys certainly know how to travel!" I said as Enl'iel gestured for me to enter first. She laughed lightly. A sweet trill that was bright and youthful… I wasn't sure I'd get used to her like this.

A colossal man stood by the open doors, looking very uncomfortable in a corporate suit. He pulled his shirt collar, loosed his neck tie, as though trying to escape its confines. He threw me a look of *hurry the hell* up as I clambered in the back. The man unnecessarily shoved Brennan in behind me. Brennan's face glowed, and he growled with anger. Brennan turned to get back out, but Enl'iel pulled his arm, planting a soft, lingering kiss on his cheek.

"Don't you mind him, now. You and I have more important catching up to do than you and Jude," she soothed, and Brennan seemed to immediately melt and forget about the driver smugly grinning at him. This must have been the Jud'ael guy they were talking about. Brennan's reaction to him matched the sigh of disgust he let slip when his name had been mentioned by Gedz'iel.

The drive was much like the first one, initially. Silence oozed from Jaz and Ben until we pulled off the M4 near Reading for a bathroom break. When Jaz got back in, she sat next to me and passed me something from her pocket. It was a picture of Shadow and Grey, with a note. I read the quickly scrawled script.

Dear sweet girl,

Don't you be worrying about your mutt and bag o' bones horse. I'll keep them fed and fat for you.

You take care and come back to us,

Alfie and Joan.

Tears hung in my lashes.

"Thanks, Jaz."

She squeezed my hand.

"Sorry for being a complete cow to you. I honestly couldn't string together enough dirty words yesterday, but…" She squeezed my hand a little tighter, "I realised after having my hissy fit that you're the one who's probably got the most to be pissed-off about right now. I'm a terrible bestie for sulking. I'm sorry. I don't know what the fuck is going on, but it seems there are lot people — or whatever — looking out for you." Jaz glanced at Enl'iel, then hugged me, pulling back when Ben got back into the car.

He was still ignoring me. Before she sat back next to him, she whispered in my ear, "I can't sulk for too long, you need to intro me to that God who's driving this thing!" Clearly, Jaz was coping okay, because her hormones were back on, all cylinders firing. Relief slid through me as she relaxed next to Ben, whispering to him here and there, seemingly telling him off as he scowled in the opposite direction.

I barely noticed the rest of the long drive, only picking out the turnoff sign to Birmingham and the Midlands along the motorway.

With scouts zapping continuously around the car for the rest of the trip, it was hard to see much outside. I wondered how they weren't visible to the public, motoring along beside us. We turned off the main road onto a narrow one, wide enough for only one car. Naked trees made a skeletal, overhanging tunnel as we drove toward a sandstone church to the left atop a small hill. We pulled into a gravel driveway beside the church. Crumbling, snow-capped gravestones skirted it. The car made a right and rolled towards an impressive, whitewashed Tudor manor. A large stone sat proudly at the head of the driveway, engraved with the name The Old Priory. We pulled to a stop next to a side entrance.

Before I got out, an elderly woman bustled out of the arched door, hastily wiping her hands on her apron. She cuddled into Jude, Kea, Koi, Brennan, and finally Enl'iel. The old woman was shadowed by a man, who of course, was as stunning as the rest of them.

I stepped out, Ben and Jaz followed quietly behind me. My heart pounded with anxiety. New people, new places…I wanted to curl up in a ball and hide, but that was not going to happen. The elderly woman clapped her hands, steepled them under her chin and made her way towards me.

"Oh, me! Oh, for the love of the Heavens! Look at her! She's a true beauty. Welcome, child. Welcome to the Old Priory." The woman hugged me tight. She smelled of flour and vanilla, and reminded me all too much of Esme with her ample bosom and motherly warmth. She held me at arm's length and surveyed me carefully. That's when I noticed it. Her eyes were clouded over — she was blind, yet she looked me over every bit as thoroughly as anyone could. How could she possibly know what I looked like?

Her soft hands caressed my face, her fingers trailed my birthmark. Although she was a stranger, she felt strangely familiar, her energy kind, so I didn't stop her. She felt down my arms and pulled my hands into hers.

"Child, you are long awaited, long loved, and forevermore so. You mind, I'll be looking after you here. Hmm…" She pinched my hip. "You could do with a little fattenin' up though! All skin and bone! You call on me at any time. My name is Eilir, my dear. Oh me, that rhymed!" Eilir laughed heartily. "Ha ha! May the blessings of A'vean be upon you!"

I immediately adored her. After a dozen or so kisses covered every part of my face, Eilir ushered me back to Enl'iel. She greeted Jaz with the same enthusiasm, but was more wary with Ben.

"A troubled soul here, I see. Buck up, young man. No time for self-indulgence. On with you, then. Let's fill your belly too. You might have a different outlook once you have one of my cakes in you."

Ben couldn't have looked any more pissed off.

"And that kind of attitude, young man, will get you nowhere with me! Hmph!" Eilir chided him.

Jaz giggled; Ben gave Jaz his best dagger eyes; she flipped him the bird.

Hands on her hips, mouth pursed, Eilir glanced reprovingly between the two.

"I'll sort these two, Eilir. I'll take them to get settled. Send down some of your best, please? It's been a long, tasteless drought without your cooking." Kea prodded Jaz and Ben away from the house, towards the church.

Eilir smiled again, "Oh me, I do love her! Come on with you now Soph'ael, the kettle's boiled." Eilir ambled into the manor with a warm chuckle, her floor-length skirt rustling behind her.

Her companion followed close behind Eilir. He wore bare feet and simple white pants, just like the rest of the Watchers.

Enl'iel ushered me into a small living room decked out with well-worn leather sofas and floor rugs. There was a musty, well lived in smell to it. It was pleasant and homey.

"Eilir is our resident cook, although she is much more than that. It was a surprise to us all that a mere human could ever teach us anything. All our young look to her as a wise, guiding light. We can't possibly do without her. You'll grow to love her so." Enl'iel patted a comfy-looking chair. "We will stop here a short while in the main house before we go down to the sanctuary. Would you care for a shower to freshen up, Sophia? Eilir has a change of clothes for you already prepared."

"Yes, thanks." I was still in my grimy, smelly clothes and felt foul. I thought on the old woman as I followed Enl'iel through the ancient house. "Enl'iel, how can Eilir see me? Her eyes look as though they are blind."

"Yes, dear, that she is. It is a long story, but Eilir was blinded by accident a long time ago in an unfortunate chance encounter with a Watcher. He was horrified by what he had done, and took her in.

Unable to repair her sight, he has cared for her ever since. Over the years, she has been taught the second sight. She can see without her eyes. Dash'iel, whom you saw following her every move, is the Watcher responsible. He has cared for her with unfailing devotion for over three hundred years. I'm sure she'll tell you about it. She loves recounting how she met him." A wistful look softened the edges of Enl'iel's face.

"Three hundred years! How could she live that long?"

Enl'iel guided me up the narrow, floral carpeted stairway to a bathroom as she explained.

"Dash'iel, Dash as we like to call him, has healed and rejuvenated her with the elements in order to keep her well. Unfortunately, the human body has its limitations, and she is now nearing the end of her time on Earth. He does not leave her side. It is no secret to anyone that he has loved her for all these years and she, him. Unconsummated love, mind you, as our laws do not allow for such relationships to occur. The Council of Eloi would banish Dash if he were ever to involve himself with a human in such a manner. They've lived side by side, in love, with a chasm between them. It is both beautiful and devastating," she finished this reverie with a deep sigh, as though she would allow the relationship to have flourished if it were up to her.

"That's so cruel. Couldn't they have been given permission? Why make them suffer like that?" I asked as I entered the bathroom. Enl'iel turned on the shower and set down a towel and soap from a small cupboard.

"Love and lust are what have led to this whole predicament in the first place. There is, unfortunately, no tolerance for it. We will call for you on the half hour for tea, and then we shall retreat to the sanctuary. Enjoy your shower, dear."

I stepped into a tiny shower stall in the small, aqua room. A round porthole window allowed a view down the length of the property to the small river in the distance. A blue barge bobbed by a dock. As I scrubbed my hair, I looked on and wondered what the pain of forbidden love might feel like.

Chapter
Thirty-Two

Just as I was pulling on a slim fitting white tee over a crisply ironed pair of matching cargos, Eilir came knocking at the door.

"Tea, child? I have a lovely brew awaiting you downstairs in the parlour."

"Yes, thank you. I'll be there in a few minutes." I pulled my grimy Docs back on. Eilir's footsteps petered away. Her cheerful humming filled the silence.

I looked at myself in a small mirror next to the circular window. Still shocked by the white hair and bright blue eyes, I knew it was me, but it just didn't look like me. Thankfully, the birthmark had settled and was now a silvery colour, like a long-faded scar. I couldn't help but run a finger along it. It was no longer raised, and it tingled when I touched it. I was buried somewhere deep inside this strange reflection.

Tea was actually a banquet of sweet and savoury delights. They were awaiting me in a pokey little kitchen, on a small table that fit snugly under the angle of the staircase. Dash'iel, yet to speak, pulled out a chair for me, like a proper gentleman. I took the offer, shy as usual, not used to this kind of treatment. As I sat, he kneeled next to me. He leaned forward and placed his right cheek on mine. A warm buzz of energy passed between us. It was such a personal and close form of greeting. It was going to take time feeling comfortable with it. I smiled awkwardly when he pulled back.

"It is indeed an honour to meet you, Soph'ael. I am at your service." His voice was deep and formal, but his smile lent a boyish charm to the youthful twinkle in his eyes.

"Thank you, I'm honoured to meet you too. All of you," I replied. Dash'iel smiled, then left with a chaste kiss on Eilir's hand. She beamed at him in a way that cast aside the years of her age, to the point that I could almost see a young girl madly in love.

"He is quite the catch, don't you think, Soph'ael?" she quipped.

I was getting quite confused by the interchange of my name. "Please, call me Sophia. And yes, he is very handsome, Eilir," I answered, to her utter delight. "Your tea and food are delicious, too. What are these amazing things?" I said as I held up a small, sweet pastry bursting with juicy currants.

"Oh me!" Eilir clutched her chest. "It's an Eccles cake. Delightful, aren't they? Can you believe they used to be illegal, because they had a drop o' the drink in them?" Eilir laughed. "I cook them for all of my special guests! Once you are settled and I can snatch a small square of time, I shall teach you to make them, if you like that is?" Her brows arched.

"I'd love to learn." Cooking was not a skill I had; memories of small fires on the stove were testament to that.

"That would make an old woman very happy. Never was able to have my own babes, so it would be such a treat!" She clapped the tips of her fingers together with delight.

"Well, I could eat them all day, Eilir," I responded through my last sweet mouthful. She waved at me with a coy look of mock embarrassment and tottered to the sink to scrub a dish.

"Eilir, I shall take Sophia to the Sanctuary now. There's precious little time, and much to do. Shall I send up some help for dinner? I believe there are a few young ones in need of a firm hand today. I'm quite sure you must have some pots requiring hard labour?" Enl'iel asked.

"Oh me, yes, I do indeed. Send the scoundrels up. I'll have them sorted in no time!"

"Excellent, and thank you for your delicious treats. Such a delight to the palate." Enl'iel kissed Eilir on the cheek.

"Oh, my sweet Enl'iel, nothing but the best for you, dear lady. Now off with you then, I've got tea to prepare." Eilir grabbed a pair of scissors and began snipping some herbs by the open back door. She sang sweetly to herself as she worked.

"Come, Sophia. Koi is awaiting you. We must commence your training today."

We left the main house and headed for the church. Up the small incline of the driveway, we entered the overgrown graveyard through an aged iron gate. The bell tower to the left was in desperate need of repair. Crumbling around the edges and pock-marked, yet it was still a thing of beauty. A small plaque by the door proudly decreed that it was built in the year 1000 AD.

A medieval, musty air hit me as we entered the church. The heavy doors protested the intrusion with an annoyed screech. Ancient wooden pews sat lonely and dusty under the vaulted roof. Gilt-framed gothic depictions of Jesus and the Twelve Apostles framed a small altar. Enl'iel guided me to the back of the building, through the aisle to a small nave. Here, the burial tombs of people long dead adorned the walls. A woman named Catherine, buried alongside her husband, Alfred, in the 1500's rested in the right wall. A marble effigy of the couple laying supine with their hands in prayer was set below an oval plaque that told of their story in Middle English. I couldn't understand anything other than the names and dates. Below our feet, a bronze medieval knight was carved into the pale stone. It jumped out against the worn tiling surrounding it.

"Are you ready, Sophia?"

"No. Not at all!"

The air pressed in on me, and not just because it was stale. This moment felt tangible, plucking at my skin, reminding me that the life I knew was being left behind.

"I promise, everything will be alright. You will see that soon enough. Destiny is so often out of our control, but how we travel that path is very much a choice," Enl'iel said, then placed her hand upon the right cheek of the effigy of Catherine. It began to glow as the twirls and curls of a mark emerged like magic on the marble cheek.

As this happened, the soldier underfoot rumbled slightly. I stepped back as the image receded into the ground and slid off to the side. It revealed another underground staircase, more brightly lit than the others, at least. How many dark holes could I visit in one week? This was becoming scarily normal.

"Come now, Sophia. You have many kindred to meet, and much to learn. Once you enter the sanctuary, you must not leave without one of us, as you are yet to know how to use the mark of A'vean to control the opening. Until you have mastered the art of transference, this is your only way in or out," she explained. "In your current state, being stranded outside would be immensely dangerous."

"What's the mark of A'vean?" I asked.

"That, my dear, is the birthmark upon your face. All those with a strong elemental connection to A'vean bear this symbol. Some are more pronounced than others. As you will discover, it provides us with an ability to connect with one another and to control the elements around us as our spirit flows through it."

All my life I'd been looking at that birthmark, a part of the real me after all, but hadn't realised it.

The entrance was dusty, appearing rarely used, yet there were fresh footprints in a thick grey layer down the first few steps as I descended into a warm, underground ground passage.

"The others brought Jaz and Ben through earlier to settle them in. I understand this is very hard on them, especially Ben. He has a troubled soul, that poor boy," Enl'iel said.

"I'm really worried about him. I'm worried for them both, to be honest. They've had such difficult lives. I'm scared this will all be too much, and that I'll lose them. Or worse, they'll get hurt."

"Give them time. They will come around. Neither have had the security of stable families, therefore they lack trust in anyone but themselves, and that's perfectly understandable. Eventually, they will realise that they have stability and trust in us. I have put in a word so that Ben will have his mind occupied. They will be safe here, and I know you will not lose their friendship forever, dear. Be patient, give them time to adjust." Enl'iel walked on ahead and left me to think of Ben the entire journey down. His cold behaviour still stung like a fresh face slap.

We arrived at a landing with a white doorway — at least I thought that's what it was until she walked straight through it. Enl'iel's hand poked back through and beckoned to me. I followed her through this veil of light, and every cell of my body buzzed as I did so. Beyond it was nothing short of amazing.

What the Library of Antiquity was to record keeping, this Sanctuary was to urban living. I'd entered a secret underground world. Multiple levels spanned out around a central shaft that descended to what looked like an endless depth. It was pleasantly warm and bustling with activity. Numerous doorways and corridors dotted the perimeter, embellished by ornate, wrought-iron balustrade. The walls were thick, with lush greenery that bloomed with huge, unusual white flowers, which lent a surprising freshness to the air. Orbs of light bobbed at various points, providing almost daylight brightness. Everywhere I looked, there were people. Many people. They were walking, flying, talking, and bustling to and fro. Ordinary things were going on. Adults carrying children and workers pushing trolleys of goods. Some sat reading books on a bench by an underground waterfall. White-haired children ran around squealing, their parents chasing after them. Teenagers huddled in a far corner, laughing and glancing suspiciously around, as though they were up to something. It looked every bit a thriving, albeit hidden, society. This display of ridiculously normal activity played out like it would in any ordinary town. Apart from the flying, the floating lights and the fact that, well, they weren't human!

"Wow!" I said.

"It is amazing, isn't it? This is the Katoika Sanctuary, a home to all. This is a place for any of our kindred who do not wish to live in the human world, and even those who do, but wish for a little respite of the soul from the madness above. It is also the chief training venue for everything from schooling our youngsters to training our military."

"You have an army?" I exclaimed.

"Indeed. The Watchers were an army, Sophia. They all volunteered for the Earth mission from various ranks from all over the universe. It was the most coveted posting of the time. If only they knew what was to come." Enl'iel sighed; melancholy shadowed her eyes, "Fortunately, all those military skills have come into their own with the never-ending war with the Daimon."

How could all this have been so very secret, right under the noses of humans? I wracked my memories, no clues… not a single recollection of this secret underground world. I followed her along a paved path around the cylindrical space and down a set of sparkling stone stairs. A number of people acknowledged us with a subtle nod, accompanied by a brief flash of their mark of A'vean. One woman embraced Enl'iel with the customary cheek-kiss as I had come to think of it. She had a small child with her who walked boldly up to me.

"You're pretty, are you a Watcher? Do you have big pterugia? What's your favourite colour?" she asked in rapid succession, in an adorable, high-pitched voice.

I knelt down, looking into her opaque eyes. Her little fingers reached out to feel the curves of my face. She squinted hard, trying to see me more clearly.

"Well now, that is a lot of questions. Let me see? My favourite colour is pink," I said, and she squealed with delight at this. "I'm not sure how big my wi… pterugia are, and if being a Watcher meant I could hang out with you, then I certainly hope I am one!" I concluded with a smile.

She squealed louder, tugged at her mother's hand, "Mama! Mama, look at the pretty lady. She wants to be my friend!" She flung herself around my neck, trying to reach up to do the cheek thing. I obliged as her little cheek, with its tiny swirls of white, emitted spurts of light that tickled my skin. My mark responded with a warm glow that smothered her face.

"Ooh, Mama, she gave me a biiig kiss!"

"Enough now, Av'ael. This is a very important guest. Please don't bother her." The mother apologised and bowed reverently. I tried to reassure her it was perfectly fine, but she grabbed Av'ael's hand and gently tugged her away. "We mustn't keep them, my sweet." The mother acknowledged me again with another swift bow, then whisked away. The little girl waved frantically as she disappeared down another staircase.

"How cute!" I waved back. "She has the second sight, too, like Eilir?" I asked.

"Yes, all Eudaimonians are born with it. It is truly an experience when we see with our eyes for the first time. The first sight is a time of great celebration. You will see a lot more of that kind of attention from the children. You are — for want of a better human term — somewhat of a celebrity!"

"Oh, no! No, I don't want that! I can't stand being the centre of attention," I complained emphatically, but Enl'iel ignored me, leading us left down another sparkling corridor. Glowing orbs flooded it with soft light every ten or so paces. An ornate sign carved into a doorway hooked my attention to my right.

Stasis, please enter and exit quietly.

A woman entered the room carrying a tray brimming with herbs and steaming liquids as we passed.

"What's in there?" I asked. My brain was full to bursting with everything new that was throwing itself at me. I wanted and needed to absorb it all, yet guilt plucked at me as I remembered the fear Jaz and Ben must be feeling. The pull was too strong though. Something urged me to know more. "May I see inside?"

"Of course, I think you will feel quite at home here, actually," Enl'iel answered with a plum look of satisfaction.

She gently pushed the door open, a finger to her lips, miming quietness. I found myself in a hospital-like room filled with small, neat beds. The familiar essence of sage, lavender, and cedar filled the air as the aromas smoked dreamily from golden lanterns hanging from the ceiling. There was no modern equipment. It was as far from my accustomed hospital ward as it could ever be. It held a Middle Ages flavour, apart from the shiny, decorative metallic sheets that served as wall coverings. They reminded me of the pressed metal ceiling in Miss Marple's.

A long, wooden preparation table dominated the centre. Mortar bowls of powders in various states of preparation adorned it. Herbs hung in abundance, drying, their pungent herbiness strong and good. Clear bottles of steeped tonics added an extra heady note. Medicines were being pounded by many people with long, herb-entwined plaits flowing down their backs. Loose white tunics adorned their tall statures, which were accented by expressions of deep and silent concentration.

A handful of sleeping bodies occupied hospital style cots.

Enl'iel touched my elbow, guided me around and explained the where we were.

"This is the room of stasis. It's a place of healing and also a safe haven for our children. All Eudaimonian children attend at some point as they pass through three stages of development called the Right of Sevens. You met dear Av'ael, who is four, and still sight impaired. At birth, we are blind, and by age seven, our eyesight has fully developed. Around the thirteenth year, we enter a natural hibernation phase for one full year as our bodies go through the metamorphic changes that bring out the gifts and powers inherited from our bloodlines. These gifts only come to fruition through a state of inertia, as it is extremely painful — something you well know. The fact that you went through this change over a matter of days is what sets you well apart from others."

My God! I didn't feel pity for myself, but relief that these children didn't have to suffer as I had. She continued with this fascinating history lesson as I listened on in silent wonder.

"Our Alchemae tend to them." She pointed to the busy men and women who moved with an ethereal beauty around the work bench. "They keep the children's mortal flesh healthy whilst they sleep. It's vitally important." Enl'iel picked up a spoon from a mixing burette;

closed her eyes and smelled it. "Lovely." Enl'iel smiled. The Alchemae smiled back and continued his work.

"Our young ones are incredibly vulnerable in this state and cannot protect themselves. Many a young Eudaimonian has been brutally picked off by Rogues and Daimon for sport in the past. That is why they all pass through this safe haven to endure the change. At twenty-one, they pass through the final transition. If they develop pterugia and any other specific skills, it will all emerge by this age. This, unfortunately, can be the most painful process; thank the heavens it is brief."

My attention hooked upon the loving attention a young girl was receiving as a woman laid moistened leaves along her inflamed spine. Small, fernlike patterns blazed across her skin, just like mine. I was glad she was unconscious for this process. I could still feel the agony of a few nights ago.

Something compelled me to move towards the rear of the room. A sheet of white, pulsing light hummed from floor to ceiling. A male passed through it several times.

"What's behind there?" I asked.

"You could say that is our Intensive Care Unit. Come." Enl'iel waved me towards it.

I followed, feeling that familiar thrum of energy reverberate through my back; I sensed a pain that wasn't mine.

As I passed through the tingly white shield of light, I gasped, covered my mouth with my hands. Prostrate upon a large bed, was Cael. Covered in sweet smelling poultices, the horrific wounds on his back were being tended by several Alchemae.

"Oh, Cael!" I whispered. I rushed to him, knelt by his side.

Surprisingly, he responded to my presence. He turned his head slowly. Heavily drugged, eyes open a fraction, a hint of gleaming blue shone through. He smiled weakly.

"Now I know I shall heal, for seeing you well," he whispered and closed his eyes.

"Will he be okay?" I choked back tears of guilt.

"He will in time; a long time. Unless he ascends," she replied and kissed Cael's head.

"Ascend?" I also kissed his head and held his hand a moment before we moved away. His life force was strong. This eased the tension coiling in my belly.

"Like my dear Brennan, Cael's wings were partly ripped from him, leaving his mortal body gravely ill. He can recover, but it may take years. Ten, twenty, or even hundreds, like Brennan. Or, if he so chooses, he can ascend his spirit and leave his mortal body behind, like Andr'eal," she explained.

"You mean die?" I grasped my mouth in shock, felt a wave of dizziness pass through my head.

"No, Sophia. We are immortal spirits. We can exist consciously without an organic body. Cael would simply move to the Cavern of Souls and await the time of rapture. The very same rapture that you will hopefully bring about for us, sooner rather than later. You may visit with him anytime, if you wish. I sense it has already restored some of his strength to see you so well. Now it is time to meet with Koi. Now that you are known and awakened, we have such little time. Time is now a precious commodity we dare not toy with. Despite your fatigue, you must begin your training immediately."

Chapter
Thirty-Three

Belial took his punishment with the honour and bravery that any soldier of worth would. He was beaten almost to the point of descendance into the pits of Hell. Any thoughts of a mortal death releasing him to the peace of the Sanctuary of Souls were long ago lost. He was a hair-breadth away from joining the A'vean filth that lived below the cracked Empyrean earth, alongside the human garbage.

Plum blood poured from his split lips and swollen eyes. His wings were dull, and a horn had cracked painfully in half.

"You have betrayed us with your failures. You could have proceeded without his permission! You are pure-born after all, Belial! Do you not have your own mind? You committed yourself to us, yet so often return with the pathetic excuses of failure." Yeqon blasted him once more with a lava-hot crack of light. The blow finally brought Belial to his knees.

"How did you fail? How?" Yeqon screamed, inches from his face. Spittle sprayed Belial's skin. He winced. He resented that deeply.

"She was awakening before you! The portal to us was open. You allowed someone to destroy your mortal vessel!" Yeqon's fingers tightened around Belial's neck. The strain of anger drained all the beauty from Yeqon. He was as ugly on the outside as his blackened heart in that moment.

"Master..." Belial breathed raggedly, the veins in his face bulged. "I... was betrayed... someone... works... against us," he coughed.

"Excuses, excuses." Yeqon squeezed harder, enjoying the flare of Belial's nose, the redness of his skin. "Meanwhile, another eternity drags by while we rot here. What was Nik'ael doing? Didn't you have a plan, Belial?"

"Yes, M-Master Yeqon," Belial coughed and spluttered as Yeqon eased his hand slightly, "He cleared the house for me... but I think Nik'ael may have changed the plan."

"Liar!" Yeqon knew of Nik'ael's own ideas. He pressed Belial hard to test him, to dig out anything Nik'ael may have failed to divulge. He needed the release of a decent fight, and Belial was an easy target. His brothers were lathering on the pressure. Yeqon needed to appear in control.

"You failed. There is no other explanation. You had her in your grasp, Belial. Either way, you should have brought her to me! Be damned Nik'ael's other ideas!" Yeqon threw Belial to the ground, at the feet of the other four imposing figures. "I grow weary of Nik'ael's procrastinating. No more. We attack now. We will hunt them down, wear them out, until their blood pours such that we could sail the Earth upon it!"

Yeqon's spies had informed him that the girl had been taken into hiding for training. Despite Nik'ael's arguments, Yeqon believed that she would become too strong, too quickly, after much heated discussion with his brothers. This latest failure tipped Yeqon over the edge. Lashing out like this showed that he was under pressure to maintain control. He appeared weak, and weakness meant vulnerability.

"Pineme, summon Nik'ael. He is to cease his mission and join us immediately. I want that wench brought in. She will not resist us once we have her in our possession. I'll enter that filthy Earthen realm myself if need be!" Yeqon spat at the thought; his spittle sizzled on the scorched ground. "Clearly, we cannot rely on anyone other than ourselves to discharge that which has been commanded. As for you, Belial, you shall have time to think about your insufficiencies. You should have overcome her. Despite everything, she should be at my feet this very moment. A little stay in the Pits should clear your mind whilst you heal." Yeqon smiled vindictively.

"No! Please, no!" Belial was shamed by such begging, though he persisted whilst on his knees; a pathetic dog.

No discussion was entered into. The red glow of Yeqon's trident split the ground, opening a great chasm. Piercing screams erupted into the humid air. Yeqon laughed with pleasure at the display. The others joined in his amusement, stamping their feet and weapons on the ground rhythmically, chanting foul curses at the beleaguered Belial.

Belial begged one last time. "Please… not there?" He looked up into their chiselled faces as he clawed at the ground. The broken horn fell from his head, blood pooled in the shell of his ear. They were enjoying his suffering, whilst Yeqon asserted his power before them. Scum, they were nothing more. How stupid he had been to join them. He was done with them. They would rue the day they cursed him to the Pits.

"Join your equals in the bowels of the Pits. You may learn something there," Yeqon bellowed.

Unceremoniously, Belial was shoved with various weapons by the Five into the chasm. Belial fell, joining the six hundred and sixty-six tortured, yet obedient, demonic A'vean souls. He fell far and deep, the screams of the imprisoned Daimon army more painful than any corporeal beating.

Chapter
Thirty-Four

Smooth, gemstone-dotted corridors led us deeper into the subterranean labyrinth. The smell of peppermint, and a door slightly ajar, made me double back. I followed my senses through the heavy wooden door and to be met with the sight of that dragon-tattooed arm holding up a Darkest Goth mag. The slop-slap of chewing accompanied the quick flicking of pages.

"Jaz!" I ran to her, "Are you okay?" I threw my arms around her.

She pulled back, threw a Mentos my way, which I playfully caught in my mouth. We both laughed.

"Finally, she makes an entrance." Jaz quirked a brow, looking me up and down.

I smiled; sheepish, "Sorry…are you alright?"

"Despite feeling like I'm buried alive and confined unless '*safely escorted*' by my glowing guard…" Jaz eyeballed the handsome, but silent sentry standing by the doorway, "I suppose you could say I'm living the life! They feed me, albeit vegetable slop, and bring me trashy mags." Jaz fanned the magazine at me, "And… would you believe there's even a flat screen in this place?" She pointed to a wall. "Gotta be possessed! No electrical connections! Not a cord in sight! Ha!" Jaz nodded, impressed.

A slim screen glowed on the wall. How, I had no clue. Dr Phil played quietly in the background. It was her favourite show. She loved the *'screwballs'* who made her feel *'somewhat normal'*… her words, not mine. I wondered how normal she was feeling right now?

A quick look around showed me she was decked out very comfortably. Despite the bare earth walls, colourful floor rugs, various furniture and a huge, four-poster bed lent a cosy feel to the place.

"How wasted is that baby?" Jaz saw me eyeing luxurious linen on the bed.

"Jaz! You're appalling!"

"I know, it's a talent!" She winked her long lashes in my direction.

"So, how are you, angel-girl?" Jaz looked me up and down as though she might find alien antennas.

"I suppose I'm okay. I'm alive, aren't I?" Nerves pulled at my smile. She seemed to be waiting for more. My thumbs circled each other. I bit my lip. *What the hell could I say?* Then I looked up sharply, a spark of joy in a moment of immense uncertainty. "Found Cael! He's here, alive. Not in the best shape, but alive!"

"Really?" Jaz sat bolt upright, leaned her chin on her hands, "I so thought he was a dead man. Can I see him?" She eyed the door, "Be nice to stretch my legs, even with Mr Personality over there tailing me."

"I'll take you when I can. That's all right, isn't it, Enl'iel?" I asked, feeling her energy hanging heavily over my shoulder, anxious to get going.

"Yes, dear, that will be fine," Enl'iel answered. Jaz eyed her suspiciously up and down as well.

"Where's Ben?" I asked Jaz. I felt like I'd been asking that question incessantly. Jaz threw her mag down and took a sip of water.

"He's next door, and luckily for him, he has that hunky Jude dude as his personal bodyguard slash jailer — whatever they want to call it. He's taken him out for a bit of bro-mancing or something. He's next level shitty at the moment." She waved her hand dismissively. "Gone to blow off some steam or something. Might pull his fat head in an inch or two!" Jaz saw the look on my face. "Don't take it personally — he's barely talking to me, either."

"I'm sorry. It's all my fault."

"Your fault? His smart-arse attitude is his own problem. Don't waste a neuron on him Soph." She popped another mint in her mouth. "You reckon he likes peppermint?" Jaz nodded at the guard. I shook my head at her impressive ability to bounce back to her predatory man hunting.

"Okay, okay. Enough now, you two can socialise later at first meal." Enl'iel scooped an arm around my shoulders. "Sophia, must have her initial training with Koi. He is waiting." She urged me back to the door, one eye on Jaz. "Jasmine, please, behave like a young lady?" Despite Enl'iel's stern brow, I didn't miss the slight upturn of her mouth. We left the room with Jaz staring at me, her smart-arsed look gone, a hollow, pale worry replacing it.

After a short walk and a spiral staircase deeper into the Earth, I found myself inside what can only be described as the largest gym I'd ever seen. To be honest, I hadn't seen many, but I was sure this was outta the ball park huge. The gym was crammed full of weights, hessian punching bags, and running tracks. Metallic walls gleamed with medieval-style golden and silver weapons. They neatly adorned the walls in descending order of size and nastiness. There was nothing modern in sight. Impressive pieces of body armour hung majestically amongst the cache as well. It could have been a training stadium for an ancient Olympic game tournament, without the nude athletes. Jaz surely would've preferred it that way, though.

A number of people were present, the first of whom I noticed were Jude and Ben. His head snapped up in my direction the moment I walked in. It felt like a siren went off whenever I entered a room. Apparently, I couldn't make a discreet entrance. After a whispered word through clenched teeth by Jude, Ben nodded my way in an uncomfortable acknowledgment, then turned his back and pounded mercilessly into the innocent sack in front of him.

Koi manifested into physical form right in front of me with a pop of light, giving me a fright. Enl'iel took her leave, promising to pick me up later. She pecked at my cheek, the way she did when she was just my Nan. The lingering aroma of English breakfast tea hung in the air briefly after she was gone.

"Sophia, it is an honour to begin your training." Koi bowed.

I did a wobbly bow too, feeling all levels of awkward.

"No, no. You do not bow to me." He smiled and guided me along.

"Foremost, I wish you to know that this shall not come easily. Your mind must be equally as strong as your body." Koi tapped his temple. "Clarity clears the body for strength and growth. You must move thoughtfully with your mind, not with the emotion of your heart. I was taught this concept eons ago, when I was a young Seraph, like so many of us here. Fighting through the many worlds of the universe to maintain peace and order, this mantra guides us through many a challenge. I wish you to repeat it often, embed the thought into your deepest self."

His words resonated with the warning from the vision of Enoch and I'el.

Beware my heart.

Koi clapped away the moment, startling me again as I digested his speech.

"Please?" He pointed to a neat pile of white clothing on a bench by the wall. "Change into your training attire, and we shall begin."

I did so in a small bathroom hewn from rock, alongside a row of natural spring showers. The steam of someone else showering clouded the air with a mineral, earthy tang.

I met Koi back in the arena wearing the white karate-style pants and a white t-shirt with a gap in the back. Heavy, comfy black combat boots replaced my Docs and had me looking half cadet, half ninja. I was painfully aware of Ben's eyes boring into me from behind, but I resisted the urge to look back. Jude's tone was getting louder and more impatient as he yelled Ben through whatever they were doing.

"Now, we shall begin." Koi picked up my right arm and palpated the lack of muscle. His brow quirked, as though the challenge was painfully obvious. "Your body has been neglected and unchallenged in your human life. Your recent transition will have left you in a physical aftershock. We must enhance your physical strength, alongside harnessing your elemental power. A little training every day, and you will be surprised by your own potential. You won't know yourself within the week." Koi let my arm drop.

"Finally, in time, the fun part — weapons!" Koi clapped his hands.

There was a gleam in his eye which suggested this just might be his favourite part of training… and whatever it was that he actually did as a Seraph… Watcher… angel… God my head hurt.

We began with a gentle jog around the perimeter to warm up. Ben's stare was a heavy blanket. But each time I lapped past him, he looked the other way.

Why did it matter to me so much?

My love of jogging paid off with Koi being very impressed that I kept a steady pace with him. We completed five laps of the track that was marked out by neatly recessed white stones. Koi rewarded me with a smile, a handful of almonds, and a refreshing mug of minted water. Some weight training followed the run. At first, I balked at the dumbbells placed at my feet. They seemed too heavy for my lanky arms. Koi had just made a point of it.

"Just think of them as cotton buds. That's all they are to you."

"Your faith is way too easily given, Koi." I stretched my arms in preparation, feeling utterly ridiculous.

"I give none of myself unless it is fully deserved. Trust in yourself, and try."

"Okay, but don't laugh when literally nothing happens." I shook my arms out. They felt like jelly. I felt the pressure of strangers watching me. I wanted to run and hide… but there was no chance that was going to be tolerated.

Deep breath in, deep breath out, repeat.

I bent my knees, keeping my back straight, as Koi had shown me. My hands locked around the weights. I faltered when I saw 40 kilograms engraved on each one.

"Uh, no way!"

"Cotton buds!" Koi reminded me.

Cotton buds! Sure thing.

I closed my eyes and felt like an idiot. Then forced myself to imagine cotton buds. Big, heavy, metallic cotton buds. I yanked hard. Nothing but an embarrassing grunt happened.

"Shouldn't I try something just a little lighter first?"

"For what purpose? To convince yourself that you are capable of less? No. Pick them up, now," Koi scoffed.

My jaw dropped in disbelief. I received no sympathy. I was going to look like a fool.

I took a deep breath and couldn't resist a quick look around. I was sure there was a whole crowd waiting for a good laugh. There wasn't, and luckily, Ben seemed to have disappeared along with Jude. Metal clanged somewhere, but I couldn't see anyone.

I gripped again and tried really hard.

Cotton buds, cotton buds, cotton buds.

I pulled up, felt nothing. About to complain again; Koi clapped.

"Ah, there you are. Welcome to your new life, Sophia."

I opened my eyes to see that my arms were well above my head, with a weight suspended in each. It was as though they were feather dusters — practically weightless. Cotton buds!

"Holy crap! Sorry, I mean, how did I do that?" I set the weights down and turned my hands over, looking at them for evidence of this amazing strength.

"It is the elemental power that courses through you. You are able to displace mass with a thought and energy surge." Koi smiled as though proud of me.

This weight session continued for some time until Koi sensed fatigue creeping upon me.

"Here, drink. Rest a moment."

Before I was at all ready, he was preparing for more.

"Now, let's actually work." A subtle smile softened his seriousness. "It's all very well and good to be strong and able to run, but what if you are running *from* something? What if something powerful and extremely fast was chasing you down?" he asked.

My body tensed; what would be chasing me down?

"Whilst you are so green, you must practise the defensive rather than the offensive. Are you ready to test those running skills?" Koi clicked his fingers. A red orb appeared with a sizzling crack. It hovered above him, malevolently humming and pulsing. I took a step backwards.

"This is a training orb. It will help you run faster, become stronger and nimbler. Your reflexes will be honed. I want you to run again, but do not let the orb catch you. I will count to three and then release it. Now, run!"

I didn't question him, as the orb seemed to spring to life. It pulsed a brighter red and seemed only to stay still because Koi's palm coaxed it into submission. I ran. Within seconds, a sharp sting struck my back. The orb was attacking me. I glanced back to see it weaving around the room, emitting horrid stinging pulses in my direction. I pounded the ground as hard as I could, but the evil thing was too fast.

"Run harder, Sophia! Think quickly, outmanoeuvre it!" Koi yelled from the distance. I ran harder, glancing back only to check its position. My breathing was labouring with the panic of this new, unknown entity in Weirdville. It zipped around me, zapping like a possessed lightning bolt. I only went a couple hundred meters before it tripped me up and I fell to the ground, exhausted and bruised. It hovered above me momentarily before gliding back to Koi, who approached casually.

"What... the hell... was that?" I half yelled, trying to catch my breath. I was irritated. I didn't realise I was going to get electrocuted. Koi offered me a hand up; I brushed him away and got up myself, rubbing at my sore arms and legs. I noticed Jude and Ben in the distance at the mouth of a doorway. Ben was staring at me openly until Jude unceremoniously shoved him out the door. It seemed Ben had met his match in brooding attitude and brute force.

Koi pulled my attention from the doorway. "Not impressive, yet neither disappointing."

"I assume that's a compliment?" I was even more annoyed. "Is that it? Is that what I have to do to train? Learn to run?"

"In part, for now. You will know when I am pleased." He turned his back and conjured more of the orbs. They danced around above him in a smooth synchronicity.

"This, Sophia, is just the beginning. When you are confronted by Rogues, as you are all too aware, they will be fast and merciless. If you come across a Daimon, speed, strength, and cunning are the least you will need until you can control your elemental power. I will bolster these strengths so that you may have at least a modest ability to protect yourself. Your training will be intense. There is little time before the Unseen and their foul hordes make their move. Your identity is known by the Daimon, your location will now be priority number one. Your safety will be near impossible to guarantee if you are unable, at the very minimum, to outrun an attack. This is why the orbs are an unpleasant necessity." Koi inclined his head, as though in apology.

I digested this for a moment, muscles clenched; fear and stubbornness had a quiet argument in my mind before I nodded to him. I dusted myself off and readied myself to continue.

For the next hour or so, I ran and dodged those horrid red devils. I was sure that they actually enjoyed it. Finally, Koi gave me a reprieve and sent me to shower and change. I was dripping with sweat and aching in places I didn't know I had. The shower was bliss. My skin a canvas of purple bruising, a surreal artwork of pain. Someone thoughtfully left a handmade lavender soap for me, just like back home. The aroma was familiar and comforting. I found a change of clothes awaiting me when I emerged. It was one of the soft, white linen outfits that most of the Eudaimonians and Watchers seemed to wear. It was comfy and loose. The outfit was less karate and more yoga retreat. Jaz would surely give me hell when she saw me wearing it.

First meal' was how they referred to brunch. Breakfast was more of a room service affair. I liked that idea a lot. At first meal, I sat with Koi in a massive hall on the highest level of the sanctuary. Whilst he ate in quiet contemplation, I studied those around me.

People were coming and going from the buffet-style line. Eilir fussed around over what to serve and when, slapped the hands of her young apprentices when they put things in the wrong places. Enl'iel sat at the far end of the large table with Brennan. They waved and smiled my way. Day by day, my hunger had grown to the point that I filled my plate with an enormous mound of roasted vegetables. The physical changes of my awakening must have sapped my energy, because I never quite felt satisfied and was constantly looking for the next snack. I noted with relief, though, that everyone else seemed to have large portions, too. I immediately felt somewhat more connected to them. As I was sticky-nosing at others, I noticed Ben sitting with Jude and Jaz a few tables away. While every pair of eyes in that room peered secretly and sheepishly at me, the one pair that I wanted to look at me didn't. It was killing me. My desperation to attain Ben's acknowledgement was consuming me. I needed to reconcile this unknown animosity oozing from him.

"How are you enjoying your meal, sweet girl?" I started as Eilir appeared out of nowhere. She piled delicious, freshly baked rolls in front of me.

"It's delicious, thank you. How in the world do you cater for all of these people?"

"Oh me, child, it's been many a year of practice, and a few good clips around the ears to the other cooks! I run a tight ship!" Eilir beamed; a twinkle of pride in her dull eyes as she waddled away to chastise some poor kid.

"Well, aren't we Miss Popularity!" Jaz slipped in next to me. "Seriously though, do you have any sway on getting a steak down here? Do they all eat like you?" She grimaced at the carrot on her fork.

I laughed and elbowed her. Jaz was a balm that soothed my worries and kept me grounded. She, on the other hand, hid all of hers.

"Sorry, but I think you're just going to have to force that down," I said with a smile.

"Hmph! And you think *you're* having a hard time!" Jaz shoved some cucumber around with her fork as though it were a piece of poison. Irreverence was her calling card. I was about to ask her about Ben again, when to my utter disappointment, Koi interrupted.

"And now it's time for session two," he announced with an amused smile. He stood, waiting for me to follow, as he greeted Brennan and a new guy as they approached our table. I'd just crossed the globe, taken a beating this morning, and they wanted a second torture session on day one. My look of appeal to Enl'iel down the other end was met with a sympathetic smile, but no intervention.

"See you later, Jaz." I sighed deeply, forced my aching muscles up.

"Not if I see you first. Be careful, Soph," she answered as Jude breezed silently by and took her back to Ben, who was also getting up to leave. Ben actually looked my way, so I waved tentatively. His jaw clenched, but he forced out a strained smile before they left together. Why bother? I thought. Fake affection seemed worse than being ignored.

I followed Koi back downstairs reluctantly, stopped him at all points of interest along the way to ask a myriad of questions, trying to delay the inevitable. Eventually, we were back in the arena. *Damn!*

"This afternoon, we are going to focus on your elementals." Koi rearranged my top, which was apparently not sitting right. "You must keep your back clear, to avoid singeing too many outfits. Eilir is the resident seamstress too, you know. Even I fear her if I've not taken appropriate care of her '*hard and endless work*,' as she likes to put it." He raised his eyebrows in mock fear of Eilir's apparent drill sergeant wrath.

The clothing's clever design allowed the ferny leaflets to be free, enabling the pterugia to emerge unhindered. It was mainly a concern for the women though, as barely any male ever seemed to wear a shirt. This was somewhat distracting, if I'm being honest. As we walked and I was thinking on this pulse-quickening topic, I noticed on Koi's left shoulder a collection of perfectly straight white lines; a barcode of scars. Brennan and the new guy breezed past us and I noted that they too had these same straight markings in the same place, just less of them.

"Calm yourself Sophia." Koi placed a hand upon my shoulder. "I feel your anxiety. It is your mind we are exercising this time, not your flesh." He smiled more broadly and clapped his hands together with anticipation. We entered a new room off the main arena.

I found myself in a very different space. It was devoid of anything other than a single, large white orb floating in the centre of the room.

"You now have the honour of being in the room of Enlightenment. Eudaimonian children who are so gifted, learn to use their elemental powers here from age fifteen. At twenty-one, if they develop pterugia, they will learn the power of flight in safety and under strict guidance. I regret that you must learn so intensely and quickly, but that is a matter simply out of our hands."

"She'll be fine Koi. I've seen her in action." Brennan appeared from the other side of the orb, holding both thumbs up to me. He had way too much enthusiasm.

"That remains to be seen," Koi responded dryly.

The other guy remained silent, watching me in a rather overtly uncomfortable way. Brennan seemed to notice this and elbowed him hard in the ribs. He responded with an elbow back. *Weird.* I paid them minimal attention after that, as I was drawn to the spectacle of the orb.

This orb was truly impressive. It generated an energy that left a tangible and visible static in the air. Just like back at the library when it was full of people, there were wisps of multi-coloured current snapping and twisting faintly above me. I felt my heart instinctively match its rhythmic pulsations.

"Sophia, Brennan will instruct you with your elemental powers. He is one of our most skilled with the orbs. His mastery of the power of E'lan is universally acknowledged. Indeed, you have witnessed his abilities already." Koi waved Brennan closer. "I will merely be here to observe."

"Can't believe you're finally here, Soph. You're going to love this." Brennan smiled his cheeky, boyish smile. He was annoyingly infectious. He pointed over his shoulder, "This mother of an orb will help you learn how to control the elements, so that you can draw and repel the E'lan around you at will. So far, you've just reacted reflexively. Impressive, but not enough to cut it in the real world of the Daimon. This orb will teach you conscious control of that power. Had you been born on A'vean, this would have been as instinctual for you as it is to us. Watchers come into existence with full knowledge, while the

Eudaimonia must be taught. I actually taught Enl'iel many years ago. She was a quick learner, just like you Soph. You need to be taught as though you grew up Eudaimonian. It'll be an honour to help you too, Princess." Brennan finished with an unnecessary and over-exaggerated bow. I heard Koi sigh with annoyance.

The other guy spoke up unexpectedly, breaking his brooding appraisal of me. I'd noticed he'd been checking me out. It didn't really feel flattering the way he squinted his eyes as he glared in my direction. His arms were tightly crossed.

"She must be trained efficiently and quickly Brennan. The militia are reporting more Rogues daily. The Daimon are ramping up infiltrations across the continents. There's no time to waste." he unwound his arms, stepped closer.

"Sophia, I'm Lorcan, First Lieutenant of the 1st Seraph Legion and brother to this smart mouth!" Lorcan playfully punched Brennan in the shoulder, acceding a half smile.

Okay.

I offered my hand to shake his, just as he bent in to do the kiss-thing, causing us to bump heads awkwardly. It was a rather embarrassing exchange.

"Sorry… hi," I stumbled my words and edged back.

"Oh, um, sorry, hi. Yeah, um, I know you're just getting used to our customs." Lorcan seemed equally embarrassed as a flush of scarlet hit his cheeks.

"Still great with the ladies there, I see, bro!" Brennan teased.

"Shove your pterugia up your…"

"Manners! You are representatives of A'vean and the great council. Act as such!" Koi chided.

They were both as human as any two brothers. I was in Wonderland. My world was a contradiction. I just hoped I didn't meet the Queen of Hearts anytime soon.

"Let's move on." Koi threw a shot of energy at the feet of the brothers who were jostling and mouthing rude remarks to each other. "Enough you two. Begin!"

Brennan and Lorcan pulled themselves together quickly after the scolding and took on a more adult air. Brennan began.

"Okay Soph, the aim of this exercise is to look into the energy orb, to acknowledge its power, to feel it, to understand it, and invite it into you. Sounds poxy, I know, but trust me, you'll understand what I mean soon enough. Don't be scared, it can't harm you. You and the orb are essentially the same—both made of the purest form of energy. You just happen to be prettier!"

"Brennan!" Koi grumped. Lorcan laughed to himself. I was just standing there, an open-mouthed prisoner to their banter.

"Alright, alright! Just trying to chill the tension, Koi. Calm down!" Brennan raised his hands in mock defence. Koi turned his back and moved a few paces away; I assume to refrain from zapping them with more fervour this time.

"Anyway, as you learn Soph, this will all become easier and more natural, until you barely even need to form a thought. The connection will be instant." Brennan concluded his less than polished intro to *How to be an Angel 101*.

"Okay, sounds less painful than this morning. How do I start?" I asked, immediately determined to make a better impression than on the running track.

"First, relax your mind. Calm your breathing and let your thoughts melt away. Close your eyes, feel nothing but the energy, just like when you heal someone," Brennan instructed.

I obliged.

"Okay. Wow! I can actually feel it. It's strong and really hot," I answered immediately, as my back began to warm, my skin to tingle.

"I think she's talking about me!" Brennan quipped to Lorcan.

"Belt up, bro!" Lorcan barely contained his laughter.

"What the hell?" I opened my eyes, losing the connection, to glare angrily at them.

"You are both asking for a one-way ticket to Jude," Koi snapped.

They both raised their eye brows in feigned fear, then apologised.

"Sorry Koi, sorry Soph," they said in unison.

"I can see why you idiots got yourselves in all this trouble!" I gave them my best dirty look.

"It's been a long time in hiding, drowning in boredom Soph. Sorry. This is actually very serious. I'm just letting off some steam. Come on. Let's get on with it then. Go on, try again." Brennan had a fairly convincing expression of deep concentration now. I relaxed a little and tried again.

"Okay, I can feel the energy again." It almost had a smell to it, a sharp, clean tang. I breathed it in. "What do I do now? It's really intense. It feels so different to before, back at home, I mean."

"It should feel different. Your body is now more attune to the pulse of the universe, so you should feel it potently within your whole body, not just your hands. You are the elements, Soph. Listen closely, your heart should beat in rhythm with the pulsations," Brennan said, a more serious edge to his voice.

Again, that was easy, since it had already happened the very moment I'd entered the room. My confidence was brimming. I nodded silently to him.

"Now, imagine that you are reaching your hand out, grasping at the light, pulling it into you."

I did this… well, I tried. Within a split second, something flung me backwards to the ground, with my legs in the air. My face was hot with embarrassment, again.

"I thought this wasn't going to be painful?" I grumbled as I dusted myself off again.

"Told you, brother, she may be the great Earth-born angel, but man, that human world has screwed her up like a pretzel!" Lorcan laughed at me.

"What the hell?" I snapped, unusual for me, but I'd just had enough of these two.

"Shut the hell up, you don't know me! You don't know what I've been through. Give me a break, will you?" This Lorcan guy completely pissed me off. "If you're here to help, then help me! Otherwise, just get out!" I pointed sharply to the doorway and a small crack of light sputtered out of my fingers, as the A'vean mark singed my face with a burning anger.

"Ah, thank you, Lorcan. You have at least been of use in something. Hmmm…" Koi still eyed Lorcan and Brennan up and down, disapprovingly.

"You have proven my suspicion to be correct," Koi said.

I looked at him, confused. "What?"

"Apologies, Sophia. I asked Lorcan to rile you. It is a skill he is proficient at. As is his brother."

Lorcan muttered a whispered profanity, but then high-fived Brennan. I gaped at both of them, prepared to punch them out happily.

"I was worried that it was anger which drove you, and so it is. Remember, we must use our minds, not our hearts. You have much control to learn. I felt your anger in the scroll chamber just before your pterugia emerged," Koi explained.

"I was thinking of Esme. It seemed to help when I couldn't make anything happen," I answered.

"Indeed, we all have struggled with this at some point, particularly after loss. However, we can work with this. We just need to channel that passion in a more controlled way. Please forgive Lorcan. He did not mean any ill intent.

I looked at the annoyingly gorgeous Watcher. "Sorry for yelling at you," I said, rather half-heartedly. Their earlier juvenile behaviour still irritated me.

Lorcan shrugged, as though it was nothing. That angered me just as much. He offered a handshake, which I begrudgingly took. I didn't understand myself at the moment. I was never one to harbour anger, hold a grudge, or have a temper. That was the sole talent of Jaz. I was Sophia, the compassionate nurse of comfort and ease. Not right now, though.

Sensing my confusion and feelings of failure, Koi took my hand in his.

"Come now, you have been thrust into a new and dangerous world, one that must seem something akin to a nightmare. All in such a brief time, too. Despite us pressing the need for expediency that your awakening has brought forth; you must not be harsh on yourself. We all have weaknesses that sometimes surprise us. Look at these two, for instance." Koi pointed to the brothers, who looked up with surprise. "Eons of experience and still little more than children at times!"

Annoyed grumbles erupted momentarily from the brothers, but they then kept a self-preserving silence.

"Insight is your greatest power, as with it you can address and overcome all such deficiencies. Now that you know this weakness exists, we can build on your strengths to harness the elements," Koi said.

After the shaky start, we practiced a while longer. Brennan and Lorcan snapped out of their ridiculous behaviour under Koi's strict watch and pushed me to the limit. I was grilled over and over until I could stand my ground with the orb and take in at least a little of its power without an immediate kickback onto my butt. All but once I was thrown to the dusty ground at some point. I could, however, feel the connection grow each time. It felt a little less forced with every new attempt. I could feel my body wanting to draw in the power. It was believing it with my human-bred sense of reality that was the problem. The fact that I could feel my body wanting to respond soothed my bruised ego somewhat.

This little routine played out for the next three days. I slept, ate, and trained. I barely saw Jaz. Ben was a ghost. I visited with Cael, who was growing increasingly more lucid. On the fourth morning, after a particularly punishing session with the nasty red orbs, Lorcan appeared.

"He's here for you."

"Who?" I asked as I towelled down.

"Gedz'iel." The worried look in Lorcan's eyes wasn't reassuring.

Gedz'iel was early. I wasn't ready.

But it was time to open the scroll.

Thirty-Five

The shadowed figure lurked outside of the church in the cool, dusk air. The evening light hid him well enough amongst the barren trees. A light drizzle cooled his temper somewhat. The call in the recesses of his mind was driving him mad. It had begun hours ago, as a distant summons. Now it was a harrowing scream, laced with threats, beckoning him to return to the Empyrean realm immediately. He ignored it, and the throbbing headache it gave him. He was done. They were backing out of the plan of attack—he knew it. Yeqon was so power-hungry these days that he made decisions based on clawing the kingship into his grasp, rather than what was actually the right path to take for their mission. He knew he could only ignore them for so long before he was tracked down. This was an enormous risk, but he had to take it. His discovery was epic—he couldn't abandon it just to bolster Yeqon's gluttonous stupidity. He couldn't believe he'd finally found the hub of their world. They'd known it was in the Northern Hemisphere, near the ancient dead portals, but they had been hunted away ferociously, always outnumbered. Yeqon and the others were holding onto the six hundred and sixty-six worst of their kind for the right moment. Yeqon had stolen them from Tartarus before the portals were destroyed and kept them subdued, waiting until the time was right. They did not want to risk a crushing loss with a hurried misstep.

Nik'ael had managed to follow her covertly. He stayed only as close as he dared. Her power drew him in, like a moth to a flame. He could be as blind as that old Welsh woman in the main house and still find Sophia. She lit up the air around her with an aura that he'd never seen before. Of all the Watchers he'd known, never had he seen such beauty or felt such power. The colours and warmth and purity that surrounded her made him tense to where he needed to lash out, to strangle the life out of something, just to release the stress. The fracture in his hand reminded him of the need to control himself. Self-inflicted pain was a representation of all that he'd lost. The other beauty that had once been ripped from his heart.

It was harder now to stay concealed. The militia were everywhere, always on guard. Back in Australia, their obscurity at the tail end of the globe gave them a false sense of security. Here, though, it was as fortified as any place could be. It was dangerous to put out a call for backup. He'd have to ride it out until he could get himself close enough to find the kind of information that would make taking her worth it. He might be forced to use other means to support his one Daimon army. Despite what Yeqon claimed and demanded, if they took her before she knew enough, it would all be pointless. Yeqon was too stupid to understand this nuance. He was a murderous thug with little brains and too much power. Who was he to judge, though?

Nik'ael again rubbed at the bracelet. It was well worn now. Some of the beads were half the size of when Neren'iel had made it, so impossibly long ago. Shame crashed through him like a tidal wave. He had betrayed his long-dead wife in more than one way. What he'd turned into, and these endless thoughts. The longing thoughts of the Earth-born that he could not seem to repress. What would Neren'iel think of what he'd become? He already knew. The thought of what he had become would repulse and horrify her. He had shamed her memory through his every action. She would have forgiven her transgressors, whereas he could not. For a moment, he let his guard down and drew away, down to the small river. He let his true form emerge. It was a relief, like taking off ill-fitting clothes and slipping into comfortable ones.

He rubbed again at the bracelet. Counting the twenty-one brown cedar beads eased him somewhat. The itchy rash the cedar now gave him was annoying. As the allergy grew, he knew it to be a barometer of his darkness. She had given it to him when his final Right had come to completion. Twenty-one beads for twenty-one years of growth and knowledge. He remembered the celebration. The whole village had put on a massive feast, as was custom for the twenty-first year, no matter what powers emerged. The Eloi council had observed the ceremony, which was also customary. Back then, they were all equal—all family. That was until the slaughter at the hands of their own. Instantly, his anger seethed out of hibernation. His head ached, and he cracked his knuckles until every last one popped loudly enough to scare the birds from the tree he hid within. It hurt, but also soothed him at the same time. The Avon River rushed wild and cold below, as did his heart.

The Earth-born was going to allow him to avenge those ancient atrocities. To avenge Neren'iel's murder. Despite what she would think of him, this had always been his single aim—to avenge her death. At what cost, though? His eternal soul, no doubt. He would end up in the pits of Tartarus. He knew that. The spiral went so deep, there was no way out now.

Damn them. Damn her. He clenched his fists and returned to his previous form. He was going to have to be extra careful now. Those around her would fight to the death to protect her. Let them. He could handle that. The thought of her death irritated him. Suddenly, it was an unpalatable thought. In the back of his mind, he was wondering how he could avoid that. Could he get from her what he needed without killing her? "Ahhh!" He banged at his head with clenched fists. He felt like he was going insane. Her blood was necessary, and he needed revenge. Yet her face haunted his dreams. What was happening to him? The wind blew hard, and a small chirp sounded beside him. He grabbed at the bird that landed too close and squeezed the life from it. There. That felt better.

Chapter
Thirty-Six

I wore no shoes as seemed the custom, unless you were training. I showered quickly after being summoned. Enl'iel met me in the change room, dressed in a more formal version of the standard outfit. Golden swirls tastefully adorned the cowl neck of the top.

The cut of the fabric was just that bit sharper, the white more intense. Enl'iel's hair flowed luxuriously down her back, daintily entwined with a multitude of herbs. She was breathtaking, and as angelic as anyone could look. She swiftly healed the extensive bruising along my arms before passing me a matching version of her outfit.

"We do not dwell so much on fashion, but do adhere to some small tokens of formality when we have a meeting of importance. It is a small show of respect for our heritage," she answered my unspoken question. My outfit bore the same golden embroidered swirls but had a little extra bling with a few clear gemstones woven through the gold. She must have seen my eyes gleam at the beauty of it. "That was Eilir's special touch, just for you." Enl'iel smiled, "She is a sweet soul."

The door opened and two Alchemae healers entered, baskets brimming with all things foliage. The females silently and expertly braided my hair with sweet-smelling flowers and oils making me feel so pretty that I was left wondering where the ball was.

The walk down to meet Gedz'iel after my lengthy day of endurance was exhausting. The journey was so deep into the Earth that a set of orbs followed us to light the way through pitch-black corridors. The walls eventually became plain packed dirt. The metallic lining had stopped many stories back. I'd stopped counting after descending the tenth flight of stairs. It would've been quite handy to have gotten a handle on the flying trick already.

Brennan had caught up with us and echoed my thought out loud about halfway down.

"Get those wings out and start flapping, Princess. You're a proper angel now. I don't like breaking a sweat like a human with all of this walking. It's not good for my pores!"

"You're such a tease, Brennan. Get on ahead and see if they are ready," scoffed Enl'iel playfully.

He obliged by springing his wings and flapping away in an instant, leaving nothing but a breeze in his wake.

We were greeted by Kea outside a set of large, dark wooden doors.

She was dressed as we were. She appeared all the more stunning with her hair piled atop her head, a crown of lavender bringing out the intensity of her blue eyes. Everyone seemed to glow from within. The beauty of their auras came from somewhere deeper than their skin and shone through.

Her demeanour seemed surprisingly more formal as she greeted us.

"Enl'iel, blessings to you. Precious Soph'ael, may the blessings of A'vean be upon you." Kea inclined her head, inviting us to enter. "Hello." It was a lacklustre effort by me, but I was in a new culture, a new place, a new world. I'd already got the feeling that there were strict protocols for behaviour in Gedz'iel's presence. I was relieved Jaz wasn't there. She'd flip the bird without a second thought. She would be the proverbial bull in a china shop.

I followed Kea through the impressive entrance, into a sort of drawing room of a forgotten era. Stiff, uncomfortable-looking furniture from a century or two ago was scattered over a myriad of Persian-looking floor rugs. A large wingback chair sat proudly behind a huge desk off to one corner. Books in the thousands lined the walls.

A stone hearth glowed brightly, lit by pulsing orbs in the place of real fire. It smelled earthy, herby, with a cosy warmth. The rest of the room was softly lit by sweetly scented candles and scattered orbs in the highest corners of the ceiling.

Sitting in that wingback chair was Gedz'iel, who looked drawn and tired. He stood immediately upon seeing me and mustered a small smile as he came forward to greet me. Five unfamiliar faces stood behind him with a calm air. They appeared all of eighteen years of age, but even I could feel the ancient energy rolling off of them.

"Good evening, Soph'ael, or as I have been informed more than once, Sophia, as you prefer to be addressed. It is pleasing to see that you have arrived safe and well. I trust you have had a taxing few days, and have already begun training, so may I first thank you for the enormous strength and show of grace you have displayed." He bowed politely. The five others behind him nodded their heads in silent agreement.

"I would like to introduce you to the Council of Eloi. They are my peers, advisors, and kindred who are here to witness the reading of the Prime Scroll. We are all here to bear witness and make assurances that not even a whisper of the contents shall fall into the hands of the Daimon." Gedz'iel motioned towards five powerfully built Watchers.

Five pairs of sparkling cerulean eyes were glued to me throughout his speech. The impressive men were dressed as Gedz'iel was; nothing but sleek white pants. They stood silently by him as he made the proper introductions.

"This is Theus, Matias, Serael, Amais, and Pathos."

As they bowed to me in turn, their white A'vean markings lit up with an unparalleled brilliance. The backdrop of their dark, earthy skin tones made the sight all the more beautiful.

I bowed in return, again not sure of the protocol.

"No, no!" Spoke the surprisingly gravelly voice of Pathos. His aged tone did not match his appearance at all.

"You do not bow to us; you honour us with your presence. We are merely here to serve and protect you, your Grace." Pathos bowed again, as did they all. The awkward flush of self-consciousness rose to my cheeks again. This was so not me.

Gedz'iel continued, "The Eloi are of the very first Watchers that were sent to the Earth. They are the last of the original influx. They lived with the first functioning humans on the African plains. Being the oldest of our kind on this planet, their penance has been long endured. For this reason, I took them into my council to guide and protect other Watchers and their offspring. You will find no greater leadership or protection than here." Gedz'iel swept his arm across to indicate the five men, "Now, time runs from us. Are you ready to open the scroll?"

"Yes… I think so. I will try my best." I really wasn't at all sure I was and struggled to find even a weak voice in the face of the task ahead of me; a task I really didn't understand. Its magnitude was well beyond me at this point. I looked back to Enl'iel for encouragement, and got it with a kiss blown from her palm in my direction.

"This is not about trying your best, Sophia. This is your birthright and destiny. Your spiritual connection to I'el alone will allow you to read that which we cannot. The words of Enoch were written strictly for your eyes only. Had they not been, we would have solved this ourselves instead of enduring such a banishment. Ours has been a curse of ignorance and the pain of abandonment. We have tirelessly protected what we do know whilst we awaited your birth," Gedz'iel said.

The glow of the orbs cast shadows across his face that brought out a different edge to him. The youthful strength gave way to a simmering anxiety beneath the surface. Gedz'iel looked almost human. His eyes were sharp and alert, burning for an end to it all.

"How long have you been waiting?" I asked.

"In excess of a hundred thousand years. Time has not moved swiftly either," he answered.

"What? That just sounds …"

"Impossible? Yes, and it has been almost impossible to endure at times," added Serael. "An eternity of nothingness eased only by sporadic wars with the Daimon," he concluded.

"So, all this time you've tried to understand clues yourselves, yet you knew even if you had a breakthrough, you still had to wait for me? That's just so cruel. Why would I'el make you suffer so much and so long?" My fingers clenched. I wanted to punch this I'el for his cruelty.

"Because our actions have caused exponentially more suffering among humans, and that is our shame," answered Pathos.

"How have you endured it? I can't imagine it at all," I said. It was incomprehensible. I found it hard to believe that I was actually awake whilst hearing this impossible story.

"To pass our time we committed to helping humanity the way we were supposed to in the beginning. We whispered in their dreams, guiding them to their own self-evolution. We pulled together what we could recall of our ancient culture as best we could and passed it on to some of the earliest developing cultures so as to preserve our own memories. The risk of losing all that we knew of ourselves the longer we were cut off from A'vean was too great. We did not know how long we would suffer or how much of our history we could retain. As you already know, beneficiaries of this knowledge were the Mycenaean culture who became the progenitors of the ancient Greeks. That is why there are so many similarities in our vocabulary. The smallest snippets of our own ancient past stay alive every time a human speaks the Greek language."

"You created the Greek culture?" I asked Pathos.

"Not quite we merely left suggestions in their subconscious. We simply embedded remnants of our knowledge into their developing culture. They lived and died under their own direction. They worshipped their own versions of Gods. They prospered and perished, paving the way for new cultures to emerge in that region. The rest, as it is said, is history." Pathos bowed his head as Gedz'iel spoke again.

"You, on the other hand, Sophia, were born with this knowledge coursing through you. You do not need to try your best. It is within you, as you have already experienced when you retrieved the Prime Scroll. Belief is all you need." Gedz'iel placed a warm hand on my shoulder, gently lifted my chin and stared intently at me, "You are not human; you are something so much greater. You must acknowledge this." He broke the intense moment as he passed me the silver chest. It immediately vibrated under my touch.

"It knows you. Answer its call. Open the chest, Sophia. I cannot, I have already tried. Please, make us wait no longer," Gedz'iel asked.

One of the five men, Theus, brought over a heavy chair and motioned for me to sit.

I settled the chest on my lap. It warmed as it continued its gentle hum. The sensation made my legs tremble. I slowly ran my hands over the pretty rectangular shape. They glowed and also began to shake. The lid swirled with fine artistry. Curls of silver engraved every surface. The edging was thick with concentric circles that seemed expertly soldered on to give the chest an ornateness that belonged somewhere palatial. As my right hand passed over a small indentation on the front, I heard a soft click. The lid popped slightly ajar, and I lifted it open. I could feel the eyes on me, the breaths that were being held. Even Gedz'iel seemed on the edge of his ancient seat.

Inside the box was a long, cylindrical tube. I picked it up gently, hoping it wouldn't disintegrate suddenly, like an ancient artefact. The heat of the bodies pressing in around me grew, as though they were at the precipice of a great moment and I was in the driver's seat.

The brown leathery tube was light and, not surprisingly, covered in swirling patterns. Unfamiliar letters scripted themselves along the swirls, which seemed to come alive as they moved across and around the tube. These words were strange to my eyes, but not to my heart, which thrashed wildly in my temples. I felt like I had been jabbed with an adrenaline needle.

I ran my fingers over one sentence and read it out loud in a careful, measured voice.

"To propomenon phugein adunation." The words fell naturally from my lips. "It is impossible to escape what is destined." The translation just blurted out of me.

I repeated the phrase quietly a few times as I continued to turn the waxy leather slowly in my hands. "It's not like you haven't tried to escape it, Soph," I quipped to myself. Across one end, a time-blackened wax seal capped the tube. On closer inspection, I was shocked to the core to see a name scrawled across it. In beautiful script was written, *Soph'ael.*

Sensing my surprise, everyone asked at once.

"What is it?" Kea and Brennan were practically breathing down my neck.

Gedz'iel knelt in front of me.

"Something troubles you. What is it?"

"No, it's nothing, it's, it's just that my name is written across the seal!" I answered. Saying it out loud seemed even more preposterous than seeing it with my own eyes. The energy in the room immediately soared. Static crackled through the air, as everyone became agitated with the anticipation of what was to come. They now knew for sure that I really was the person that they had been waiting for. I knew, for the first time, that I was who they said I was.

"Do I just…?"

"Yes, Sophia. Break the seal," Gedz'iel answered.

I tried picking at it with my stubby fingernails, but it was rock hard, and they were no match for it. I twisted and pulled at it next. No one made a sound or move to help me. This was my puzzle to solve, apparently. I ran my fingers over and over it, looking for a crack or weak spot. My intention was to avoid damaging it by being too rough. I stopped for a moment to think, fixating on what was written across the cylinder. I repeated them over and over in my mind with my eyes closed until I suddenly felt something burning me. I hadn't realised that my hands had lit up. Melted wax drizzled through my fingers and down my leg, drying instantly in little clumps on the ground.

The collective intake of breaths heightened my excitement. I did it!

I took a minute to let my hands dull and cool before I tipped the cylinder upside down, catching an aged, rolled document. I stood back up and went to pass it to Gedz'iel, but he motioned for me to open it.

"No. You alone must read it," Gedz'iel commanded.

Making my way to the desk, I slowly unravelled the delicate parchment across it. I winced at the crinkling and crackling sounds, terrified that it would rip or break apart. I pressed on though until I had beneath my hands a one-meter long document. The words on it were perfectly written in a careful hand, so neat and precise that it seemed almost impossible that someone could have done it without the aid of a printer.

"Shall I just read it out loud?" I asked.

"Please?" Gedz'iel stepped closer, the skin of our arms touching. The power rolling off him seemed to transfer to me, giving me a jolt of confidence, clearing my head instantly of the last remnants of doubt.

I glanced down at the words, and began to read.

"The Glory of A'vean shall dwell upon thee.

As I stood in awe at the foot of the great alabaster mountain, glistening among the range along the horizon, the mighty and most revered Great Lord spoke unto me of the dishonoured Watchers. It was benevolence He spoke of, unto mine ears alone, honoured and bound by veiled secrecy. 'Enoch, righteous man of men, come hither and hear mine words. Cast them to the furthest reaches of the Earth, until such time as the righteous and worthy are enabled, by purity of soul alone, to read unto themselves of the manner of their salvation from eternal torture and banishment.' Henceforth, the seven Archangels made worthless pleas for the Watchers of A'vean, for their absolution and forgiveness. The Glorious Throne thundered in rage. For a time, His wrath was wrought upon the Earth through flood and plague and ignorance for generation upon generation. The progeny of lust suffered until such time as He sought out the Council and pronounced. 'Nought have I shown mercy upon those Watchers who have henceforth disgraced and dishonoured themselves amongst man. They, who created abominations with the blood of women, have shamed all. Such as it is, suffering among them and mankind alike, has been great. The unnatural offspring have risen above their misery and flourished. So greatly and with such dignity have they endured execration that it yearns at my heart to offer absolution and peace, for are they not of my being? As they suffer in their ignorance, so do I. For unlike the Daimon, evil runs not through them like a purging fire. Thus, once more, all realms of A'vean may again be availed to Watcher and mankind alike. For such time that purity of soul and intent courses through the flesh and blood of a Watcher born of the Earth, legate of the disgraced, that the key to hence unlock the portal between Earth and A'vean will itself avail unto them.'

'The blood of truth shall open the gates. The righteous of heart and soul may emerge unto the glory of the seven mountains, and dwell within the falling waters of eternal life. They may once more eat from the Tree of Life and walk with the Angels evermore.'

'Be warned of he who draws blood with ill intent. Beware the wrath of the Titans of Tartarus that shall thunder upon you like a rain of fire, lest he test the gate with an unclean soul. The Earth-born angel shall, of her will alone, draw of her blood to seek the wisdom lent hitherto by the reverent and obedient Enoch. For only the pure and true may seek to understand that which will unlock eternal freedom and rapture at the foot of thy throne.'

The great Lord called me forth, and blinded by His light, I bowed and fell, submissive at His feet, for He was light and power, but could take the form of man if He so chose.

In mine ear He whispered unto me. 'Hear my name and shout it from the highest mountains and deepest seas. I am I'el, creator of all that is and ever will be. I give mercy unto those that preserve life, those that allow all to be as they were created without judgment or harassment. Aggress against me and know thy anger. Kill not your fellow man in my or any other name, for that which tortures man, tortures me. Show sorrow of the heart for your transgressions. Love of all that live among you, and thy heart will fill with love once more.'

And so it came to pass that I'el told unto me the secrets of passage between A'vean and Earth. The accursed portal that was to be closed evermore was now, by design, free to be sought and open, but only by the most righteous One. And to the Earth-born, a time predetermined, her birth shall be. The first place of pilgrimage shall be far. Mine words and devices you shall find to be corrupted. Trust not all who adore you. The Unseen shall harass, trick, and covet you.

Tread with caution through the quest you must endure. Strength shall come to you, but compassion, as your weakness, will render you anaemic in the eyes of evil.

The land upon which thy parents were born shall be your first passage. In yonder resting place of your father's mother lay the words of I'el. From the sprig of bloom did thy father descend. He, thy father, who shall be hunted by the lion and boar to protect you, has waited there, afore your birth and ever after. Through denial of birthright, he has protected you. Follow on in glory and strength of thy father and thy predecessors who sacrificed all for you. Your challenge is great, the weight upon thy shoulders immense.

Three chests of knowledge must be sought. They will lead you to the door of A'vean. All-seeing that I am, humbly through the Lord I'el, in mine eye I see treachery among the most exalted. Heed this warning that discord and malevolent forces shall interfere with mine works. The Kaladai shall be corrupted.

Paradoxes lie everywhere. Mere mortals shall redeem mine works.

The Devil will guide you; an Angel shall destroy you."

There was utter silence in the room as I finished reading. My head thundered. *Treachery.* It was not the most positive of revelations. It seemed to give and take all at once. The effort of translating the ancient text had been less natural than I was led to believe. I was stunned with myself that I had read these strange symbols out loud in English, as though I'd spoken the language every day of my life. The true A'vean language, the language of the Creator, ran through me as naturally as my blood flowed. In all that I'd read though, the one thing that clung to me was the reference to my father. Was I finally going to find out about my parents? Who were they? The skeleton in the closet that was my parents' identity seemed precariously close to revealing itself from the cobwebs of the past.

Were my parents alive, in any sense of the word? These Watchers and Eudaimonians were impossibly old—eternal. Therefore, my parents could still be alive. If so, where had they been, and why had they not made contact with me? Overthinking again, nausea burned my throat.

Deep breath in, deep breath out, repeat.

Gedz'iel broke the silence, his voice solemn.

"Well done, Sophia. You have begun what shall become our triumphant return home. Repatriation is more important to us than you could ever imagine. I honour your courage and belief in yourself, though I sense that belief still wavers. Be patient. It shall evolve and strengthen every day."

Everything suddenly felt suffocating. Gedz'iel blurred. The air felt thick and every sound exaggerated. Brennan breathed too heavily behind me. Enl'iel noisily twirled a wad of hair around her fingers. Kea's bracelets were clanging like cymbals. I could hear every sound as though it was plugged into an amplifier. The thudding of my heart pulled it all together into an irritating symphony in my mind. I barely tolerated the booming of Gedz'iel's voice.

"There is much to consider within this scroll. The references to traitors disturbs me greatly. Return home all of you. Consider Enoch's' words with the wisdom of your years. Assist Sophia in unravelling their hidden meaning. Be on high alert for anything that may cast doubt upon any of us. This pains me to even put into words. May we stitch our story together in fullness without malevolent interference, especially from within." Gedz'iel bowed towards me, as did everyone else.

"Please don't do that. You don't need to do that." I was mortified by the excessive attention as the room continued to swirl.

"Accept who you are, Sophia. We honour and protect you," Gedz'iel replied. The others mumbled their agreement.

Thrum, thrum, thrum.

The resting place of my father's mother.

Thrum, thrum, thrum.

Kaladai, Portal, key.

These words wove themselves through my mind amid all the noise.

"Enl'iel, she is weary. She is yet to attain her first psynostris. Take her and administer a resting tisane. Our time is short, and her strength must be rallied. She must be strong. I fear taking her out into the world with the threat that awaits us. There is a worrying movement in the Underworld. Some Afflicted have been picked up from the underground in central London. They are preparing for something, and we too must be prepared. Have Koi intensify her training, we must stay ahead of the Daimon. Arm the humans."

Thrum, thrum, thrum.

Psynostris, my father's mother, my father's mother.

Thrum, thrum, thrum.

Gedz'iel and his five companions flashed out of existence. The room fell silent, but it was still chaotic in my head, and the noise followed me like the after effects of a rock concert as I made my way silently back to my bed.

Chapter
Thirty-Seven

Sleep was torturous. I tossed and turned, tangling the sheets around my thrashing limbs. Vivid dreams stole rest from me.

Clawing hands, screams, and burning flames licking at my feet, terrified me. Eyes — black eyes, green, red, orange and blue eyes — flashed at me, pinned me to the bed. A beating drum thundered through the room, vibrating up through the bed, resounding painfully in my head. A presence was near me, hovering over me, touching me. The beating drum pounded harder as a hand caressed my face. "Mine," whispered into my thoughts. For an eternity, my eyelids rebelled against me and refused to open as I screamed at myself to wake up. This presence was heavy, and lingered as it ran fingers slowly down my arm, wrapped them around my hand. Was it here to hurt me? It didn't feel like it, yet it was certainly not welcome to violate my personal space. I continued to scream wildly at myself to wake, as this dream-invader left me numb and limp with the fear of its intentions.

Finally, my body listened to my mind, and my eyes flung wide open, scanning every atom of space surrounding me. It was still and dark with a quiet and intensity that only the night brings. Within seconds, my pupils had adjusted to the dimness of the space, and my body froze just as it had in slumber. The soft glow of my mark illuminated something. A shadow hovered silently, unearthly, inches above me. It had been there all along, not just in my dream. Dark and featureless, a malevolent red aura cloaked it, and my newly sharpened sight could not seem to penetrate it. Wings that spanned far into the room gently flapped. Red and orange sparks sputtered silently from them with each movement, floating away and disappearing into nothingness. To my surprise, despite the rigid state of my limbs, I felt no malice from it towards me. The shock of its reality kept me quiet and still. I realised almost instantly that this dark visitor was not angry or dangerous in that moment, and that it was not there to hurt me. At least for now. It was sad, deeply sad—desperately sad; a loneliness that left a hollow pit in my stomach. Despite myself, I felt compassion for it, overwhelmed with an annoyingly incessant need to help. As these thoughts passed through my mind, it reached out a silhouetted hand and gently caressed my face with a hot palm. At this point, I realised that the drumming, though still present in the background, had dulled considerably, replaced with my heart thrashing against my ribs.

"Who are you?" I asked. No answer, but it drew its hand quickly away. "Do you need help?" I asked again. This time, it responded by gliding slowly away until it stood by the doorway, its head hung low and wings retracting into nothing more than a mild glow behind its back. It was clearly a male by the sheer width of his shoulders. The muscled arms were far from hidden by its veiled disguise. "Who are you?" I asked one last time, just as a wave of nausea punched me out of nowhere. I pressed on my stomach, swallowed it away.

When I looked back up, it vanished in an instant in a sparkling display of red and orange fireworks. A sulphurous odour remained and stirred the nausea back up. Fear slithered along with that nausea and I pulled the blankets up to my chin, glancing around the room for more intruders. After satisfying myself that I was alone, I took a sip of water from the glass by the bed, suddenly feeling extremely parched. Unnerved by the incident and the darkness, I called to the dormant orb by the doorway to light up. It responded by bathing the room in a soft and comforting glow, alleviating the thickness of the atmosphere. It was a handy trick Brennan had shown me. Apparently, he was the master of these things. I fought the urge to call for help. I felt like I needed to keep this to myself. After a lot of contemplation and no conclusions about the creepy apparition, I eventually drifted back into another fitful sleep.

By the morning, I was achy and exhausted when Brennan, Jaz and Ben came by to pick me up for training. I didn't even have time for a shower to dull my pounding head before Jaz palmed me an apple and an Eccles cake, saying that she was allowed to watch me '*kick some butt*' in training this morning. Ben followed on silently down the corridors and staircases, broody as usual. He was looking gaunt, almost haunted. He appeared unwell, but seemed to still have a strong energy. This place was not good for him. He was an independent spirit who had never dealt well with being told what to do. I bet, if he hadn't been surrounded by supernatural beings, he would have been out of there days ago. I felt on the edge of saying something to him a number of times, but forced myself into silence each time. Jaz on the other hand, despite her regular bitching, was looking amazing. For the first time in years her face was clean of the heavy makeup. We had no chance to bring personal things with us due to our sudden departure, so she was forced to go *eau naturelle*. She looked fresh and healthy. If only she saw her natural beauty, inside and out, as I did.

"You look like crap Soph, no sleep huh?" This apparently was Brennan's way of saying good morning.

"Well thanks. That's truly the way to a girl's heart!" I slapped my chest dramatically. "No, I didn't sleep well at all. Even if I did, I seem to feel constantly exhausted anyway," I said.

"Ah, that'll pass Princess. You're adjusting. Sometime soon you'll need far less sleep. When you reach psynostris, you'll feel a whole lot better."

"Gedz'iel mentioned that word last night. What is it? Not more pain?"

"Nah, it's actually awesome. Psynostris refers to wakefulness. We need minimal sleep. A rest every few days is all it takes to keep the blood and bones going. In our natural state, we never sleep, not required. Very handy when you want to party," he joked.

"I can't imagine that at all. No sleep?" I gaped, disbelieving it.

"Too true. Just a few hours a week. It will come to you soon enough, probably the second you clock over to twenty-one."

"Wow, I want me a piece of that magic! Could you imagine it Soph? Non-stop all-nighters!" Jaz slapped my back.

"Yes, but the trade-off Jaz, is that you have to play like us and fight the Daimon and plenty of other nasties," Brennan toyed with her.

"Oh, you can shove that then. I'll stick with bed and a hot guy instead," she quipped.

"Jaz!" I gasped and rolled my eyes.

"Oh, you love it!" Jaz answered, not too far off the mark, and we laughed.

"So, Princess, I thought these two Saturnines could watch you train today. They've been cooped up so long, they've forgotten how to smile!" Jaz elbowed him and told him to shut it, but thankfully did so with a playful edge. For some reason, when she was tense, so was I. When she relaxed, I softened too.

"If you play nice, I'll grab Lorcan and some scouts and take you all skyward this evening for a little fresh air. We might not see the sun, but at least it will be out of here, and hopefully we can have a little fun. What do you say, kids?" Brennan slapped his hands, rubbed them in anticipation.

"I'm not a kid, angel-boy," snapped Ben.

"Angel-boy! Nice work man!" Brennan said. "I'm so wounded."

"You're behaving like a kid, bro. Say sorry, you jerk!" Jaz snapped at Ben with a punch on his shoulder. Ben remained silent and sullen.

"Nah, no harm Jaz. It's cool. Takes more than that to rattle me." Brennan looked down at Ben, "Dude, we're on the same side. Want to get out of this place tonight? Have a break from all these weirdos down here?"

"For real?" Jaz asked.

"Of course! You think a guy can't party?" Brennan looked wounded.

We were all silent with the surprise of the opportunity as we stared at Brennan, mouths open.

"Anyone going to join me? Do I have to have my own, lonely pity party out in the big wide human world?" Brennan gestured his hands wide.

Brennan was just too damn light sometimes. The gravity of what was going on seemed a little lost on him. But perhaps it was just his way of getting through yet another day of a very long existence.

"Yes! I say yes!" I answered for us all. Jaz jumped with excitement; Ben showed the emotion of a corpse. I needed to breathe some fresh air. I wanted to run, needed my muscles to burn and ache, not from being chased by orbs, but the freedom that running through the hills and trees allowed. When I ran, I usually contemplated my worries, and boy, I had a few big ones now. From the moment I saw Cael in St Xavier's, to this very second, I'd been propelled through a whirlwind of chaos. There was no time for questions, no time to say, *'no thank you, I'll check out of this option.'* I quietly coveted the chance to allow the twisting in my guts to unravel by releasing the pent-up stress that I was loath to share with Jaz and Ben. Not that Ben seemed interested in me at all. Despite his behaviour, my hurt had calmed a little, and I understood the stress he must be feeling. I looked at him, just catching him glance away from me. He wanted to talk; I could feel the desperation of unsaid words. I'd try to be patient and let him come to me in his own time. Still, I craved for one of our nights in, where we would talk for hours about everything and nothing during movie marathons.

"I'll do anything to get out of this place. It's like being buried alive," Ben finally ground out the words, like they were glass in his mouth.

Brennan reached for a high-five, but was left with fresh air from Ben, so he looked to Jaz, who obliged with a firm palm slap.

"I'm in, thank God. Can we go shopping? I'd kill for volume pump mascara and a steak sandwich, extra rare!" Jaz added that last part with a nudge on my side to tease me.

"I'm sure that if you promise to control that temper of yours, I can talk Her Majesty into allowing a shopping trip. Behave, Jaz, okay?" Brennan responded as we took the final staircase down into the training room. She twisted her hair around a finger and looked innocently at him, as though she had no idea what he could mean.

"Her Majesty?" I asked

"Enl'iel, Princess. She's the head honcho. Her word is *the* word around here when Gedz'iel isn't in. Even has Koi in a tail spin at times!" Brennan pushed through the heavy doors, revealing a handful of red orbs. They hovered in the air, waiting for me with what I just knew was glee.

I swallowed the last of my breakfast pastry as I eyed them cautiously. Koi was in the centre of the room.

"Holy crap, what are those things?" Jaz whispered.

"Sit back and watch. You'll be glad you're spectating, trust me," I answered as I buffed up my courage and walked in with as much attitude as I could muster. I wasn't ready for yet another pounding. Jude was over to one side with a young girl, bashing the life out of a wooden dummy with a nasty-looking silver and gold weapon. Lorcan was standing behind him and gestured to me, but when I responded, he called out, "Not you, Ben! Send him over for some fun." I turned to tell him, but Ben was jogging over already, a surprising smirk on his face. He had the look he got when he had an old motorcycle to pull apart and repair from scratch. Jaz was already chatting with a flame-haired human girl in fighting gear. I watched Jaz as her attention was frequently diverted to Jude. How her wild hormones still raged in this situation was an absolute mystery.

The orbs escorted me over to Koi, and the anticipation of failure had broken out into an early sweat down my back.

"Good morning, Sophia. I trust you slept well?" His brows knitted. "Hmmm, no? I sense you have not. Your mind is troubled. Is there anything I can do?" He asked and cheek-kissed me.

"No, I'm fine," I lied. "Just nervous. I want to do better today," I said truthfully.

"And so you shall. You have improved each and every day," Koi laughed and gently patted me on the back.

Brennan wandered past us as he headed towards Jude.

"You'll be okay, Soph. More of the same, but this time you actually have to beat them!" He winked annoyingly at me.

"Hope you're not betting your life savings on it," I called back.

"Just our eternal salvation, Earth-born!" An eaves-dropping Jude shouted from fifty feet away as he sliced clean through the middle of a training dummy.

"That is far from helpful, Jude. She learns quickly, her energy is immensely strong. It's her self-confidence and trust in her own abilities that needs more attention. That kind of comment is counterproductive!" Koi snapped.

"Apologies, Master Koi. I'm sorry, Sophia. That was uncalled for." Jude said, eyes averted to the ground.

"I love a man who can apologise," cooed Jaz from the sidelines. I scowled at her as Jude bowed in contrition, immediately turning from me and speaking to Ben.

"Want to have some fun, human?" Jude handed Ben a dangerous looking sword that was nearly as long as he was tall.

"Hell yeah!" Ben pumped one fist into the other with more life than he'd shown in days. He was bug-eyed as he gingerly handled the massive weapon. He turned it over, the sheen of it flashed across his sallow complexion. I wasn't sure that it was a good idea, but if it helped him out of the funk he was in, it couldn't be all bad. I glanced back at Jaz. She dropped the apple she'd been gnawing on as she gawked at Jude with unabashed lust when he removed his sweaty shirt. This would only end in disaster. She was looking at him the way human guys drooled over her. She was non-existent to him, not to mention that she didn't know about the non-fraternisation clause between our species.

The orb session was actually not as bad as expected this time around. It started off shaky, with my butt being zapped black and blue within minutes, but then something just clicked. The third time I ran from them, I realised that if I concentrated on the energy pulse thrumming through me, I could draw on the instinctual anger of being attacked as this energy surged. These regular beats of E'lan running through my veins were hypnotic, drawing me away from my erratic emotions into a brief place of calm. Because I knew I was safe and not at risk of death in this controlled environment, I could take the time to allow this calmness to harness the anger into something I could control. Whilst dodging a close shave to my face as I reached the halfway point of the circuit, I surprised the orbs by tumbling forward into a tight ball. I spun around and landed on my knees, facing them. In a flash, I thrust out my hands and threw a white-hot arc of light their way, as easy as if I'd pitched a baseball. Two were both hit with this one powerful blast from my hands. They illuminated a bright white colour, stretched out into long, thin vertical lines of light, and then just blipped out of existence.

"Oh no! Did I kill them?" I panicked immediately, but was met with applause and laughter.

"Sophia, well done. You have caused no harm. These training orbs are not alive, so to speak. They are useful energy pulses that we create, and have no sentient sense of self or the ability to feel pain, fear, or discomfort. They have fulfilled their purpose, and you have used them perfectly. I am beyond impressed with your progress in such a brief time. Your innate abilities are surging through you like reflexes. Within the week, I believe we shall be able to inform Gedz'iel that it will be safe enough for you to venture out from the security of this sanctuary." Koi made his way over to where I was still kneeling on the ground in surprise and relief. He offered his hands to hoist me up, and I noticed then the pale white tattoos across his fingers as they grasped my hands. I'd originally thought they were scars, but I could now see that they were letters. *Love* was tattooed across the knuckles of one hand, and *hate* across the other.

"Interesting choice of words on your hands, Koi."

"Ah yes, they are a reminder to me of the intertwining of the two most powerful emotional energies. Love and hate are really the same feeling. They both have immense power to cause pain and heartache, but they come from completely different points of contention. It is easy to confuse the two, and the Daimon like to use their intensity against anyone they can. These tattoos remind me of a time when I was very near to losing myself. I look upon them to remember. It is important to keep the two emotions separated, as when they become blurred, like a lover scorned, there can only be an undesirable outcome." Koi glowed as he explained, his fervour only enhancing his beauty. But his eyes told a different story, as though the words recalled pain. I wondered what he had been through. Had he lost a love? Had he been the spurned lover? He ran a hand though his short hair, "Now, we continue."

Koi pushed me harder after that. Each time he produced a red orb, I managed to bring it down, but not without racking up a few more bruises. Lorcan joined in, watching my steady progress with an intense interest.

After I'd banished what felt like the hundredth orb, Koi invited Lorcan to instruct me in physical combat. I was a little alarmed at this, to say the least. Not to mention exhausted. When I protested, Koi explained why.

"You will not always be running from and fighting the foul zombie creations that are the Rogues, Sophia. You will come across a Daimon or two sooner than you'd care to. And it may not be conveniently after you have rested, either. Indeed, attaining the state of psynostris would be better sooner than later for you. Encountering Belial was not a pleasant experience for you, I'm sure, and he certainly chose to attack when your defences were lowest." Koi's eyebrows arched. "As you can well appreciate, a Damion's strength in all elements and reflexes are far superior to Rogues. Lorcan, will you instruct Sophia in a physical training battle, as you do with all the newly awakened?"

"Of course, Master Koi." Lorcan bowed respectfully. He cleared his throat as he fiddled about a moment, smoothing out his already perfectly smooth training pants. He seemed nervous. His broad, bare chest moved in and out with measured, deep breaths. His boyish face flushed as he smiled briefly at me, revealing charming dimples on his cheeks. He was a Watcher, a powerful being, but seemed more a bumbling teenager in that moment. With the previous smart-mouthing forgiven, I tried to help him out of the extreme awkwardness he was exuding.

"I'm really nervous, Lorcan. You'll explain exactly what I'm meant to do? I've never even had a self-defence class before!"

"She's a crap fighter, kicked her arse in high school!" Jaz called out with a whoop. She paled as Koi approached and had a word to her. I giggled to myself.

Lorcan seemed to relax. "It's an honour to teach you, Sophia. This will be a breeze for you after what I've seen today. Your human upbringing doesn't seem to have scarred you too much," he said. I didn't share his optimism as he motioned for me to walk by his side. We headed to a doorway across the running track, past Ben and Jude, who stopped briefly to watch us. Jude swiftly pulled Ben's attention back again with a swot across his back with the flat edge of a sword. Ben responded with a well-placed expletive retort. I wasn't so sure this was what Ben and his moodiness needed — roughhousing with Jude, who was clearly his own personal fan club.

Through a darkened doorway that was lit spontaneously with well-timed orbs as we entered, we arrived in another, smaller room, dug out of the cool earth. It was dim, and would've been pitch dark but for the faint glow of angelic light illuminating from the millions of crystals pin-pricking the walls. The orb light refracted this ethereal glow, giving up what the area contained. It smelled old, like time stuck to the air.

The room was a train wreck of debris, as though a building had collapsed there long ago. Partial stone edifices lay in various states of decay, creating a maze of tunnels and hidey-holes. Shards of clay pots were scattered everywhere. Barely-there wooden beams lay criss-crossed over some of the remains. It was an archaeological mess and delight, all in one.

"What is this place?" I asked in awe.

"An old Roman city, more than two thousand years old, I think, and looking its age, I'd say. It's dark and pokey, great for hiding in. We use this place to teach battlefield stealth and hone both physical and elemental reflexes. It's kind of like laser force, but you actually get hurt here… sometimes. But you won't, I'm sure! Watch out, though, you'll still find the odd skull rolling around the floor!" Lorcan shrugged and seemed to look around for one. That little gem gave me a chill, so I focused on something else.

"You know laser force?" I was surprised by this information, even more so than the impressive remains.

"You think we don't get out much? I often head into the human world. Laser force is wicked! Don't mind a game of football either, when I can fit it in. You like the game?" Lorcan asked.

"Not really to play, but I followed Australia when they were in the World Cup. Ben loves soccer. I've had more than my share of 3am games to watch over popcorn with him."

"Well, he can't be as big a tosser as I thought he was if he's into the world game! Oh, sorry," Lorcan said when I grimaced at the insult to Ben.

"It's okay. He's being an idiot at the moment."

"That's putting it mildly." He kicked at nothing in particular on the ground and cleared his throat. "Anyway, there's more to being a Watcher on this outpost of a planet than slashing Daimon and protecting beautiful… um…" Lorcan immediately flushed, coughed again, and mumbled something in another language, then walked on ahead, trying to ignore what he had just said. Awkward was the standard in my life now, apparently. I pretended I didn't notice what he said, not wanting to make him feel any more embarrassed. I did enjoy the warm feeling the compliment stoked in me.

"All right, Sophia," Lorcan began, his voice finding a deeper, thicker English lilt.

"Just call me Soph," I interrupted. I hoped the familiarity might break the suffocating tension oozing from him.

"Right, okay, um… Soph, how this normally plays out is like fighting the orbs." He pointed at the surroundings. "We use the ruins as an obstacle course, and the objective is for you to steer clear of me and actually hunt me down without me catching you first." Lorcan moved towards a half-collapsed stone doorway with the Roman numeral XII carved above it. "We start at door twelve because… well, we just do. Not sure why." He smiled and raised his perfectly sculpted white eyebrows charmingly. "Since you don't know how to dull your energy too well yet, I want you just to pretend to attack me. Aim at the ground near my feet. Please don't actually zap me, you might just kill me!" He chuckled. I didn't follow suit. It wasn't an amusing thought, knowing that I could accidentally kill one of them. Anxiety surged, causing my back to burn and head to ache. That old friend called *'run for the hills'* tried to emerge, but I managed to ignore it, but only just.

"I *will* zap you though, like an orb. No mercy!"

A devious smile spread across Lorcan's face. I could almost have been sucked in by his boyish charm if he wasn't describing his intention of attacking me.

"So, if you can catch me off guard, you need to engage me in physical combat. Wrestle with me, kick, punch, scratch—anything. Don't be afraid to hurt me with your fists. This is what I'm trained for. Sometimes we can't, for various reasons, use the elements of E'lan, so we have to be prepared to fight however we can, and physical strength is always on our side. This is also why we carry weapons if we know we are going into combat; everything helps. Daimons are proficient hand-to-hand fighters. They also have some nasty weapons, so we need to keep pace with whatever force they will use against us." He tossed a dagger from one hand to the other, seeing me wide-eyed at the lethal-looking edge of it.

"Haven't you ever wondered where humans got the inspiration for weapons in the first place?"

"Not really," I said.

"Look no further than Yeqon and Lilith. Now there's a match made in literal Hell!" He sneered at the mere thought of them. "We've always used weapons on the more violent places across the worlds, but they were never intended for Earth." Lorcan shook his head in disgust, pausing to slip the blade back into his belt. "Unfortunately, Daimon often like to play with their victims for their own sadistic amusement. They even keep some in their own realm to hunt for sport. That's a place you never want to end up in. They won't necessarily kill you immediately, so you must know how to fight with whatever resources you have, whether that be your energy, your fists, a chromious blade, or a rock on the ground. I know you haven't trained like this before, so this will be a sort of get to know you session, in order for me to see what you're capable of, and where we'll need to focus."

"I have no idea how to fight. I've barely ever swatted a fly! I suppose, like everything else at the moment, I'll just see what my bizarre instincts happen to dish out!"

"That's the way, positive thinking." Lorcan smiled, as I swallowed back the horror of the potential blast ending my life, and I felt a sense of relief.

"Soph, I'm giving you two minutes to hide. Then I'm going to hunt you, while you hunt me. The winner gets the other's Eccles cake from Eilir tomorrow! Fair?" His unusual accent was playful now and snapped the tension that coiled my muscles into springs. Although a fish out of water, I was safe here, I felt it, despite the less than pleasant training methods. I took a cue from his casualness.

"No way! I'd rather give you my bank account PIN number— Eccles cakes are too damn good!" I took off at a run through doorway twelve, smiling to myself as the sound of his friendly jibes about who the winner would be faded into the distance.

Chapter
Thirty-Eight

The hunt was on. I squatted behind a stack of huge earthenware urns in the middle of the war zone, as Lorcan had called it. It was almost pitch black in the tunnels, so I let a little warmth enter my face to emit a small glow from my A'vean birthmark. It was becoming easier each time to draw upon this energy. I didn't need to visualize it, just a slight twitch to my cheek seemed to be all it took to call it up and let it out. At least that was going well.

The ruins were deadly silent, but for the distant clanging of Ben and Jude playing with those awful weapons. Drawing on every suspense movie I'd ever seen, I kept my back to the walls and edged ever so slowly on tiptoe around the corners of the crumbling buildings. My soft glow cast deep shadows across ancient graffiti and artwork etched into long-forgotten remains. The ground was uneven, covered in partly buried debris. I remembered Lorcan's quip about skulls, and tried to imagine it was only pottery shards cracking underfoot. The vile memory of the Prime Scroll chamber prevented me believing it was merely rubble.

A rush spread through my chest as I felt my way around the labyrinth. I had to admit, it was exciting, like playing a grown-up game of hide and seek. The sound of splintering wood had me double back to where I'd started. I thought I heard a mumbled expletive and felt a rise in the static in the air. I could sense Lorcan's energy nearby. My cheeks warmed as my mark lit brighter, and my hands tingled with the thrill. I felt like a lioness waiting to pounce. Some new, deep-seated instinct threatened to emerge.

Deep breath in, deep breath out, repeat.

My glow dulled compliantly. I didn't give my position away. A smile broadened across my face. I edged carefully around a huge, mouldy wooden beam, ready to strike, only to find a little glowing orb bouncing around. Was that left by Lorcan to tease me? I turned back, nearly tripping over a decayed wheel. The static in the air weakened as he retreated. He was hunting me, not the reverse. This was his game. I needed to change that. I stopped a moment and closed my eyes, took another trademark deep breath and let my mind relax. I reached out with my senses to feel the surrounding energies, like Koi had been teaching me with the giant orb. To my left was a cool calmness, and to my immediate right there was a quiet sizzle of electrons. I moved silently that way, one side step at a time, and it became stronger. My skin prickled as I became more accustomed to when my own kind were near. My face flared up unexpectedly.

I stopped again and tried to calm this unintended beacon. I visualised a gushing waterfall. Only my power was the water falling over the cliff face, away and down into a deep lake below. I let that elemental energy flow away as I willed myself invisible. My face and hands settled relatively quickly. My body was cool, still, and quiet. Each time, it was easier than the last. My confidence blossomed a little.

I was so deep in the ruins now, not a wisp of light present. I crept closer to the buzzing; Lorcan was nearby. I could hear rapid yet controlled breaths. Could he sense me? He didn't seem to move from his position. I was squatting behind two large stones, heart pounding and holding my breath. The air was alive. I peeked around the corner and that was my mistake. He was there, saw me, and threw a nasty sting of light that bit my hand before I jumped back into the darkness.

That made me mad. He laughed. I rushed back around just as Lorcan was retreating. I kept pace with him, my agility jumping and ducking around the mess of obstacles both surprised and delighted me.

It spurred me on. Like a flash of lightning, he zipped in and out through the corners and corridors and mess. He glowed, revealing himself, as though he wanted me to catch him. He was toying with me. Making it easy for me to find him. That made me mad, too. I wanted to show him that I could do it without his help, so I stopped and ran the other way. His energy stopped, too. I think that confused him—he thought I would take the easy option. They all thought I was too human, too weak. Perhaps it was true for now, but not forever. My university lecturers thought I was too introverted to succeed as a nurse. I rose to that challenge, and I would rise to this one.

I quickly made a quiet circle back past the two big stones, over to where I thought he'd stopped. He was there. I could feel his energy from behind the damp walls. I managed to keep my own energy so low that I felt darker than the veil of blackness surrounding me. He wouldn't be expecting that. Despite the excitement of the chase, I maintained a calm control. My waterfall was working, and I let it keep flowing through my mind. The static buzz was teasing my hair on end as I edged up to another toppled doorway. It led out of the tunnel I was hiding in. Lorcan breathing softly, mere paces away. I was nearly jumping out of my own skin with the thrill of catching him first. I counted quietly to three, then sprang from around the corner, straight into Lorcan's back. He yelped in surprise as we toppled to the ground. I had him face down for a just second before he flipped me over. I was flung a few feet away. I slammed hard into an unforgiving rock.

"So, we're playing dirty?" I puffed and pulled myself up.

"As hard as you want it!" he said, and threw a thin bolt of light at me. I dodged it just in time; sharp stone pellets blew out from the disintegrated rock behind me. I lunged forward. He met me head on, quickly outmanoeuvring my flailing kicks and punches with his martial arts skills until he flung me down hard. My back screamed as I came to rest across a beam of wood.

"Ow!" I yelped. Lorcan hesitated. I swiped my foot out and tripped him up, bringing him crashing down on top of me. Dust puffed up, making me cough and splutter. Once it settled, I wiped my eyes with my free hand to see him staring intently at me, mere inches away. His eyes swirled, studying me whilst I was pinned beneath him. Our breaths were rapid as we tried to catch them. I wriggled and squirmed, but he was too heavy. His thick arms imprisoned me.

"You're more impressive, more naturally gifted than I could have ever imagined. I didn't expect you to be able to hunt me. You dulled your energy signature to invisibility. You are indeed an angel of the highest order." His breath was warm, sweet and soft. The pulse in his neck quickened. He shifted slightly, so that his weight was not so heavy on me.

"Are you going to let me up?" I asked, feeling suddenly self-conscious of his lingering proximity.

He didn't answer, he just stared silently at me. This unexpected awkward moment made me babble, a skill I actually was proficient at. "You know, I think I've earned that Eccles cake."

"Indeed," he said softly.

"I'll share if you let me up right now."

"Only a pastry?" He asked, his voice dropped lower, his eyes lingered.

My heart froze.

"Um… Lorcan, I'm tired. Please, let me up?" I wriggled my other arm free, but he moved to grab both of my hands and pinned them back by my sides. His mark glowed strongly; it swirled all the way across his forehead and down to the edge of the right side of his jaw. He just stared at me, taking in my face with his ethereal eyes, his head tilting subtly left and right.

"Lorcan, please stop. You're making me feel uncomfortable. Please, let me up?" I pleaded. The fun had just been sabotaged.

That seemed to snap him out of whatever this moment was to him. He pushed up wordlessly and turned his back to me, shoulders sagged.

"Lorcan, sorry…" I began.

"You've nothing to be sorry for, I'm sorry." He shook his head. "Go get changed. You'll need to have Enl'iel attend your wounds." His tone was flat, the warmth and fun a mere memory. He walked away through the mess we'd made, melting into the shadows towards the main arena. He didn't look back.

Why were guys so difficult? I shook my head and laughed a little at the ridiculousness of what had just occurred. Was Lorcan embarrassed or annoyed? Who knew? If only guys, angelic or not, would actually communicate! I had to navigate the maze and find my own way back to the central arena, left alone to ponder the aftermath of his hormonal outburst.

I followed the clanging that echoed off to the left and emerged where we had started. Jaz remained just inside the main entry watching Jude and Ben still go at it with swords that looked like they could kill at a hundred paces. Otherwise, it was empty, but for Koi who, with a look of deep concern, immediately took me back to the Stasis room for healing. He counselled me on my progress as we walked.

"I hear you fought well. You have minimal injuries; this is commendable with an opponent such as Lorcan. He informs me you exceeded his expectations. You are becoming exponentially stronger by the day. Just a few sessions down, and already you are able to begin the process of controlling your elemental power. Lorcan was very impressed with you."

"He said that?" I asked, rather surprised after *the* incident.

"Indeed, Sophia. He informed me that you hunted him with stealth. Your fighting technique needs more finesse, but he said you are much stronger and more resourceful than you realise. He will continue to train you every morning and evening from now on."

My hair bristled a little. That was going to be comfortable. *Not.*

We pushed through the Stasis room door to find Enl'iel readying a bed with some poultices, bottles of things I didn't recognise, and a tall glass of water. I gulped it down before saying hello. The room was not as full as the first time I visited, but I noticed the white veil of energy still blanketed Cael's bed down the back.

"Oh, my word, look at you! Master Koi, a little gentler, please? You're every other colour than skin!" Enl'iel exclaimed.

"The cost of learning, and learning well. The orbs and Lorcan might consider themselves less fortunate on this occasion, my dear Enl'iel. She has performed impeccably today for one so unsure of herself." He leaned in and bid me goodbye with a bow and a kiss on my hands.

As a female Alchemae brought a cup of herbal tea for me to sip, I noticed my swollen fingers. They were cut and scorched. I felt achy and sore all over. It even hurt to sit. This was barely injured according to Koi? I stared intently at my crimson, chipped finger nails when exhaustion set in. Enl'iel spoke soothingly as she dropped essences of this and that all over me.

"Stop doubting yourself, Sophia. A week ago, this was but a fairy tale to you, and look at you now. With barely any introduction, you have fought off our orbs and matched wits with our best trainer. You have read the ancient language and begun to unlock the secrets of Enoch. You have defended yourself against both Daimon and Rogue. Imagine where you will be a week from now! Acknowledge your successes, believe in yourself, and confront your challenges was grace and fortitude. When you thought yourself a mere mortal, you exuded an enviable confidence in your ability to heal. You have that and much, much more now." She poured her energy into my aching palms as she spoke, instantly relieving the pain.

"I know what you're saying is true. I can feel the changes in me. And today, I did feel more in control, I kind of enjoyed it actually."

She smiled at this revelation.

"I'm just so uncomfortable with all of the attention and people acting so weird around me. I miss normalcy, I miss my friends." I sounded like a whining child, but I was too tired to care.

"There is no more *normal* in your vocabulary, and I'm sorry for that. However, you will adapt… you must. Accept that your kindred reveres you. You are precious to us all. As for Ben, I know that's who you are referring to." She dabbed dried blood from my knuckles.

And now Lorcan, I thought quietly.

"Ben will come around. I know his behaviour is hurting you, but you must understand that his human sensibilities and masculine stubbornness are a brick wall in front of his common sense at present.

Give it time. He loves you, and he will open his heart to you again," she soothed.

My cheeks burned when she said that he loved me. What did she mean by that? She was already distracted with preparing me a plum tea while I read too much into her offhanded statement. He couldn't love me, well, especially not now. I thought of Koi's tattoos and unrequited love and then mentally slapped myself around.

Stop it Soph!

"Now, finish this, and then take a shower. I see Koi didn't let you refresh after training!" She screwed her nose up a little. I must have stunk like a men's locker room. "Afterwards, I believe Brennan is taking you, Jasmine, and Ben out for some fresh air? You will enjoy that, but stay cl…"

She didn't finish her sentence as the door burst open. Ben was shoved through the door, Jude right behind him. His left arm held high in the air by Jude, who was trying to stem the flow of blood cascading down. Jaz was close behind, cursing at Jude with all of her extra special expletive words for apparently causing this injury. Brennan was trying to hold her back.

"Hands off!" she screeched at him as she struggled in his grip.

"What happened?" I visually assessed Ben for any other injuries. His aura was dark with anger. He was holding his breath, on and off, almost gasping. He was pale, sweaty, and tense with pain. All my aches were suddenly distant memories.

"I'm fine, Soph. It's just a scratch," Ben spluttered. The sound of my name spilling from his lips made my heart skip a beat. I immediately helped him sit on my bed, whilst Enl'iel called on the same Alchemae for a multitude of herbs, lotions, and bandages.

"This fucking idiot sliced my brother! Almost in friggin' half!" Jaz punched Jude in the arm, hard enough into his back that he stepped out of her way.

"Will someone stop this howling human before I silence her myself? My ears are about to bleed! He has a scratch, that's all!" Jude growled in her direction, making Jaz back off slightly. She gave Jude her filthiest look as she garnered a renewed tenacity and shoved Brennan away from Ben, taking over the task of maintaining pressure on his arm to stem the bleeding.

"You cut my brother! I don't care who or what you are, just back the fuck off!" Jaz then gave her complete attention to Ben and helped as Enl'iel and I inspected the wound. It was deep and gaping, far from a scratch.

"It was my fault, sis. Leave him alone. I insisted on using the weapons. I forgot how strong these—uh, these guys are. I forgot they aren't normal," Ben said, gasping through the pain.

Jaz's renewed accusing glare had Jude smugly back off towards the door. He matched her glare with a frightening scowl, unflinching, cross-armed. Now there *was* a match made in Hell.

"Jude?" Enl'iel questioned him with her own look of annoyance.

"Apologies, human. Steady on with the insults, though," he said in an overtly forced, softer voice, far beneath the might of his presence. His face brimmed with annoyance, which told me that apologies were not his forte. I felt Ben bristle when he referred to him as *'human'*, but Ben kept himself quiet. The strain of pain over-ruled his need to continue a pointless interspecies war of insults.

"Whose idea was it to let Ben near the weapons? Hmm?" Enl'iel questioned Jude and Brennan further, each of whom was looking at the other accusingly. It was like two bulls in a paddock pawing the ground at each other, daring each other to cave and drop the other one in it.

Lorcan entered the room at that moment of standoff, adding to the delightful feeling of discomfort surging in the air. I felt instantly awkward as he averted his eyes from mine. I concentrated on dabbing at Ben's wound with some gauze as tea tree and calendula essences were dropped into the gash. Ben winced, barely restraining a groan. Lorcan had put his hands up in defensive innocence to Enl'iel's questioning whilst Jude surprisingly acquiesced, "I have dishonoured us all with my lack of judgement."

Enl'iel chastised him further with a few choice words as he took his leave, mumbling something about heading to London to check on the troops that were stationed there.

"Don't go far Jude, you will be needed here," Enl'iel called after him as he slammed the door behind him.

"Brennan, you're not off the hook. Don't look so vindicated. You are just as much to blame," she snapped.

"But…" He looked to be eluding the truth but conceded, "Ah, it was fun while it lasted, though, wasn't it buddy?"

"I'm not your God-damned buddy!" Ben grimaced as he lashed out through gritted teeth.

"Shhh, calm down Ben or you'll make the wound reopen," I soothed.

I snuck a covert look at his face. We were so close, yet I felt worlds apart from him. Ashes and spice tinted the salty sweat pouring from him.

His wound would, under normal circumstances, need surgery and an impressive number of stitches. It would still take some time to heal, but I knew we could repair it our way. As Enl'iel dropped the last essence in, some of his blood dripped down onto her hands. She paused a moment, looking so concerned that I panicked quietly to myself. She looked off into the distance momentarily, seemingly in thought.

"Lith'eal, please, would you fetch me some more bandages?" Enl'iel called to another Alchemae in the back as I wiped the blood spatter from Ben's face and neck with a damp gauze pad. My fingers accidentally touched the scar on his cheek. He jerked back, nearly opening the wound up again just as Jaz had started bandaging it.

"Don't!" he snapped at me.

His ridiculous anger shocked me. I lost it right there and then.

"What? What the hell is your problem, Ben? You've been an iceman to me for days! When is this going to stop? I'm sorry about what's happened. I'm sorry my life has turned into a freak show, but believe me, it's certainly not been my choice. I'm sorry you've been dragged into it. Don't you think I'd much rather be home right now, hanging out with you guys like we used to? Like normal? Don't you think I want everything to be normal, too? Well, it's not, is it? So just get the hell over yourself! I'm just trying to help you. Stop being an idiot!" My hands fell away from him. I looked away. I caught a barely hidden smile tip the corner of Enl'iel's mouth.

"You tell him, Soph. God, you've got a thick head, Ben. Grow the hell up! You're being such a dick!" Jaz snapped, forever the number one ticket holder of my fan club.

Enl'iel cleared her throat as she tried to ignore Jaz's colourful language, whilst Ben stared at the floor with thin, tight lips.

"Apologise to Sophia, human, or next time I'll take to you with my own sword, and with purpose," growled Lorcan. I'd forgotten he was even there. "Her wounds may not be of the flesh, but they run deeper than yours. Apologise, now!" Lorcan seemed bigger and scarier as he let his wings unfurl like an angry gorilla puffing out his chest.

"Okay, okay, fine. Back off!" Ben looked at me, not apologetic, though… more conflicted. "Sorry, Soph. Just give me some space and time, okay? It's not you, it's me."

"Oh my God! I can't believe you just said that, Ben! It's like the worst breakup speech in history, and you guys aren't even—hang on, are you two?" Jaz's eyes were nearly out of her head with intrigue.

At the same moment, both Ben and I belted out a firm, "No!"

His over-enthusiastic denial had started the blood seeping again through his half-wrapped bandage. His face paled. Enl'iel was reinspecting it with a deepening furrow of her brow. I was already tense again with concern, Jaz's statement long lost on me now.

"What is it? You look so worried," I asked as she unwrapped it again. She stalled a moment, then called for a eucalyptus and lavender poultice. "It's just deeper than I thought. Ben, I know you are frightened, but will you allow us to heal you with our elemental energy? The blade that struck you can often fester flesh very quickly. It is created of a substance that affects not only the flesh but also the spirit. I sense your energy to be very low, which is perhaps why this wound is so unpleasant. Do we have your permission? It will not hurt, I promise." Enl'iel's face pinched with concern. She held his hand tight.

Jaz poked Ben in the back, "Use a brain cell and let them help you." She poked him one more time for good measure.

He scowled her way, then nodded his assent quietly. Both Enl'iel and I immediately laid our hands across the oozing wound. I felt him hold his breath and tense. Jaz was wrapping up the briefly used bloody bandage as our hands illuminated. She scuttled in closer to him, watching us with intrigue, her eyes wide. We let our joint energy flow into his arm. I concentrated deeply, as the negative energy oozing from him was intense. I drew it up and cast it out of me. The wound knitted together. He winced and groaned slightly, making me falter.

"Concentrate," Enl'iel urged. Her intensity was incredible, her concentration unparalleled. I heard Jaz draw in a breath as she watched the wound fuse almost completely back together. We stopped when there was just a small, one centimetre gap to allow any fluids to drain out. Sweat poured down Ben's gaunt face. It wasn't meant to hurt, but he seemed drained to exhaustion. I wondered about these weapons and the power they had.

"Wrap that clean bandage over the small wound that is left Jasmine," Enl'iel instructed.

"It's okay, bro, all done. Hang in there." Jaz wiped his brow lovingly, then bandaged the small wound close to his elbow. Her voice was gentle as she helped him through this moment of pain. She kissed him on the cheek as he leaned into her and sighed.

"Now, Jasmine, dear. Bandage over the wound with this fresh gauze, twice a day. Would you like to monitor it for me? You are a capable young nurse," Enl'iel asked.

"Sure, of course." Jaz faltered a moment. "Hang on! Your voice, it's so familiar. You sound just like… but no, you can't be! You're not, but… but how?" Jaz squinted with a confused and suspicious glare at Enl'iel as she finished the last few wraps of the bandage.

"Watch me, dear," Enl'iel said as she briefly flashed her old *'Nan'* visage at Jaz.

Jaz nearly jumped out of her skin, just as she fastened the bandage securely. "Holy mother of… seriously? Nan? What the…?"

Enl'iel smiled quietly to herself with amusement.

"I only just found out myself, Jaz. I'm shocked, too, and I lived with her!" I said.

"Concealment is one of my many talents," Enl'iel said with a girlish shrug.

Jaz gave her a tweak on her arm, just to make sure was actually real.

"You guys take freaky to a whole new level. Funny, I was wondering what happened to Nan. I didn't want to ask you, you know, in case she'd been…"

"I'm here and perfectly well," answered Enl'iel. Jaz's face was enamoured.

"Impressive, very bloody impressive!" Jaz said with a satisfied nod.

"This is getting more entertaining by the minute. Are we finished here?" asked Ben dryly, apparently unaffected by this new and paranormal development.

"Indeed, we are, Ben. You need to get out of here for a while, get some fresh air, and perhaps some decent manners back into you. Brennan is going to take you all topside. However, it will only happen if you rest first. I will bring you some analgesia shortly. Please inform me if you are in pain Ben, you do not have to endure pain whilst you are in my care. Now, freshen up, eat, rest and then have a nice break. But, do as you are instructed—all of you—for your own safety and ours, or you shall not be allowed out again." Enl'iel stood and took the tray of used medicinal jars to the central table, then disappeared behind the veil of light concealing Cael.

Brennan took the other two away to rest and get ready. Lorcan followed behind them. I was just leaving for the showers when Enl'iel called me back, emerging from Cael's isolation zone. "Wait a moment, Sophia," she asked. "Take this." Enl'iel passed me a bracelet with a white pearl-like oval stone inlaid into a silver setting.

"Gedz'iel returns tonight to send you on your quest. You need all the help you can muster before you begin this journey. I do not know what lies before you. This, dear, is part of your Soul Stone. It is but a remanent of the one your parents gave you upon your birth. When children of our kind are born, they receive a Soul Stone to protect and soothe them. It is a gift from the spirits of the Cavern of Souls, the most ancient and revered sanctuary on Earth. These stones are a gift to celebrate a birth. Unfortunately, because of who you were, there was much haste and panic after your birth, and your stone was lost, other than this small piece that snapped off. I was to give it to you at your twenty-first reception, but circumstance has not afforded us that luxury. You will notice that all of the young children carry them around to soothe and protect themselves from negative energy," she said.

I recalled immediately that little Av'ael had held one in her hand, but it had been the size of a glowing plum.

"Please, give this other one to Jasmine. It is but a small cutting of my own stone. It may calm her unruly anger. Her soul is damaged, and I can only hope that one day peace will enter her heart and blot out the darkness." She placed in my palm another delicate bracelet with a tiny, asymmetrical wedge of stone set in it. "Please, tell her it is a token gift from me, nothing more. Lord I'el forbid that she accepted help from anyone or anything!" Enl'iel added with a resigned shake of her head. She absently fiddled with her own Soul Stone necklace as she spoke. It was a habit of hers for as long as I could remember, usually when she was worried about something. "Off you go now. Enjoy your small slice of freedom while you can." She disappeared back through the veil to Cael.

I looked around the Stasis, rolling the two soul stone bracelets over my palm. Only now did I notice the glowing Soul Stones laying upon the chests of each slumbering teenager. I turned to leave just as I heard a slight commotion. Glancing back, I noticed a young girl surrounded by what I assumed were her parents. She was waking from her hibernation, it seemed. There were tears of joy, hugs, and laughter. The word reception was mentioned, as an Alchemae began to assess her condition. I felt like I was eavesdropping on an intimate moment, so I slipped from the room, wondering how different things may have been if my parents had been in my life.

Chapter
Thirty-Nine

Freshly showered with a single silver braid running over my shoulder, I made my way through the bustling mass of people, thankfully unrecognised this time. Anonymity suited me. I could have been in the downtown area of Melbourne, Sydney, or even New York—the hustle and bustle of the subterranean population was surprisingly similar. As I finally made it back to the central entry level, I noticed for the first time, a floating platform one storey above us, just hovering there, as though it were in space with no gravity. It looked like a chunk of earth had been dug out and tossed up there. Old roots hung down like scraggly hair as it gently bobbed up and down. I stepped back as far as the surrounding wall would allow in order to crane my neck up to see what it was. There were flashing lights appearing and disappearing atop it, and a faint, warm glow was emanating from it. As I wondered at this new marvel, I felt a tug at my leg.

"Hello, pretty Sophia. What you looking at?"

I glanced down to see little Av'ael, her dull eyes glued intently on me.

"Well, hi there, little one. I was just wondering what the floating rock up there is?"

"Oh, that's our sys—syth— Zitos stone! I'm not allowed up there until I'm twenty-one. Are you allowed there? Mama told me it's pink!"

"Well, I haven't seen it yet, but I hope to soon. And if it is pink, I'll be sure to tell you."

She squealed excitedly at this and ran off to her mother, who was calling her away. So, there was one of these here, too. Noting all of the flashing energies coming and going up there, I assumed that was how they entered and exited without using the church. I eyed it a while longer, then made my way to the Sophia exit, translated as the door for those unable to control their powers.

"Hey, Elsa!" called Jaz, who had decided I looked like the Snow Queen now that I had white hair.

"Oh, you just kill me Jaz, so funny!" I smirked, wishing for my rainbow locks back. Brennan laughed, Lorcan stared, and Ben looked anywhere but at me. Two new faces giggled at the comment, and I rolled my eyes. What and who now?

"Excusez-moi, Sophia, but it is a compliment. You are very pretty, as is Elsa. Bonjour, I am Kristen, and this is my brother, Thomas," said an olive-skinned girl about my age. Her brother was the polar opposite in appearance—pale, blue-eyed, and golden blond. I snuck a quick look at their eyes and could see instantly that they were human. I put my hand out to shake, and Kristen laughed.

"Brennan, 'aven't you taught her 'ow to greet someone properly? Does it take a mere 'uman to do it?" Kristen leaned in and did the cheek-kiss, although with her, there was an absence of any elemental connection. No buzz, just the warmth of her skin on mine. Her hazel eyes sparkled with kindness and strength as she stood back, and I felt her to be an instant friend.

Thomas followed suit. "It's an honour to meet you, and will be an honour to protect and serve you," he said in a smooth, more understated French accent.

"There now. What other angelic customs must we teach 'er?" teased Kristen.

"Yes, yes, pull your head in, l'enfant," Brennan answered.

"Ooh, you 'ave been practising your French, formidable!" Kristen responded, clapping with sarcasm.

"Don't get too excited *Petite Fleur*, it's one word at a time, sweet pea." Brennan turned back to me. "Princess, these two balls of Parisian cheek are part of our extended family. They're descendants of the humans who took refuge with us after the great flood and pledged their allegiance to us. We protect them, train them, and they in turn, work with us, particularly with reconnaissance, in the human world. They are invaluable, even with their rather large egos."

"Huh! Will you listen to 'im? I learn from the master!" Kristen replied as she playfully swatted his arm.

Both Kristen and Thomas then extended an arm and bowed to me with huge grins, revealing long bows and a quiver of arrows on their backs. It was all very Robin Hood. I wondered why guns weren't an added accessory to the expansive cache. All these ancient weapons seemed understated in the modern world. As if reading my mind, or the fact that I was caught staring at his munitions, Thomas spoke.

"They are silent, deadly, and do not attract human attention. Could you imagine the commotion if we fired an Uzi every time we saw a Rogue?"

Okay, fair point.

"And, modern weapons don't knock them down. Every weapon outside our elemental energy must be chromious lined or tipped. It brings them down every time. Plain old metal just doesn't cut it," added Brennan before gathering us closer.

"Okay, Ben and Jasmine. You guys will stick with Kristen and Thomas. They will guard you, along with Kea, into Tewkesbury, where you can shop, hang, or do whatever you want to for a couple of hours. Stock up on whatever you need. I don't know when you'll get another opportunity. Stay close, and do everything they say." Brennan warned with an uncharacteristic seriousness.

"That is the best thing I've heard in days. I seriously need me some makeup. No zombie-things around up there, though?" A genuine note of fear-stained Jaz's voice as she pointed to the ceiling.

"Jude has already secured the route with scouts. You should be perfectly fine. Just try to be on your best behaviour, okay? It took some quick talking to keep Jude here a little longer to help after what happened before. So, Ben, keep your trap shut, at least around Jude! Jaz, you will be just fine. Don't worry, Mini-Princess." Brennan gave her a brotherly peck on the top of her head. She blushed and surprisingly hugged him, perhaps a second longer than necessary. She craved love, this girl, but sought the wrong kind in all the wrong places. If only she'd accept more than just the type wanting to get up her skirt. When this rare moment of comfort for her with Brennan was over, he waved his hand across the veil of light that protected the entrance to the church, and the aged stone staircase was revealed once more.

"It's safe to go on through now. Never try to sneak through the veil—your arse won't thank you for the sting," Brennan laughed as he urged us along.

As I exited through the heavy church door with Lorcan and Brennan, Kea was already revving a dark-coloured car for the others to drive them to town. I waved to Jaz as she cradled Ben's arm while he got into the car first. Unfortunately, it was late afternoon when we emerged, and being winter in the UK, it was already very dark out. I felt disappointed that I wouldn't get to see sunlight today. Just a smidge of the sun on my face would have been bliss.

Jude reappeared briefly as they got in the car, ignoring Jaz with a practiced ease as he called in a few more scouts with a high-pitched whistle. "There's been a bit of Daimon activity in Birmingham, just want to bolster up a few more lead scouts to clear the way," he said to Brennan as he flashed out of sight, heading up the disappearing Jaguar with twenty or so scouts zooming in formation on either side of the car as it wound away through the darkness.

"Okay Princess, ready for a little R&R?" Brennan asked as he passed me a gorgeous pair of new running shoes. "Want to see if you can outrun a Watcher?"

"How did you know I like to run?"

"I am the best! But I've also been your neighbour for your entire life. Forget so soon? But we'll stick with the simple fact that I am the best."

I scoffed warmly at his ridiculously large ego and strapped on my runners within two breaths. I took off after him down the narrow, paddock-lined road. We ran for a couple of kilometres before he jumped a wire fence and headed off south of the church, across a field of sleeping cows covered with a fine dusting of snow. A few beasts lazily raised a head to check us out, chewing away on a previous meal. I scrambled over the derelict fence while he jumped it like a pro, leaving me far behind.

The second I stepped onto this field; I felt a heavy thudding in my chest. A steady drumming, like the dream I'd had the other night. I felt pain that wasn't mine. Desperate screams fought for dominance in my head. It took my breath away for a second or two. Brennan shouted out something rude to me about my fitness from the distance. I shook my head as I leaned over, resting on my thighs. The thudding continued heavily in my chest. I tried to brush it off and pushed myself onward, attempting to ignore this uncomfortable intrusion. To distract myself, I recalled the passage of Enoch's words about my father. Sprig of bloom, lions and boars—whatever that meant. I hoped Gedz'iel knew what that mouthful of confusion was all about. As the thrumming continued, I wondered why Enoch couldn't have just said things plainly—but of course, that would have just made life way too simple. Mulling over this, I pumped my legs so hard that all I could hear was my heartbeat as I drowned out the unwelcome sounds with exertion.

I pulled up behind Brennan, still marvelling at how he'd recovered. A few days ago, he was the paralysed photographer across the road, and now we were running cross-country together. Despite the incessant and covert noise intrusion, my body felt alive. The sting of burning muscles invigorated me, leaving me wanting more. My steady breaths plumed white in the freezing air.

"Just down the hill and over the river is a surprise for you." Brennan took off again, barefoot, like a flash.

We reached the small stretch of rushing water and made our way across to the other side on a conveniently located, very rickety rowboat.

I wasn't sure how it even stayed afloat. There seemed more holes than wood on the floor. The thrumming in my head was almost insane as we climbed up the other slippery bank in pitch darkness. At first, I said nothing, there was enough drama going on. We walked down past a derelict outhouse of some sort toward another paddock lined with huge, white trimmed fir trees. I had to say something then, though. The screaming in my head was out of control.

"Can you hear that?" I asked.

"What, Princess? Why are you yelling at me?"

"Sorry, am I? It's just so loud. That drumming sound? I'm sure I can hear someone calling for help or something. I don't know." I rubbed my cheek, which was threatening to sear right off my face. I couldn't let my power show outside, lest I attract something unpleasant, so I pushed the feeling as far back down as I could. It eased off the further we walked away from the old building.

"No, I don't hear it," he responded, concern replacing his smile. "I don't feel any negative elementals around here. The E'lan is stronger near the sanctuary, so perhaps you are picking up on another Watcher in the vicinity. Strange… I can normally feel my kin if they're nearby. You're more powerful than me, though. Your antennas are probably picking up someone far off, clever little angel." He reached a hand out to me. I took it. "Stick close though, just in case, Princess. If anything happens to you, I'll have to deal with Enl'iel, and that is not a happy option, trust me!" Brennan laughed and cringed all at once. We pushed through the line of thick firs as a misty rain fell, cooling off my still warm face. He pulled me closer, pointing out into the middle of a darkened paddock.

"Do you see it? This is your surprise. You have twenty minutes. Knock yourself out!" He gently pushed me forward as my eyes adjusted to the darkened space, revealing a sight that brought a well of tears to my eyes. A piece of normal stood there, swaying its long, grey mane. A stunning horse, almost identical to Grey, grazed lazily in the distance. He looked up suddenly, and it felt like he was beckoning to me as he nodded his head up and down, stamping his hooves into the cold, hard earth. I glanced back to Brennan, who waved me on, and then bent down to squeeze through the perfectly kept wooden perimeter fence. This amazing creature let out an attitude-filled whinny and pranced over to me like a supermodel. We met halfway, and like instant friends, he nuzzled into my shoulder, wriggling his upper lip, looking for a treat. I smelled that beautifully familiar, equine aroma. I hugged onto his muscular, Arabian neck and felt his warmth and strong heartbeat. If I'd closed my eyes, I could have been home. He shoved at me impatiently with his head.

"Okay, okay, you want to be friends?" He pawed at the snowy ground before ripping up a small mouthful of frozen grass that peeked out between the white patches. "May I?" I asked, as I'd always done of Grey.

More hoof-stamping and swishing of his tail followed. Without another thought, I grabbed a luxurious handful of mane, swung up onto his wide back, and said, "Go for it!"

And he did. Straight into a full, bounding gallop around the large, foggy field. He threw his head in that high-strung stallion kind of way, and I revelled in each loping lurch. Moonlight lit our path in a magical glow. With my legs squeezed tight against his ribs, I let go of his mane and threw back my head, letting the cold air rush past me, sending my hair wildly about. I felt instantly connected to him. I kept my eyes closed as he ran, and the longing became stronger and deeper by the second. Time slowed down, the air became thick, and the sounds around me slowed and deepened.

Home, I thought, I just wanted to be home. Suddenly, I thought I could hear someone urgently calling my name. Who was it? What were they calling me for? I was in heaven here. *Leave me alone.*

"Stop!"

Was someone calling for me to stop? No, I'm not finished yet. The thundering hooves faded.

"Wait, Sophia. No! Stop!"

I ignored these calls. I was going to enjoy every second of this tiny piece of normalcy, squeezing it out for as long as I could. The thrumming in my head was dissipating, the burning in my face had gone, and silence and peace surrounded me. My body tingled as the stallion took me away. Numbness overwhelmed me, a feeling I gladly accepted. Cool, warm, cool. Silence, blackness, stillness. The loping feeling suddenly stopped. I realised with a sense of confusion that the horse was no longer beneath me. I could no longer hear anything as something yanked me from within, backwards through a starry cosmos, away from the beautiful creature, away from safety, away from anywhere.

Chapter Forty

It had been for but the breadth of a hair that Nik'ael had not been discovered today. He was not sure that he could move around or even near the Sanctuary any longer. His care factor had taken a nosedive as his loyalties wavered more than they had in a thousand years. He had always struggled with his inner Daimon. Destruction was never quite as palatable to him as it was to the others who had switched alliances. Guilt had always gnawed at him after each and every terrible thing he had done.

He was at a crisis point. Seeing her so close, yet so impossibly distant pulled at every fibre of his being. His fingers worked at those beads almost constantly now, the worry and frustration wore them thin. Concealment and the proximity of all that chromious was near killing him as he watched the others drool over her, be near her, touch her. He had a death wish. He knew it. What more could he expect when deep down in his dark heart, it was not just Yeqon he was deceiving, but also himself?

He wanted Ben out of the way. His presence had an effect on her that had become far too distracting for both her and himself. He needed, for his own self-preservation, to remove Ben from the equation. Having Ben fawning privately over her, and so closely, was impossible to deal with any longer. Perhaps then he could regain his perspective and lust for vengeance. It would hurt her, and that stung him. It would hurt Ben more, but he could live with that. Ben was nothing. This handy topside excursion had been exactly the chance he needed. Brennan and Enl'iel would be done-for once Gedz'iel found out that they'd let Sophia out of the sanctuary. He bristled with satisfaction at the thought of that smart mouthed Brennan getting zapped to this side of nowhere.

Without Sophia nearby just now, he could concentrate better, and deepened his cloaking as the scouts increased their presence tenfold upon approaching the small town. He stood outside the Tewkesbury Bell Inn, pressing into the wall and assessing the layout of the main street for escape routes and points of ambush. Leaning Tudor buildings still stood proud with heraldry flags lining the length of the main street. He remembered this place from the 1400's, whilst King Richard was being tormented into doing things he didn't want to do by Anjou'elle and Neph'reus. Richard had fought hard, like a nobleman should, but he was hopelessly overpowered. He was no match for those evil vixens of the underworld. Nik'ael chuckled smugly. Those were interesting times. The aristocracy was so riddled with the perversion of Daimon influence back then. Even the rare good-hearted king could be a pawn for the Unseen and their stupid games with humans. He momentarily wondered to himself just where those two devilish women had gone. They hadn't made so much as an elemental blip on the radar for centuries. Suspicious.

As the scouts swarmed every dark corner, the village came alive after hours with the local half-breeds opening up the shops for their own kind. He almost admired their little network of bartering that spanned the globe. Never a thing was in want. Whilst humans starved for the simplest things, the Eudaimonians just gave each other whatever it was they needed, no matter the value. Perhaps if humans possessed less innate greed for material wealth, this world would not have been so easy to send to Hell. That was the irony he witnessed on Earth. Everyone was so scared of death and going to the wrong place, yet the real Hell was the one they'd created for themselves through war, greed, and oppression.

He called for Belial again as he shadowed Jasmine near the pharmacy. Belial never took more than a few minutes to respond, yet he had ignored all three summonses today. He knew that he'd scorned him back at the cottage on the mountain, but there was a purpose in that, though he'd not had the time to fill Belial in. Even so, Belial was but a guard dog, and not too smart. Like himself, Belial also had divided loyalties. It oozed from him, so he could never be sure how much he could be trusted.

Back when Belial's daughter was born, after a dalliance with a human woman, Belial almost lost his way, nearly running back into the arms of the Watchers. He'd actually fallen in love with the human and fathered two children with her. The first was a son, who had disappeared after the woman was locked away in Bedlam Asylum for being insane. The stupid woman had announced to medieval England that an angel had fathered her child. She'd nearly burned at the stake for it. Belial searched for his son fruitlessly, on and off for years. He eventually rescued the woman in a midnight raid on that horrendous human institution and kept her alive and young for three hundred more years. He had fathered another child with her, a daughter. The woman had finally gone truly mad from the mix of negative and positive elemental powers coursing through her. She ran off to the south and flung herself from the white cliffs into the ocean. The tragedy brought Belial to his knees. It was a love Nik'ael understood. He'd had that with Neren'iel. If it weren't for his own quick talking to draw Belial back into the fold, the brothers would have long ago thrown his butt into the depths of the Pits. Belial owed him, and he needed him to pay his debt right now.

He listened in the distance of his mind, while the humans dined at a kitschy, 1960's Chinese take-out. The laminate and chrome table was piled high with food, and Jasmine was glaring at Ben.

"Don't even say it!" she threatened him with a pointed chopstick.

"What? I just didn't think you ate that stuff," Ben answered.

"If you ever tell Soph that I like tofu, your lips will be as fat as your head!" She showed him her fist as she shovelled vegetables into her mouth. Nik'ael liked her a lot. She amused him to no end.

As the group rose and left, he knew the time was near.

He smelled them before he saw them. While he was watching Jasmine back in the pharmacy, he sensed the slightly foul, metallic tang. Only his highly tuned hearing picked up the ragged, rapid panting coming from the shadows of the alley ways. It oozed from their pores. He knew this was the opportunity he needed to get rid of Ben, to create a bit of mayhem. It would make Sophia vulnerable, and possibly dangerous, but might also push her powers to the point that could bring this situation to a head. If he had more leverage of his own, then hopefully she would be putty in his hands and the brothers would have to sit up and acknowledge that his way was the correct way.

The chain around his neck hung heavily against him, not in weight, but in the oppression of his sensibilities. What he was about to do went against every grain of goodness left in him. What little there was, anyway. He'd seized the opportunity back in Melbourne. When the secret cavern below the library was collapsing in on itself, he had swooped in and out, gathering exactly what he'd been looking for. He was now a few chess-moves away from checkmating himself to a one-way ticket to Tartarus if he was ever caught by I'el. It was cannibalism—there was no way to pretty it up. It churned in his stomach, but he needed to do it. He fiddled with the bracelet, begging for forgiveness that was wholly undeserved.

The handful of bone-thin youths he'd seen slip down the lane towards the Avon Barges were his targets. Their deathly pale skin and fidgeting movements confirmed who they were. Addiction and toxins oozed from their ravaged bodies. Ragged clothes hung from their skeletal frames. Desperation shown in every fleeting glance they made up and down the street as they looked for a quick hit. They would be puppets for him; he would be their God whilst he was their supplier. While the others moved to shops further down the street towards the Abbey, Ben quickly darted down an alley behind a boarded-up bakery.

He took a breath, hesitated momentarily, then undid the concealed vial and sprinkled a few grains of the iridescent contents along the ground leading back to the pharmacy where the unsuspecting Jasmine was browsing somewhere in the vicinity of her brother. The smell of the Thanratos made him retch as he bounced back into the strategic position that put him where the action would happen.

Jasmine swung a string bag filled with hair dye and wore a new set of earbuds blasting Pachelbel's Canon when he heard the panting of the addicts edge closer. It had taken them mere seconds to pick up the scent. Ben held a stack of auto magazines and a bag of mixed nuts that he was slowly chomping on. The Afflicted were mere feet away from them all, under a veil of shadows. He'd heard them licking the angel bone dust from the pavement, and it disgusted him. These vile leftovers of his own kind were but a means to an end on this occasion.

Within another thirty seconds, a few scouts had picked up the scent too. They zoomed in a panicked but controlled figure-eight around the unaware shoppers. Kea, instantly on alert, called out to everyone to head for the car. An immediate and exciting feeling of fear filled the air as people scattered. Kristen and Thomas cocked their bows and assumed a deadly-looking stance. Chromious arrows were held at the ready as their keen human eyes darted everywhere, looking for the enemy. Jasmine was initially oblivious to the scene, her face buried in a magazine and temporarily deafened by the music in her ears. Ben would be taken out, no question; the numbers were on Nik'ael's side tonight.

Fifteen Afflicted emerged from the damp shadows into plain sight. He acknowledged them with a subtle nod of his head and a flash of the vial around his neck. He found their leader, a tall, scrawny, white-haired woman who moved like a marionette. Her previously bright blue eyes were dulled to a sickly grey. He communicated telepathically with her to explain what he wanted and what they'd get in return for their compliance. She smiled wickedly, and her eyes gleamed in the lamplight as she licked her lips. Her group panted hysterically in turn. They hooted and hollered loudly, sounding like crazed soldiers heading in for the slaughter of battle. There was nothing remotely Eudaimonian left in these wretched beings, and even less was human. They were simply non-entities, stuck between two worlds, but ultimately destined for nothingness.

He gave the word, and they attacked without hesitation. Elemental energy surged on the night breeze. The air crackled with electricity. The street lights flickered on and off, buzzing and hissing with the negative pulsations. Screaming like nails on metal, the Afflicted charged. Thomas and Kristen let fly with a barrage of well-aimed arrows. Christmas decorations exploded from the street poles as casualties. Red tinsel fluttered to the ground, symbolic of the blood about to be shed. Kristen, despite her small stature, took out two with a single arrow as it penetrated so forcefully that the same arrow still had enough power to kill another Afflicted attacker coming up behind the first. Kea was in full power. She threw out crackling bolts like a machine gun. The suburban Eudaimonians were cowards, quickly closing up shop and retreating instead of helping their own. Typical, Nik'ael thought. Jude appeared briefly and chased down two Afflicted towards the river. Thomas took a pounding by a growling, towering male as Ben cowered in temporary safety behind him in front of a closed shopfront. Half bald with the fits of self-mutilation, the haggard Afflicted pounded into Thomas with iron-like fists. Thomas' combat training shone through, though. Even without the benefit of ethereal size and power, he was agile, strong, and cunning. With a slight, close-lipped smile, he flipped the male to the ground with a twist of his legs and put an arrow through its empty heart before it could blink. The arrow entered so forcefully the creature was pinned to the ground. Chromious metal descended these creatures instantly, just like a Rogue. Numerous bright balls of blue flame smouldered over the pavement, leaving nothing but a stinking pile of ash behind. Ben was slack-jawed at the horrific sight.

Nik'ael had once used these chromious weapons himself. He both admired and cursed them all at once.

Jasmine, with a hand over her mouth and eyes wide, had run to hide with Ben in the doorway, having finally noticed the fray. Mascara and lipstick tubes rolled across the road, resting in the wet gutter where she tossed her bags away. Her movement conveniently drew the attention of one of the Afflicted to Ben's position. The beast made a clicking noise and whistled. The last six made a beeline for Ben. Jasmine screamed wildly for help.

"Where the fuck is everyone? Help, help us!"

"Get down Jaz, get down!" Ben yelled at her.

Ben stood protectively in front of her, too foolhardy and macho to hide any longer. The dull sound of classical music drifted up from the footpath from the hastily discarded earbuds, lending an eerie, distant soundtrack to the show. Ten more Afflicted emerged from across the street, attracted by the fight, engaging Kea, Thomas, and Kristen in battle. Jude was back and took them out one by one from the other side of the street. The small force picked the foul creatures off quickly, but not before one of them got to Ben. It dragged at him with sharp, claw-like fingers.

"Ben! No! Help us!" Jasmine screamed. Nik'ael had never seen her cry in all the time she had befriended Sophia. He felt a twang of pity for her. She was gutsy and loyal—qualities that some of his own kind could benefit from.

"Run Jaz, get out of here!" Ben put up a pathetic attempt at fighting off his assailant, but he did not resist for long, knowing there was no chance of success. He was pale and grunting with the effort of self-preservation as he stood his ground momentarily in front of Jasmine. Always, Ben protected his sister. They did not touch her, though. They had what they came for. She screamed and scratched and kicked at the thing that had a grip on her brother's shirt. Ben shoved her back with his elbow.

'Get back, run! Get away from these freaks! Go!" he yelled at her. Ben glanced back at her solemnly, and his free hand pushed her harder, back into the doorway, out of harm's way.

Nik'ael listened as Ben screamed in frustration at her again, "Run, Jaz!" He groaned and cried out. "Remember," Ben struggled harder,

"I've always loved you, sis. No matter what happens, nothing will ever change that. Get the hell outta here!"

He shoved her back again as she sprang forward to him, then let his legs slacken, allowing the thing to take him. Despite the barrage of energy pulses coming its way from Jude and Kea, the Afflicted managed to drag Ben off through the mayhem, into the shadows, towards the river and oblivion. Nik'ael's mission here was accomplished for now. He put a shaky hand to his head and transferred away to the maniacal screams of Jasmine assaulting his ears.

"No! Not my brother, no!"

Chapter Forty-One

Heaving breaths, wet and warm, ruffled my hair. Crisp air coated my skin in coolness. As I became more aware of my senses, I screwed my hands into fists. The crunching of dry leaves instead of cold snow disturbed the otherwise silent blackness around me. Through a veil of matted hair, I opened my eyes and lifted my face slightly, bringing a few leaves with it as they had plastered themselves to my face. The warm breath was on my neck now. I stayed prone, not sure what to do, not sure what had happened. I held my breath and just listened. Something flew overhead. A branch snapped in the undergrowth, alerting me to things lurking in the dark surrounds. I concentrated on the breathing, focusing on the rhythmic sound. It was soft and smooth, not particularly threatening. Despite the fact that it seemed to be safe, I let my face warm, just in case. My arms and back began to defensively burn of their own volition, preparing to pounce. My instincts seemed to kick in, whereas my common sense was yet to catch up.

A sudden sloppy lick to my arm quelled my racing heart in an instant. A whimper confirmed it as a paw pressed into my arm. I looked up to see, of all things, Shadow.

"Shadow? How did you get here?" I sat up slowly, confused, clearing my eyes with a swipe of my forearm and checking myself for injuries. My face crinkled with the anticipation of gashes that, surprisingly, were not there. My dog nuzzled into my chest as it dawned on me that I was not where I thought I was.

"How did I get here?"

A descending full moon beamed across the landscape, highlighting softly swaying gumtrees. I was somehow back home. *How?* I found myself down the back of my property, laying by the small stream that had dried to its summer trickle. I sat up amid the canine-licking fest, trying to fathom how I came to be here. Everything seemed surreal. The ground was cool and firm. A bat flew quietly overhead. The tepid wind was just audible as it brushed through the trees. Shadow's unwashed aroma was certainly unmistakable. I cautiously stood, dusting myself clean of the prickly leaves and noticed a slight mist developing, which hid my feet from view.

"C'mon boy, keep me company." I scratched the top of his head as I took in the surroundings more thoroughly. Listening and feeling, instinctively with my increasingly sharp hearing and vision.

"Stay close." My voice seemed too high-pitched with the uncertainty of simmering fear as I babbled away to my fluffy body guard. The energy in the air was all too wicked. Shadow pressed protectively into my legs as I walked, the glow from my face lighting the way through the dense bush. I was wobbly and unsure in my steps. Whatever happened had taken something from me.

I figured I had better get down to the Zythros stone to call for help, so I headed for the shed. That was my first mistake. Within seconds, Shadow had his hackles up. A deep growl rumbled from him as he bared his teeth. He stood protectively between me and something up ahead in the dense undergrowth. Without thinking, I let my face glow brighter to see what was there. That was my second mistake. Out of a woody clump of unkempt lavender scrambled a decomposing, one-armed Rogue. The foul thing was grunting incomprehensible threats in between apparent retches, as though it was ill. Fortunately, the bushes were full and aromatic with their summer blooms, so I could swallow away my own need to vomit. As I backed away, a memory suddenly emerged of 'Nan' telling me as a child that lavender kept bad spirits away. That's why I was surrounded and bathed in it daily! Lavender made these horrid things ill.

Shadow lurched at the creature while it vomited black fluid uncontrollably. It flung him like a rag doll to the side, but not before Shadow had pulled off the bottom half of its single, flailing arm. It was now thankfully unable to grasp at me as it lunged in my direction, teeth bared and eyes bulging. Its lack of arms gave me the split-second of time that I needed to draw enough elemental power from the air to throw a small but effective bolt at it, turning the monster into nothing more than a pile of stinking ash. The short amount of training with Koi and those awful orbs was starting to pay off when I actually needed it.

That success was mistake number three, though. Like a moth to a flame, my power surge was a beacon that caused the ground to rumble. Like snakes writhing underneath the surface, the ground moved unnaturally. Skeletal arms began clawing their way up. Faceless limbs grabbed at anything they could as they emerged with a frightening speed. Shadow rebounded, snapping and growling like a hellhound at everything he could that was trying to dig its way free. It was a sickening scene. I didn't know which way to move. Hands and faces were being ripped to bloody shreds by Shadow, but they just kept rising, undeterred. I stamped on a few, making crunching sounds I would never forget. Fog rolled in thicker now, blanketing the ground, making it difficult to see the enemy. Their stench thickened with a foul domination of the sweet summer air. Shadow disappeared in the sudden whiteness. I called for him as I cautiously backed up further; the ground rumbling yet again. I turned to run, and cold things grabbed at me. My wings emerged. They were useless though as they seemed to falter with the intense fear I was failing to overcome as I tried to run. I wriggled my shoulders as I fled, encouraging the damn things to do something. I didn't give up though; I kept trying to fly. Unsurprisingly, I only managed to fling myself face first into the ground, landing eye-level with a skull with one dull, bloodshot eye glaring at me from under a bed of dried leaves. I punched at it furiously and blasted it at close range. I got up and ran as hard as I could, wings long forgotten. At least I knew that I could trust my legs to move fast. I screamed for Shadow, hearing his barks and yelps in the haze.

From somewhere in the darkness, a frantic, screaming whinny rang out. Hooves thundered. Out of the trees ahead of me burst Grey, with Shadow in hot pursuit. They both laid into the attackers with teeth and thrashing hooves. I took the unexpected opportunity to keep running, knowing that my only hope right now was to get to the shed and down into the cavern to use the stone to call for help. Something grabbed painfully around my ankle as I was mere paces away from the rear of the shed. It tripped me up. I could smell the sweet pond water, hearing the trickle of the little waterfall that ran down from the top of the garden as I seemed to fall in slow motion.

My head smacked against something hard as I fell. The warmth of the blood that trickled down my face brought on the reality of the danger in full force, sending my heart into overdrive. The panting and gurgles seemed frenzied now, as though the appearance of blood excited them. I struggled with the iron grip, kicking at it with all my strength. I was surrounded by a handful Rogues in various states of decay. It was distressing to see that some were even children—young and old, male and female, of various races and ethnicities. It appeared that anyone could become a Rogue. The perpetrators of these horrors were beyond evil.

This split-second of sorrow was quickly washed away by the salivation of the one that held me.

"Just one bite!" it gurgled though lips that barely moved, pushing the others into mass hysteria as it clawed further out of the ground. I threw a well-aimed bolt at it, taking out half of its head, but it held tight as brain matter fell sickeningly to the ground. My fight or flight mode was on and hot. My now frantically flapping wings luckily threw up a decent gust of dirt and leaves as I kicked at the leftovers of this thing that had hold of me. The flying leaves and dirt caused enough of a distraction as they all spluttered and coughed that I could throw a few more bolts out unencumbered. I ashed one or two more as I finally kicked the head clean off the one gripping me. I scrambled away, coughing back the urge to throw up.

Shadow and Grey had worked their way up to me by kicking and snarling through the throng, holding the rest back. Seeing them under threat, with blood pouring from Grey's neck, caused a primal scream to surge from within me. Lava-hot, the energy oozed from every pore of my body. I was glowing from head to foot, ashing anything that touched me or them. I screamed for Grey and Shadow to run, fearing for their lives. Despite my apparent superpowers, more foul things kept emerging from every square foot of ground, they didn't fear me. How many had been lying in wait, and for how long? The thought was horrifying.

A yelp from behind had me spin. I was now mere feet from the peeling green door. Despite being Ms Earth-born Saviour, I was clumsy and tripped over myself, only to come face-to-face with another corpse that took a handful of my hair, burning his flesh as he touched me, but he didn't let go. I yanked back just as a set of hooves came thundering down around my head with a precision that stamped the burning, gurgling face back down to where it came from.

Hurry, Earth-born! The command was implanted privately into my head. I flipped over to see Grey standing over me, and all seventeen hands of him looked down at me with eyes that were — *knowing*. In a brief lull of quiet, I sat back, panting with the exertion of the fight and looked up at the strangely calm horse. Shadow reappeared and licked my muddied face. His breath stank of garbage and his teeth were stained with dark, clotted blood. "Good boy, thank you," I kissed his muzzle.

After a quick glance to check on the progress of the Rogues up the slope, I heard another command. *Run, leave this place!* I looked up at Grey again, and for reasons I couldn't explain, I thought the voice was coming from him. He stamped his feet as though to maintain my attention as he shook his head, then his whole body. His entire body simultaneously shimmered and blurred in and out of focus. As he reappeared, crisp and clear, I almost forgot what I'd just been running from. He had changed from a stormy grey to a solid, shiny black, with a lustrous white mane and tail. Swirling blue eyes looked down at me as wings of light, just like mine, slowly flapped from near his withers. With a swish of his tail, in my mind, he spoke.

Jump on. I shall get you to safety. The ground here is alive with evil. Grey shook his head with impatience and pawed at the ground. I didn't hesitate as I heard the gurgle of new things nearby. I grabbed hold of his white mane and swung myself up, easily done with a surprisingly helpful flap of my own wings. *Hold on,* he communicated to me. With a sudden lurch, we were skyward, flying away into the dawn light, away from danger, and further away from what I knew as reality.

Grey—whoever or whatever he was, flew smoothly over the landscape. This left the creatures on the ground confused and they receded back within the ground and undergrowth. Eyeing the ground below to make sure it was now safe, he circled back to the old shed as I clung tightly to him. He, too, knew that's where I needed to be. Grey landed softly near the door and withdrew his wings. He nudged me forward with his soft muzzle. *Run, Earth-born! Run fast to the Zythros stone.* Grey turned and screamed as horses do, just as he faced the onslaught of the new wave of Rogues crashing mercilessly through the tree line. Shadow reappeared and launched at a woman who was raking craggy nails up and down her bloodied thighs. Her white hospital gown was filthy and torn as she searched for a target. Grey reared up and charged, dispatching her into a fleshy mess as more came in for the attack. I stood frozen momentarily, one hand on the peeling green door. *Go, my friend. I will hold them off for you. Run now!*

I did what Grey said as the melee erupted into a screaming, bloody fervour. I ran inside to find that the wooden door had reappeared over the opening to the underground sanctuary. I knelt down to pull at it, immediately remembering that there was no handle, just the rusted keyhole… and the key to it was long gone. How was I supposed to open it? I punched at the door in frustration as I panicked. Is nothing easy? I searched frantically for something to wrench it open, digging through an assortment of rusted tools. I heard a surge of gurgled panting and an equine scream that made my blood run cold. I looked out the window, rubbing a hand across the grime. Grey was surrounded and being scratched at from all angles. Shadow bit at every decaying leg of the ever-increasing army. There must have been ten, maybe fifteen of them. There was no thought in it. I ran back outside, surprising them with my reappearance.

Grey snorted in annoyance and screamed in my mind, *Leave! Now!*

"I'm not leaving you to die, Grey!" I threw out as much energy as I could draw off the morning breeze. I took out three in one go, then flapped my wings to lighten the darkness and stir up the undergrowth again to cause more confusion. That, I could do. This light of mine also helped to singe what skin was left on a few others, leaving them nothing but horrific, mobile skeletons. I couldn't fly, but I could use these puppies to ash these devils away, bit by bit. I ran at the Rogues, taking them by surprise again, which made taking them out all the easier. They seemed seriously stupid. They lacked combat skills and forward thinking, and didn't know what to do when I rushed them.

"Get away! Argh!" I yelled and screamed, madly waving my arms and wings, convincing myself that I could be intimidating. Some did back off. I felt cocky and brave, until I heard a yelp and a crunch. A huge male had picked up Shadow and bit into his neck. To my abject horror, it appeared to drink his blood, then throw him to the ground, limp. Dead. The beast roared and beat its chest with a crazed bloodlust and renewed strength. Blood dripped down its faced, onto its chest that bore a stitched, vertical surgical wound up the sternum. As one, Grey and I attacked. He turned his rump and booted off its filthy head, whilst I ashed it with minimal effort but great satisfaction.

I ignored the new rumblings underfoot as I ran to Shadow's lifeless form. Grey paraded, a guard in front of me, daring anything else to advance as he arched his neck and stomped his huge white hooves. I knelt down, pulling the huge ball of fur onto my lap. Shadow's life force was gone, and nothing but the dissipating warmth of what was my most loyal friend remained. I hugged him tightly.

"No! No, my precious boy, no!" Sobs choked me. Hot tears blinded me. I screamed skyward, "Why? Why do we have to go through all of this? Why can't you just come and help? Damn you!"

My sacrilegious screams went unheard, but it helped emotionally to let it out. As I saw Grey through the blurring tears struggle to hold the next barrage back, fiery anger consumed me. What more was I to face? No time to adjust, to heal, or mourn. I burned with resentment.

I whispered to Shadow, "Go on, boy. Find your place in the stars."

The new Rogues had wriggled fully free and were advancing too quickly. A kookaburra laughed nearby, as though the scene was all too funny. I hated that bird. I hugged Shadow briefly and laid him gently down. To prevent those things from getting at him again, I turned my face away as I incinerated his body, keeping him safe from further defilement. He became one with the earth immediately.

The air felt empty now, and so did I. Grey trotted back and placed his head over my shoulder. He nudged me backwards to the shed.

You are going to get yourself killed before you can save your kind if you do not do as instructed. He invaded my thoughts again.

I answered, teeth clamped firmly together, chin trembling.

"I will not let another one of my loved ones die for me, including you, whoever you are!"

We slowly backed away, mirroring the tempered pace of the Rogues, not making any sudden moves. They had slowed somewhat, as though now aware of the force they faced. Soulless corpses that seemed worried about being killed; the thought struck me as strange. They took a step forward for each two we retreated, silent footsteps making no sound other than their grotesque, bubbly breaths as we slowly circled round to the shed.

Sophia, I am your Grey, but I am also your guardian. When I arrived on Earth, my mission was to serve and protect those of A'vean. You are my final mission. So, as a soldier, if I have to die to protect my charge, you must accept this fact as do I. There is always a place for me upon the fields of A'vean, be it in body or spirit. He nuzzled warmly at my ear, then took a mouthful of my singed shirt, pulling me backwards.

I will miss that four-legged flea farm. He was acceptable company, Grey snorted mournfully as he nosed me towards the shed door.

"Me too, Grey. Me too," I sobbed, just as a loud crack behind us made me jump.

The Rogues screeched in what seemed like mass panic as we turned to find, of all people, Lorcan. He dusted himself off casually before he threw out a warning bolt of light, blasting away half a dozen Rogues in one go, causing the others to retreat a fair distance.

"Well then, if you were trying to run away, you need to brush up on some military stealth, Sophia. I could track your elemental signature from Jupiter. Very sloppy. Hansel and Gretel were more subtle." His tone was clipped, but not cold.

"What?" I was surprised to see him, grateful to see him, but also immediately pissed off, "Oh God, I'm sick of this! Just to let you know, I have no freaking idea how I got here!" I yelled, my tone clocking in somewhere between furious and hysterical.

"Chill, will you? Keep stepping back slowly while they are unsure of themselves. I know this was not your doing, so to speak. You've accidentally transferred yourself through emotional longing. Why you chose a Pegasean beast to fret over, I have no idea!"

Grey stamped his feet in disgust at the insult, but nudged me to Lorcan, who was backing up towards the door just like us.

Go, Earth-born, he is a tracker. He has come to return you to safety.

"What about you?" I asked quietly, alarmed.

He responded by flapping his wings wide and bright, rising into the air. *Don't you worry, my beautiful friend. I will be near, and we shall meet again soon. Thank you for the peppermints, by the way. I particularly loved the peppermints!* With a kick of his hooves, Grey was gone in a flash, taking out three more Rogues in his wake; a shooting star across the dawning sky.

"Always one for drama, that lot. Unfortunately, they have the annoying habit of being loyal and useful," Lorcan mumbled as he grabbed my hand.

"Let's get you back to England. I'd say after this, your life supply of Eccles cakes are mine!"

His humour was lost on me.

Lorcan kept close. Wings wide and pulsing, the four remaining Rogues retreated into the bushes, patting at their rapidly eroding flesh. He drew me into his chest, but as his wings began to envelop me, we were thrown off balance, falling to the ground on top of each other as the ground beneath us lurched like an earthquake had struck.

"Well, this is becoming a bit of a habit, don't you think?" he quipped as he looked down at me, all too close for comfort. I was full on about to smack him out when we were distracted simultaneously by the pond bubbling, as though suddenly at boiling point. In a nanosecond, he pulled me to my feet and shoved me back so hard that I fell straight through the green door, landing face first on the ground inside.

"Get down into the sanctuary now, Sophia!" Lorcan yelled just as something sharp flew past my head, so close that it nicked my ear. I pressed my earlobe and coughed the dirt from my mouth as my eyes landed on six huge, pulsing arrows of white energy embedded in the splintered wood on the back wall. Lorcan was yelling at something or someone and blasting crackling bolts in rapid succession. Inside, the shed walls flashed bright with each blast.

"Ha! He's sent one of his dogs in! Too weak to chase down a mere girl himself. Typical!" Lorcan berated someone. A deep, seductive voice that drew me to the small window again, hunched over with just my eyes peeking over the sill.

"Your insults mean nothing to me. Yeqon cares little for anything other than her blood. As a loyal servant, I am more than happy to oblige whilst he attends to other leverage." This new, huge male loomed intimidatingly. His ashen hair blew in the breeze of his grey wings. A large band of Rogues emerged wet and rotten from the pond behind, flanking either side of him. What leverage was he referring to? Something deep within me twinged. A warning, but for what?

"You were more fun twenty thousand years ago, Pineme. Get bored?"

Lorcan took a step back, which accidentally drew the focus of this devil in disguise to the window. For a nanosecond, he saw me. In that paradoxically long, drawn out moment, his dark eyes bored into mine with zero emotion. He drew up his bow and shot six more arrows in my direction. I threw myself to the ground, landing on the door in the floor as glass shattered everywhere.

A metre-long fiery bolt had wedged itself deep into the ground. The force that it took to get it into the concrete-hard dirt floor must have taken immense strength. The earth sizzled around it.

"You fool! If you kill her, she's no good to anyone!"

"I believe we only need her blood." Pineme smirked.

"You have no idea what you need, idiots!" Lorcan retorted.

"We need her to get vengeance, and that is all." Pineme's voice was deceptively calm.

"Run, Sophia! Get to the stone, get down there now!" Lorcan commanded with the same calm as the evil one. Cracking and popping filled the air once more as I raked at the handle-less door.

I still had no key for the lock. I pulled and pushed at the damned door from every possible angle. The groaning of the newly advancing Rogues had quickly made me frantic. I kicked at it, punched it, and tried to dig it open with my bare hands. Nothing worked. I could tell Lorcan was hopelessly outgunned as I saw him slowly edging closer to the shed through the shabby reflection from a square of polished tin on the wall. As my fear grew, so did the heat in my body, and my wings unfurled wider of their own volition. A bolt of energy was fired inside, reflecting off of the tin and blasting upwards, blowing the roof clean off.

I screamed at Lorcan, "I can't get in! It won't open!"

He was now fighting from the doorway. His size was such that I could see his wingspan and feet, but not his shoulders from my vantage point.

"Bollocks, Sophia! You know exactly how to open it. Whatever you did to get into that Scroll chamber is what you need to do now! Hurry!" I heard him groan as he took a shot and stumbled. "Don't even think of it, just get out of here!" he warned as I moved to see how injured he might be.

I turned back, just as another flurry of arrows flung past him, one slicing down my arm. I grabbed at the wound, the glistening blood trickling quickly down to my fingertips.

Blood.

Blood!

That was it.

I crawled to the door and let the crimson droplets fall, one drop at a time, onto the rusted lock. Instantly, a resonating boom shook the ground. The door shimmered and hazed away until it evaporated into nothing but a dark void.

"I'm in, Lorcan! I did it!" I screamed through the frenzied cacophony of Rogues now scratching at every side of the shed. One had climbed the side and was peering down at me from where the roof had been.

"Go! Run for your life, I'll meet you there! Run!" Lorcan yelled.

I threw myself down those stairs, missing three or four at a time as I heard the Rogues overhead. Lorcan couldn't hold them all back alone, not to mention a Daimon as well. I could hear the echoes of these foul creations falling over each other to get to me. The gurgles and groans were tormenting as I fell and slipped down a flight or two at a time. I tried a few awkward flaps of my wings. They worked for a second until I smacked myself clumsily into a wall. I tried to run, fly, and run some more, with limited success. When I finally reached the golden gate, I slammed it shut quickly as I saw the filthy creatures scrambling around the corner from the stairwell, each one for himself, trying to get to me first. The gate had no lock. How could I keep them out by myself? I was frantic, grabbing at my head for an idea. The murals pressed in on me. They were judging me, telling me that I was the wrong person for this. I was weak… they'd made a mistake. Normal. Boring. Average. Their jewelled eyes bore down on me as I imagined these words.

"No!" I yelled back, "I'm not!"

Then it struck me. "Brennan, you gorgeous genius!" I called out loud as the eyes went back to blank, stony stares.

I flung out my right arm, channelling all of the anger, hurt, and fear towards the gate. I also let in for the first time, some self-confidence. "I can do this!"

My mark raged, but this time it felt fantastic—empowering even. The burn up my spine was like wine to my tastebuds.

"Burn, you evil bastards!"

The elemental burst that shot from me was so strong that it flung me backwards, like the kickback from a shotgun. I watched as the energy hit the golden bars. A hum instantly followed, vibrating the metallic barrier like a giant harp playing a deafening tune. The decomposing hands reaching through the bars smouldered, and they began to retreat slowly back, unaware of what was coming. Like a sonic boom, a solid white atomic light lit the corridor. Within seconds, it was all over. The dust settled, and there was nothing but silence and the sickening smell of burnt flesh left behind.

Brennan's security system had actually worked. If only that self-indulgent show-off had been there to see it.

I looked around, and I nearly threw up as I suddenly realised that Lorcan had been following me. For a moment, I thought I must've incinerated him, too, until a light tap on my shoulder reassured me otherwise.

Behind me, with an expression of awe on his face, Lorcan quietly said, "You really are our saviour!"

With that said, he enveloped me in his wings and transferred us home.

Chapter
Forty-Two

As Lorcan's wings retracted, I sensed an immediate and panicked urgency in the Sanctuary as everyone in the main area ran. I looked down from above as they carried bags, pulled children hurriedly along, and wheeled those in stasis down to the deepest levels. Even the greenery reacted, with the large, white flowers closing as if in self- preservation. I watched the frenzied scene below from where I'd arrived, next to the pink version of the Zythros stone. The monolith was alive, vibrating with the sounds of a million voices humming within it. My head snapped around as my name was called sharply from behind me.

"Sophia! If you were not so valuable, *you* would be in the highest order of trouble with the Eloi council right now, much like Brennan is! Come now, we are in crisis!" Enl'iel waved her hands in anger. She was wearing white training gear, complete with chest armour. There were pacing footprints in the dust on the floating deck. She must have been waiting for me.

"Bring her down!" Enl'iel ordered. Lorcan flew me down to the first level, landing amongst the hustle and bustle by the door to the main corridor that led to the lowest levels. Enl'iel transferred down with a simple touch to her temple.

"Go search for Brennan. Tell him that he'd better be ready before Gedz'iel or I get there. Go on, now!" Her face was florid.

Lorcan disappeared in the customary flash of light. Without so much as an *'Are you okay?'* from Enl'iel, I was dragged in an uncomfortable silence, apart from her huffing and puffing, until we had descended into a stuffy library in the depths of nowhere.

Awaiting us was the council of Eloi, silently surrounding Gedz'iel, who languished casually against the desk, arms folded. They were still and emotionless on the outside, but their auras were fiery, sparks sputtered behind them. All six of them had their wings spread wide. Like Enl'iel, they were dressed in battle armour. Their hips heavy with weapons. Kea, Jude and Koi stepped back as Gedz'iel surveyed all present.

"Welcome back, Earth-born. You have caused quite the stir—you and young Bren'ael." He cocked his head to the left, where Brennan slouched in a winged chair. He looked like a teenager stuck in detention after school. Brennan smiled weakly at me.

Gedz'iel rose from his position slowly and methodically, grazing his short hair on the orb-powered pendant light above. His armour clanged menacingly. He looked to Enl'iel.

"You, of all people, should have known better." He cut her silent before she could respond by turning his back on her. He faced me.

"Foolish choices. All of you!"

There was a group cringe as his cool temper brought us all to attention. "Relaxation outing! At a time such as this? You, Sophia, have no business being above ground where the enemy slither in every crevice and under every rock! Fools, the lot of you!" Gedz'iel turned his back on us all, breathing slow and deep as if to maintain control of his anger. He leaned heavily on the edge of the desk, his wings flapped slowly, fanning a warm draught across the room. The calmness of his voice, cool and sharp, was gut-wrenching.

"I…" I began to explain myself, but was immediately cut off by Gedz'iel's sharp tone. It seemed more deeply punctuated with that indistinct European accent most of them seemed to have, especially in his heightened state of anger.

"It matters not *how* or *why* you did what you did. The fact is that the act of your transference has caused waves around the globe. The energy signature you left was so strong and unrefined that it has alerted and drawn up all manner of evil to the surface. They are close enough to us now that they may as well knock on the front door!" Gedz'iel bellowed the last part. He was furious. His energy drew goosebumps to my skin.

"We are all but completely compromised now because of your inability to control your emotions. We have been forced to dispatch the strongest among us as sentries and scouts. Our weakest are hiding in the lowest chambers. Our young ones in stasis, the next generation, our most vulnerable..." His fists clenched, "Our young ones are at heightened risk now because of you!"

I cringed whilst Gedz'iel paced back and forth. He glared at Brennan, then beckoned Koi and Kea over. They spoke briefly in whispers. Koi shook his head many times before bowing and stepping away. Kea seemed to also plead a case with him before taking a step back and standing by my side, giving me a reassuring rub on my shoulder. Just her touch was enough to ease my anxiety. I couldn't help babbling another explanation.

"I'm sorry Gedz'iel, I don't know how I transferred. One minute I was riding a horse, and the next, I was face-down in my old backyard!"

"And because of it, our hand has been forced! Lorcan nearly paid with his mortal life, hunting you down. We are ill-prepared to search for the prophecy of Enoch, but we must move forward prematurely due to your stupidity." His tone now dripped with anger. "You should have foreseen this, Bren'ael. You've lived by her side for twenty years. Your softness is a weakness, as is hers!" Gedz'iel didn't hold back the insults as he stared the supplicant Brennan down.

My attempted apology had clearly fallen on deaf ears. Not a soul, not even Brennan supported me. I gritted my teeth and balled my fists. How could I have known I had the power to do this? In the blink of an eye, they'd expected me to absorb a lifetime's worth of knowledge and training. Without question and drowning in fear, I had followed this freaky twist in my life. I'd ridden a rollercoaster of shock and awe, allowing nature and trust in those around me to take over. Absolute trust is what I gave them. The least they could have done was cut me a little slack. Two weeks ago, I'd been working the early shift and window-shopping for Christmas presents in the village, and now, I didn't even recognise myself in the mirror. My face had become red hot, the skin tingled with rage.

"Sophia, calm yourself down," Enl'iel said in the least motherly tone I'd ever heard from her.

"Calm down?" I yelled. My eyes burned with fury as I looked around the room. "I've questioned nothing! Not a damn thing! I've accepted everything you've thrown at me. I've been terrified, attacked, injured, and through no fault of my own, I mess up! If I hadn't been kept in the dark for the last twenty years, I might've had just a little bit more preparation for such an occasion as this! Whose fault is that, huh? Not mine! A little truth more than five minutes before my body whacked out on me, and I might not feel like I'm on a suicide mission, blindfolded!" I kicked the chair beside me. To my surprise and delight, my newly emergent strength had it sail clear across the room, smashing into pieces against the far wall.

With nothing left to say, I shoved past a room full of shocked silence, slamming the heavy door so hard that it left a crack right up the middle. I didn't care. I was beyond pissed. I ran through the corridors, ignoring the call of my name. Up a level or two, I stretched my wings that had popped out again without an invitation. I pumped them a few times before ramming into some poor sod laden with boxes as he came around a corner. I apologised and quickly helped him up, then ran the rest of the way. At first, I just ran randomly to blow off some steam, then an idea came to me.

Exhausted, I slammed the door shut and leaned back against it, breathing out my anger. My trembling hands glowed strong and bright as I rubbed them across my face, clearing my eyes of unwelcome tears. Enough crying.

The room was quiet and empty except for them. *Yes!* I thought. The red orbs hung in the far corner of the training room; their glow reflected across the array of weaponry hanging along the wall. I flicked my hair back over my shoulders and shook out my arms. Before any common sense could take over, I called out.

"C'mon you little bastards, give me your best shot!"

They just hovered in frustrating ignorance.

"C'mon, attack me! Do it!" I screamed at them, flailing my arms and egging them on. Still nothing. I stamped my foot and threw out a small, sputtering shot of energy. It landed just below them, refracting off the wall, down into the ground. Just that act itself felt good, releasing some tension and anger. I looked at my hand a moment, turning it back and forth, marvelling at what it could do. Then I looked back up, surprised to find that the orbs had disappeared.

A sudden static energy teased at my hair. I turned slowly, only to see that the bunch of red nasties had snuck up right behind me. Clearly, my tantrum had finally got their attention. It didn't feel such a good idea now that they were looming ominously over me. I took a step backwards in a moment of hesitation. But then my lingering anger overcame the self-doubt enough that I stuck out my chin arrogantly and taunted them.

"Bring it on!"

I was under siege immediately. All five launched their nasty stings at me as I ran, ducked, and rolled like Koi had taught me. I came out of a roll roughly after copping a blast to my heel. I shot a stinging rebuke back. It knocked one orb out of existence. Their hum intensified as I darted around behind wooden training dummies. Dodging in and out of them, I avoided most assaults. My heart raced with exhilaration. My wings felt increasingly strong and purposeful. They grew brighter as my confidence soared. I was still a little dizzy, feeling drunk from the unexpected transfer, but I was mad on the buzz.

The remaining orbs grouped together, then formed into an arrow pattern. They chased me down through the dummies and out into the open. They were fast and methodical, with robot-like precision. My body stung all over. Despite this, I stood my ground and gritted through the pain as I doubled-backed to the dummies and headed deeper underground, descending to the ancient ruins that I'd trained in with Lorcan. I managed a few flaps, and had actually become airborne for a short time. My unsteadiness was a surprising bonus. Their accurate attacks flew by me as I wobbled wildly all over the place. This advantage gave me enough time to hide behind the door of an ancient home. It was dark and musty inside. Unfortunately, the orbs found me within seconds, and zoomed straight in through a sliver of space between a crushed window frame. They surrounded me in the far corner by an upturned urn. An eerie red glow spilled across the tight space. For some reason though, they'd stopped firing at me. In a move I didn't anticipate, they collectively threw out what seemed to be shackles made of a fiery, red energy, and bound my arms to the wall. As much as I struggled, I couldn't move.

"That's not fair! You're fighting dirty! Let me go!" I yelled and struggled against the bite of the shackles.

"What in I'el's name is going on in here?" Koi ripped the door from the last of its hinges and stormed in like a thundercloud. The orbs retreated, and my shackles immediately dissipated into thin air.

"Thank you," he said as they buzzed away.

Covered top to toe in dirt, fresh blood and bruises atop the old, I looked away as Koi and the entire group from the meeting room entered the small, dark space. They all looked relieved, some immediately annoyed. Koi glared at me; his eyes turned an icy blue. His mark glowed vibrantly, pulsating like a vein, throbbing with anger.

"Are you trying to get yourself killed, Sophia? These orbs are capable of dealing a deathblow if they sense a security breach. You're lucky they recognised who you are and called to me. Foolish child!"

My cheeks blazed. I couldn't look at any of them. I was annoyed and humiliated, all at once.

"We all understand the immensity of the stress you are under. You have lost your dear friend Esme, may her mortal soul one day rest on the plains of A'vean," Koi swiped a palm across his mark and raised his hand, palm up, as did they all. I assumed it was a gesture of respect. "You have faced terrible creatures and dire circumstances whilst discovering who you truly are. But are you so naïve to think that we would not support you in this? You are not alone. The pressure is high, but the bond here is deep. Running off like a human child having a tantrum is beneath you, Sophia. You are a sensitive soul, but this show of aggression is surprising. I thought better of your inner strength." Koi's unexpected lecture stung more than the orbs.

I struggled with my emotions, kicked the ground, and grunted.

"You know *nothing* about how I feel! You were born knowing who and what you are. I've had it flung in my face, out of the blue!" I pushed off the wall, wincing at the bruising on my arms. "I've gone along with you all without question. I've not made even a ripple of fuss. I haven't been able to mourn Esme, not even offer her a proper funeral. Besides seeing all that I have, I now come to find out that I have parents somewhere, but nobody tells me who or where they are. I have powers that I can't control because I was kept in the dark my whole life. So, until I get a few answers, you all can decipher that damned scroll yourselves!" I shoved past the still shocked group and marched back to the main arena, stopping to lean against a wall of golden swords.

I couldn't believe I'd blurted all of that out, but I was seething. It seemed that the more this power emerged, the more untapped anger arose in me as well. I had always been calm and level-headed. This transition was turning me into someone I didn't like. Every pulse pounded as I tried to calm down. It seemed when faced with a real threat, it was the rawest emotion that fired me up. My wings were just settling back down when Enl'iel approached, placing a hand on my shoulder. I jerked away.

"You should have told me earlier, Enl'iel. I would have had more time to adjust. I thought I knew you; I thought I knew a lot of things, but my entire life's been a lie."

"I know, Sophia. I am very sorry for that. I understand how you must feel. We did what was best for your physical safety, but perhaps not your emotional wellbeing," she responded calmly. "We shall give you the answers you need as best we can. We all seek answers, and we can learn these together. We are all one of spirit and family, Sophia."

I refused to look at her as I turned my back and peered at my distorted reflection in a golden blade.

"Sophia, come now. We must move forward. I sympathise with your plight, but for the sake of our survival and our home world, you must push these emotions aside." Gedz'iel's deep voice preceded him. He waved his hands over the burns on my wrists. The pain ebbed away and I felt my power surge back. He held my hands in his, then tilted my sullen face so I was forced to look at him. I didn't dare resist.

"I feel your pain, I truly feel it as my own. It is a burden shared by us all. You are like a daughter to us, as we have all watched and protected you for all of your precious life. Unfortunately, we do not have the luxury of time at present, as the Unseen are on the move. We are both the hunters and the hunted now. We must rise against the Unseen with the first strike. If they were to use their spies to get ahead of us, to compromise our path to the portal—if that happens, I cannot guarantee we could protect humankind from whatever they plan. If, somehow, they were to open the portal, anything could come through. It is a gateway to the universe, Sophia. It is a wide and densely populated universe. If they were to get their hands on you, they would force you, one way or another, to do their bidding. Come now, help us, help yourself, and help the humans, who we were sent here to protect." Gedz'iel took a step back, giving me space to think. All of their eyes were on me. I didn't want to listen to him, but it all made annoying sense. Even Brennan looked on hopefully, giving me a reassuring nod. They were all now so irritatingly calm.

"Fine," I gave in and Gedz'iel led me from the training room. My hand felt warm and safe in his.

Deep breath in, deep breath out, repeat.

"Will you tell me everything? Not in a day or a week, but now?"

Gedz'iel stopped a moment by the heavy doors before we re-entered the library.

He placed his large hands on my shoulders and looked down at me. I was barely a foot shorter than his imposing stature, yet I still felt small. He leaned down and placed his glowing mark to mine. "A K'ufili—a kiss for my kindred. A gesture of love and oneness." He actually smiled. I instantly felt a warmth stirring inside of my chest. A calming feeling. I was immediately more relaxed.

"Sophia, you think yourself so insignificant. Ordinary, to put it in your own words. Well, inside that ordinary girl is something extraordinary. I regret that you have been blocked from discovering this gift through your concealment. In time you will come to see how inexplicably un-ordinary you are." Gedz'iel held my face in his hands, rubbing his thumb gently across my cheek, like a wise, old magi, disguised in youthful beauty. "Be at peace with who you are," he said, followed by another K'ufili. We re-entered the library.

My instant thought was, *but ordinary was good and safe*. It was my motto, and I didn't want to let go of that. Could I be ordinary and extraordinary at the same time, like an A-list Hollywood star who had it all, but chose to live a simple, unimposing life away from the limelight? It seemed an unlikely and almost conceited thought, not at all how I thought of myself.

"Enl'iel, her mind troubles her still. Perhaps you might give her a small measure of comfort before we proceed any further?" Gedz'iel beckoned her over.

"Of course," she answered, her eyes downcast and not meeting mine. The sting of his chastisement was still evident in her demure tone. The glisten of a tear on her cheek tugged at my heart. Guilt trampled my lingering anger.

She took my hands in hers. "Sophia, I want you to close your eyes and concentrate on nothing but a moment of pure joy," she instructed.

I regarded her briefly, wondering how I could conjure up anything even remotely jovial at that moment.

"Please, dear, trust me," her eyes were unashamedly moist now. She hurt as I did. I melted and finally closed my eyes.

She placed her hands on either side of my face, "Now, think of this special moment. Think of it, and nothing else."

I searched my memories for something that couldn't be tainted with sadness, a time that was pure, innocent, and happy. It came surprisingly without effort. I recalled the day I sat with a five-year old girl in the Paediatric ward. She had just beaten leukaemia. Whilst her parents cried with joy in the corridor with the doctors, she sat with me and brushed my hair into rainbow plaits and ponytails.

"Nurse Sophie, are you a real fairy? I think you are. Do you know the tooth fairy? Does she sparkle like you do? You always sparkle when you visit."

She'd asked me a million questions that afternoon as we played hairdressers. Had that innocent child seen something in me that I didn't see myself?

I suddenly became aware that I was smiling. I felt a shiver rush through me. My eyes popped open. I sucked in a sharp breath.

"What did you do to me?" I asked in a slightly accusatory tone.

"Look, dear! Look!" Enl'iel guided me to an oval-shaped mirror by the doorway. I could hear a lot of hushed murmuring behind me. I looked at the image reflecting back at me.

"Oh my God, Nan… sorry, Enl'iel! How did you do that?"

The reflection showed a much more familiar face—comforting and ordinary. It was me, just me, with my rainbow hair restored.

"It will only last as long as your power is kept within. You will learn the art of concealment in time, as we all do. For now, I gift it to you," she kissed me K'ufili-style and led me back to Gedz'iel.

"And there she is, my old Princess!" Brennan practically shouted from the sidelines.

"Does this help?" Gedz'iel asked.

"Actually, as stupid as it seems, this hair does make me feel a whole lot better. I feel like me again," I answered, as I ran my hands through the multicoloured mane. "I remember when Jaz first put the bright green through it. School wasn't impressed," I giggled to myself.

"I am pleased to hear this. Now tell me, what it is that you wish to know?" Gedz'iel asked.

His immediate compliance boosted my feeling of security. I began to feel that perhaps I really was part of something, and not just an outsider dragged in to be used and cast aside.

I could only think of one pressing thing to ask.

"Who and where are my parents? Also, I want Jaz and Ben with me. Besides this…" I gripped a fistful of hair as evidence, "…They are all that's left of my old life. They are the only people who I trust to have never lied to me. I need my friends." I thought I'd asked politely, but I could literally feel the hurt of the insult to Enl'iel. It hurt me as much as it hurt her as I heard the sharp breath of shock from where she stood behind me.

"Very well," Gedz'iel answered just as the doors cracked open. Eilir entered, humming as she busied herself with setting up tea and cakes. "Not now, Eilir," Gedz'iel said, firmly but kindly.

"Oh, pish posh, you won't be savin' anybody on an empty stomach! Now, eat and drink, before it gets cold." She tut-tutted to herself as she shoved a cup under Gedz'iel's nose. He took it gently and kissed her cheek, as did they all. It appeared that they truly adored her. I noticed her limp had worsened. Dash was ever her shadow, helping her walk, despite being slapped away by her when he tried to do too much.

Gedz'iel put his cup down after drinking it like a shot of espresso. "Soph'ael… Sophia, tonight we hope to discover the location of the next piece of the puzzle, but we must unravel Enoch's clue first. You have made a valid request, and along with my brothers…" he indicated the five Eloi members, "…I believe it is of no service to any of us to keep anything hidden from you now." Gedz'iel pulled a chair for me to sit in. The light orbs suddenly seemed loud and irritating. This unexpected moment was almost too much, and he began without further delay.

"Your mother is a Eudaimonian of great lineage. She, Sarun'iel, has links going back to the time of Adam and Lilith. She gave birth to you and another child twenty years ago."

I fell back deeper into the chair, "Another child? I have a sibling?"

"Yes, a twin brother. So powerful was the elemental signature that emerged from your first cries that Daimon gathered from far and wide. All manner of evil crawled from their cesspits and hunted your parents down. Your family were unaware of exactly who or what you were until it was too late. They had been living amongst the Hidden, Eudaimonia who wish to live as humans. They use little or none of their gifted A'vean powers. This made them invisible to us until that night. Their unpreparedness allowed them to be overwhelmed by an ambush under the cover of darkness. Thinking quickly, your mother caused a diversion, running off with a bundle of blankets into the woods whilst hiding you away with the midwife. Your father ran with your brother. As far as we knew, your father was overwhelmed by the Daimon, and your brother was either captured or killed. The midwife saw this unfold from her hiding place beneath the cottage, through a cellar window where she hid with you." Gedz'iel paused a moment for me to absorb it. Every muscle clenched; my fingers clawed the arms of the chair.

"After a time though, your father returned to the cottage with the body of your mother, who had lost her mortal life protecting you." I physically shuddered, felt the sting of my nails split against the chair.

"Your father has not been seen since that night. It is believed, with no evidence of his ascendance, that he still searches the world for your brother after sending you away to safety with the midwife. That very midwife stands before you today." He pointed to Enl'iel. She acknowledged this revelation with a bow of her head. Tears welled in my eyes.

"You knew them? What was my father's name?" I asked quietly.

"Yes, Sophia, I knew them briefly. They were kind and gentle. They lived simply. In hundreds of years, they had never conceived a child, so when you and your brother were born, their joy was unimaginable. Your father's name, as you may have heard before you entered the

Scroll Chamber, is Rik'ael, but around the village, he was known simply as Richard of Woodville," she answered.

I was floored. I had a brother, a blood relative, and possibly a still living father. My heart then lurched again in grief for the mother I would never know. A mother who gave her life for the survival of her children. I was blinded by my rapidly welling up eyes.

"You said my mother is dead, but speak of her as though she's still alive!" I blurted out.

"Indeed. She continues to exist somewhere in the Cavern of Souls. Her immortal spirit has dwelled within the stones of the Earth for twenty years," answered Gedz'iel solemnly, before he continued. "We have searched for your father, and your brother, too. They unfortunately have left no trail behind, even for our best trackers, such as Lorcan. We have, thus far, entreated no message from your mother. Lorcan was dispatched just this past hour to Peru to appeal to her, begging for any information she may have. Whilst we cannot physically visit the Cavern of Souls, sometimes the departed can contact us if we are in its vicinity."

"Peru? What? I, I can't think! I… err… can I see Ben and Jaz now, please?" The fabric of the chair ripped; blood pooled around my nail beds. I needed my friends to help me make sense of all of this.

Silence engulfed the musty room. The orbs seemed to glow even brighter. The smell of earl grey tea and vanilla sponge intensified, and hearts beat more rapidly all around. I could see coloured auras surrounding everyone, but some were brighter than others. Gedz'iel's was golden. The council of Eloi, who stood silently behind him, were bathed in pinks and blues. Pathos had licks of orange around his head. Everyone else was surrounded with a spectrum of rainbow light. Tension radiated from them as the assorted auras flickered erratically. Only Gedz'iel and the council remained calm and static. I felt feelings that were not my own next. Fear, regret, anger. It was like I was tapping into them all. The silence was achingly long as I studied each face. Brennan was picking his nails with a small dagger by the hearth, head down. Enl'iel was ashen and looked at me with sorrowful eyes. Kea motioned my attention back to Gedz'iel.

"That is not possible right now, I'm afraid. I'm sorry, Sophia. Jasmine is recovering from shock in the newly relocated Stasis room. Unfortunately, whilst you transferred, there was an attack. She witnessed young Ben abducted by a horde of Afflicted. I am certain it was at the behest of a Daimon. I am much aggrieved to tell you this," Gedz'iel said.

"What?" Barely a whisper, my voice was almost eclipsed from the shock. My body slumped; my skin numbed. If I could have sunk down any lower, I would've disappeared into the fabric of the chair. I wasn't mad or sad, or anything other than cold with emotional paralysis. I ran my bloodied fingers across the armrest, tracing them along the dark, sculpted wood ends. It was smooth until the bump at the end, like my life had been, until recently.

For a moment, I stared bleary-eyed around the room. It brimmed with paintings of all eras and styles, yet my attention was drawn to a familiar, concentric circle in a modern-looking painting directly ahead. Silver and gold circles overlapped each other against a black backdrop, and these swirling patterns absorbed me. I thought I heard my name, and then felt a pressure on my shoulder. The circles danced, enticing me in. One seemed to grow and pulse wildly before it emerged from the confines of its silver frame. I ignored the others, which were snapping in and out of the picture in turn. The large one was pin-pricked by a small light. Soon, the light grew into a swirling mass of pink, blue, and gold-flecked hues that swirled and sparkled.

An eye—His eye—burned down upon me once more.

Silence.

Chapter Forty-Three

I was shaken from the trance by Brennan,

"Princess, come back now."

I blinked as Gedz'iel came into focus. He knelt in front of me with Matias and Theus. Serail and Pathos just behind them.

Gedz'iel looked intently at me, his warm hand steady upon my glowing, trembling one.

"She has connected with I'el, may He forever be blessed. Her eyes turn as his." Gedz'iel touched his hand to his mark, looked to the ceiling, and raised his palm. It was the same sentiment I'd seen frequently over the past few days, whenever I'el was mentioned. I remained numb as I watched his reverent gesture. The tinkering of china, as Eilir waddled past with a butler's trolley, registered somewhere in the distance.

"I get it," I said after a few moments as my head space cleared.

I slowly stood up, and they all backed away. Everyone held his or her attention achingly enrapt on my next move. I turned and looked at each and every face as my pulse thundered. Intense expressions met my gaze, all brimming with anticipation. They looked on silently; patiently.

"I get it. I understand now, somehow." I furrowed my brow as I heard myself. The words kept coming, I just didn't know from where.

I paced a little in front of the hearth. "I know what I am. I am more than a key. I feel some kind of link between this world and His."

A surge of energy swirled around me. I felt the warmth of their smiles brighten the room. "Whatever happened just now has left something behind, like some kind of strength or connection. I don't know, it's just something. I don't feel the same." I ran my hands through my hair nervously, feeling ridiculous saying these things, but also knowing that they were absolutely true and needed to be acknowledged out loud. "I know I have to embrace this and fulfil a purpose, no matter what the human in me says." I spoke to no one and everyone, perhaps more to myself.

I rubbed my eyes. They felt strange. There was an ache in the back of them. I walked back to the mirror. My irises were a more intense blue than before. They sparkled and seemed to be moving… yes, the blue turned clockwise.

What the hell?

My eyes were swirling, a biological cosmos coursing around my pupils. It was terrifying, exciting, and grounding all at once. It cemented in me the acknowledgment to myself of what I was and pushed back the last of my lingering doubts.

I rubbed across the soul stone bracelet for strength. "I will serve you and do my best to save you all. However, you need to do something for me. I won't rest until I find Ben and hunt down anything or anyone that has hurt my family." Thoughts of Esme brought tears back, "I need you all to promise me that we will see this through together, and seek justice for all those who have been hurt. We serve each other, we are one and the same, or we are nothing."

I was quietly taken aback at my own sudden confidence. I was always a follower, and yet here I was, demanding vengeance and servitude. Had I not been so high on energy at that point, I may well have run out and hidden in embarrassment.

Everyone inclined their head as I finished speaking. Their marks all glowed in perfect acquiescence.

"Sophia, you indeed are the daughter of I'el. You finally feel our eternal connection of oneness. We work and live as one, and so in turn, your needs are our needs. We will seek that which is important to you as it now is important to us," Gedz'iel said.

"Thank you," I turned to Enl'iel.

"Is Jaz going to be okay?" I asked.

"Yes, she will recover. She is shocked, but comfortable, and has received calming tisanes to help her rest while her emotional wounds ease. Gedz'iel has deployed scouts to search for Ben. Kristen and Thomas captured two Afflicted, and Jude is interrogating them as we speak," she responded.

I grabbed the last steaming cup of coffee from Eilir's trolley as she waddled by with perfect timing. I gulped it down. Hot and sweet, with a touch of bitter at the end, which befitted how I felt. Warm and comforted, but disgruntled to the core about the hand dealt to me.

Eilir beamed and passed me an Eccles cake, "Eat up, sweet pea, you can't be doing great things on an empty stomach now, can you?" I took the sweet pastry and leaned down to kiss her grey head. I couldn't stomach it right now, but I took a small bite to please the sweet old woman.

"Oh me, I love this one. Now, Dash, go get yourself some decent fightin' clothes on. I suspect you'll be needed here, rather than by my side." Eilir gestured Dash out the door with an authoritative flick of her hand.

"Eilir, no! I will stay with you, as always," he responded, placing a loving arm around her shoulders. She leaned into him and patted at his chest. This gentle giant alleviated, for a moment, the evident strain that walking was having on her.

"Oh, go on with yer! We both know the time has come for you to stand with your brothers and sisters again. You've looked after me long enough. No more 'o this guilt. You've given me a longer 'an happier life than I ever would 'o had if I hadn't run into you that night. Never has a woman been gladder to be blinded by a man!" Eilir laughed heartily. "You go on now, I'll be here waitin' for you. Always 'ave been, you know that." Eilir fumbled around with her apron and dabbed at her unseeing eyes.

"She speaks the truth, Dash'iel. It is time to put personal needs and regrets behind and stand with us. You have cared well for this gentle soul. Dearest Eilir, I will see to it that you are relieved of your duties as required, and rested." Gedz'iel placed a glowing palm across Eilir's spine, giving her aged body an instant and visible relief from her pain.

"Yes, your Grace, I understand." Dash bowed as Eilir pushed at him to let her go. He took up a post with Brennan and Kea by the hearth. The glow of the fiery light gave away the strain of pain in his face at the sacrifice.

"Let us move on now, please?" Gedz'iel guided me back to the desk. It was time to be strong and grown up. The scroll lay open across the desk.

Deep breath in, deep breath out, repeat.

"We have awaited you many a millennium. I honour you and offer you my unwavering service." Matias took my hand and bowed, then offered me a K'ufili kiss. I accepted and the spark that passed between us; it emboldened me with a jolt. "My gift to you, Soph'ael, is courage." Matias stepped back and pushed the scroll towards me.

"Okay, here we go," I said, more to myself.

I ran my fingers across the cracked, stiff script. The words seemed to swim across the page and jump out at me. The harder I stared, the more three-dimensional they became, as though I could pluck them from the air. I picked up the tea-coloured sheet, inspecting every inch. I read through it slowly to myself, lingering over the reference to my parents. The resting place of your father's mother. This was where we needed to go. But who was my father? Rik'ael was a name, but where did that lead us?

"Lorcan is trying to connect with my mother's spirit?" It felt weird saying that.

"Yes, Sophia. Hopefully, she will extrude herself from the crystals to speak with him," Matias replied.

"Extrude herself?"

"She dwells, as do others, within the crystalline walls of the Cavern of Souls. A place of safety and contemplation for those of us who have ascended the human form, but cannot return to A'vean," he answered.

I placed the delicate paper back down, gently smoothing it out as I did so. It crackled like dried leaves, but thankfully remained intact.

"Clearly, my father is key in this passage. How could no one know how to track him or his family? You knew him once, Enl'iel. Don't you know even one of his family members who could maybe help?" I asked.

"I knew Rik'ael, who, as I said, went by the human name of Richard, for only the briefest of times. I knew nothing of his past; he was very secretive. Your parents chose to live a hidden life as Gedz'iel explained. They only contacted me for your birth, as the one thing we must come together for is a new birth. A human cannot deliver a child for a Eudaimonian, as the energy the birth exerts could very well kill them at the worst, and blind them at the least." She gestured toward Eilir as evidence. "I knew Rik'ael a mere few hours. It is the only reason we even know his name. He is a ghost to us. Your mother's lineage though, when we briefly re-discovered her, was indeed a surprise. Her lineage commands great respect. It appears though, her love for him drove her underground and out of our lives long ago," she answered.

"Okay, well what about my name, Woodville? If he gave me that name, it must have been for a reason, to link me with my heritage. Should we follow that lead and see if we can track him down? Can't we Google his name or something?"

A cough-masked laugh echoed from someone in the room. Pathos broke the stony-faced silence that the Eloi had perfected and chuckled at my comment.

"You think that's funny? I don't hear you making any useful suggestions!" I snapped. There was a touch of Jaz running through me today.

"Indeed, Pathos, show some respect. She learns more of our ways every minute. Sophia, we are never documented in a traceable way, as the humans are. We have called for Rik'ael across all the realms in and around the Earth, with no response," Gedz'iel said. "He has never been known to anyone in our community before, and this is why it is so difficult to trace his lineage or query as to your ancestors. It is as though he arrived out of thin air. Such is the problem with the Hidden — if we don't know them, we cannot find them, and if we cannot find them, we most certainly cannot help them. Perhaps there is more in the scroll that we are not seeing. Can you read it once more?" he asked.

I nodded and looked over it again. I read aloud the section pertaining to my father.

"It just makes no sense," I said.

"We are all here for this exact reason. You translate and we will decipher.

Not everything weighs solely upon you, Sophia," Gedz'iel answered.

"Thank goodness for that, we'd be here for another century."

"More truth in that than I care to entertain, Princess!" said Brennan with another annoying wink. I glowered at him.

"Read that section about the boar again, please?" Gedz'iel instructed.

As I again mentioned the reference to the boar and the bull, Eilir, who was stacking cups, slapped her hand across her knee and clucked out loud with a whoop and a laugh, "Oh me! You are all so big and handsome, but lacking the sight!" She tapped at her temple, smiling to herself, "It's right in front of yer pretty faces. Don't yer read the books? Lordy, 'yer lived through our entire history, and blimey, you've near well influenced half of what's gone on! Yer should've picked it right up!" Eilir chuckled again as she re-tied her apron and shook her head at her own amusement.

"Eilir, what are you talking about?" asked Dash with surprise.

"Oh, my love, it's 'er name! 'Er name is the clue. I may be mere peasant-born, but I've had a good deal 'o years to pass the time with books. Woodville and sprig 'o bloom is what gave it away. Sprig of Bloom is the Frenchy description for the name Plantagenet, an' Woodville, well that's the name 'o the lass that married the 'ansome King Edward IV. He was one those Plantagenet kings. Elizabeth Woodville had many a bairn, Sophia's' father must be one of them.

Queen Elizabeth, she was always rumoured to have a touch of magic about her. A Queen of England, ha ha! That's her dear old Gran!" Eilir pointed straight at me.

None of what she said at all registered. It was too confusing, too ridiculous. So, in Sophia tradition I focused on something completely irrelevant.

"Eilir, don't think me rude, or that I'm questioning you, but how do you read books?" I asked, completely unable to digest what she had just blurted out.

"Why, dear, Dash reads them to me, my love. Think he's read me every book ever put to the press!" she answered. I was hanging onto her every word as she continued.

"Oh, me, sweet Sophia, your 'o the line 'o the Kings of England! Oh me! The Plantagenet kings! That last bit about the boar, that's old mad King Richard's standard. So then, who was 'ol Richard hunting down, as the script says? I wonder? Could it have been yer dear old pa? If he were as powerful as any 'o this lot here, I'd say he was all too valuable. A good reason to be hunted by the old boar, Richard!" Eilir chuckled away, her Welsh drawl becoming thicker and more enchanting as her memories flowed through. She blushed, seemed delighted in helping us. I silently took in her massive revelation as she patted down her grey skirt and lace apron. The irony of a room full of immortal beings and a blind, elderly human apparently cracking the case wide open wasn't lost on anyone as we all regarded her with open-mouthed admiration.

"But why would my father be hunted down by a human king? If he was brought up Hidden or human, as I was, who would know about him?"

The Eloi named Amais spoke next, "Master Gedz'iel, Sophia, may I?" Gedz'iel nodded, so Amais proceeded. "I believe Eilir speaks a truth. I recall being present for a reception of youths in the human fifteenth century. Master, you were away, guiding lost souls to the Middle Realm. We were called upon numerous times during this period of festivity to deal with a number of Daimon infestations within the human aristocracy. Do you recall Neph'reus and Anjou'elle?" All in the room, other than Eilir and I, reacted immediately with disgusted acknowledgment.

"At that time, they were known to be hunting amongst areas suspected to be settlements for the Hidden. They were looking for anyone who could even remotely be considered the Earth-born. They had their dogs sniffing around for energy signals in every valley and forest. There were rumours at the time that the British royal lines had Eudaimonian blood running through them. For years, those two preyed on all the royal families, trying to get close," Amais nodded to himself, paced around the room.

"Anjou'elle drove King Richard mad with her infestation of his mind. What reward she received from Yeqon, I could not guess, but I knew then there was more to that particular act than the mere passing of time for her. With Richard, she pushed a decent human into a crazed monster. Matias and I were called to the chamber of Edward IV on the eve of his death by Jacquett'ael who only then revealed herself to be the mother of Queen Elizabeth. That enlightened us to the hidden Eudaimonian heritage of Queen Elizabeth and King Edward. By the time we arrived though, he was far too ravaged. His pterugia were gone —he had been ambushed in the night. King Edward ascended well before his time. He was a strong kindred, one who had fought well to protect his family. There was the pungent stink of Daimon in his chamber, leaving no doubt that one or both of those vixens had been there. This is when Elizabeth went into hiding with her children, knowing that her true self was no longer a secret. Until that moment they had lived quietly. Hidden in plain sight in the ruling ranks of humanity. Elizabeth's sons and daughters were now targets. It was just prior to the Great Undoing of the Unseen, when we managed to push every known Daimon back into the Empyrean realm. It all makes perfect sense now." Amais tapped his temple, his mark glimmered brighter.

"Elizabeth must have secreted away her most powerful child, and that must have been Rik'ael, Richard, your father. Her name before she was married to Edward had been Elizabeth Woodville, your name, Sophia." Amais smiled, it suited him.

There were more than a few *oh's* uttered. My skin tingled. Something seemed to crack open inside, something previously unlocked, a history, a connection… a family. I smiled back at Amais; my heart raced a little faster. I nodded, and he continued.

"It was about the time King Richard became unstable. He was obsessed with Elizabeth's sons. Anjou'elle and Neph'reus must have known something of her son's power and wanted to circumvent nature. Perhaps to possess your father until he revealed himself as the Earth-born or fathered the Earth-born."

My head felt tight, dulled like it was stuffed with cotton wool. I pressed my hands to my mouth, as though to hold everything in when I felt like I might just fall apart. The air buzzed with power, plucked at my skin, as though to let the truth seep within me.

Brennan circled me, tapping his lips, brows furrowed.

"This makes it all fall into place. There seemed to be no sense in what they were doing at the time. The word back then was that they were just toying with the humans for amusement. It was always their calling card, but really…" Brennan let Kea take over.

"They had intel, they had a plan, and they very nearly got what they needed. They very nearly took possession of the Sophia's bloodline!" Kea shook her head, she sighed with relief.

Eilir clapped her hand on her bosom.

"Yes, yes, that's it! Oh me! Her father must 'av been one of the princes, you know Dash, the princes in the tower!" The energy piqued a little higher, elemental light snapped above us. All the hairs on my arms prickled. Eilir wandered nearer, fingers steepled beneath her chin.

"Old King Richard wanted those boys gone, good and proper, but everyone thought it was to save his crown…was it really him or those beastly Daimon?" Eilir nodded to herself, her milky eyes had a shine of wonder in them, "There was always the rumour though that the boys got away. Hmm—I wonder?" Eilir nodded some more, then pressed on her back and sat down with a groan.

There was a deep, thoughtful quiet as we all digested this.

I recalled reading about the princes in the tower in high school history. They were supposedly murdered by King Richard III. Could they really have been Eudaimonian? Could one of those much-discussed children be my father? Could he have somehow escaped a Daimon and survived?

Now I paced. "So, my father escaped his possessed uncle and found his way into the Hidden society of Eudaimonians?"

"Ooh, she's smart as a whip!" cooed Eilir, still rubbing her aches and pains.

"If I may, Eilir, dear sweet lady, you are in fact a most amazing soul. You have pulled together the facts for us in a most incredible way." Amais buffed her ego until she blossomed with rosy cheeks.

"Eilir, you are as amazing today as the day I met you," Dash whispered as he set a glowing hand across her back, easing her pains once more. My ears were attune to the smallest of sounds, and the love in his voice had a life of its own.

Amais took his place back with the Eloi, behind Gedz'iel who white-knuckled the back of a chair with a look of great contemplation.

"Brennan, you know what to do?"

"Consider it done." Brennan bowed. I looked back to the rippling amber of the hearth to see him hugging into Enl'iel. He kissed her cheek, then her lips, then walked over to me, placing a quick peck on my head. "I've always called you Princess. Who knew it was for real? Ha! Now we know exactly where to go. Time to get this party started!" Brennan shook the casualness away and assumed an unfamiliar seriousness.

"Your Grace, I'll take my leave with Koi to gather the ranks. I'll arm the humans and send out decoys. Recall Lorcan, and send him my way as soon as he returns. We could use the battle smarts of a decent Seraph and tracker. He can lead the human infantry with Jude. Jude may join us when his interrogation of the Afflicted is complete." Brennan bowed at Gedz'iel's orders and let his mark glow brightly.

"Sophia, you must go to the armoury. We leave for Windsor tonight," Brennan ordered, no smile, no jokes, just a stiff nod.

I wondered why we were suddenly heading to Windsor, but the room was moving before I could ask more questions.

Gedz'iel then took control of the strangely escalating situation. "The council and I shall go to the perimeter of the Empyrean realm to secure extra sentries. We must prevent as many leaks as we can. I feel a shift in the elements." He glanced to the ceiling as though he could see this shift. I saw nothing.

"We have no time to waste. Move with caution and haste. Sophia, listen to your elders, use your resources. Your powers grow ever stronger, but please remember that you are not in the least alone. Rely on your kindred where you can. Enl'iel, guide her with a firm hand until she reaches maturity, whilst she remains unstable," Gedz'iel said as he and the Eloi blinked out of the room in a brief flash, leaving me frozen, like a deer in headlights.

The heat of their auras remained long after they had gone. Everything began moving in fast forward. The energy in the room was high. Heartbeats raced with anticipation. They pulsed under my skin as though we were all connected. It felt like a hybrid of excitement and fear. Enl'iel and Kea beckoned me to follow them. A human resident with red hair helped Eilir out and down the corridor in another direction. I could hear her protestations of not needing an escort echo back through the shadows. I quickly grabbed Enoch's scroll, rolled it tight, and stuffed it back in its cylinder and into my right leg pocket. The diamond dagger had taken up permanent residence in the left one.

Before I could blink, I was back in the huge training room, where armoury of all styles was being handed out to a roomful of people. The multinational, variously sized human contingent of hundreds, stood in orderly ranks, assembled by the door to the room of ancient ruins. Whilst they jostled with an electric excitement, they were being handed quivers, swords, and shields. Once armed, a cord with a glowing stone was placed around each neck. The lofty Watchers and Eudaimonians were arming up with the impressive chromious arrows and golden swords. I was thrust toward a woman with plaited hair entwined with lavender and other strong-smelling herbs. In fact, I noticed that all the Watchers and Eudaimonians wore the same hair decor, as though they'd just stepped from a fairy-tale forest.

A breastplate was snapped around my chest. An unseen stylist yanked at my hair until it, too, was threaded full of herbs and braided down my back. I turned around to find that my hairdresser was Kea.

"All the protection you can get, honey. Daimon loathe the smell and energy of cedar and lavender, as you should well have guessed by now. It makes them so sick that they can't hide or maintain their disgustingly clever guises. That's one thing you'll learn—Daimon are quite the masters at concealment. You can easily think you're seeing a perfectly harmless human, when you're actually face to face with your worst nightmare. I've been fooled before." Kea pulled down the string sleeve of her scoop-backed top to reveal a jagged, silvery scar that cut through a few of her energy leaflets where her wings emerged. "Note to self, if someone starts gagging for no reason, back off, or blast them to Hell. Literally! Otherwise, you'll very likely get your pterugia ripped out." She winked at me and then moved on to help someone else.

I gulped, chewed my nails, my mind a flurry until I started at the snap of my name.

"Sophia, front and centre!"

Kea spun me around, pushing me in Brennan's direction as he called me to join him upon a stone platform under more infamous red orbs. I moved stiffly in the heavy gear, the steps a challenge. He drew the attention of the masses by thumping his chest plate with his sword a few times. The metallic clang immediately drew the crowd into attentive silence. I felt a thousand eyes on me as he began to speak with a presidential impact. He didn't sound the least bit like himself.

"The time is upon us that we finally begin the journey home. The Earth-born saviour is here to serve us, as we serve her. Our singular aim is to escort her, protect her, and fight alongside her as she clears the path to A'vean. Daimon scourge every realm, every corner and continent. Crush them. Descend as many as you can so that Tartarus may have fuel to burn for eternity. Fight like the warriors that you are today, my kindred, like the warriors you have always been." Brennan rallied everyone until they roared with rapturous approval.

"If we are forced to ascend in order to protect Sophia, then we must commit to this now. If she succeeds, we shall be reunited with our home, where we belong. We will once again be afforded the luxury to move through the universe at will, no longer a prisoner in this small, forgotten galaxy." Brennan pumped a fist to more cheering. "We rally together as the kindred that we are. Enough of us have ascended for no good reason, other than a scuffle with bored Daimon. If we are to dwell in the foundations of the Earth, then let it at least have a reason and purpose. We continue today with what has already begun. We continue today on our path to freedom!" Brennan beat his armour again.

The final roar shook the room as weaponry banged rhythmically against shields and armour plating. Wings lit up the naturally dark space. The well-trained humans looked down with perfect timing to protect their vision from the stunning but dangerous display.

"This is our Saviour. Never was there a more precious being on the Earth. We honour her for who she is, with our unconditional protection and guidance." Brennan thrust a sword into the air. Another huge roar erupted, as weapons were raised in kind and orbs were flung from the hands of Watchers and Eudaimonia. The humans in the back, headed up by Kristen and Thomas, were no less enthusiastic. They now wore metal helmets, their eyes protected from the glare by a film of black. They too, jabbed swords and shields in the air. Gold and silver flashes reflected throughout the cavern. I could feel their nervous energy and hear a thousand heartbeats drumming in my head. For the first time, I didn't feel that familiar twist in my guts that the embarrassment of excessive attention drew. I felt bolstered, strengthened by the comradery. I think I actually smiled.

Koi appeared next to me and addressed the army.

"My kindred, two Daimon and a hoard of Rogues have been seen within this county. We move, now. You all have your orders. Cover every square foot to flush them out and away from Windsor." He left the platform. I followed him to the bottom of the stairs, where he met Lorcan, who'd arrived back from his search.

My mother, did he find my mother? I tried to follow Koi, but Brennan grabbed my arm. "Not now, Princess. I know what you want, but we need to focus on one thing at a time. Lorcan has his orders, too." Brennan pulled me back up the stairs and raised his sword-baring arm, along with the other, and created an enormous orb.

"Upon the orb, as it dulls, we transfer out. This mass movement will cause enough distraction and confusion among the Daimon and Rogues that Sophia should be able to safely reach her destination undetected. To our beloved sons and daughters of the Earth, take caution and heed your leaders. Waste not a drop of your blood, if you can help it. Conceal yourselves so you may move unheeded, unnoticed. We thank you for your unwavering support of us, mere visitors to your home." he stabbed his sword towards the roof. "Nik'e—to victory!" he shouted, like some mythical hero.

The orb pulsed, as though it was counting down. As it pulsed, the Watchers and Eudaimonians altered their appearances. Hair, skin, and eye colours morphed from one thing to another. It suddenly looked like a room at the United Nations, except that they were all wearing the same battle armour. At the exact same time, they all shimmered slightly and these fighting clothes disappeared under a veil of concealment, leaving them looking like they were dressed in street clothes.

"Wow!" I gaped at the magic of it.

"I'll teach you that someday, Princess," Brennan whispered in my ear.

After counting ten pulses, the orb dulled to almost transparency. With the exception of me, my small contingent, and the humans, everyone else blinked out, en masse. Brennan was left behind, staring down at me, his glistening chest plate heaving from the thrill of what was to come, "Let's go, Princess. We've got a Queen to dig up!"

The neighbour from across the road seemed a mere memory.

Chapter
Forty-Four

Branches heavy with fresh snow weighed over the human legion before they were led away in groups of twenty by Jude and Lorcan. They wore street clothes over their armour. That familiar drumming returned to my head the moment I'd set foot outside, and I could've sworn those distant screams for help from the previous night were haunting me.

Several mini-buses parked up the gravel drive towards the Tudor house. They were emblazoned with Gloucestershire Tourist Company, a clever way to send out people in many directions without raising suspicion. Kristen and Thomas escorted them, appearing to be in some position of leadership. Koi, Kea, Brennan, and I left in a black Jag. Enl'iel stayed behind as caretaker of Jaz and the others who were in stasis, and the otherwise vulnerable.

"I feel kind of ridiculous, dressed like a Roman soldier and riding in a Jag." I plucked at the uncomfortable outfit. Humour seemed inappropriate, but I was aiming for a little stress relief. The air was suffocating with tension.

Brennan smiled, "I'll have you know it's actually the inspiration we gave to the ancient Greeks—let's not let the Italians think they have all the fashion kudos!" His trademark smile and wink flashed brightly again. "These clothes protect us. They allow us to move quickly without disturbing our pterugia and this armour damned well saves a lot of us from ascending these flimsy bodies." He flopped his hands as though they were useless. "The ancient human empires quite liked our style. Where's the fashion sense gone these days? Skinny jeans just don't cut it when you're trying to roundhouse a Daimon!"

He mimicked a sharp karate style move. I ducked, then laughed. He laughed too.

"Point taken though, Princess. These days, we look more like a costume party with nowhere to go!"

Brennan plucked at his loose pants, "Luckily, this particular car is chromious lined, all the better to ride in virtual invisibility to the Daimon than walk around, dressed in this getup. If not a Daimon, we'd probably be attacked by the local lads looking like this!" Brennan winked again. There was another hint of the irreverent neighbour I once knew.

"You don't do serious much, do you, Brennan?"

"Serious? Who needs serious, unless it's absolutely necessary?" He thumbed over his shoulder. "That carry on back in the cavern? That was to muster some courage and cohesion. It's what I used to do. I was a marshal. I rallied and organised the troops. Lorcan and Jude would train them for wars in other worlds. I'll let you in on a secret Soph. There are so many effed-up places across the universe, there's little enough time for fun, so I'll take humour over angst any day."

"Here, have a drink," he passed me a chilled water bottle.

"Close your eyes for a bit. We'll have to take the long route just in case, but hopefully we should be left alone. The Daimon and Rogues should be too distracted with the energy signatures blasting across the northern lands right about now." Brennan pointed to the violet horizon as another day ended.

Through the setting sun, faint blasts of light blurred across the sky.

"And there you go, like bees to honey!"

"Won't that put others at risk who live in those places?" I asked. Guilt gnawed me.

"Nah, don't worry. They've all headed to wastelands, moors, remote shorelines and such."

Koi emerged from a contemplative silence. "We never place innocents at risk if it can be helped, Sophia. Except for you, my dear girl. It is unfortunate that what you are requires so much risk. I am most regretful for this." He bowed his head in apology.

I plucked at a loose thread on the edge of my pants. "It's okay, Koi. I know it's not your doing. It's not anyone's doing. I suppose I could blame fate if I need to point the finger, but what's the point? It's happening and I can't stop it. I trust you guys to help me. It is what it is!" I sighed in defeat and snapped that thread away.

Koi actually smiled. A warm, handsome, beautiful smile. "I will do all I can to prevent harm coming to you," he said. I felt his pulse relax with relief as though I had taken a burden of guilt from him.

We drove for quite a long time, but I couldn't rest. Sleep was not my friend. My rhythms were so disrupted. Spending so much time underground and barely seeing the sun was messing with any possibility of rest, not to mention the world-saving burden weighing heavily on my shoulders. When I did close my eyes, I couldn't switch off the sounds. Voices, heartbeats, breathing. Every day it seemed I was more in tune with frequencies that no human could or probably should hear. I nibbled on some crackers to quell the growl in my stomach as I read the scroll again to pass the time. *The resting place of your father's mother.* Everything had happened so quickly, from me reading the unreadable scroll, to Eilir making the connection and the mad rush to leave. I'd had no time to ask what was to happen next.

"Koi, how do you know we need to go to Windsor?"

"Ah. Well, there is a story to that. It begins at Eltham Palace and ends in Windsor Castle. As the truth revealed itself through our precious Eilir, all of the pieces fell together in an instant. We are all too familiar with the happenings during the time of King Edward IV, and his brother, Richard. We all knew these monarchs well. His wife, Queen Elizabeth was a very powerful Eudaimonian. She chose to live in hiding once Edward IV ascended. The elemental powers of

Elizabeth children were known to be particularly strong. We entreated Elizabeth to join us, to live in the caverns, but she felt her children had a higher purpose on Earth. She felt they could make a difference in the lives of humans by leading them in peace, through their own aristocracy. However by Neph'reus and Anjou'elle's activities forever altered whatever plans she must have had. Neph'reus is a woman you never want to meet and Anjou'elle is an Empath who can sense the powers and vulnerabilities of others. We already knew they was using the all too vulnerable and newly minted Richard III to get to his brother's children. She managed to kill off a few of Edwards young to simply absorb their power. I can't say if they knew any more than that about them. Anjou'elle and Neph'reus, have coveted the lack of connection with A'vean. The chaos they've caused for no other reason than boredom, is a list too long to recount. They are just as dangerous as any Daimon you could ever come across, especially as their motives have never quite been clear. They have not been seen or heard from since that time long ago. This could be a good or a bad thing. I do not know which yet. Silence can be both golden and deadly."

"Do these women want me, too?"

"I would say they are equally as dangerous to you. Would they want you for the Unseen or themselves? That I am unsure of. They have used many a soul as a pawn to bargain with in the past. We only hope their long-standing absence means they have been descended and you will never cross their path," he answered.

Great. This was a fantastic twist.

"So, the Windsor connection? I still don't understand."

"Forgive me, I tend to over-elaborate. I thought perhaps some more background might bring more sense to your understanding of things. This revelation about your parentage has brought great clarity. It pulls everything together. Because we knew Queen Elizabeth Woodville prior to her ascension, we know exactly where to look for her, your grandmother. She lived at Eltham Palace and was buried upon her mortal death at Windsor Castle."

My mouth was hanging open again. I now found myself entwined in one of history's greatest love stories and betrayals. It was so bizarre. King Edward IV married a commoner, Elizabeth Woodville. From this, my father was born. He must be Richard of Shrewsbury who was supposedly one of the twins in the tower who disappeared and was never seen again, feared murdered by the usurping Richard III... or so it seemed. The rest was history... human interpreted history.

My father must have changed his name as he went into hiding, only using the Woodville name to connect me to my lineage when I was born. I sat in a car, over five hundred years later, marvelling at this almost ridiculously unbelievable revelation.

The drive to Windsor castle took a couple more hours as we detoured country lanes and back roads in case we were being followed. Since I remained wide awake, I received a brief history of the English monarchy from Brennan, who felt the need to contribute to my understanding of all the monarchs as he sang their names in a ridiculous but funny rhyming song. After a time, we all quieted, and I gazed into the shimmery beauty of my diamond dagger as I contemplated my links to royalty. Ordinary... I was so far removed from that comfy old friend; I couldn't even remember what it felt like anymore.

We finally pulled up to a quiet backstreet in Eton, just near the river. Tourists were still out in numbers, snapping the iconic academic district under a velvety night sky. The long, Union-Jack-lined-street featured old shopfronts with stiff garish clothing in the windows, leading the way to the impressive stony Windsor castle facade.

We covered up in thick winter coats to conceal our clothing and blend in better with the crowds. Kea slapped a woollen hat on my head, tucking my long plait into it. They all changed their appearance, taking on various eye colours and warming their hair to blonde, brown, red... every colour. I was vastly jealous and impressed.

"Try to keep those baby blues low key, Soph. Don't want to draw too much attention." Kea elbowed me gently. Other than shutting my eyes, I wasn't exactly sure how I could do that, so I kept my stare fleeting, never looking at anyone or anything for too long.

One of our tourist buses pulled up behind us. Kristen and Thomas took the humans ahead of us to scout around the area. It felt so bizarre calling people humans, when I'd identified as one for so long. Truly surreal.

Unused cameras dangled from their necks whilst weapons hid at the ready, concealed under their heavy street clothes. I felt like I needed to be out front, taking charge, protecting them, and making decisions. But frankly, the only decision I'd been capable of making was to accept and move forward with this curve ball in life. I had to follow the others' lead. I had no idea where to go or what to do.

"The standard is down, her Highness is not in. This makes things a little easier," Kea commented.

"How so?" I asked as we turned the corner out of a small road and onto the street directly opposite the main castle gate.

"Fewer guards to deal with, Soph. We'll wait a little longer until the tourists die down. Then we duck in, break into St George's chapel, and meet your grandmother. "That's where Elizabeth is buried," she answered, her smile appearing all too casual.

Kristen reappeared. "Everyone is deployed. We are ready when you are." She bowed discretely, then turned away and pretended to snap photos along the cobblestone street.

"In here, Soph. Let's grab a drink while we wait." Kea tugged my elbow as I drew my gaze from the impressive thousand-year-old castle. We entered the Whitehorse and Wagon pub opposite of the castle's exit gate. Just as we sat down in the window bench seats, Kristen traipsed back in with a satisfied smile.

"Mademoiselle, you look like the cat that caught the mouse," Brennan quipped.

"Oh! 'Ow well, you know me, monsieur! I 'ave just 'ad a very interesting little chat with the guard over there," she pointed to a portly officer who was looking around for someone, his mind clearly not on the job.

"There is an old tunnel under this pub that used to move supplies to the castle. It 'as been backfilled, but you two boys can do your thing, no?" Kristen arched her perfectly plucked brows.

"How did you find that out?" I asked.

"Oh, a little Kristen charm goes a long way, Sophia." She batted her lush lashes, stuck her head back out the door, and waved at the guard. He immediately blushed, acknowledging her ever so carefully whilst sucking in his belly, attempting to stand taller. It was quite funny to see him gobsmacked by her, smoothing down his uniform and puffing out his chest like a proud pigeon.

"I couldn't charm a fly to a steak!" I joked, half believing it.

"Oh, it's not about 'ow you look or who you are. It's about making people feel good about themselves. And you, Sophia, make people feel good without even knowing it. You just cannot see this gift you 'ave. Now, I will talk with this lovely barman while you three find the cellar. I will follow on soon." She sauntered over to the bar and had the young guy entranced in seconds, asking him to show her how to use her camera. She could've been Jaz's sister.

When he was well distracted, I followed them past the bar. I tucked a stray piece of hair back up under my hat and took some initiative. I asked a man with Manager on his name badge where the restrooms were. I thought that would cover us for heading out back in a group. I sensed his heart quicken and heard the blood rush through his veins. There was also a peculiar feeling of connectivity between us. I felt compelled to let my mark glow just slightly. A quick flash of blue in his eyes told me he *was* my kindred. He nodded for me to go down the back hallway. *Wow!* As we headed towards the rear of the pub, the manager quickly put up the closed sign, announcing a plumbing problem to all the patrons and other staff.

"Well done, Sophia. Sometimes the smallest things bring the largest rewards. You are already able to sense your own kind, a great gift." Koi commended me in a whisper.

I suddenly realised that I'd used elementals in public, but before I could panic, Koi hushed me with a finger to his lips. "It was but a mere blip. I did not even notice." He patted my shoulder reassuringly as we moved on.

The manager followed us and introduced himself as Stev'ael, then added, "Just call me Steve."

"The guard was correct. There was a tunnel under here five hundred years ago. But it was filled in, quite solidly, I'm afraid," Steve said as we descended creaking, wooden stairs into a keg-filled cellar. It was damp and musty, the air an extra level of freezing.

"Are we safe using elementals down here?" I asked.

"Absolutely, unless there are any monsters lurking in the dark. Steve?" Brennan asked jokingly.

"All good here. Haven't seen a Daimon in years, not to mention the other filthy blighters."

"Excellent," I said, more to myself. I threw off my jacket as did the others and stretched my arms. The armour felt less cumbersome, but no less ridiculous. Nerves and excitement intertwined, revving me up into an internal frenzy; my guts writhed. Jaz would've loved this. But then that made me think of Ben, and my excitement waned. My heart beat an altogether different rhythm. The fact that he'd been taken by mind-altered monsters was just too awful to contemplate. My guts churned the other direction.

I'll find you, Ben. I promise.

Chapter
Forty-Five

"Sophia, I believe this is meant for you." Koi waved me over to a corroded medieval gate. A dinner plate-sized padlock with a concentric circle engraved upon it hung from the gate.

"Seems I'm expected everywhere!" I sighed in resignation. The heavy, circular chunk of metal hummed when I picked it up. I immediately concentrated all my energy on it. The lock burned red, then white hot, and the ensuing light caused a blinding flash. The lock was disappointingly still intact.

"Interesting," Koi murmured as he inspected it more closely. He turned it a few times. "Chromious. It appears that it requires a different form of energy to release it."

"I don't… oh." The dagger banged knowingly against my leg. I slid it out of the pocket and into my sweaty palm. Drawing my own blood, even a drop, was harder than I imagined.

"Just like in the scroll chamber, Koi?" I asked. How much of this stuff was going to be spilled?

"I believe so. Forgive us for the sacrifices you make." He bowed away after offering me a K'ufili.

"Hmmm," I huffed. With the dagger in my right hand, I closed my eyes, bit my lip, and jabbed the sharp end into my thumb. The sting was unpleasant but tolerable. A thick, iridescent drop sprung quickly. I let it dribble across the engraved portion of the lock. It languidly drizzled through the indentations, filling up the concentric design in a ghoulish, sparkling display. Once the blood had filled the pattern, I waited hopefully as I pressed on my thumb to stem the bleeding. The moment my blood congealed in the metal indentation, the same red and white heat lit up the room once more. When the light faded, the last of the lock was crumbling away, rusty particles dusted floor.

Brennan had the gate screeching open within seconds. We all stepped through, where we then faced the wall of solid, packed, freezing cold earth.

"How will we get through, Master Koi?"

I turned to see that Thomas and Kristen had appeared with several human troops. Their stealth was impressive.

"Ah, Thomas, I trust you have finished the deployment?'

"Oui. We are covered in all directions. We can assist you here if required."

"Thank you, Thomas. If you can, keep your group in and around this building, please?" Koi asked.

"As you wish." Thomas made a quick bow to Koi.

Thomas turned to Kristen and the small group, giving instructions. Kristen went back upstairs with the humans, whilst Thomas took up a sentry post halfway up the stairwell.

"How will we get through this?" I asked.

"We will use our collective energies to vaporise the blockage. Kea, Brennan?" Koi looked at them expectantly.

We stepped through the iron gate; our feet sank into a muddy floor.

"You two know what to do?" Koi asked Kea and Brennan.

"Sure do."

"Yep."

"Sophia, on my count, we are each going to focus a single energy pulse at the same time into the centre of the blockage. Timed well, and given that there are four of us, this should clear the tunnel. Are you ready?" Koi asked.

"Yes, I think so," I mumbled.

"You know so," corrected Kea. "Positive thinking, kid."

I smiled at her optimism.

"I will count back from five. That should be enough time to draw your energy forth. Deep breaths, Sophia, and relax!" Koi instructed as he gave me one of his rare smiles.

"Okay." I nodded. I was already calming my mind and feeling for E'lan in the freezing air. It was there, vibrating steadily, invisible, but as palpable as if it were a snug blanket wrapped around me.

Koi began counting.

"Five,"

Deep breath in.

"Four,"

Tingling in my arms.

"Three,"

My body heats up and my wings unfurl.

"Two,"

I draw it all in, accepting the power.

"One,"

I exhaled.

Four arcs of lightning exploded from our palms and disappeared into the centre of the wall. The energy blew back wildly, every small hair on my body stood to attention. For a moment afterwards, it was eerily dark and silent, until the dirt and rock imploded upon itself with a loud boom. I intuitively flapped my wings to blow the dust and debris away from me. Rocks rolled over my feet, and we all coughed a few times. Once it was all settled, I marvelled at the now clear passage.

"Now that's teamwork!" Brennan said as he retracted his wings. I tried to pull in mine with no luck. He saw me looking back at them in frustration, wriggling my shoulders impatiently.

"Relax your shoulders, breathe and will them in," he said. I tried this. It worked somewhat as they collapsed slightly inwards but were stubbornly refusing to disappear completely.

"It'll come Princess, don't you worry."

"I'm not so sure about that." I peered over my shoulders at the stubborn, glowing appendages.

"Just do what I say," Brennan said as he placed his hand across my spine. "Now, close your eyes and breathe in." I did as he said. He rubbed down the length of my back and in an instant they had retreated.

"Impressive Brennan," Kea commented.

"I know!" He smirked, and he nudged me towards Koi who was inspecting the inside of the tunnel.

"Look, we are near an ancient portal. The elements have come to greet us," Koi pointed ahead.

Before I stepped in to see what Koi was talking about, I couldn't help but notice all of the white scars down his back. Craggy, silvery lines crisscrossed around his pterugia openings. Battle scars, I feared, just like Gedz'iel. Other markings seemed to be ornate tattoos, the meanings of which I didn't know. They were as beautiful as they were mysterious.

I followed Koi's gaze. The tunnel glistened with all manner of gemstones. It resembled twinkling Christmas lights at night.

"What is this?" I was nothing short of amazed as we made our way over the rubble, moving carefully along the tunnel. I ran my hand along the energised walls. Pins and needles rushed my fingertips.

"The earth here has seen our power before. It is alive and connected to us, which tells me that this may be close to one of the ancient, long-dead portals. One from the beginning of time," said Koi.

"Profound," said Kea.

"Awesome," said Brennan.

"Wow!" I said.

"The crystals are attracted to our power. They have greeted us," Koi explained.

It was a stunning sight.

We made our way quickly through the glittering darkness, coming rather suddenly to a vertical ladder that we climbed up and out of through a heavy metal grate. We arrived in a circular room. It was damp, cold, and musty. The stone-stacked walls were ancient. There was nothing in the room, other than a well, sunken deep into the ground.

"Where are we?" I asked in a whisper, but my voice echoed.

"We are in the Keep," answered Thomas, who had followed secretly behind us.

"Why are you whispering?" Thomas asked me.

"I don't know," I answered. It just seemed a place one needed to whisper in.

Koi looked momentarily alarmed at his presence, but Thomas was quick to alleviate his worry.

"Master Koi, all is well. I took the liberty to follow on, in case I could assist you with any guards inside the castle grounds," he explained.

"Thank you, Thomas. And yes, we are in the Keep, the central stronghold of the castle. I believe we need to make our way out through the gardens and over the dry moat wall. St George's chapel is just outside, in that direction," Koi pointed the way, as though we could see it from our position behind thick stone walls. "Thomas is correct to be concerned about the human guards. We would not wish to be seen digging up a Queen. The attention would surely draw the Daimon, not to mention upsetting the royal family."

Digging up my own grandmother was a sickening idea to contemplate. I feared what I would find, but also equally feared the sacrilegious act. Yet, this was all predicted by Enoch. It must be the right thing to do, however unpleasant I found it. *Right?*

A glowing blue light caught my attention, distracting me from my ethical dilemma.

"Brennan! What are you doing?" whispered Kea, "You will draw attention with that thing! Turn it off!"

"Rubbish, it's just a phone! Actually, the smartphone is one of my favourite things humans have invented." He held up the backlit device for us all to see. "Unless you guys can pull the blueprints for this place out of thin air, we're going to be fumbling around in that dark chapel among a hundred graves," He poked the screen. "Look here, thanks to Google, I've got the layout of the chapel, as well as the exact position of Edward and Elizabeth's burial chamber. Once we're there, we can be in and out quickly." Brennan flashed the phone to each of us individually to parade his find. Koi grumbled at it with a look of suspicion. Clearly, he wasn't a tech head.

"You have a phone?" I shook my head in surprise, "I thought you guys knew everything! Well—almost everything."

"If that were the case, Princess, we wouldn't need Enoch, you, or five-hundred-year-old bodies!" *Fair point.*

"Look, Koi, it's a clean run, in and out." Brennan appealed as he pointed to the screen again, showing the exact position of the tombs.

"Indeed, that is most forward thinking of you, Brennan. The quicker we are in and out, the safer Sophia will be. But put that thing away now, lest we are detected by that light!"

"Master Koi, the exit doorway over there is monitored with a security system. It needs to be disengaged," Thomas reported.

"I've got it! Here, Soph, you check out the floor plan while I sort this." Brennan handed me the phone. The screen showed a black and white line drawing of the current burial places for both the recent and long-dead nobility within the chapel. A beeping alarm sound drew my attention. Brennan was breaking a sweat trying to disengage the alarm before it blared and announced our presence to the world outside. He gave it a few small power bursts at various points. All of a sudden, a long, high-pitched squeal sounded for a few, breath-holding seconds. Then all went quiet until an electronic click was heard as the door to the outside unlocked.

"Damn! Those humans are getting more ingenious with those bloody things. That was almost embarrassing!" Brennan grumbled.

We snuck out of the Keep ever so slowly. Not a glow, or even so much as a warm breath passed between us, so that the dark remained our friendly concealer. Thomas was shivering within seconds. Despite his heavy coat, the nearly freezing temperature was getting to him. He made no complaint, though, even when Brennan offered him his own coat that he'd slung around his waist.

"It's just a costume for me man, here, take it."

"It's no problem. The cold keeps me focused." Thomas waved him away.

"Alright then." Brennan shrugged.

Thomas seemed on high alert. His eyes darted everywhere, ready at any moment for anything.

Kea stuck close to me as Koi and Brennan snuck ahead, keeping low. She pulled me close to her side as we made our way across the steep sloping flowerbeds. A waterless moat between the Keep and the wall was all that separated us from the rest of the castle grounds. We all quickly shrunk under the cover of shadows behind the wall, just as a trio of red-clad guards appeared, flashlights in hand. The stamping of heavy boots in the distance told me that there were plenty of eyes, ready to spot us. Once they had passed, we climbed quickly and fluidly over the ancient wall and squatted again, listening for more guards. The diamond dagger poked into my shin whilst the soul stone on my bracelet warmed me from the outside in. I rubbed it, and the smooth little piece of stone calmed my nerves whilst sending a bolt of heat racing up my arm, which caused my mark to suddenly light up.

"Who goes there? Wallingford, is that you? If you're playing funny buggers again, I'll be writing you up this time!"

I gasped and covered my face with my hands. Kea pulled me into her. With one gentle touch, she dulled my mark back to nothing. "We really need to work on that when we get outta here," she whispered.

"I'm sorry!" I whispered back. "God, I'm such a failure!"

"Oh, stop being a drama queen, we've all been there. Now, shh!" she whispered again.

"Sir, I'm at my post. What are you on about?" called Wallingford through the walkie-talkie.

"I saw a light by the Keep," said the first voice. "I'm going to check it out, stand by," he ordered.

Fantastic, I blew it again!

A flashlight clicked on nearby. At the same moment that the torchlight hit our huddled group, someone lit up like a mini atomic bomb blast. Koi flew over to the guard in an instant and dragged him back to us. He was stunned and rigid as Koi laid him carefully on the ground.

His large bearskin hat had fallen off. Koi whispered in the guard's ear whilst resting a glowing hand across his forehead. The guard seemed to suddenly emerge from his coma-like state. Koi stood him up. I held my breath as Koi put the walkie-talkie to the guard's mouth.

"Base, this is Stanford, over. Just a few squirrels, over."

The guard holstered the walkie-talkie and then knelt down right in front of me. He fumbled around looking for something. I reached for his hat and silently passed it to him. He looked up at me; in fact, he seemed to look through me. He took the hat, stood up, put it on, and then marched away, toward the southwest exit.

"What did you do to him, Koi?" I asked.

"A little mind bending. Only sparingly do we use this tool to protect ourselves from discovery. He does not know what he saw. Now, let us move on."

We approached the beautiful chapel from a side entrance. The huge, ornately designed wooden door was barricaded with a metal gate. Koi made quick and quiet work of it, heating the steel to its molten point, which allowed the locks to drip away to the ground. As he pulled at the remnants of the frame, it squeaked loudly. We froze. The noise could've woken the dead. Luckily, the guards seemed to have moved to a different section, so we quickly squeezed through the narrow slit and pushed through a wooden door into the church.

"Remind me, Sophia, that the first thing I teach you when we get back is how to transfer! And properly, not randomly!" Koi muttered, slightly annoyed. He walked purposefully across an aisle. He stopped, turned, and retraced his steps, "It's a damned labyrinth!"

"Yeah, it kinda looked more straight-forward on the floor plan," quipped Brennan. The place was impressively ornate. Pillars and banners, statues and plaques punctuated the night-shrouded surrounds. The overly busy decorations made it hard to connect the right way forward with the floor plan at hand.

"Pass me that wretched device, Brennan, will you?" Koi held his arm out impatiently. I couldn't help but giggle as Koi had to defer to a human gadget to find his way.

After turning the phone every which way and arguing like a married couple, they indicated forward, and then to the right.

We followed solemnly through a candlelit corridor. There was a prominent plaque marking the resting place of the current Queen's mother. We then made a turn into a smaller, inner chapel.

"I believe she lies somewhere in here," Koi assumed, as he picked up a thick altar candle to light the way. I grabbed one, too. The floor was crammed with memorial engravings. I looked down, just as the tomb of King Henry VIII illuminated under the glow of my candle. I was both surprised and elated. This brief tour was like Hollywood boulevard for me. The Tudor period of British history was my favourite. I couldn't help myself. I knelt down and grazed the lettering with delighted wonder.

"Princess, look! Over here!" Brennan whisper-shouted.

"Come on, Soph. Let's get this done," Kea said, pulling me up.

By the far wall, surrounded by marbled engravings, was a simple granite inlay on the floor that revealed the names Edward IV and Elizabeth Woodville.

My heart skipped a beat.

"This feels so wrong," I said.

"Worry not. You are expected in this place," said Koi.

"Take out your dagger, Sophia," he instructed.

I pulled it from my pocket.

"Without question, it will be only you who can touch this sacred place. Do as your heart tells you," Koi motioned for the others to step back and give me space.

I grasped the dagger firmly, knowing all too well what was coming and it wasn't my heart speaking. I knelt over the grave, resting my palm on the cool stone. The gilded letters warmed under my touch. Everything that was connected to me seemed to react when I touched it, by either warmth or vibration. It was a welcome consistency where all else seemed quite random, aka stubborn wings! I sighed, then took the dagger and pricked the tip of my thumb again without the same hesitation as before. Red oozed down the blade, coating it thickly. I didn't wonder what I had to do next. I just did it. My body worked as though it innately knew what was required; destiny drove it now. Another unexpected piece of random experiences, but at least it was doing something helpful this time.

I jabbed the point of the now crimson blade into the thin mortar space between the gravestone and the surrounding tiles. Energy flowed down my arms and into the dagger, which glowed white and hummed. I dragged the sharp point around the entire perimeter of the stone. The floor chimed as the blade scraped musically along its course. Once I had completed the perimeter, I stood and waited. Everyone waited.

The floor hummed; the air prickled with power. The stone memorial sank fluidly into the floor and slid off to the side, out of sight. Inside the tomb, candlelight shone upon two coffins, each featuring the effigy of the person within. I hesitated… it just felt so very wrong.

"Go on, you are not disturbing anything," Koi reassured me.

Easing myself down into the cramped hole was no easy feat. It was dark and menacing, the stale air hard to breathe. I got my bearings with one foot balancing on the lid of each coffin. Creepy was the only way to describe the situation. I leaned down to run my hands over the marble faces and hands in repose. It was then that I saw a faint engraving along the side of her face… Elizabeth's marbled face, a mark identical to mine. I touched it tentatively. The cool stone was a poor substitute for a motherly touch, but it seemed as though it was as close as I was ever going to get, so I savoured it.

I stilled my quivering lips as a hot tear slid down my cheek. It rolled slowly across my now fiery mark and dropped silently onto the marble face. There was a sizzle and small spark as it made contact. This brought me out of my emotional haze. The lid rumbled. I moved quickly, edging back as far as the tight space would allow. I looked up at the faces peering down at me.

"What's happening?" I whispered.

"You've unsealed the tomb, Princess. Just stand back and watch," said Brennan with an uncharacteristically reverent tone.

I looked back down as I felt my feet lose traction. The lid over Elizabeth shimmered. It undulated and became hazy. I moved quickly to the edge of Edward's coffin, just as the other lid liquefied and vanished in the same way as the door in the shed.

There, below me, lay a thing of awe and beauty. The diamond skeleton of my grandmother in silent repose, glistening with perfection.

Clasped in her hands was a scroll.

Chapter
Forty-Six

"Oh my God! I gasped.

"Unbelievable!" exclaimed Brennan.

"Blessed be her eternal soul," Kea said solemnly.

"I have never seen such a thing! It's amazing," said Thomas.

"Sophia, quickly, take the scroll. We cannot linger," urged Koi.

I was frozen with wonder as I looked at Elizabeth. My vision clouded. I felt woozy and thought I was going to faint. I knelt down to steady myself, and accidentally grazed part of her bones. Electric sparks shot through me like I'd been injected with adrenaline. My heart galloped wildly as my vision slowly cleared. As I blinked the last of the cloudiness away, I was overcome by the sight of a flesh and blood woman lying where the skeleton had been. White hair neatly curled up beneath a delicate golden crown. She was dressed ornately in a lace-embroidered white gown. Jewels dripped from her ears. She opened her blue eyes and smiled. Elizabeth spoke in my mind.

Beautiful child of mine son. I have awaited you an eternity. Feel thy love I have for thee.

My heart raced even faster as a wave of warmth, of pure love ran through me." I smiled. She smiled.

Take from me this scroll to illuminate your journey. It is but an arrow to guide thee. I await success and repatriation with thee, my beloved granddaughter, amongst the plains of A'vean. Beware thy love of loves, sweet child. Beware thy heart. Thy heart is full and vulnerable. The Unseen shadow thee and shall use thy purity to bring thy fall. The way forward is incomplete. May caution be your tutor.

She smiled at me once more before she vanished. Nothing but the sparkling skeleton remained. I blinked rapidly, searching for her.

"Please come back?" I whispered, my lashes full, eyes bleary once more.

"Hurry, Soph! The guards are on their rounds. Grab the scroll!" Kea called in the distance of my mind. I shook my head to clear it, wiped my eyes dry. I slid the cylinder from Elizabeth's bony fingers that were now open, unclasping the scroll for me to take easily. Sitting underneath it, caught between the tiny hand bones, was a small necklace. I picked it up, too. The thin, golden chain carried a delicate, teardrop blue opal. I quickly clasped it around my neck, just as hands yanked me up and out of the tomb.

"Sorry I took so long. I needed a moment."

"What do you mean? You were in there for thirty seconds, max!" Brennan said.

"You're kidding! I… but I saw…"

Koi pulled me aside as the granite floor restored itself, resealing my grandparents in their mortal resting place.

"She communicated with you?" Koi asked, somewhat surprised.

"Yes," I answered, as we moved carefully out of the small, inner chapel.

"Your power grows infinitely stronger by the day. Convening with the ascended is a gift of the highest order," he nodded approvingly.

We retraced our steps carefully back through the Keep and tunnel into the pub. Kristen was waiting for us, sitting on a bench seat and laughing animatedly with the Steve.

"I can't believe I saw her. It was as real as anything could be. I think she was expecting me, too. It was just amazing," I recounted.

"Was she beautiful?" asked Kristen.

"Like an angel," I embedded Elizabeth's face into my mind. It was the closest thing that I had to my mother.

"Indeed, she is an angel," Koi said.

The screeching of car tires outside the pub stopped the conversation.

Through the window, I saw Jude race out of the car and head towards the front door. Showing no respect for the lock, he rammed right through, leaving it hanging from one hinge.

"Get in the car, now! Rogues are rolling out all over the country. Let's make like last night's news and get outta here!"

We followed him without question and crammed into a different car.

"Keep the energy low. They're within miles of us. Something or someone has tipped them off. They shouldn't know we're here!" Jude fumed, as he floored the accelerator.

"Ged reckons there's been a double agent among us for a while. I'el better protect him if I find out who he is!" growled Brennan, as he rammed one fist into the other. I held on for dear life as the car took the corners at alarming speed.

"Who would do that? One of us? How could they?" I asked, confused, now grabbing the seat in front of me to keep steady. "It doesn't make sense. To help the Unseen is to guarantee that they don't get back home!"

Brennan yelled over the screeching and revving of the car, "True, but perhaps they've been offered something that's more tempting? We've been here so long that the memories of home have faded. Too many temptations and fascinations here. It's not hard to imagine the promise of something tangible that they can have now over only the near impossibility of getting home. There are some who don't want to leave, even if…"

The car screamed around a corner and accelerated faster, cutting off Brennan. Then it rocked, as something crashed into it. Kristen screamed. Jude swerved, and I slammed into the door. My face lit up with the spike of adrenaline.

"Keep the face in blackout mode, Soph. That was a Rogue we just hit!" yelled Brennan.

I was hyperventilating, tried to breathe deep to quell the glow, well I tried to. The current situation was too frantic. I ended up just holding my breath and hoped for the best. Just as my face calmed, my damned wings started to emerge in reflex to the danger. The car must have looked like a lighthouse on the rocks as we sped down the motorway, with me trying to dull the glaring light.

"Soph, stop it, you're going to let the entire universe pinpoint us!" Kea screeched, as we swerved another zombie thing that flung itself at us from an overhanging tree branch.

"Shit! I can't control it! Koi, I need help," Jude yelled.

"Thought these were chromious lined? Brennan yelled.

"No... had to lift this one," Jude struggled with the wheel. "Argh, the bastards are coming from every damned direction!" He swerved again. The four-wheel drive bounced twice over lumps on the road. I didn't even have to wonder what they were.

"Sorry, sorry!" I panicked as I kept trying to shove the wings back in. A decomposing face slammed into my window. The skin and bone shattered with the impact. I screamed in revulsion. How could they match the car's speed?

Jude swerved again, and the car rolled. Kristen screamed, then went silent. The car rolled four or five times down an embankment before crashing into a tree. It felt like slow motion, a dream. It was a dream, until we were stopped and the pain began. Thomas was yelling as he tried to pull his leg free from under his crushed seat. I was hanging upside down above a front seat, wings still showing. Koi, Kea, Jude and Brennan were gone. I could only hear the panic of Thomas, and my rapid breaths. Petrol was strong in the air.

"It's okay, Thomas, calm down. We'll be okay," I could just reach him. "Grab my hand."

He did. We could just wrap the tips of our fingers together. I concentrated on soothing the fear and pain emanating from him. His aura was faltering. I drew it in and sent him some warmth and strength. This took my mind off myself and allowed my wings to finally retract, leaving the car in pitch darkness and silence.

Then I felt a little shuffling.

"Thomas? Are you okay?"

"Yes, Sophia. I'm fine. Thank you. I am still stuck, but you have eased my pain," his voice was markedly weak.

The car rocked unexpectedly. I smelled it before I heard it. I scrambled down from the upturned seat with a few twists and wriggles. I was fairly sure I had a dislocated ankle, yet that pain evaporated as a flesh-less hand smashed through the window nearest me.

I lit up again, but just enough to find Thomas in the dark, and I let myself fall across him. I twisted in the tight space and shot a bolt of energy at the foul creature. It sizzled into nothing in an instant.

"Stay quiet and still," I whispered to Thomas as I covered him like a shield. He did as he was told, though I think he'd actually passed out.

Another lurch, and the car rolled upright. I was ready for another Rogue as I righted myself quickly, staying across Thomas.

Nothing came.

"Come, Sophia," was the last thing I remembered as I felt a hand on the back of my head.

The next thing I recalled was waking up. I was tucked under a knitted rug in my little room in the sanctuary, and Elizabeth's scroll was tight in my grip.

Chapter
Forty-Seven

Nik'ael had searched for Belial for hours. His thoughts of returning to the Daimon realm were quickly tempered by a sharp survival instinct.

Something was not right. He knew he was vulnerable if he returned to that cesspit now. Someone or something was triggering the Rogues. It should have been him, but it wasn't. If he didn't know who or what it was, then there was most certainly something very wrong with the plan. He had never been out of the loop, until now.

He kept his distance in the trees lining the drive of the Tudor manor. He saw the battered car pull up. He also saw them carry out the two humans, but Sophia was nowhere to be seen. His heart did a flip in panic. Was it about his or her safety? He didn't know. The small vial rolled in his hand. He knew they'd been to Windsor—the Afflicted spy was more than willing to tail them for two sniffs of his precious container. He didn't, however, know what they'd found there. The defilement of the air with the aroma of Rogues told him it must have been something worth chasing them down for. It must have been the next piece of the annoying, bloody puzzle.

He ignored the distant yells, calling for him. They could wait. He would finish this himself and prove that he was equal to the task, equal to them. Nik'ael felt closer than ever to the last hurdle. He didn't want to leave, but he had to. His mind relaxed, his wings unfurled, and her rose into the air. He reached a lofty height above the snowing clouds. He made his way towards Windsor, to try to find what he was missing. He was just one step behind now. His heart raced as he glided away. It was not from the effort of physical exertion, but from the inner turmoil and effort it took to quell the unruly, disobedient emotions inside. As he disappeared through a bank of thickening clouds, he let out a desperate, primal scream that sent birds flying in all directions.

He didn't notice the figure following his same flight path.

Forty-Eight

Lorcan hovered by my bedside. Not literally, but he paced worriedly nearby. The scroll that remained in my hand brought memories of the past evening crashing back.

"Time to get up. Eat your breakfast and quickly. Enl'iel will escort you from the dining hall. Meet her there. Then we are to meet Gedz'iel in the library to read that scroll," he said.

No, *how are you? Glad you're alive.* He was blunt and to the point.

It was the first time he'd spoken to me since he'd left for the Cavern of Souls. He left quickly before I could ask him if he'd found my mother. I felt immediately gutted that it meant he probably hadn't. I dressed quickly, wondering how I'd gotten into my nightwear and hoped that had been Enl'iel's doing. I downed a bowl of fruit salad and a lifesaving black coffee on the move. A backpack had been left by the door. I shoved both scrolls in it, located the dagger in my pocket, and left, following the trail of Lorcan's sea breeze scent.

I met Enl'iel in the dining hall which was practically deserted. Long, empty tables were the only evidence of a once thriving and bustling underground community.

"Good morning, Sophia," Enl'iel kissed me in a human way with a peck to my cheek. "How is your ankle?"

I'd forgotten about that. It felt normal, totally pain free, "Was that you?"

She answered with a smile. "You were rather battered. I am so pleased you are safe and feeling better." She blinked away a tear and smoothed away a stray hair from my face.

"How did I get back? Last thing I remember, I was upside down in that car!"

"The others chased down most of the Rogues who attacked you. Koi got back to you just as you vaporised one. He righted the car and transferred you here. He had to sedate you in order to dull your energy for a safe trip. Your power is very strong now, and is growing rapidly as your birthday approaches. How you develop so fast is beyond our understanding. The enemy is getting closer for every day that you grow, Sophia. You are a beacon for danger."

"You mean the Daimon?" I grabbed another coffee as my skin crawled at the thought.

"Yes. They are sending so many of their bloodhounds out now. They somehow know that you are in this region." Enl'iel looked troubled as she poured herself some tea.

"There's a traitor. How can we get ahead when one of our own is a double agent?" I asked, as I stirred an extra sugar in my coffee, taking a seat at the closest table. While I quietly crossed off those whom I thought couldn't possibly be guilty, Kristen appeared opposite me. Her head was bandaged. There was evidence of healed bruises around it, already faded to green and yellow.

"'Ow are you?" she asked "Nervous? You look tense, like you 'ave been caught wearing last year's fashion!" She smiled, and so did I. Her candour was refreshing.

"This isn't how I thought I'd be spending Christmas. I'm not nervous about my ability so much as what the next scroll is going to say!" I answered.

"I expect this 'as been confronting. You 'ave been thrown in at the deep end, as they say. You suddenly are living in a fantasy movie. Don't you worry though, no matter what is to come, we all 'ave your back. Thomas and I know these vile creatures well. We 'ave many reinforcements. We 'umans are very 'andy. Daimon cannot sense us.

You see 'ow they did not notice you slip out to Windsor? We kept them busy for hours yesterday. You trust me, okay?"

I nodded, "Thanks for seeing me as a person and not just a means to an end."

"Oh no! Is that 'ow you feel?" Kristen's sweet face was an impressive masquerade for the huntress that lurked beneath.

"A little. Would I be as valued if I was not the Earth-born?"

"Oh, la verité! Sophia, you are loved for who you are, not just what you can do. Yes, you 'ave a special purpose, but if that disappeared tomorrow, I would still lay my life down for you. You are kind and loyal and respect life above all else. That, by itself, makes you truly special." Kristen smiled broadly, reached out, and tapped my hand gently.

I felt like a selfish kid, needing an ego massage every five minutes to keep me going. I vowed to myself then and there to stop sulking and just get on with it. No more overthinking. Just ride the wave I was on, with as much confidence as I could muster.

"Your brother doesn't have the same accent as you," I commented.

"That is because 'e was raised on the move with our Papa. Papa was an instructor for the human militia. Thomas travelled and learned with 'im."

"Where were you then?"

"In the countryside. Anjou actually. Mama trained me and many others. We were part of a group who hunted the Demon Countess, Anjou'elle. She 'as not been seen for so long that we disbanded a few years ago to prepare for your awakening.

The Demon Countess? That title made Anjou'elle seem exponentially worse. Her name was popping up all too frequently.

At that moment, Theus interrupted us, of all people. I'd never seen any of the Eloi move out of the library, aside from my little temper tantrum in the training room.

"With respect, Soph'ael, it is time for you to open the next scroll for us." He offered me his soft brown hand. Mine hand slipped comfortably into it; his fingers curled gently around mine.

"I will meet you there Sophia, I shall just check in on Jasmine."
Enl'iel blinked out with a brief flash. Kristen, Theus and I made a quiet journey down stairs, each in our own contemplation of the next move in this game.

Back in the library, I was sat in the same chair, with the same faces peering down expectantly at me. Except for Eilir. Her lack of presence was glaring. She seemed part of the fabric of this world, and without her bustling around, it just seemed colder.

I opened scroll the tube and let the brittle paper slide out. It wasn't sealed like the first which provided for a lot less drama. As I unravelled it, I was surprised to find it adorned beautifully with intricate decorative illumination. It was a far cry from Enoch's simple scroll. It resembled a medieval biblical manuscript. The script was ornate, the opening letter of the document an exaggerated gothic C entwined with red and white roses. Down the margin were faded crowns, drawn by a skilled hand. The necklace I'd retrieved from Elizabeth's palm burned against my neck as the scroll came into contact with my skin. I read aloud, and with a renewed confidence this time.

"Child of mine son, feel the love of thy heart, through time and distance.
Evil is near and known, but unknown.
Beware the devil beside you.
Heed the humans who adore you.
Thy father, mine own son, his love does not unravel for you in his absence.
We are all of but one origin, alas no longer of one spirit.
Evil has sliced through the core of our heritage.
The key to salvation is in your soul, protected deep within you.
Your blood runs pure, misunderstood by thy enemy.
Seek that which your blood shall resurrect.
I share the divine words of Enoch with thee:
"The Kaladai is the key to be bathed in your purity.
Thrice created, twice destroyed and hence scattered in pieces by the disciple of learning.
His words shall guide thee in the end from deep within his earthen retreat
Find the circle most misunderstood.

I came out of the haze of the reading; having heard every word I'd said clearly this time.

"How would Elizabeth know what Enoch had written?" I asked as they all moved about with contemplative agitation.

Gedz'iel and the Eloi continued to pace the room, digesting the words.

"I suspect it is a combination of sources. Uriel, who walked the Earth with Enoch for a time, shared some universal knowledge with me as he may have done with others. It may also be visions from I'el. As you yourself have experienced Sophia, I'el can communicate across time and space. Throughout our extensive history, He has made revelations to those deemed worthy, either directly or through an archangel such as Uriel. Only the smallest of snippets, however. Just enough to push us along, but not enough for a Daimon to gain an advantage if one were to come across such information. Not enough to redeem ourselves alone. I received such a vision eons ago. This is how I knew of the Prime Scroll chamber, and how it was to be opened. A few revelations have made their way to the ears of the Unseen, though. Traitors lurk among us as you now know. The attacks on you in Windsor are evidence of this." Gedz'iel explained. He ceased pacing in front of me.

This strong, imposing Watcher oozed exhaustion. His fight had been long. It was easy enough to see that in his drawn expression. The endless suffering of isolation they had endured made me angry. Why would I'el enforce such an extended punishment? I didn't much like I'el right then. I gently placed my hand on top of Gedz'iel's in sympathy. The buzz that exchanged between us was incredibly strong; reassuring. He placed his other hand across mine and smiled. We shared this silent moment before he nodded. "Thank you, Sophia."

I picked up the scroll again and ran my fingers across the words again, drawing their meaning out of the parchment. They leaped off the page, moving and spinning and dancing in front of me. Teasing me. Three-dimensional images popped in and out, wanting me to decipher their meaning. I'el's words through my grandmother, they were meant for me. I believed immediately that I would understand them, that I could and should understand them.

"Clearly I'el wants you to return. He wouldn't do what he's doing otherwise. It can't be that hard then, can it?" I asked no one in particular. One sentence loomed at me, begging to be understood.

"The circle most misunderstood. This is where we need to go, but where and what is it?" I pondered thoughtfully.

Amais spoke, "It most assuredly refers to an ancient portal. In the beginning, there were many, however over time they were reduced to just four. The Southern portal is that of your homeland, Soph'ael. The others were the North, here in England, the Middle East, and South America. They were disabled one by one, long forgotten by all. Now, somewhere, there is just one."

"The Giants Dance and the Disciple of Learning! Does that mean anything to you, Amais?" I asked.

"That I am not so clear about. The Disciple of Learning would appear to be a person, the Giants Dance is more perplexing."

"Why not just say it as it is?" I was annoyed.

"Here, here!" Brennan piped in. I looked his way, only then noticing what he was doing.

"Brennan, you're brilliant!" A blue light glowed in his hands.

"That's just stating the obvious, Soph."

"Oh, pull your head in! Have you ever heard of the word modesty? Can I borrow that a second?" I pointed to his phone, exasperated with his perpetual facetiousness.

He moved to pass it to me.

"What is that thing?" asked Pathos, just as I was about to take the phone. He leaned in for a closer look. His eyes narrowed in suspicion as he eyed the device.

"You are so last millennia, Pathos! It's a smartphone, man!" Brennan teased.

Pathos huffed and gave him a look that could have cut most to the bone. Brennan tapped at the screen giving it a small zap of current, not noticing his glare at all.

"Brennan, Sophia, how can this be of help to us?" Gedz'iel asked, he stepped forward with interest also.

Just as Brennan was about to slap the phone in my hand, the door banged open.

"Where is she?" A familiar voice demanded in a barely withheld scream.

"Jaz!" I exclaimed, jumping to my feet, nearly dropping the scroll. I shoved the phone back at Brennan. "Hang on," I said to him.

"Soph, you gotta get me outta here! Ben, where is he? Do you know? Can you find him?" Her eyes were dilated, glassy and desperate. She pulled away from the Alchemae who ran after her. She was dressed in ill-fitting, standard issue white clothes, which hung from her too thin frame. I hadn't noticed her weight loss prior to this. She was pale and gaunt.

"Get me out of this fucking place, Soph!" Jaz was stopped by two sentries at the door as she strained to run in my direction. She broke down and cried like a small child, falling to her knees.

"Let me go, for God's sake, please let me go?" She begged in a way that was alien to the Jaz I knew.

I put the scroll gently down and rushed to her. They tried to stop me.

"Get out of my way!" I demanded.

They did.

She completely broke down in my arms. A thousand tears of every emotion poured from her, drenching my shirt. Her grief made me stronger and even more determined to make right what was wrong in the world for so long.

Enl'iel entered the room at a run with a tray of medicinal supplies and got just a little too close to Jaz. She may have been hazed by the tisanes they'd clearly been giving her, but she was sharp enough to turn and slap the tray right out of Enl'iel's hands. Glass and fluid sprayed everywhere.

"No more of your bloody hocus pocus! I want to find my brother and go home!" she sobbed desperately.

"It's okay, Jaz, no one will force you to take any more medicines," I glared at Enl'iel and the other Alchemae who were calmly picking up the mess. Jaz's hair was threaded with bits of herbs and she smelled like a flowers and sweat. Her voice was thick with the remnants of drug-induced sleep. I knew they were just trying to protect her, but this would not fly with her for much longer. I decided I was going to be her wing woman, so to speak, from this point on.

"You can stick with me Jaz, okay?"

Someone tried to object, but I put up a hand to hush whoever it was. "But you have to do what you're told. No more flying off the handle, okay? I'm having enough trouble controlling myself. They promised to help me find Ben. We *will* find him… *I* will find him, and then I promise, I'll get you home," I said.

She considered me for a moment through her lush, wet lashes as she crumpled on the floor, exhausted. I cuddled her. Enl'iel passed her a cup, but Jaz went to swipe it away.

"It is just water, Jasmine," Enl'iel said sympathetically.

I took it first and had a sip.

"Water, au naturel! Have some." I passed her the cup and Jaz gulped it down. After a few moments, she seemed calmer.

"Don't bullshit me, Soph. These people, or whatever they are, have no interest in my brother or me, for that matter. Why would they bother looking for him? They want you and your magical shit, that's all."

"Perhaps they don't have interest in him, but I do. I love you both, you're my best friends, and I'll do everything I can to protect you and to find him." I had a sudden flashback to the cavern, where I swear, I thought Ben was going to kiss me. I lost track of my thoughts for a second.

"Soph?"

"Sorry, I was just thinking about how important you both are to me," I mumbled. It was the truth mixed with a longing that I couldn't reveal, even to myself. I snapped out of the reverie, stood and pulled her up, "Can someone get her into some decent clothes, please? She'll need some protective gear too. She's coming with me."

"Jude, remove the girl," ordered Gedz'iel.

After Jaz was hurried just outside the doors by an incredibly annoyed Jude, Gedz'iel immediately questioned me.

"Sophia, this is not wise. She is human, and a liability to you. For us all."

"You take other humans into battle. I'll make sure she's out of the way," I countered.

"Indeed, we do, but they are well trained in our ways. But with her fragility, this is a heavy weakness that may weigh dangerously between you and us all. She is strong willed, but I see the pain that courses through her. She is impulsive and explosive. Her temper makes her vulnerable, which in turn makes all around her so. She is safe here. She is not a trained warrior. No one can guarantee her life out there." He pointed to the roof.

"Gedz'iel speaks the truth, Sophia. We know you mean well. But she can be impulsive, as you have just seen. How are you going to control her? She has been sedated for her own safety," Enl'iel added.

"Her outbursts will put others in danger. She could cause more trouble than I care to consider. This is no time to pander to childish tantrums, Sophia. She is not our responsibility, and if we face battle, I fear she will become a casualty. Enough children of the Earth have bled for us," Gedz'iel was grave, but I was indignant.

"Jaz has been bullied and harassed for half of her life! She's the product of a crappy childhood. If you just give her a morsel of trust, put that trust in me. You'll see that she can shine like a diamond when she doesn't feel like a caged, wild animal. Please?" I looked at him, hoping he could see in her what I did.

"And who is going to watch her? You cannot," Theus spoke. "Your responsibilities are too great. You cannot afford to be distracted by a human."

"Give the human a chance. She may well be helpful as an undetectable scout." Pathos joined in the debate.

"Pathos, with respect, you do not know this human. She is volatile," Enl'iel cautioned.

"Her name is Jaz, not Human!" I snapped.

"Indeed, we do not intend any slight. What may be of benefit though, is that she is invisible to the Daimon. She is of no interest to them at all. If we place a scout nearby her to read her thoughts and emotions, her eyes and ears in the right place could well be of value. If you wish to keep her, Soph'ael, she must earn her place. Left here though, I believe she would be more of a liability. Her escapee habit could compromise the safety of the Sanctuary." Pathos concluded.

Before I could say another word, Brennan spoke up.

"I'll sort it. Just leave her to me. Poor kid's been dragged into this mess. I'll make sure she's taken care of. You're in, aren't you Jude? A little paying it forward old friend?"

Jude glowered at Brennan from the doorway where he'd quietly reappeared. He clearly didn't want to air whatever dirty laundry there was between him and Brennan. He sighed in a resigned, yet clearly non-gratuitous way.

"Brennan, this is foolhardy. Your responsibilities to Sophia and your kindred come before this girl," Gedz'iel warned.

"Don't worry Ged, have I failed you yet?" Brennan gave the now bristling Gedz'iel a confident smile that bordered on irreverence. Gedz'iel's dark expression said as much.

"One mistake by that girl, one foot out of place and you alone will answer to me Brennan," Gedz'iel conceded.

"She will be invisible, I swear," Brennan added as he winked at Jude.

I beamed at them both. That was the best I was going to get.

"Just keep her safe, okay?" I asked.

"You know *I* will," Jude responded with as dirty a tone as one could muster. He leaned heavily by the doorframe, arms crossed. "Tell her to keep her mouth shut, her head screwed on straight and she will be fine." Jude nodded his head towards the corridor. "Off you go… hug or something." he jerked his head towards me.

"I'll be back in a minute." I headed for the door feeling Jude's none too pleased stare as I ducked past him.

With Jaz now safe under Brennan and Jude's watch, I stepped out of the room to find Jaz being consoled by that same red-haired girl that kept her company days before.

"Thanks. What's your name?"

"Rosalyn," she bowed sharply.

"Oh, for God's sake, don't do that!" I rolled my eyes and put my hand out.

"I'm Soph, thanks for looking after Jaz."

She shook my hand shyly. "You're most welcome, Soph." She smiled sweetly. "I can take her to refresh and change if that is your wish?"

"That would be great, thanks," I turned to Jaz as Rosalyn stepped away.

"Jude will make sure you're okay. This is the only way you can stay and be safe, do you hear me?"

"He doesn't look too thrilled." Jaz glanced over my shoulder at the doorway. Jude's back blocked us from a heated discussion between the Eloi about me having too much opinion.

"Well, can you blame him? You just need to be civil, not friends, just civil. Otherwise, they will sedate you again. I don't know how much I can push them; I think this was a pretty good deal, Jaz. You owe Brennan big time."

"You promise me you'll find Ben and I'll do whatever I'm told," she agreed.

"Jude, did you get anything out of those Afflicted about Ben's whereabouts?" I called out, realising I'd heard nothing about them.

"One expired quickly, the other responds to nothing. I have had no success unfortunately. They suffer so much already that any means of persuasion are rarely successful." He shrugged. The inference of torture was disturbing.

"Well, one way or another I'll find him, I promise." I hugged Jaz and secretly hoped that was not an empty promise. Jaz wiped her tear-reddened nose and pinched her cheeks, instantly looking a little brighter.

"Fine," she sniffed. "At least my prison warden over there is eye candy," she whispered as she crossed her arms and gave Jude a sweet-as-pie fake smile.

"Stop it will you, this is serious!"

"I know, can I put it down to being slightly off my face? Don't drink the tea, I'm serious!" Jaz had a point; her eyes were heavily dilated. I could forgive her practically anything at that moment.

"Get some rest and eat something. You're skin and bone. I'll be with you soon. You absolutely must do what you're told, or I'm going to get my butt kicked, okay?"

"Okay," she agreed. We embraced again before she disappeared down the corridor with Rosalyn, Jude begrudgingly in tow.

"Hurry up Human, I haven't got all day!" he growled impatiently.

"Hands off, Freak!"

Less than ten seconds and the truce was already broken. This could go so very wrong, and that was without any Daimon. Those two might just kill each other.

"Enough now, return to the scroll, Sophia," called an impatient Gedz'iel from within the library. I re-entered just as Brennan started complaining.

"Where's my damn phone? I put it on the desk!"

"What? I was going to check out something on the web. Find it Brennan, it could be important!" I exclaimed.

"I put it right there Soph!" He pointed to the edge of the desk.

"Forget about such trivialities, Bren'ael. They are but magic tricks," scoffed an unimpressed Pathos. "Perhaps you would not have misplaced it had you not been so caught up in babysitting humans."

"Argh," Brennan was clearly annoyed as he hunted for it for a few more minutes, until Gedz'iel ordered him to stop and focus on the scroll.

"We will decipher it ourselves Brennan. Stop now and help us."

We worried over the ancient words for a while. I examined each illustration, every word and full stop. All in the room held the scroll. Each of us tried to extrapolate meaning from the same line, The Giants Dance. For some reason that one line drew us all in. If only Brennan had his phone on hand.

"Hmm, perhaps we should recall Eilir?" Gedz'iel mused. They all laughed lightly at that.

"Master Gedz'iel, perhaps some training to clear our minds?" suggested Matias.

"Indeed. Combat is an excellent refreshment."

The next few hours were punishing.

Combat with Lorcan and Brennan was more than brutal. The soft approach was long gone as I was flipped, rolled, kicked, and zapped. Brennan received a few good strikes from me though, underestimating the improvement in my agility.

"When did you get so damn good?" He breathed heavily as he came out of a commando roll, rubbing the kick I'd managed to plant on his thigh.

I raised my eyebrows in mock confusion. I was still too scared to use my elemental power in full during practice, despite them encouraging me to have a go at it.

"You really need to use more elementals though Soph, you have to get that fire power down to a precise art," Brennan said. "I want to see how strong and accurate you are. C'mon now, give me a quick blast to the hand." He licked his lips, crouched and looked on expectantly.

"But you said I could kill you if I did that, Lorcan!"

"Did you say that, bro?"

Lorcan's cheeks bloomed crimson. Then he fessed up.

"Didn't want her getting a big head too quickly. Besides, she needs the stealth and physical combat practice more."

"You tricked me!" I immediately let a zap fly out. It cracked so hard onto Lorcan's armour that he was flung to the ground.

I stood over him, "You're an idiot!"

Brennan was nearly crying with laughter, "Man, you have a way with women!"

That was when I saw Jaz enter the arena with Jude. Expecting a firestorm to erupt, I watched nervously from a distance.

No yelling or shouting ensued, however. She simply followed him to the mats and proceeded with his warm-up. They began with some basic self-defence. She was swift and focused. I moved in just close enough that I could feel her energy. She was centred. Calm. Each time she fell under Jude's moves, she got straight back up. There was fire in her aura, but not towards him. Jaz inspired me.

I moved onto the orbs, feeling motivated by Jaz's impressive effort. For the first time, I ran an entire lap without a single sting. Koi congratulated me as I took out all but one orb.

"That burn from within is working with you today, Sophia. This is progress." He nodded, nearly smiling again.

The success of finding Elizabeth had boosted my confidence all round. I had opened and read two scrolls. I knew I was capable of more. After a quick break to eat, Lorcan tapped me on the shoulder.

"Our turn. Let's go." He turned his back on me and walked away. Ouch! I must have really stung his ego. For the second time. I wasn't looking forward to this.

"Give him hell, Princess!"

I gave Brennan a thumbs up.

Back in the ruins, Lorcan disappeared immediately into the shadows. I stopped and listened. He was going to get me good and proper if he could; payback for humiliating him.

At first, there was just silence. Only the distant sounds of weapons practice in the other room.

Then there was something, a thrumming, pulsing, rhythmic vibration. It tickled the tiny hairs on the back of my arms. I melted into the shadows of a crumbling colonnade for cover. The burn within me rose, but I swallowed it back down. Waterfalls flowed through my thoughts as the feeling dissipated. I would call for it when I wanted it. It would behave itself until then… I hoped.

I jumped as I felt a shift in the air nearby. The breeze of wings rustling the stale air. I held my breath and grabbed a hold of Elizabeth's necklace. It was hot. As my hand closed fully around it, I sensed something pull in my gut, like plucking a guitar string. My grandmother spoke across distant realms to me, her voice echoing in my mind.

"From within you, I dwell. My strength is your strength. Where you see yourself, so you shall be."

Darkness and silence reigned again. I snuck out of my hiding place and received a nasty sting on the back of my knee.

"Got to do better than that, or you'll be toast within the week. Try harder, Sophia!" With that rebuke, Lorcan was gone again in a flash, lurking somewhere else, ready for the next strike.

I was mad now. He was being a jerk. I breathed through the burn and snuck through the rubble, listening for him again. The faintest hint of ocean mixed with cedar hung in the air. He was sweating. My senses were becoming so precisely honed that I could sense someone's proximity just by the lingering of their scent. It reminded of Ben. Ashes and spice. I missed that.

I ducked away and back towards the colonnade until the scent dissipated. I wanted to blitz him this time. I needed to prove myself to him, and also to myself. I grabbed the necklace again and thought of Elizabeth's words. I imagined myself standing behind Lorcan. I squeezed my eyes shut and willed it to happen with every atom of myself.

Everything became dull. Something yanked hard behind my bellybutton. The ground disappeared. Blackness became blacker until it was peppered with pinpricks of light. Silence, then a thud. I suddenly had a mouth full of dirt. I looked up, spitting it all out, just as a very surprised Lorcan turned around to see me.

"How the hell…"

Before he could say another word, I jumped up and zapped the hell out of his smart mouth. He flew backwards onto the ground before recovering quickly, just as my wings unfurled.

"Come on, let's play for real!" I teased as I forced his sorry arse down again.

"You transferred! How did you do that?"

"Granny taught me!"

Chapter
Forty-Nine

With a thorough examination of my necklace by the others after Lorcan rather humbly reported what I'd done, no one was the wiser as to how this connection occurred.

"It is not a soul stone, but it is also not a stone I have seen before," said Koi. "Whatever it is, its vibrations are beyond ancient."

"It could well be a relic of the old world. Keep it close, Sophia. Its purpose is clearly for your benefit," Gedz'iel added.

I could barely keep my hand from it for the rest of the day, constantly twirling it through my fingers.

We finished the session with a cool-down run with the human battalion, which was actually fun. They were so competitive. They tried to outrun us, even though they knew it was impossible. The bond that we shared was incredible. Generations of families served and protected the Watchers and Eudaimonians in secret, for no reason other than a deep love and kinship that spanned the history of time.

I met Jaz for the evening meal, and she looked exhausted. Jude was nearby, an eye constantly on her. Watching for any wrong move, I imagined.

"Well, my faculties have finally been cleared of that god-awful stuff, at least. That dimwit over there is not so bad, either." She pointed her fork at Jude. "He promised me he would find Ben."

"Well, that's a change from the other day. Friends now?"

"I wouldn't go that far. He's tolerable, nice to look at, but just tolerable."

She was feeling low. I could tell this by the fact that she was eating a vegetarian meal without complaint.

"Promise me, for your own safety, you'll listen to Jude, or whoever you're with? I don't want anything to hurt you."

"I'm a one-woman trip to destruction for anything that touches me right now, so those things better stay the hell away," she said.

I giggled, "I've never wanted to cross your path! I remember year seven all too well!"

"So you damned well should! You know who's boss!" Jaz smiled. "You okay, Soph? For real?"

"I'm going with the flow." My fork circled the plate.

"Seems like that's all you can do with these people," Jaz said.

Two more days of training followed, but brought no progress with the scroll. We were convinced the Giants Dance was the key to understanding where we had to go, but with Brennan still hunting for his phone, we were blind to outside help. Apparently, it was too dangerous to head outside until we were armed with knowledge as well as weapons.

I walked through what I'd seen and done in Elizabeth's tomb over and over again, trying to remember something I might have missed. Nothing jumped out.

I took a walk with Jaz for a break. Today was the day before the winter solstice. I knew this because I heard some sentries discussing the different shift change times for the shorter day. It was just days until Christmas, which was about the right time for the shortest day of the year. That was hinted at in the verse too. When the moon lingers long. I felt the pressure, we all did. What would happen if the solstice came and went before we figured it out? Would the prophecy still work?

Jaz and I found ourselves at the entry level, sitting amongst the lush but flowerless foliage. It was the most outdoorsy place I could find since above ground was off limits. The warmth from the huge light orb, when my eyes were closed, felt almost like the sun. It would have to do for now. The sound of the waterfall behind us added to the effect, and for just a few moments, I felt relaxed; you could almost suggest happy. Jaz sat quietly beside me.

I was running those verses through my head again when I heard the delightful squeal of a child nearby. Surprised, thinking they'd all been moved to safety, I looked up.

"Who's the munchkin?" asked Jaz as she sat up, hair askew.

"Oh, that's little Av'ael. I met her when I first got here. She's a sweetie."

"Yeah, I suppose, if snot and dribble is your thing."

"Stop it! You were small and cute once, too."

"Never! I was born screaming and haven't stopped." Jaz snorted a laugh. "What's she doing over there anyway?" Jaz pointed to the little building Av'ael was constructing out of dirt and stones. "Looks pretty damn good for a kid!"

I started explaining that she could see a little bit, when I caught sight of her construction as well.

"Actually… what is that?" Av'ael's back was to us, so we walked over to where she was playing by the far end of the waterfall. She was plucking stones out of the small pond and using them to build a circular structure. She only noticed me when I peered right over her shoulder.

"Pretty Sophia, pretty Sophia!" Av'ael hugged my leg.

"What are you making there, Av'ael? It looks very impressive."

She beamed, clasped her hands under her chin, and swayed in coy shyness.

"Oh, I don't know! I had a dream last night and a nice man showed me how to build it. Mama is taking soooooo long, so I'm making it for the man now," she said as she picked up a finger-sized stone and placed it down to complete a circle.

"It's pretty cool, kid," said Jaz.

"Thank you. What's your name? You look sad."

"Uh, I'm Jaz, pipsqueak. I'm fine, don't you worry." She ruffled Av'ael's hair in a way that didn't impress the little girl as she tried to push her soft white locks back into place. She took her soul stone from her pocket and cuddled it to her face.

"This is for you, Sophia," Av'ael pointed to the structure of concentric grey stone circles.

"For me?"

"Yes, the man in my dream told me to make it for you."

"Who was the man in your dream?" I asked, just as her mother called from down the nearest corridor.

"I don't know. He had pretty rainbow eyes, though," she answered.

"Come, Av'ael. Oh, my goodness, forgive us, Soph'ael. Blessings to you," she said as she recognised me.

"Oh no, please, it's no trouble. We were just admiring Av'ael's artwork.

"See, Mama, she's the nicest Lady-Watcher ever!"

"I hope she was not interrupting you," the mother said.

"Not at all. In fact…" I knelt down and looked intently at the tiny sculpture, "Jaz, what does this remind you of?"

Jaz squatted next to me. Av'ael took a step forward and ruffled Jaz's hair. Her hands slid down Jaz's face and felt the rise and fall of her features.

"Hey kid, what're you doing?"

"I'm feeling how pretty you are." Av'ael's white eyes glimmered. "You're pretty in there." Her fingers slid down over Jaz's heart.

It was a moment of pure innocence, and it left Jaz speechless.

"Come, darling. Leave these ladies alone now. May the blessing of I'el be forever upon you." Her mark glowed warmly as she picked up Av'ael and disappeared down the corridor. We were alone once more.

In the vast silence, we circled the rubble masterpiece.

"Why is it so interesting?" I asked, more to myself than to Jaz.

"Beats me. Kind of cute kid, though."

I looked up in surprise.

"Don't say a word. Repeat that to anyone, and I'll have to kill you!"

"Understood, Jaz." I smiled as I looked back at the intriguing circles.

I stared intently at the stones. My heart skipped a beat as I quickly pulled the scroll from my backpack. The bag was an almost permanent attachment now. I dared not let the scrolls out of my sight.

Could it be? Could I'el have connected with a small, blind child? I wondered with a growing excitement.

I inspected the page again. Not the words, but the colourful artistry.

"What is it Soph?"

"I don't know. Well, actually, I think I might know. I'm just looking for…" I sucked in a breath.

"What?"

"Look!" I ran my hand down the margin, along the line of coronation style crowns, until my finger rested on the one that was third from the bottom of the page.

"It's a crown. Yeah, okay. There's a whole bunch of them," Jaz said.

"No, look at this one!"

Jaz looked closer.

"Oh! It's not a crown. It kinda looks like…"

I cut her off, "Jaz, I think it's Stonehenge! The clue is in the scroll and Av'ael's little building has somehow shown us too! Can you see it?" I pointed to the scroll first and then Av'ael's creation. "Look, an outer and inner circle, with the alter stone in the middle. She's even tried to put the lintel stones on the top. She's a miniature genius!"

The circle most misunderstood.

No one had ever really deciphered what this ancient structure was, that much I knew to be true.

I dragged Jaz at a run until I finally found Brennan, with Koi. They were visiting Cael in the Stasis room. Cael looked much better now. He was mainly asleep still, but the wounds were healed to silvery scars. His leaflets had been obliterated. I didn't know if he would be able to fly again. Despite my own excitement, my heart lurched in grief for him. I kissed his cheek gently. He stirred, so I stepped back through the white veil, excitedly beckoning Brennan out.

"Brennan, have you found your phone?" I whispered.

"Ironically yes. Would you believe it was stuffed behind a loose stone in the library hearth! Some smart arse is messing with me! Anyway, what did you want it for? You wanna make a call? Who is he? I'll need to shake him down first, with this and this!" He held up each fist, one at a time.

"Stop messing around. I think I know where Elizabeth's scroll is sending us!"

Brennan pulled the phone from the leg pocket of his pants in a nanosecond and fiddled with it to power it up.

"God, do they ever wear shirts around here?" Jaz commented, trying not to look like she was gawking at the roomful of sleek muscles.

"Feisty, aren't you!" Brennan stretched his chest out, showing off. If Enl'iel were here, she'd cuff him over the ear, at the very least.

"Okay, what am I searching for?" he asked, his typing finger ready.

"Oh, just give that thing here!" I snapped and snatched the phone from his grasp.

"You can't use one finger to type. We'll be here a week." My thumbs were armed and ready to go.

"I'll not take offence to that and continue to save your backside!" he said.

The screen was dull. "A little more power, please. Quickly!"

"You're feisty, too! Okay, okay, keep your knickers on straight," he said as he pointed at the phone. A small spark arced out of his finger, hitting the middle of the screen, giving me an immediate signal to the outside world.

"Brennan, do not ever mention my knickers again!" I grumbled as I typed a search into the device.

I waited a moment. It took a little longer for reception this deep down in the Earth.

"Yes! That's it! The Giant's Dance is an old term for Stonehenge!" I jumped up and down with excitement. I typed in tomorrow's date as well and waited.

"Tomorrow is December 21, the winter solstice, the night when the moon lingers. It's the shortest day of the year. Just as the scroll said. We have to get to Stonehenge by sunrise tomorrow!"

I raced out the door in search of Gedz'iel, with the others on my tail.

421

Chapter Fifty

Brennan and I hunted everywhere for Gedz'iel. He'd left a few days ago to monitor Daimon movement. He hadn't returned yet from the perimeter of the Empyrean realm, the Daimon realm.

"Can't you just call him back?"

"Not that easy, Princess. It's one of those funky places, like the Bermuda Triangle. Nothing works like it should. The energy is thin in the atmosphere, because the Daimon suck it all up into their hellhole. This makes it hard to use our power or get messages in and out. We might just have to use the muscle and brainpower we have here if old Ged doesn't return ASAP," Brennan explained.

"It could work in our favour if he actually stayed there. He's an expert at monitoring whatever is slithering in and out of that place. He would know by their movement if something of significance was occurring, and news of that would bring him straight back," said Lorcan, who'd appeared in the doorway of the deserted library, peeling an apple with a small dagger.

"Everyone who helped the other day is still on standby. We have all the backup we need, but we should probably still try to get through to Ged."

"Don't let him hear you call him that again, Bren. He'll deck you, like this!" Lorcan threw the apple so hard that it was obliterated when it hit the side of Brennan's head. They tussled a little, like teenage brothers, before I stepped in.

"That's enough! Both of you, we've no time to mess around. I want everyone available called back and ready to go first thing in the morning. I have to be there before dawn. Now cut it out and get yourselves together!"

They both stopped and glared at me. Then clapped. That annoyed me immensely.

"Just do it. I'm going to find Enl'iel."

They mocked me further with a salute, but disappeared with a touch to their faces, off to do what needed to be done.

I looked around the ancient room. It was so quiet, yet spoke loudly to me of an incredible world hidden in plain sight. I wanted to spend hours here, going through all the books to learn of the heritage I'd only just discovered. The dagger banged against my leg, reminding me of what I needed to do though, and that began with finding Enl'iel.

This time I tried something different. I wanted to prove something to myself. No one else was here. I'd dropped Jaz back at her room on the way down, so I couldn't make a fool of myself in public. I closed my eyes and concentrated really hard on Enl'iel, wishing myself to be with her. I stopped for a moment and opened my eyes, looked around the room to gather some reassurance that I was not under anyone's glare, then shut them tight again and concentrated. I placed my right palm over my mark and let energy flow from it onto my skin. Snaps of electricity zapped across between my face and palm. I pictured her long white hair, her warm smile and sparkling eyes. My body began to warm. Then my stomach churned. I sharpened the image of her face as clearly as if it were right in front of me, and willed myself to be with her. My mark scorched.

I was jerked into blackness—quiet, cool, tepid, then warm. Just as suddenly, I was met with the brightest of light again. I came to an ungraceful thud. I opened my eyes as someone grabbed my arm to pull me up. It was Enl'iel.

"Sophia! You have transferred! Did you mean to?"

"Yes! I did it! Oh my God, I can't believe I did it again!" We were standing in the corridor, leading to the training rooms. She was in her fighting gear. Word must have travelled quickly. She hugged me as we continued to move at a brisk pace.

"Brennan told me that you discovered the meaning of the words, and then gave orders for action. I am so proud of you."

"I only hope I can keep it all under control!"

"You have more control than you know," she said as we approached the entrance to the training arena.

We were met there by Koi, Kea, Brennan, and Jaz.

"Where did you get to?" Kea asked. "Found this one wandering on her own," she jerked her head at Jaz.

"Yeah, you forgot me back in my room Soph! God!" Jaz rolled her eyes. "I kinda rock this outfit though!" Jaz was dressed in protective gear as well. She looked like a warrior-goddess in all the white and metal. I hoped she didn't need any of the gear. I really hoped that she wouldn't see fighting at all.

"Sorry everyone, I took a different route," I said.

"She transferred to me!" boasted Enl'iel.

"No way! Well done, Princess!" Brennan high-fived me. There were glowing marks of approval all around as we walked quickly through the milling troops of Eudaimonians and humans. A large contingent of Watchers stood up on the stone platform at the head of the room. They observed solemnly the mustering of troops. There was still no sign of Gedz'iel or the Eloi. I was hoping that wasn't an ominous sign.

Jude approached just as we were about walk up the steps.

"I will take you from here," he said to Jaz.

I faltered. Panic set in over the decision to let her stay near me. Near danger. I knew she wouldn't tolerate any other choice, though.

Whilst she was eyeing him off, I pulled Jaz to the side.

"You will listen to Jude. Don't be a hero or a hothead. If you get yourself killed, I'll kill you myself!"

We hugged goodbye. "Yes, fucking ma'am," Jaz saluted, then looked serious for a moment. "Just find Ben, please?"

"I will, I promise," I said.

And then Jaz was gone, lost in the mass of people and the promise that she would be safe.

Dash followed Jude, and it was the first time I'd seen him dressed like the Watcher that he was.

Lorcan appeared at my side.

"Will Dash be okay? He hasn't fought for a long time, right?" I asked, rubbing the gooseflesh from my arms.

"He was a Seraph warrior in his time. He will mirror Jude with the humans. Don't worry, he will be fine," he said.

Upon the platform, there many people now gathered. Thomas and Kristen were loud enough that I heard them shouting orders to the human troops under the direction of Jude. He, who I could just make out, had a firm grip on Jaz's arm. She was not going to be able to move a centimetre with Jude by her side. I was relieved and somewhat amused by that thought.

A line of Alchemae healers entered with trolleys laden with food, water, herbs, and lotions.

"We're in for the night. We eat and sleep here tonight," said Brennan. Weapons clanged and banged as they were sharpened and adjusted. A few groups were in the ruins, practicing stealth tactics. The popping of elemental explosions rumbled underfoot.

Kea suddenly pulled me aside, "We've had word from Gedz'iel. At least one of the Unseen has left the Empyrean realm. This is not good news. We want you to rest for a few hours. Tomorrow most likely will be hideously more challenging and dangerous than we had anticipated. A dozen humans have been lost to Rogues overnight already. They're buffeting their front line on the outskirts of the county. They know we're on to something. They're trying to distract us with small, frequent melees."

"Couldn't Gedz'iel have stopped them from leaving that place?" I asked.

"Gedz'iel is powerful, Soph, but they are originally our kindred, ancient souls who are equally as strong."

That knowledge was humbling, and the thought of rest ridiculous. I needed more practice.

"I can't rest while everyone else is preparing!"

"Yes, you can, and you will." Kea pulled me into a small room carved out of a sheer wall of rock at the back of the platform. The room was hidden behind a simple white curtain. I didn't think I was tired until I saw the bed.

"It's only three hours until we must leave, anyway. It isn't long, but enough to rest your body, if not your mind. You, of all of us, need your rest."

My shoulders slumped. I complied. It was just easier. I'd gotten things started, which was a feat in itself. I didn't want exhaustion to defeat me just when I was needed tomorrow.

As Kea turned to leave, I asked, "Do we really have a traitor among us? It's the only way they could know we're about to make a move, right? Who would do such a thing?"

"Someone with a grudge. That's how it all started so long ago with Yeqon and Lilith."

I sat on a small cot. It squeaked and sunk under my weight.

"I've heard that name. Who exactly is she?"

"She's a girlfriend you really don't want. History says Eve plucked the forbidden fruit. Well, history forgets Lilith. Anyway, rest up. I'll make sure Jaz plays nice with Jude. If not, I'll keep her under my wing… literally!" She smiled and left.

My head was in a tailspin. Roaming Daimon and spies among us. I lay down, pulled a blanket up to my neck and played every face through my mind. I could not find fault or suspicion with anyone. I tortured my thoughts with the worry until sleep thankfully crept up on me without warning, and I drifted off.

Horns and pitchforks poked at me. I ran through stinking wastelands. Hands grabbed at my legs as they reached up through cracks in the dry, packed ground. Smoke made the air hazy and unclear. There is a flash of white hair, then black hair. Blue eyes, then black. Someone is following me. I trip as a hand catches my ankle, and I fall hard. I'm yanked back with an iron grip. I try to summon some elemental power, but nothing, not even a molecule of energy, would arise. I am empty, powerless. I am being pulled down into the earth by this strong, huge hand. I release a silent scream. My skin scrapes and rips open as I'm being dragged across shards of rock. I claw desperately, with no effect. Finally, I tip backwards as the ground gives way. The hand releases me and I fall backwards into a long, dark abyss. I pray for forgiveness for failing, for letting everyone down by dying in a stinking hellhole. I close my eyes, awaiting the inevitable thud. It doesn't come.

Instead, I am cocooned in strong arms. Heartbeat pounding, nervous, anxious. Whoever is holding me is doing so with great fear.

"Don't speak."

A deep, throaty, familiar voice.

I panic. I struggle to escape, at all costs.

The arms tighten. I am trapped.

"You are safe."

Too familiar. Everything brightens slightly when a light is struck. A flame burns on a dirt wall in a sconce made of—God—was it a leg bone? Red and orange lick away the darkness.

I struggle a little more in the muscular arms.

"Do not resist if you wish to live. Quiet yourself, and you will be safe."

I crane my neck back to see who this voice belongs to. Who my captor is. My eyes adjust quickly. I blink a few times. A curved horn. Another horn, broken in half. My heart thunders in panic now. I force myself to look at the face that gazes down upon me. He is beautiful. He is perfection.

He is Belial.

I awoke from this nightmare thrashing at someone, drenched with sweat.

"Get away! Get off of me!" I yelled at whoever was grabbing my hands.

The pressure was immediately released. I sat up, rubbed my eyes clear.

"It's three in the morning, Soph. Time to get up," Lorcan stood over me.

He couldn't wear any more weapons if he tried.

"What are you doing here?"

"Why so surprised? I'm hardly the bogeyman. I was sent to wake you. Get up, we leave in thirty."

Lorcan glared at me a little too long before he turned to leave. I looked down to see that at some point, I had wriggled out of my clothes and was just in my underwear. He swallowed too hard, the pulse in his neck quickened. The scent of salt was on his skin, sweat glistening in the orb light as he lingered by the curtain. I hastily pulled a sheet over myself.

"I need to get dressed. Would you please leave?"

"Of course." He pushed a chair out of the shadows as he left. It had fresh clothes on it.

After dressing, I ran out of the room quickly and bumped into Kea. The place was bright and alive, with orderly squads awaiting the orders to move out.

"Great, Dash came to wake you?"

"No, Lorcan woke me," I answered, confused.

"Oh, I asked Dash to… never mind. It doesn't matter. Here…" She handed me two Eccles cakes that were hot and smelled delicious. "Eilir insisted that they were sent and warmed up for you. All the way from her safe house in Wales. You *are* the charmed one."

I ate quickly as everyone started to mill around the entrance. All manner of protective gear was strapped back onto me, the breastplate being my least favourite. But Kea combing lavender oil and herbs through my hair was by far the highlight. I felt heavy and awkward in the outfit, but smelled amazing. The gauntlets seemed over the top, but apparently, they came in handy for weapon deflection and punching down Rogues in an emergency. It was all a bit Wonder Woman to be honest.

There was some shouting off to my right. Of course, it was Jaz, escaping Jude's clutches. She dashed through the crowds, making a beeline for me.

Enl'iel chased her, but she got to me first.

"Just wanted to see you before, you know, whatever it is you're doing!" Jaz huffed, out of breath. She dragged me into a tight hug. Her body was shaking. "Don't get hurt, Soph." She squeezed a little tighter.

"I'll be fine, you just watch yourself. You've already run off from Jude, and we haven't even left yet!"

"I know, I just needed to say…"

Enl'iel finally caught up with her. "I just wanted to say… uh… Soph, you rock that sexy goddess look too!"

"Come, Jasmine. Back you go, or it's another special drink of tea for you," Enl'iel grumbled.

Jaz mumbled something extra crude as she went back down to the arena. She peered back at me. There was genuine fear in her eyes. I nodded to her. *I'll be ok,* I mouthed the words, not at all believing my own promise.

Brennan, Koi, and Lorcan appeared from three sudden flashes of light.

"Ready, Sophia?" asked Koi, who gleamed in gold and silver armour, as did we all.

"Let's just get out of here before my nerves fry."

Chapter
Fifty-One

Cool night air nipped at my skin, and I pulled my camouflaging jacket more snuggly around my body. Despite my elevated body temperature, I could appreciate how cold it was, and I worried for our human soldiers. Close to seven in the morning, the motorway behind us was quiet. Maybe one or two cars had sped past since we emerged to hide between the monolithic stones. It had been another long, evasive trip. Replaying that dream of Belial in my mind and worrying about Jaz had me on edge. I fidgeted along the rim of my armour, feeling certain I'd made the wrong decision keeping Jaz near, but facing off a great white shark would be easier than leaving her behind. I was so scared that she'd run off to look for Ben at the first chance she got.

Ben, where are you?

Brennan scouted the outer circle of Stonehenge, while I concentrated on tracking the energy within them. The soft pulse underfoot had drawn me in from miles away. It was getting stronger by the minute, as though beckoning me to know it. The air was alive here with an unearthly buzz. The E'lan was the most powerful I'd felt. It teased my skin, slipped within me, seemed to poke around, lingering… snooping on who and what I was.

The closer we'd got to Salisbury, the more irritable I'd felt. I'd tried to the point of exhaustion, to keep my power dulled to the minimum for the entire trip. I didn't want any more stuff ups. This wasn't easy with the unpredictable grasp I had on controlling myself. I imagined waterfalls, waterfalls, waterfalls! I think I held my breath more often than not, lest I light up like a one-woman firework display.

Elizabeth's scroll crackled in my pocket as though it were alive, aware of its surrounds. Its words burned with encouragement; its power knew I was close to something of great significance. Kea and Koi were down by the Avon River. They were patrolling the area whilst Enl'iel kept a distant watch on the other side of the motorway. Jude should have been there already to run an advanced reconnaissance, but he was nowhere to be seen. Not a footprint was in the snow to show that anyone had passed through, and this worried me.

My heart raced with apprehension. It pounded in my throat, rushed through my temples. I allowed a faint light to emanate only from my face in the grim pre-dawn light. I kept my hands clasped tight, lest they betray me and spark to life. Heat radiated within me, each vein, every artery pulsed warm and comforting; an extra barrier against bite of winter. As I circled though the stones, I wasn't one hundred percent sure what I was looking for, but I knew I would find it. I simply had to.

Brennan whispered inside my head, *Heads up, Princess. A mist is rolling in. The Rogues are coming.*

How the hell do you do that? I thought back at him, knowing this was an ability I was yet to understand or conquer. Of course, there was no reply. I looked up to see the grey blanket slithering over the landscape towards us. I'd learned from experience that they liked to emerge from sudden influxes of thick fog, masking where and how they arrived. It was as though they literally appeared out of thin air, clawing their way up from the ground, like the walking dead that they were. This time, though, despite the fog rolling our way, I knew they were not too near, as the stench of decomposition had yet to accent the air.

I recalled the instructions of the scroll.

Light the way as dawn arises… The East beckons…

The light would lead the way. I was yet to know what this light was, but I did know it meant waiting until sunrise to find out. I was hoping it would be as simple as the first sunrays highlighting the place amongst the stones where the next clue was concealed, but it felt like we didn't have much time to wait. It would be another half hour or so before the first hints of winter sun hit the ground, and the pressure of attack and the lives already lost weighed too heavily upon me. If I could circumvent the prophecy just a little to cut out some time, I was going to try.

I called back in a muffled whisper to Brennan, "Anything? I'm feeling a vibration, but it seems to be all around us. The ground is humming." I bent down, placing a palm to the ground. The shudders within it pulsed up my arm.

Yeah, there's definitely something here, Princess. We're in the right place. It's just where to look without drawing those bastards out. Damn it, it would be a slam dunk if we could light this place up!

The mind-talking made me slightly dizzy.

"I know," I sighed with the frustration of it. "Let's just keep poking around. I want to find this thing before the others get here. I don't need them in any more danger."

"Okay!" he whisper-shouted back to me. "Sorry about the head invasion, Soph." Brennan must have sensed that it unsettled me.

I inspected every inch of the stone circle, in awe at how the great stones dwarfed me. Nothing seemed to jump out or look even remotely like a secret something could be hidden somewhere. There was no ancient swirl or scrawl to be found. It was the polar opposite from the symbol riddled scroll chamber.

The ground was sticky with the mud of recent rain. It sucked at my feet as I crunched through a thin layer of icy snow, leaving me ankle deep in a cold, black sludge. Logically, I knew that if we were supposed to wait for dawn and I knew which direction East was, I could try to work out a general search area for the location of the next artefact. Based on the scroll, we believed that sunrise would cast a ray of light across Stonehenge from the eastern horizon, hopefully landing somewhere near the location we needed. The general hum of the ground was confusing, though. It didn't seem to be drawing me anywhere specific.

"Which way is East?" I whispered again as I came up behind Brennan.

"If you're standing by the Heel Stone, facing the henge, it should be at a slight diagonal to the right," he whispered in soft white plumes.

"What if I just head in that direction? I might come across whatever it is by luck?" I shrugged and pointed to what we thought was east.

"You really want to walk out into that fog, in the dark, with no clue if you're going to find it? Be patient, Princess. The prophecies were given to us for a reason. Let's follow them through, sometimes we need to have a little faith," he answered, all too sensibly.

This winter solstice sunrise was the key to finding the next part of this puzzle. I could feel the desperation inside me to end this nightmarish adventure. This was not the way I'd ever envisaged seeing the world—running and hiding under constant attack, wracking every neuron trying to figure out ancient riddles. I needed to be strong and patient. Thankfully, I had ancient teammates to guide me, beings who had a patience and depth of character I could only dream of.

A rumble, ever so slight, shook the ground. Brennan fell in close; pulled me back protectively behind him.

"We're not going to be alone for long," he announced ominously.

"We have to get to this thing! I'll dig through the ground with my bare hands if I have to. Just where is it? What is it?"

"We have to ride it out 'til dawn. If the prophecy said sunrise, then there's a reason for that. If we were meant to take shortcuts, I'm sure we would have worked this out a thousand years ago, Soph. Let's dull down and just wait at the Heel stone. The second that sun is up, you get yourself onto that altar stone so you can see where the sun points to. You're the key to this so make sure you meet and greet that sun. Okay?"

I nodded.

We huddled closely in front of the large, bluish Heel stone. It was impressive, both in its size and mystery. Another rumble underfoot was followed by the faint whiff of something rotten. It swept in on a newly emerging breeze. The temperature dropped; snow began to fall. My hair whipped up in the breeze. Pent up, nervous energy buzzed between us. Crackling electrons sparkled sporadically in the air around us.

"There aren't enough of us here! You and I can't fight a horde of Rogues ourselves!" I felt panicked, despite the cold, sweat guttered along my top lip. The two of us arriving here alone was not ideal, but travelling in numbers was a risk as well. We were more detectable when in large groups, but a group sounded much safer right about now.

"Speak for yourself! I'm quite impressive as a solo performer!" Brennan smiled and pulled me into his side in a brotherly hug. He spat snow from his mouth, shook flakes from his hair, "Don't worry, Princess. The others aren't far off. Five, ten minutes max. And remember Koi, Kea and Enl'iel are nearby, we're not so alone. The Rogues will pinpoint us instantly if they transfer here, you know that by experience. We all have to stay on foot, unfortunately, and be patient if we want to remain invisible to the enemy."

The sky was starting to lighten now, the pale violet of the horizon seemed clearer than the air above us. As dawn approached, there was another earthy rumble, quickly followed by a blinding flash of lightning in the distance and a loud crack of thunder.

"What was that?" I craned my head apprehensively around the stone, looking for the source.

"The reinforcements have arrived!" Brennan fist-pumped the air, and then gave the sign of thanks to I'el, touching his hand to his face and raising it to the sky.

I noticed an immediate change in the atmosphere then. The air cleared as the fog rolled away to the South, towards the light. The cool breeze dulled, the snow stilled, and was once more the air smelled sweet and dewy.

A new and faint whisper tapped in the back of my mind.

Got your back, kid. Don't make me regret putting my faith in you.

It was Jude's all too familiar, vexed tone.

It was growing painstakingly close now. The waking sun lipped the horizon with a deep orange glow. Silhouetted flocks of screeching birds flew haphazardly overhead. They emerged from the South, as though frantically fleeing something.

"That'll be the troops," Brennan said, indicating the frightened flock. Jude had definitely drawn the evil out towards himself and the human battalion. I worried momentarily for his safety, but then I reminded myself that he'd survived longer than written history. I'd heard Jude had even fought with the troops of human wars just for fun. He was strong and cunning... probably a little unhinged. I felt less sure for the poor humans, though. I hoped Jaz was tucked away somewhere safe.

I stood and bounced up and down on my toes to let the blood run back into them after crouching for so long. Who knew when I might need to run? My eyes never left the darkness in the distance, lest I miss something. I felt strong, physically. My training had given me a strength I'd never imagined I could have. My muscles were tense and ready to spring into action, and the heat in my veins burned, yearning to explode. But would it be enough?

Deep breath in, deep breath out, repeat.

Footsteps in the distance caught my attention. I peered into the faint blue light behind us.

"Someone's here," I whispered. We crouched down again behind the stone. I strained my eyes against the bluish backdrop, looking through the shadows cast by the giant stones. I knew someone was behind one of the monoliths on the outer circle, as I saw a darkened figure dart behind it.

"I'll go check it out, it's probably just a homeless guy. Plenty hang around here, trying to make money from the tourists. They're probably just getting in early. I'll give him a nap for a while, that'll keep him out of trouble," Brennan said.

"No, I'll go! I've got to start doing things on my own."

"If it's not what you're expecting, best if I'm there too, Princess." He made to stand but I grabbed his arm and pulled him back down.

"No, it's only a few feet away. I'll call if there's a problem, okay?"

"Then take this." He passed me a curved chromious dagger. "I know we haven't touched on weapons yet, but just in case, even a small nick with that thing will slow anything down, giving you enough time to get away. Ram it wherever you can, if need be. I'm right here anyway. I've got your back as always." Brennan passed the shiny blade with a nod of encouragement.

I took the weapon which was heavy for its size, and shoved it down the band of my pants.

"I'm sure it will be nothing, just like you said, a wayward tourist hunter. I don't want some poor human hurt, let alone killed by whatever is surfing in on that mist. Hang on, how do I put someone to sleep?"

"Easy as. It's a skill the young ones learn with the second right of sevens. You'll kill it. Look here." He cupped his hand behind his own head. "You just have to get within a foot of someone. You feel for the brainwaves that surge and fluctuate within this space around their skull. You can slow them right down by sending a small, gentle pulse of energy out. Just like when you heal. It works in an instant with humans, a little longer for our own kind. Don't try it on a Daimon or a Rogue!"

I gave Brennan a reassuring squeeze on his arm.

"Okay, hold the fort, big guy. I've got this." I didn't really think I had it, but I needed to rely on myself more. I hated the dependence I had on everyone else. Just like nursing school, I was going to learn on the run with practical experience… I hoped.

"Yes, Ma'am!" Brennan saluted me with a dimple-rich smile again. I kind of adored him, in a completely big brother way of course. "Make sure you're on that stone before the sun is up, though," he said, gesturing to the horizon. "We've got one chance at this. We need to get in first, before the Daimon just nuke everything while they look for what we're looking for."

"Promise. See you in a minute." I snuck away.

With feather-light steps, I cased the perimeter, passing one stone at a time, pausing, and then moving on. As I passed the altar stone, I could hear and feel the beat of a heart. It was rapid, panicked, and disturbingly familiar. My stomach lurched, a wave of nausea rolled through me, making me stop for a moment to still the feeling. The ever-increasing ground vibrations from the encroaching battle heightened my sense of urgency. I listened hard and heard panicked breaths, which suddenly stopped for a moment, as though this person was listening, too. After a sharp intake of that breath, the breathing continued. The familiar emotion of fear blanketed me. It chilled me, and my mind was screaming to turn around and go back to Brennan.

Instead, I felt for the dagger and crept forward, willing my energy to remain down so as not to give away my position. I was fairly certain that whoever was hiding was not a homeless person. He or she was emitting a different feeling altogether. My head ached like a hacksaw was working through it. I hadn't felt this way since I'd arrived in the UK. Something was very, very, wrong. I was only two stones away when I decided to double back and approach from within the circle.

Koi's voice returned to the back reaches of my mind.

Know your enemy's position at all times. Attack first and fast. The element of surprise is most powerful.

I was sure I was going to throw up any second; I rubbed my stomach in an attempt to settle it. The feeling was overwhelming, but I pushed forward. Whatever was ahead had to be fairly questionable because of the effect its negative energy was having on me. I came up silently behind twin stones connected by a massive lintel. I couldn't tell whether the pulse pounding in my head was from whoever was hiding, or my own. Brennan was trying to whisper to me from afar, but I couldn't listen to him with all the noise already banging about in there.

A sharp intake of breath and sudden movement had me sprinting into action with an animal-like instinct. I was around the monolith in less than a second, unfortunately losing the dagger as I grabbed for the person trying to flee. My arms managed to get a good tight grip around their neck. We wrestled to the ground, grunting, panting, and struggling.

The cold snow melted under the heat of my rising anger, as I couldn't help the release of my energy. I glowed, hot and furious, above this mysterious being who was surprisingly strong. He definitely couldn't be human. He grunted and groaned while trying to fling me from his back, but I had his large, muscular torso flat on the ground, pinned underneath me. My legs wrapped around his, with one arm crooked around his throat, while the other twisted his left arm up behind his back.

"Who are you?" I asked, close to his ear through gritted teeth. As I heaved for breath, the scent of ashes and spice enveloped me. I gasped, shocked, and jumped immediately back, letting him escape from my grasp.

He scrambled quickly from under me and turned around. He sat, panting heavily as he wiped mud and slush from his face with the back of his hand. His bare chest heaved from the effort of our struggle. He looked up at me with emerald green eyes that glistened in the very first rays of the sun.

"Ben!"

Chapter Fifty-Two

With the initial shock at seeing Ben, I nearly forgot my purpose at Stonehenge in the first place. The sun was rising, the heat of it kissed my skin and I needed to be on that altar stone. I grabbed Ben by the arm, dragged him wordlessly along. He didn't resist as my mind raced with confusion. I pulled him into a full run to the central altar stone—the heart of the henge. I jumped up on it with the lightness of a cat and pushed him down at the base of the stone. I glared at him, both furious and scared all at once.

"Stay there! I don't know what the hell you're doing here, but just stay there!" I snapped; confusion ran hot under my skin.

He coiled away, but didn't move. A loud buzz cranked up to blaring in my head. It hurt, made me wince. The ground rumbled, and the stone beneath me hummed as a fuller sunlight hit my back. I looked up at the sky as snowflakes fell again. They descended from a single cloud formation, surrounded by pink and orange hues. Humming and rumbling and voices all invaded my mind. I shouted out loud, my hands pressed firmly over my ears.

"What do I do?"

"Light it up, Princess! Light it up!" Brennan appeared, running around from behind a leaning stone.

Inside my head, a million voices screamed at me, on repeat.

Light up, light up!

I glanced down at Ben. I hadn't seen him for what felt like an eternity. He glared at me. His expression was unreadable, but his eyes never left me as he stayed crouched, motionless, on the ground.

I closed my eyes, relaxed my body with great difficulty. I let the warmth in my veins unfurl, allowed it to escape the flesh and blood that contained it. The heat spread quickly throughout me, up my legs and down my arms, my face pulsed with heat. My spine screamed to break free as the burn coursed down it. I breathed in and out slowly, vaguely aware of Ben, feeling his heartbeat match my own.

My wings burst from my back and fanned around me. Surprised at how quickly I could do this, I dared to open my eyes. My breaths were hard as I scanned around to see what was happening. Ben was now standing, looking at me oddly, his head tilted to one side. I could have sworn his expression was love and hate intertwined. Brennan was just behind him, regarding him with confusion before drawing nearer to me.

"Something's happening, Soph, hang in there! Look!"

Brennan's eyes followed something through the henge and across the landscape to the Northeast. I followed his line of vision. That's when I noticed that the light of sunrise refracted from my wings to the stones and back again in a complicated pattern of light, converging into one piercingly bright light that reflected off the altar stone and carved a path through the still dark horizon. It hit something far off in the distance. There was an increase in the Earth's magnetic field, a hum like the rev of a jet engine whirring before take-off. A white light exploded up into the remnants of the night sky, followed by a brief but ear-piercing explosion. This strange light lingered in the air like a beacon.

Enl'iel, Koi, Kea, and a few others emerged through the stones at that moment.

"Sophia, you did it!" Enl'iel reached up to help me down with the broadest of smiles.

"Come now, let's follow the path of light. We must hurry, Jude is outnumbered, and we will be inundated all too soon!" Panic shook her voice, which made me panic, too. Enl'iel slid to a stop when she caught sight of Ben, and swung her focus in his direction.

"Ben! How did you get here?" She pulled him close, looked him up and down for sign of injury. He remained silent, but compliant. Her face reflected the same confusion I felt. She took off her coat and put it around him.

"That's a very good question," I said, still bitter for the worry he'd put me through, and the nagging feeling that there was so much more to this than I cared to know.

With no more time for words, as the clang of metal and screams of mortal wounds edged closer, we ran.

And we ran fast. We veered with an inhuman speed towards the pulsing beacon. I had my hand vice-tight around Ben's wrist as he silently kept up with surprising ease.

"What do you think is over there?" I puffed as we ran.

"Looks like the old henge they call the Durrington Walls," Enl'iel answered.

The mist was rolling in again. Thankfully, it wasn't too thick yet. The dawn light began to dull to a stormy grey as we crossed the couple of kilometres between the two ancient sites. Over another motorway that bisected this area, we arrived to find the dissipating beacon being replaced by the emergence of a swarm of little glowing orbs.

Keepers.

The fog was thickening rapidly now and full of stench.

"Hurry, Sophia! Follow the Keepers, they will guide you," Enl'iel urged as she pushed me forward and hung back, taking over my grip on Ben.

"Watch him. Don't let him out of your sight!" I looked at him quickly, urging him to explain himself. He was so distracted by the screams and flashes of light in the distance that he hadn't even registered our exchange. He looked frightened.

"This young man will not leave my side. Now go!" Enl'iel yelled over the noise.

With one last lingering look at Ben, I ran toward the bustle of orbs to find the rubble of an exploded rock scattered along the chalky ground. The Keepers buzzed around me in an instant, as though they were excited to see me. A kindred feeling emanated from them, but also one of urgency. The thicker the fog became, the faster they swirled around me, shielding me. A couple zipped away and then back again, as if urging me to follow.

"Get the hell going, Soph!" called Brennan from the distance, "They're coming, and it's a bloody swarm!"

I glanced back, saw Brennan running towards the fog. He threw off large white orbs that exploded into a thousand shards of white-hot arrows that sprayed down towards the oncoming enemy. "I'll cover you, now run!" Brennan fired continuously as I ran after the little lights, whilst he disappeared into the malevolent fog. The others must have joined in as the sky behind me was lit up less by the sun than the by angelic war munitions. The clash of weaponry was all too close as the encroaching battle neared by the second.

I stopped looking back and followed the Keepers at a furious pace. They buzzed ecstatically. They drew me toward the Avon River as the wind whipped up suddenly and ferociously.

My breath was catching in the frigid air, but I didn't falter. The clouds above swirled faster and darkened from grey to black. Lightning crackled across the sky. The smell of rotten eggs and decay was an assault to my senses and a frightening warning. One last glance behind me had my legs working even harder. The stinking fog was now at my heels. Tendrils were reaching out to grab at my feet. Or were they fingers?

I skidded to a halt at the river's edge, heaving for breath. Guttural screams that were way too close sprung hot tears down my cheeks. The snow was thick and icy along the banks, the edges slippery as I followed where the little spirits were guiding me. The rushing water melded with the howling wind, drowning out the distant screams. My Keepers darted out over the water and hovered under the naked, white-capped branches of a willow tree that hung long and low. It brushed sorrowfully over the water. The storm that brewed was loud, the wind rustling through the dormant branches. In the back of my mind, I heard warnings to hurry.

The Keepers dove in and out of the water, inviting me to do the same.

Without hesitation or question, I kicked off my boots and singed coat and dove into the freezing water.

Despite the murkiness, my vision was crisp. The little lights swam in front of me. I realised with a shock that I felt no need to breathe. It startled me, and I thrashed for a moment until I was drawn along in the current, encouraged by the little white guides. They hovered over a spot on the bottom, and I felt around through the slimy silt. A fish rushed past, scaring me half to death. I dug in harder as the Keepers became frenzied while they lit up the slimy hiding place.

When I was elbow-deep in the sludge, I hit on something hard. My excitement built; my heart pumped furiously. I dug fast, and within moments had pulled a metal box from within its watery grave. I could tell by the feel, by the engravings under my fingertips, that it was the same as the Prime Scroll box. I clutched it to my chest and floated quickly to the surface.

I emerged about fifty metres or so from where I dove in. The climb out with heavy, waterlogged clothes and armour up the icy bank was hard going whilst holding the chest under my arm. The Keepers surrounded me and worked together to levitate me up and out safely onto the bank.

"Thank you," I said, reaching out to them. They danced across my palm with a warm, tickling buzz. The keepers then dulled down rapidly and disappeared, leaving a fearful energy swirling around me. Biting rain fell, turned the snow to slushy mush. The dawn sky sparkled with the E'lan. Sounds of fighting, the smell of death was all too close. I screamed out for Enl'iel, Brennan—to anyone that I thought could hear me.

My mind was chaotic, like radio static. Voices yelled frantically, I leaned forward, tried to hear something… anyone. A voice, a call in the background became louder and more frantic.

Run! Run, Princess! Run!

Shoeless and dripping, I pulled myself through the slush and ran in the opposite direction of the fray. I wrapped my wings around myself, encasing my body, protecting it from the cold and the danger, and didn't look back. My instinct was to do exactly that, yet I now knew better than to ignore such a warning.

Angelic lightning struck the ground in front of me. Mud sprayed in my face, I slid to one side, rounded the scorch it left and ran harder, not knowing where I should go. I sent a hot blast haphazardly in the direction the shot came from. There was no point hiding now. I had to defend myself. There was no more running away, no hiding from that which was baying for my blood.

I tried to transfer away. Slipping and sliding across a foreign landscape, fear slithering head to toe, gasping for any sense of how to survive. I thought of the sanctuary. I envisioned Cael, the sweet smile of little Av'ael, anything far away and safe, but my panicked mind couldn't get a firm grip on any one thing. I felt my body try. The strange backwards pull in my gut faded in and out twice, but the effort was pointless. The power just wasn't there. So, I ran as hard as I could to anywhere but where the screams were coming from, and it felt cowardly.

The warmth of the sun was now completely dulled by the wild weather, the sky as black as night, a new kind of cold slicked across the landscape. I felt sick again, my stomach lolled and ached, acid burned my throat, slowing me down. Dread coated every breath.

I pushed myself until I arrived back in the middle of the henge, under the eye of the great sarsen stones. They were charred, the white snow spoiled with sulphurous piles of ash and splashes crimson. I was momentarily mesmerised watching that blood seep across the purity of the snow, someone's life force dissipating into nothingness. It was heavily and strangely silent within the confines of the henge, even the wind quelled its howl. But not in my mind. The chaos of screams continued, none of it made any sense.

I followed the blood smear. My footsteps crunched too loud, I hunched down, crept slower. A body lay pressed against a great stone; bloodied and lifeless. I knelt; his dark skin was cold; dead cold. He was human and ripped to shreds. Tears welled in my lashes, immediately flaking into icy droplets down my face. I closed his eyes, placed my hand over his heart. I silently prayed to whoever might be listening to take care of his soul.

The ground rumbled, the shockwave of the war pushed at me. They were getting closer. Through the pillars of Stonehenge, the light show blazed near the river. The guttural sounds of Rogues and the screams of my kindred caught in the storm. The horror swirled around me. My lips quivered; I shivered, held the new artefact close to my chest, and forced myself up. Shock was setting in... I had to get away.

I spun, dug my feet in… and smacked straight into someone. I fell heavily backwards to the ground, hit my head on the altar stone. A hot trickle of blood ran down the side of my face. I tasted it in the corner of my mouth. For a moment, I was dazed, until a voice cut through and snapped me sharply back to reality.

"How ironic, the blood of the Earth-born upon an altar of sacrifice," a calm, measured voice sliced through the air.

Through bloodied lashes, still clutching the box, I scuttled backwards, numbness taking hold when I saw him. I wanted to scream, but shock robbed it from me momentarily.

A huge, horned figure, dressed waist down in black, glowered at me, A bloodied trident in his hand. His scarred, crimson-drenched chest heaved with cruel laughter.

Behind him, there were four others just like him emerging from the shadows of the stones. Dark, white-streaked hair and beautiful beyond words, yet the power surging from them was the deepest form of ugliness. The swirling storm encased us, lightning pierced the sky, clouds surged in a bilious roiling circle overhead. We seemed separated from the rest of the world.

"Get away from me!" I scuttled further away, tried to sound as defiant as I could in the face of utter dread. I found my feet, peered through the surrounding darkness, not sure of where to run.

"Who are you?" I couldn't seem to move far enough away.

"Dear, dear, if you don't know who I am, you are very much the poorer. A disservice has been done to you that you remain so naïve. Yet, it serves us all too well," he laughed, the ones behind him silent.

I grit my teeth, my heart thundered too hard, my chest hurt. Fear milled into anger.

"Stop with the Oscar performance!" My wings surged with power. "Who you are!" I screamed and edged further backwards, taking care not to move too quickly, like a mouse cornered by a cat.

He was in my face in an instant, teeth bared and smelling like the remnants of a long dead fire.

"I am your worst nightmare, Sophia, Soph'ael, Earth-born… stupid child!"

Thwack. My head flung sideways as his fist met my face. The sting was blinding. I clutched the box tighter as I tried to clear my vision, blinking rapidly, not wanting to let him out of my sight.

"Yeqon, just get on with it. Your theatrics bore me," said the one to his left.

The name turned my blood to ice, but I'd really known who he was. Evil rolled from him like the stink of a corpse.

"Know your place, Ged'erel. I've waited an eternity for this, and I shall have my fun." Yeqon's black ringed irises glowed red and seared into mine.

"I'll have that box, and I'll have you, too." Yeqon spat the words as though I was nothing.

He lurched towards me, his strength beyond mine. The chest was in his hands… but only for a moment.

"Argh," he roared. "The damn thing burns!" He threw it somewhere behind him, and the smell of his burnt flesh gave me a gruesome satisfaction. I smiled.

Thwack. Another slap across my face.

"Cover it up and bring it with us," Yeqon commanded. "Damn them!"

My energy was building up, my strength returning, and I let it grow. It had saved me before, just when I needed it. My eyes burned, my chest heaved, and my wings fanned wide. Their light revealed the beasts who'd hunted me down. Five of them. Five enormous men… then my heart sunk as I realised exactly who they were. The Unseen.

"Ah, it has just dawned upon you? You're disappointingly slow. I would put that little power show away that you're brewing, too, it could get a bit messy," Yeqon growled, hot breath and spittle fanned my face.

"Pineme, bring me the girl!" I heard her before I saw her.

"Jaz!" I screamed in horror as she was dragged out of the shadows. Her body was bloodied, her armour gone, she was bound hand and foot, screaming.

"Kill them, Soph! Kill these fucking animals!" She was smacked into silence.

"What an awful creature she is, so unbecoming," Yeqon said, as Jaz was thrown to the ground at his feet. He raised his glowing weapon above her. "You will do as you're told and come with me, or I will gladly use her head as a drinking vessel."

"No! No. No, okay, just don't hurt her, please?" Pain surged through me; a new kind of pain squeezed my heart. "I'll do whatever you want!" I gave in so easily, my heart absolutely my weakness. Tears pricked anew. I would never be able to watch another suffer… never, and that would always be my weakness. My body dulled, my coiled muscles slackened, no longer ready to pounce.

Yeqon smiled and smacked me across the face a third time for good measure. The sting was excruciating. Blood pooled in my mouth. I bit back new tears, yet my chin trembled like a traitor with the effort.

He scooped me up, held me aloft, dangling me by my arms. Yeqon kicked Jaz out of the way, her body rolled back into the shadows. I gasped; the tears won.

"By I'el, that felt good!" He laughed in my face and then spat at the ground with disgust.

Yeqon looked up to the sky, "Did you hear that, old man?"

As I dangled in his grasp, a new voice and a familiar heartbeat entered the chaos of my thoughts. Suddenly, I was flung from Yeqon's grip to the ground.

I pushed up, dazed, tried to see who it was.

A figure slithered around Yeqon, wrapped itself around him, cooed in his ear. A woman. She was tall and thin, with an alabaster complexion. As my vision cleared, I saw her more crisply. Long legs wrapped in tight black pants, thigh-high red stilettos. Spindly arms rubbed lustfully across Yeqon's chest as she dug talon-like nails in, drawing drops of blood. He growled at her, but gathered her in closer, planting an aggressive, deep kiss on her all too willing mouth. She giggled like a child, looked down at me through long lashes and eyes smudged black. She was as beautiful as she was scary; a killer porcelain doll.

"You have him?" Yeqon asked the sultry woman as she licked and kissed his neck. She growled, licked the length of his jugular from collarbone to ear. He half-smiled, his eyes never left mine. He didn't return the lusty affection.

"My love, my life, I have hunted him down." The woman disappeared for a few moments, then reappeared with a hunched, shadowed figure. She flung it to the ground in the darkness near where Jaz lay. I could smell blood. A lot of it.

"You may partake, my queen. Well done." Yeqon beckoned her back to him and bent his head to the side, offering her his neck.

I couldn't help watching as she bit into Yeqon's neck. Like a car wreck, it was impossible to look away. The storm thundered overhead. He groaned with pleasure as she drank from him. Her head moved rhythmically back and forth as she drew circles on his chest with her fingers. It turned my stomach. I couldn't help myself. I threw up. Wiping my mouth with the back of my mud-caked hand, I looked back to see that she'd finished, and they both laughed at me. She teasingly, seductively licked her lips clean of the iridescent red dribbles, mocking me openly. Large, clear, and dangerous eyes burned like a sunset as she glared at me. She then sauntered away casually, without another word.

"You are lucky I don't rip you to shreds, boy!" Yeqon suddenly growled at the figure groaning in the dark. His hunched over back faced me, and the light too dull to see who exactly it was that rewarded that woman with a meal of blood. A light began to glow from his hands which were running up and down Jaz's body. I recognised it as the light of healing. This confused me.

Who was this? *That smell, that heartbeat!*

"Don't touch her!" I yelled at the silhouette.

"Quiet!" thundered Yeqon

The figure healed Jaz to the point that she stirred, but he laid a hand across her head and quieted her into a sleep.

He addressed Yeqon.

"You don't need the human girl. We have what we need. Let *me* deal with the chosen one, as I promised."

The voice cut me to the bone.

"Boy, you test me! Do you wish this trident through your chest?"

"Have I not brought her to you? Have I not done all that you have asked? Thousands of years of your bidding. Murdering and interfering. Never once have I wavered. Just leave this one, please? She is an innocent." He pointed his glowing hand at Jaz.

The one named Ged'erel spoke, "You have become weakened living amongst the humans, Nik'ael, and you show mercy where none is warranted. It is sickening to see."

The womanly figure appeared again from behind Yeqon. She towered over the disgraced accomplice and pushed viscously at his back with her stiletto heel. He fell, but caught himself before he crashed onto Jaz by unfurling huge wings of murky light. They flapped hypnotically. Sparks of orange, red and green flicked from the edges of his immense wings. I'd seen those before. *No!*

"Indeed, Nik'ael, you have done our bidding. But you kept the Earth-born to yourself for too long. You have disobeyed your master for your own selfish desires. You wish to keep her for yourself, but she is *not* yours!" The woman screamed so loud that even the thunder seemed to meow like a kitten. "Do not deny it! I can see into your weak, half-breed heart." She inspected her hands for a moment. "I broke a nail hunting you down, you worthless dog!" She spat the words in a high-pitched trill. I remained speechless, my mouth dry, my heart breaking. Surely, I must be dreaming.

"I was trying to gather as much information as I could, Lilith. You know all too well that we are forsaken if we act too soon!" The traitor answered as he cowered from her threatening stature in the dark.

"You don't fool us. You have fallen for her, as we all fell at some point," Yeqon laughed heartily and looked around. "Is that not why we are all here in the first place? For a woman? For a man. For a lover?" Yeqon asked. They all laughed as the slithering Lilith wrapped herself around Yeqon again. "Admit your weakness, and you shall suffer little. Lie to me and Tartarus shall seem a luxury compared to the pits of the lowest realm!" Yeqon pointed at Nik'ael.

"Lilith, partake of the girl. Perhaps that will persuade the truth from Nik'ael?" Yeqon peeled the sultry vampire from his chest.

"Ooh, yummy!" Lilith made her way to Jaz. I froze in horror.

"No! No, stop! Yes, all you say is true. I've fallen, but I have never indulged in it… in her. I have struggled through this and I have not failed you yet. *Please*, allow me to send the innocent away and I will do as you wish, without hesitation." Nik'ael was on his knees, begging. His hands raked wildly through his hair. I squinted hard, but still could not make out his features. My heart didn't really want to… it already knew.

"There, was that so hard? You are as weak in your heart as she is." Yeqon inclined his head to me. "By the soul of I'el, I do not understand you, boy. You are lucky I have the smallest morsel of pity for you. I will pay for this with incessant moaning for weeks, Nik'ael. Lilith, let her go. I've got no more time for this. You've had your fill on me."

The awful, bloodsucking woman dropped Jaz heavily to the ground, whinging with disappointment.

"Get on with it then, Nik'ael. You have by the rise of the Empyrean evening to bring Soph'ael to kneel before my feet. This is your last chance. Do not disappoint me."

Yeqon walked away. They all followed him casually, slowly disappearing into the thick fog.

The shadowed figure immediately tuned back to Jaz. I remained frozen, like a coward, stunned by what I was seeing and feeling. His wings glowed brighter now, a purer white and immensely beautiful. It seemed impossible that they could belong to someone who was working with the devil. He kissed Jaz's head and then waved his hands quickly over the length of her body. In a sudden flash of light, Jaz was gone. I screamed.

"What have you done?" I came out of my state of shock, anger surged, my veins lit like rivers of light. I rose from the ground, unfurled my wings, but he was in the air and on me in a flash, my arms pinned to my side in an iron grip. The devils were gone, so this was *his* show now. I struggled violently, clawing to get my hands free enough to blast him to Hell.

"Let… me… go!" Our wings thrashed and clashed together. The familiarity weakened me each time his wings grazed mine. I awaited the pain of death, which didn't come. His strength eclipsed mine. I realised quickly that while I was fighting against him, he was merely holding onto me. Not hurting me—just holding me close to his bare, burning chest.

Ashes and spice.

The scent sapped my remaining strength. Our heartbeats matched, thrumming in sync, as they had countless times before. Only now, it was the last thing I wanted to feel. I couldn't look at him. The winds howled through the stones that watched on like voyeuristic spectres. I could no longer hear fighting. My heart screamed behind my ribcage as he drew me impossibly close, wordlessly. His breath on my ear was calm and measured. It both intoxicated and frightened me. He was both my safety and my danger all at once.

Nothing separated us now. Skin on skin. He was shaking.

Ashes and spice

The soft touch of his hand drew my face towards his.

Don't look!

"Please, no," I cried, my voice weak.

He bent his head down. His wings enveloped us both, forming a warm barrier from all that was real and unreal. I felt suffocated. He hesitated ever so slightly, his breath faltering as his heart hammered next to mine.

"Just once," he said softly, breaking my heart in an instant.

Each beat like it was the last, my mind was paralysed with denial. He gently caressed his face against mine, a K'ufili shared. A small cry of grief escaped me as he cupped my face with both hands. The screaming in my head was shoved far away as his tear moistened lips met mine. Soft and tentatively at first, as if testing the waters of a deep pool. Then the kiss deepened, firm and panicked, as if there was no time left for us… there was none. The urgency surging from him drew me further in. I matched his passion. I was disgusted with myself as I crumbled. The fire between us burned. Embraced within the stone circle, surrounded by the storm, I was desperate and hungry for this feeling. A feeling I had pushed down and away countless times, convincing myself it wasn't real, that I didn't need it… that I couldn't have it. I pulled at his neck and drew him as close as we could possibly get. He groaned with pleasure. How could something so dreadfully wrong feel so perfectly right? There was a certain kind of desperation in this forbidden act between an angel and a devil.

He pulled slightly back. The smell of burning flesh hit me. My armour was burning his chest. It seemed to alert me to my senses, as I remembered that evil could not touch chromious metal. I pulled sharply away and slapped him with every ounce of strength I had left, leaving a hand-shaped mark across the white scar on his face. I knew now that it had never been a scar at all, as his mark burned white through the inflammation. I looked into his sorrowful, emerald eyes. I was breathless, I was destroyed.

"I'm so sorry, Sophia."

With these words, his emerald eyes flickered cerulean blue and then turned black as night.

"Ben…why?"

His wings wrapped around me and I was dragged into oblivion.

The End

Thank you for reading Awaken.
To continue The A'vean Chronicles,
please scan for website link to
book 2,
Surrender

453

Acknowledgments

I want to thank my amazing family for supporting me as I ventured into the world of writing. I have the best fan club under my own roof. Thank you to my beautiful children for putting up with the many times I've pulled the car over and said, *"Quick, I've just got to write an idea down!"* Each of you has made mum feel so special because you share your pride and excitement in what I am doing.

Thank you to my husband, who is not a book worm, yet has lovingly read through my many versions of this book and ensured me that I was going to succeed. Thank you, and I love you dearly.

To James and Becky of Platformhouse Publishing. I cant thank you enough for the stunning covers and formatting. You have turned my book into a thing of beauty.

To all my readers who have supported me, thank you for stepping into the world of indie books. If I've entertained just one of you, my goal has been achieved.

About the Author

G.R. Thomas is an Australian indie author of fantasy and gothic horror. An avid reader since childhood, it has only been well into adulthood that pen was put to paper to capture the stories that have always been her mind.

In between working as a theatre recovery nurse, being mum to three beautiful children, wife to an ever-supporting husband and running a hobby farm, writing is the passion that glues a very busy life together.

<u>Follow me</u>
Please keep up to date with what I'm up to on social media:
Instagram: @grthomas2014.
TikTok: @grthomasindieauthor
Website: www.grthomasbooks.com
Facebook: G.R. Thomas Author

If you enjoyed this or any of my other books, please leave a small review on Amazon, Goodreads, or wherever you prefer to review the books you enjoy. Reviews are the gold dust that make books sparkle and are forever appreciated by authors.

Thank you again, for reading Awaken.
G.R. Thomas